A YEAR at
The FARM on
MUDDYPUDDLE LANE

Heart-warming, uplifting
romance

Etti Summers

NEW BEGINNINGS

CHAPTER ONE

Dulcie Fairfax nearly squealed with excitement as she drove along the quaintest little high street she had ever seen. Picklewick was a gorgeous village, and she was so excited to think that she would soon be living here.

Actually, she wouldn't be living in the village as such, but just outside, on a farm. How much outside she had yet to determine, but she didn't think it would be very far. She had Google-mapped it of course, just to check the distance, but looking online wasn't the same as seeing it in person, was it? And driving wouldn't be the same as walking. She dearly hoped the farm would be close enough for her to be able to walk into the village. She didn't want to have to drive everywhere, and neither would she be able to afford a taxi if she wanted to pop down to the little village pub for a drink of an evening.

Ah, there it was, The Black Horse. The pub looked even cuter in real life than it had on the internet and if she hadn't had her hands firmly clamped on the wheel of her recently-purchased mint green Fiat 500, she would have clapped them in excitement. She couldn't wait to get to know the locals – her fellow villagers, she amended hastily, because as of this morning she *was* a local.

It was a hard thing to get her head around.

Yesterday she had been living in Birmingham, in a rented flat: today she would be living in Picklewick in her very own home.

Dulcie let out an excited giggle, still not able to believe her luck. In fact, she probably wouldn't believe it was real until she had the keys in her hand, and even then she might have to pinch herself a few times. She didn't see why the solicitor who had done the conveyancing couldn't have given her the keys when she had signed the contract this morning, but he had informed her that the previous owner was insisting on meeting her at the property to hand the keys over in person, so it looked like she would have to wait to get her mitts on them.

To be honest, she could have done without meeting the guy. She just wanted to move in and savour the knowledge that she was now a property owner. Her, Dulcie Fairfax, who had never owned so much as a dolls house, was now the proud owner of Lilac Tree Farm. All thirty-seven acres of it – whatever an acre was.

Technically, she knew how big that was – she had read that it was the equivalent of sixteen tennis courts, but that information didn't help in the slightest. Neither did seeing a copy of the deeds with the farm's boundary highlighted. She simply couldn't envisage its size.

As per directions, Dulcie drove through the village, rather more slowly than she would have normally done because she was too busy trying to glance at the shops to either side of the street. Soon though, she had left the last house behind, and almost immediately, the vista opened up to reveal fields, and above them rolling hillsides. Everything was startlingly green and incredibly lush, and she wound the window down and took a deep breath of amazingly fresh air. She was reminded of the camping holidays her family used to go on as a child, although that was usually to the seaside and not to the heart of rural England. And this was quite rural indeed – far more rural than she was anticipating, she thought as she glanced in her rear view mirror to see how far she had travelled from the village.

To her consternation, all she could see of Picklewick was the square turret of the church in the distance, and she swiftly dragged her eyes back to the road ahead, feeling out of her comfort zone. It was all well and good visiting a place like Picklewick for a weekend break and marvelling at how lovely it was to get away from it all, but she suspected it was another thing entirely to live here, and a worm of unease squirmed in her tummy.

As she continued to drive along the B road leading out of the village, she kept her eyes peeled for a turn-off on her right-hand side, and when she spotted the sign for Muddypuddle Lane she slowed down and drank in her surroundings as she made the turn. The lane was a roughly tarmacked track leading up the hillside, and in the murky distance she could see a cluster of buildings on the right, which she assumed was the riding stables she had noticed on Google. To further backup her assumption, horses grazed in the fields on either side of the lane and a faint animal aroma wafted up her nose through the car's open window.

For a moment she panicked, as it suddenly occurred to her that there might be animals on the farm. Big ones, like sheep and cows. But then she remembered that the contract thankfully hadn't included any livestock. She owned the house, the barns and all the outbuildings, and thirty-seven acres of land which was mostly pasture, plus a small woodland, an orchard and a stream. Oh, and the farm also came with grazing rights on the hillside above. Not that she would ever use those rights, but it was nice to know she had them, just in case.

The hillside couldn't be seen at the moment as it was encased in mist, and neither could she see a farmhouse. Everything above the stables was invisible, and once more her stomach turned over with worry. Was there really a farm up there, or had this whole thing been a huge hoax? That someone might be playing a nasty trick on her passed through her mind, and she scanned the surrounding fields, wondering if a camera crew was going to jump out at her and record her horrified reaction for the whole world to see. Or worse – someone might be luring her to a grisly end!

Passing the stables (the animal smell was more pronounced here and she promptly wound her window back up) she glanced over at it and was relieved to see people leading horses across the yard. If she was about to be done away with, there was a chance someone might hear her screams.

Debating whether it would be prudent to cut her losses, turn around and go home, she was about to do just that – even though she had given up her flat, so didn't have a home to go back to – when she saw the shadow of a building up ahead on the left. Drawing closer, the building became a cottage, with a light shining in one of the downstairs rooms, and in the distance, on the opposite side of the lane, several more buildings hoved into view.

Dulcie's heart fluttered when she saw a worn and battered wooden sign that said Lilac Tree Farm, and she realised that she had finally reached her destination. Her former worries were shoved to the back of her mind as excitement surged through her once more. This was it! She was finally going to see what she had won!

She hadn't been able to believe her luck when she had opened the email informing her that she had won a dream farmhouse in the country, and she'd had to read it several times and had even forwarded it to her whole family for their opinion, before she had tentatively conceded that maybe, just maybe, she had actually *won* something. Dulcie never won anything. Ever. No matter what she entered – from a raffle in her sister Nikki's school summer fete, to a giveaway on social media – she had never won anything. Until she had won this farm.

She had entered the raffle (or was it a lottery? – she hadn't been too sure) out of sheer desperation. Her family, her brother Jay especially, used to tease her for entering so many competitions, but who was doing the teasing now, eh? She was! Not that she was crowing about it, but she did feel quietly smug. Her life was about to change dramatically and for the better, and all because she had purchased a ticket to win a farm.

Of course, she would have to carry on with her boring job for the time being because she still had bills to pay, but a bright new future beckoned and a more exciting life in the country lay ahead.

After the news had sunk in and she had checked that it wasn't a scam, Dulcie had spent all her free time between then and now pinning images to Pinterest and building board after board of lovely things. Things such as kitchen accessories for all the jam-making, baking and pickling that she intended to do; old-fashioned metal bedsteads and nightstands with china jugs on them; real fires and Aga ranges with baby lambs in boxes keeping warm in front of them.

Okay, maybe she would give the lambs a miss, because she wasn't too keen on sheep. The closest she'd got to one was petting a woolly head as it had tried to butt her during a visit to a city farm when she was a child. Dulcie had studiously avoided the creatures since, which hadn't been difficult considering that sheep were few and far between in the Bournville area of Birmingham where she had lived until yesterday.

The car juddered into a pothole the size of a moon crater, and Dulcie swore under her breath. This lane was badly pitted and she was forced to haul the steering wheel from side to side to avoid them, just when she wanted to concentrate on the farm up ahead.

She hoped it had a thatched roof. From the photo advertising the raffle, it had been difficult to tell. The focus had been on a large planter that had once been a stone trough of some kind but was now reincarnated as a flowerpot. A ginger cat had been sitting in front of it, washing its paws, and a bottle of milk (a real glass bottle with a metal stoppered top, would you believe!) stood next to it. The farmhouse had been a soft blur in the background, but she had been able to make out a grey-coloured stone building and sunlight glinting off the windows. There had been several arty photos of the interior – beams, flagstone floors, vintage hand-painted tiles framing an open fireplace, and quaint wooden cupboards. It had looked idyllic.

A house like that would surely have climbing roses growing around the door, and a wood pile for the fire that she would light in the winter. She knew her property had a stream running through it, an orchard and meadows, and she imagined dancing barefoot through the grass, trailing her hands along the tops of the stems, sunlight casting a golden glow over everything. She would be wearing a white flowing dress and have flowers woven through her hair, and—

'You've got to be kidding me!' Dulcie slammed her foot on the break and the car skidded to an untidy halt. Her eyes widened and her stomach did a nasty forward roll as she took in the scene in front of her.

There was no thatch. There were no roses climbing up the walls. There *was* a stone trough though, she saw, having almost collided with it, but it didn't contain the riotous tumbling mass of flowers she had expected. The plants were limp and lifeless, and hadn't been watered for some time. There was no sign of the cat, either.

The house itself was built out of grey stone and had a grey slate roof. The front door had a little v-shaped porch over the top of it with a window to either side, and there were three further windows on the top floor. The farmhouse looked boxy and solid, and not the least bit how she had imagined it. She knew that the blurb had said the house was rustic, but there was rustic and there was run-down. If she didn't know better, she would have said that the place was derelict.

However, there was a large black SUV sitting menacingly in the middle of the yard, looking totally out of place, and leaning against its bonnet with his legs crossed and his arms folded, was one of the most attractive men Dulcie had ever seen.

♥

Otto York heard the rumble of an engine coming up the pitted track long before the vehicle came into view, and for a moment he thought it might turn into the stables. But when it kept on coming, he nodded. This must be the new owner, and although he was curious who this unknown woman might be, he wasn't looking forward to handing the keys over, because that would mean the end of his family living and working on Lilac Tree Farm.

It was the end of an era, and it saddened him immensely.

He blamed himself. He was the last of the Yorks, apart from his father, Walter, and he should have taken more interest in it. Selfishly, he hadn't given the future of the farm a second thought when he had buggered off to catering college seventeen years ago, and he hadn't given it a great deal of thought since. Too busy following his dream of becoming a top-notch chef, he had immersed himself in all things culinary and had ignored the farm.

His dad had always seemed so capable and strong. Although his father was in his seventies, Otto had stupidly assumed he would go on forever. Even when Mum had passed away, his dad had carried on stalwartly, and although Otto knew he missed her dreadfully, his dad had continued to work the farm as he had always done.

Otto grunted as the engine noise faltered for a second, and he guessed the vehicle must have hit one of the many potholes which cratered the lane. Nathan, the general manager of the stables down the road, had been promising to re-tarmac it for some time, but hadn't got around to it. Otto wondered whether he should offer to lend a hand, to get the ball rolling so to speak, because how else would he occupy his days now that the sheep had been sold (apart from Flossie, who Dad hadn't been able to part with) and the farm had a new owner as from this morning.

He also supposed he should try to get a job, since it didn't look like he'd be returning to London and his position as head chef in one of the best restaurants in the city anytime soon. How could he when his father needed him here?

If Otto was truthful, his dad had needed him here years ago, but Walter had been too proud and too stubborn to admit it. Otto was forced to admit that his father had been struggling for a long time, but Otto had selfishly refused to see it.

Good lord! Otto screwed up his eyes as he squinted at the car emerging out of the mist. A green Fiat 500 bounced into view, its suspension handling the uneven surface of the cobbled farmyard with a jauntiness which wasn't reflected on the face of its driver, whose eyes were wide and whose mouth was in the shape of an O as it skidded to a stop.

The woman didn't look at all pleased, and she looked even more unhappy when it began to rain just as she cut the engine and got out, the mist turning into the kind of drizzle that didn't seem to warrant an umbrella but soaked you all the same.

He watched her glance skywards and frown. Then her eyes met his and he was shaken to his core.

She was bloody gorgeous. He guessed her to be in her late twenties, slim yet curvaceous, with a face a model would envy – and he'd seen enough of those in his time, although why anyone wanted to come to his restaurant simply to pick at his food was beyond him.

Okay, maybe not model material, because she was no stick-insect and she didn't have that haughty air models seemed to cultivate, and neither did she have the razor-sharp cheekbones; but she did have glossy dark hair that bounced on blazer-clad shoulders, a flowy white top that failed to hide her figure, and long legs encased in a pair of skinny jeans which ended in impossibly high heels.

His gaze was drawn to them as he wondered how the hell she was going to walk across muddy cobbles wearing those, before creeping up her body to reach her face again.

Her eyes had narrowed and the set of her lips told him that she'd clocked him checking her out.

It wasn't something he usually did when he met a woman for the first time, and it put him on the back foot. So he did the only thing he could think of. He narrowed his own eyes, hardened his jaw, and waited for her to come to him.

She tottered towards him on those ridiculous heels, and he was about to introduce himself when she stumbled and uttered an ear-piercing shriek as a hen fluttered out from underneath his car, squawking loudly.

His hand shot out to catch her and he gripped the woman's arm firmly, not wanting her to face-plant the cobbles.

She wobbled precariously for a heartbeat, before finding her balance.

But when the hen clucked and strutted around her feet, the woman let out another shriek and flapped a hand at it.

'Shoo! Go away! Get lost!' she cried, hopping from foot to foot like an ungainly stork, as the hen, oblivious to the ructions it was causing, tried to peck at the shiny gold buckles on her ankle straps. 'Make it go away,' she pleaded. 'It's attacking me.'

'It's not. She's hoping you've got food for her.'

'Well, I haven't. So there,' she added.

Otto took pity on her. He released his grip on her arm, hoping she wouldn't fall over, and clapped his hands a couple of times.

The hen took the hint and scuttled off into one of the barns, probably to join the other hens who still resided at the farm. By rights he should have sold them off, but they had been overlooked in his haste to sort everything else out.

'Better?' he asked, somewhat sarcastically. Lilac Tree Farm's new owner might be as attractive as hell, but she was no farmer. Everything about her, from her cute little run-around to her four-inch heels, screamed city girl. Of all the people who could have won the farm, why did it have to be someone who didn't have a clue what they were doing?

Good luck, he thought. She was going to need it.

With a loud sigh, he said, 'Am I right in assuming you're Dulcie Fairfax?'

'Yes. What is that chicken doing here?'

'What did you expect? This *is* a farm.'

She glared at him. 'Are there anymore?'

'Another two.' He took a breath and bit back his sarcastic reply. After all, he had stressed to the solicitor that the farm would be transferred to the new owner without livestock, so maybe he was being harsh. Perhaps he was doing her an injustice, and the hen scurrying out from underneath his car had simply startled her.

In an attempt to appear more friendly, although all he felt was sadness and resentment that a stranger was going to be living on the farm where he had grown up, he said, 'I hope you'll be happy in your new home,' and held out a bunch of keys.

Warily, she took them from him, her gaze scouring his face. 'Thanks.'

Otto hesitated for a moment, wondering whether he should say something more profound, like 'take care of it', then he grunted at his stupidity. The farm belonged to Dulcie now. It was up to her whether she made a go of it or not. It was no longer any concern of his.

CHAPTER TWO

Dulcie hurried to unlock the door to the farmhouse, anxious to go inside.

Her reason was fourfold. First, she wanted to make sure that these really were the keys to her new home and that the man in the yard wasn't some psycho who had lured her here under false pretences: which reminded her – she must get all the locks changed as soon as possible. Second, she wanted to get out of this annoying rain. Third, she was desperate to see inside the house; and last, but not least (*definitely* not least) she wanted to escape from the gaze of her farm's former owner.

She couldn't believe the way Walter York had looked her up and down with a scornful sneer on his face. She knew his name because it had appeared on the contract – and just for the record, it didn't suit him, she decided. And the way he'd behaved when she had been startled by that blasted chicken had been downright mean. There had been no need for him to be so sarcastic about it. Even though in her daydreams about the farm she might have envisioned collecting fresh eggs every morning, call her naive but she hadn't expected a close encounter with the creature that actually produced those eggs.

He could have been a bit more welcoming, she thought. Then she decided it didn't matter. It was unlikely their paths would cross in the future, and if she never saw him again, it would be too soon. Talk about being unfriendly. He had taken grumpiness to a whole new level.

Which made her wonder why he had insisted on meeting her in the first place. He could just as easily have left the keys with the solicitor for her to collect when she signed the contract, so she suspected that the real reason he'd wanted to hand them over in person was to check out the new owner.

What a jerk!

She was glad she'd met him though, if only so she knew to avoid him in future. She certainly wouldn't forget his face in a hurry. Good looking didn't begin to describe him, but he knew it. Haughty, arrogant… there were probably a few other choice words she could think of, and as she was mulling them over another one popped into her head – *disturbing*.

But she wasn't entirely sure why – unless it was the incongruity of the state of the farm, compared to his appearance.

Dulcie had noticed how well-dressed he was. He looked like an image of how she thought a gentleman farmer should look, and she wondered why he had raffled the farm off instead of selling it. She was aware that all proceeds were going to charity, so perhaps he had hoped to raise more money this way, which was extremely altruistic of him and she had to admire him for that, but she was also envious that he was wealthy enough to be able to afford to make such a grand gesture.

He certainly appeared to be well off, what with that car and those clothes. And the stuck-up attitude was very lord-of-the-manor, leading her to wonder if he actually did live in a mansion. He was also well-spoken, his voice crisp and clipped, with no discernible accent. She had a feeling he was used to barking out orders.

From the doorstep Dulcie watched his car glide out of the yard, irritation gnawing at her. Trust his car to *glide*, when hers had juddered and jarred over those blasted cobbles. She didn't think her poor car's suspension would ever recover and she hoped she hadn't done it any permanent damage.

The SUV's tail lights disappeared around the corner, and suddenly the world became all the murkier for their departure as Dulcie abruptly realised that she was on her own, in the middle of nowhere, with only a chicken for company.

Dear god, what had she let herself in for, she wondered, as she backed inside the house and firmly closed the door.

Then she turned around to see what her new home had to offer – and immediately wished she hadn't.

She was standing in a dingy hall whose dominant colour was beigey-brown, with a worryingly steep and narrow staircase at the far end. There were two doors leading off the hall, one to either side, and Dulcie tentatively pushed open the one to her left to reveal a sitting room containing a pair of wing-backed leather armchairs that had seen better days. The thought of sitting on the cracked and scratched cushions made her shudder. Still, they looked clean enough, as did the rest of the room. It was just a pity everything was so worn and old-fashioned. She quite liked the fireplace, though. A chunky black stove was recessed into the chimney breast and a pile of chopped wood was stacked neatly by the side, and she remembered the tiles surrounding it from the photos when she'd bought a ticket.

Two of the walls were whitewashed stone, and heavy beams stretched across the ceiling. It would have been quaint if it wasn't for the woodchip wallpaper, the stern grey flagstone floor (which wasn't quite as appealing in real life) and the heavy burgundy curtains.

A door was directly ahead, and Dulcie walked towards it, her eyes darting here and there as she entered a kitchen, taking everything in.

Her heart sank again. She hadn't been expecting anything ultra-modern and sleek, but she had at least been hoping for farmhouse style. This kitchen was more *rubbish-tip* style: the whole thing needed ripping out and replacing.

Trying to look on the positive side and not give in to the tears that were threatening, Dulcie told herself that the room was a lovely size, and that the tatty stand-alone dresser and assorted cupboards would do for now, until she could afford to replace them with a proper fitted kitchen. If she ever could afford to replace it, that is, because on her meagre wage she would be lucky if she could even cover the day-to-day running costs of a property this size.

Dulcie bit her lip to hold back a wail. She had been so looking forward to living here and so excited about her brand-new life in the country, that the run-down reality of what she had won made her want to cry. Perhaps she should cut her losses now, put it on the market and get rid of it? With the proceeds from the sale, she would have enough money to buy something nice. Something more modern, that wasn't in the middle of nowhere. How much was a place like this worth anyway, she mused. Dulcie couldn't begin to guess, but surely she would get a fair bit for it if she sold it?

Telling herself not to be too hasty and that she shouldn't make any knee-jerk decisions, she explored the rest of the house.

The kitchen had a walk-in pantry, the shelves stripped bare, but in her mind's eye she could imagine jars of pickles and preserves lining them, and for the first time since she had driven into the muddy farmyard, a flicker of excitement ignited in her stomach.

Perhaps she was being unrealistic to have expected her farmhouse to look anything like those gorgeous images she had on her Pinterest board. And although her house was a far cry from how she had imagined it, at least it was *hers*. And to put an even more positive spin on things, she told herself that this was a blank canvas, to decorate and design as the mood took her.

Just off the kitchen was a utility room – at least, that was what she would use it for. At the moment all it contained was a row of pegs on the wall and a bucket in the corner. It had a door to the outside though, so it would be a perfect place in which to hang coats and leave wet boots to dry.

Dulcie peered through the small window to the side of the door, noticing that the glass was clean, and she wondered whether Walter York had given the place a once over with a duster before relinquishing the keys. She doubted it somehow. He didn't strike her as the type to get his hands dirty; he probably had staff to do that for him.

A garden lay to the rear of the house, although it was seriously overgrown, and a path ran through the middle of it, disappearing into the mist. Another frisson of excitement travelled through her as she wondered where it led, but exploring the outside would have to wait. She wanted to see the upstairs first. Anyway it was raining, and her umbrella was buried in one of the boxes in the back of her hatchback.

The utility room had a second door and she opened it cautiously, hoping it didn't lead to a cellar. Dulcie wasn't keen on cellars – you never knew what might be lurking in them. Ooh, look it was a downstairs—

Aargh!

A flurry of brown feathers and a volley of indignant squawks greeted her, as another one of those blasted chickens shot between her legs.

Dulcie recoiled in alarm, her heart hammering as she choked back a scream, and she put her hand to her chest, willing herself to calm down.

It was only a chicken. Surely she could handle this?

But it had horrid scaley legs like a reptile, and long talons at the end of its toes. And it was *looking* at her. A beady eye watched her warily, as both human and bird froze.

'Shoo?' Dulcie's voice was hesitant, more of a timid request than a forthright command.

The chicken uttered a low clucking sound and bobbed its head in response.

How had it got in, anyway? And what was it doing in the bathroom? Shower room, she amended, as she took her eyes off the horrid creature to glance around the room. Oh, god, she hoped it wasn't the only bathroom. The thought of having to traipse downstairs in the middle of the night if she needed a wee, filled her with dread. Maybe that was what the bucket was for, she suddenly thought, horrified.

The chicken chucked again, although the noise was less of a cluck and more of a throaty warble.

She would worry about bathrooms later: she had a chicken to deal with first.

Slowly, so as not to alarm it and run the risk of it attacking her, Dulcie sidled towards the back door. A key was in the lock, so she turned it, grateful when she heard a snick as the mechanism engaged, and she eased the door open, then retreated to a safe distance.

The chicken stared at her, and she stared back at the chicken. For a moment Dulcie thought it was going to refuse to leave, but then its head shot forward, seeming to pull the rest of its feathery body with it as it took a step towards the door.

As soon as it was safely outside, Dulcie slammed the door shut, then turned her attention to the open window in the shower room, and closed that firmly, too.

Look at the mess the creature had made, she thought, eying a snowstorm of shredded white paper which was all that was left of a loo roll, except for the empty cardboard tube which still hung on the holder. Some of the decimated tissue paper had been scuffed into a pile, and for one awful moment Dulcie feared that the chicken had done a poo on it.

Wrinkling her nose in disgust, she peered at the mess and wondered where in the numerous boxes in the car she would find some rubber gloves, when she realised that the poo was, in fact, an egg. A brown egg which was still warm, she discovered when she picked it up, and she smiled. Her very first egg.

It was as though the chicken had left her a welcome-to-your-new-home present, and her heart thawed a little towards it.

Gingerly she carried the egg into the kitchen and left it in the sink whilst she explored the rest of the house.

The remainder of the downstairs consisted of a nice-sized living room to the other side of the hall, and even before Dulcie had ventured up the stairs to the first floor, she was imagining how it would look if the hideous carpet was replaced with floorboards or quarry tiles. She would keep it as a family room, she decided. It was large enough for a couple of big squashy sofas, or an L-shaped one might be a good idea, considering how big her family was and that they would no doubt all want to come for a visit at exactly the same time.

The smaller sitting room, the one off the kitchen, could be turned into a dining room, although the kitchen itself was roomy enough for a table, and one was already in there. The last person to have lived in this house was an older gent, and the solicitor had informed her that much of the furniture had been left in situ and was now hers, so she decided that she would drag the table into the dining room.

Dulcie was grateful for some of the furniture because furnishing a house this size was beyond her immediate means, yet she ungratefully wished that the heavy dark-wood wardrobes and chests of drawers which were in all five of the bedrooms, were a bit more stylish. Still, they would do for now, although she had every intention of making the purchase of a new mattress to go on the brass bedstead in the master bedroom her number one priority. She would have to sleep on the old one tonight though, and she prayed that the former owner hadn't breathed his last on it.

No wonder Walter York hadn't removed any of the furniture but had left it for the new owner – aka Dulcie – to dispose of. He probably hadn't wanted the hassle. So now it had become her hassle instead.

He might have warned her that the interior of the house needed a complete overhaul, though. He also could have informed her that there was a chicken in her downstairs loo. But he hadn't said a word, and she wondered what else Walter York hadn't told her.

She soon found out when she tried to call her mum to let her know that she had arrived safely, only to discover that there was no phone signal. None whatsoever.

Damn Walter York.

♥

Otto's dad pounced on him as soon as Otto stepped inside the door of the former stockman's cottage that was now his father's (and his) new home. Thank goodness Otto had made sure that the cottage and a small paddock hadn't been part of the deal when he had raffled off the farm.

The farm had actually belonged to his father, Walter, and Otto had had a devil of a job trying to convince him that it had to be sold – because how else would the farm's horrendous debts be paid off? Besides, his dad was no longer in any fit state to work the land and run the farm. And even if he had been fit and healthy enough, Walter was the other side of seventy, so how much longer could he have continued?

'Well, what's she like?' his dad demanded.

It was only April, so the weather wasn't the best, and in the short amount of time between driving down the lane from the farm and arriving at Muddypuddle Lane Cottage the drizzle had turned to rain. His dad was sitting in front of a roaring fire, with a blanket tucked around his legs. He looked frail and unwell, and Otto's stomach turned over. His dad was improving slowly, but he had a long way to go, and Otto wasn't sure he was out of the woods yet.

'Young, clueless,' Otto replied, running his hands through his hair to shake off the droplets of rainwater. A dog's nose booped him on the leg, and he bent to pat her. She was a black and white Border collie by the name of Peg, and his dad had owned her since she was a pup. It would have devastated him to be parted from her. He would have also been upset to be parted from Flossie, the sheep he had hand-reared last year. Walter had formed an unusual attachment to the lamb, so much so that he had visibly shrunk when Otto had informed him that he had planned on selling her along with the rest of the flock.

Otto had relented and Flossie now lived in the small paddock to the side of the cottage; although she did have a tendency to prefer being inside the cottage itself and could often be found lying on the rug next to his dad's chair in the sitting room and happily chewing the cud, much to Otto's consternation. It was bad enough having the dog wandering in and out of the house, and Puss too, when the cat deigned to pay them a visit. A sheep was the last straw.

'How young? She's not on her own, is she?' Walter sat forward, concern on his craggy face.

'She appears to be.'

His dad began to fret. 'She's not going to be able to manage that place on her own. You're going to have to help her. I would do it myself, but…' He ground to a halt, not needing to say anything further. They both knew that Walter not being able to do it himself was the reason why he had to get rid of the farm in the first place.

'No chance,' Otto spluttered. He'd be damned if he was going to go running up the lane every time Dulcie Fairfax flipped her lid at the sight of a hen. If she couldn't cope on her own, she should have thought about that before she bought a lottery ticket.

He caught his dad's expression as he went to make a cup of tea, and Walter's grumbling followed him out to the kitchen.

Otto knew that letting the farm go had been hard on the old man, but what else could he have done? By the time Otto realised that his dad was struggling and discovered that he had run up huge debts, including getting a mortgage on the farm, it had been almost too late to pull back from the brink of bankruptcy. If that had happened his father would have lost everything, including the cottage they now lived in. Walter would probably have ended up in a rented house where he wouldn't have been able to take either of his animals. It would have destroyed him.

Otto had returned to the farm to try to save it, but after having it valued and realising that even if the property achieved its full asking price, it wouldn't be enough to pay off all his dad's creditors, Otto had almost lost hope. Until, that is, he had seen an advert on tv. It was for a prize draw to win a rather expensive house.

With little real hope, he had begun to look into how a prize draw such as that worked, and he had been amazed to discover that it might be a way out of their situation.

And so, after a great deal of research and a lot of soul-searching, Otto had eventually offered the farm up as a prize draw, with the proceeds (after all the debts on the farm had been paid) going to charity.

He hadn't honestly expected much interest.

But there had been loads, and the lucky winner was now settling into the house that had been in his family for generations, and where he had grown up.

To say he felt resentful was an understatement, but Otto just had to suck it up and get on with it. Today was the start of a new normal for him and his dad. With the farm no longer their responsibility and the transfer complete, Otto could try to look to the future, starting with getting a job. He knew it might be quite some time until he returned to London and the restaurant scene – his dad needed him here – but he couldn't not work. For a start, he needed the income, and for another, he had to keep busy. The thought of not working in a commercial kitchen and not being able to conjure up mouth-watering dishes made his heart ache. He was a chef and a damned good one, and he didn't know how to do anything else.

But the issue was, cheffing usually involved unreasonable hours, and long ones too. And the only eateries in Picklewick were The Black Horse and a couple of cafes, which meant he would have to look further afield for a job as a chef. But if that was the case, once he factored in the commuting time, just how much would he be able to care for his dad if he was out of the house for hours on end?

There was one small ray of sunshine in the cloudy sky which was Otto's life right now, and that was his dad's health. His father might hate that the farm had gone, but even in the short amount of time since he had moved into Muddypuddle Cottage, Otto could already see an improvement. His father seemed brighter, more with it, and not so frail or forgetful.

Maybe it was the stress and worry that had been making him ill, and if that was the case then Otto might be able to think about going back to proper cheffing work in the not-to-distant future. However, it would be a while yet, so he'd better ask around and see if he could find something local to tide him over.

♥

There was nothing else for it: Dulcie would have to get in her car and drive to somewhere that *did* have a signal. Apart from venturing outside or going into the attic (she had eyed the hatch set into the ceiling at the top of the stairs with horror) she had tried everything without any luck, to get a signal.

She had wandered into every room in the house, peering intently at her phone and praying to see some bars. Just one would do – she wasn't greedy – but even after standing on the beds, waving her arm out of all the windows, and going as far as to clamber onto the toilet seat and stretch the phone above her head, she still couldn't raise a peep out of it.

Reluctantly, and keeping her eyes peeled for marauding chickens, Dulcie shot across the farmyard and dived into her car, wishing she had worn her raincoat – although how much use it would be in this deluge was debatable.

With great care, she steered the Fiat out of the yard, her attention glued on the dirt track as she tried in vain to remember where the most lethal potholes were. The problem was that they had filled up with rainwater, so it was difficult to tell a deep hole from a shallow puddle, and she inched down the lane with a great deal of caution, until she reached the turn-off to the stables. Coming to a standstill, she risked a glance at her phone and her heart leapt when she saw the screen.

Finally, she had a signal!

'Mum? It's me, Dulcie!' she cried, as soon as her mum answered.

'Oh, hi love, can I call you back, I'm just in the middle of—'

'No, you can't!' Dulcie shouted. No way was she going to sit in the car for goodness knows how long and wait for her mum to phone her back. 'It's now or never,' she said.

'Calm down, Drama Queen. I was only going to—'

'Mum, I'm sitting in my car in the pouring rain. I need to speak to you *now*!'

'Are you lost? Have you broken down?'

'No. I found the farm okay, but there's no phone signal.'

'Is that all? I thought something major had happened.' Her mum chuckled and added, 'Although, I suppose the farm not having a signal *is* the end of the world for you.'

Dulcie rolled her eyes. Her mum was just as attached to her own mobile. It was the easiest way to keep in touch with all four of her kids.

'Anyway, I thought I'd let you know that I've arrived safe and sound,' Dulcie said, huffily. 'I'll leave you to get on with what you were doing.'

'It can wait. Now that you're on the line you might as well tell me what the farm is like. And how was your journey? Have you eaten?'

Ah, this was more like it, Dulcie thought, wondering where to begin. She'd start with the easiest questions first. 'The journey was fine, and I stopped off for a sandwich and a coffee on the way. As for the farm…' She was desperate to share her disappointment with her mum, as well as her concern that she might have bitten off more than she could chew, but she didn't want to worry her. Anyway, she had only been here an hour, which was hardly long enough to get a proper feel for the place. And the reality was never going to live up to her expectations – Dulcie knew she shouldn't have spent so much time on the internet, gazing at photos of gorgeous barn conversions and baby ducklings…

Instead, she said, 'It's raining at the moment and there's a lot of mist, so I haven't had a chance to look around yet, but it seems very… *farmy*. There are loads of fields and from where I'm sitting I can see horses.'

'I thought you told me that there wouldn't be any animals?'

'I expect they belong to the stables. Remember me telling you that there was a stables nearby? I showed you on Google Earth? I've had to drive as far as that to get a signal.'

'Have you seen the house yet?'

'I have.' Dulcie nodded, even though her mum couldn't see her.

'Well?'

'It's rustic…' she began, wanting to pick her words carefully.

'Oh, I'm so pleased! That's what you were hoping for,' her mum said.

It was, but Dulcie hadn't anticipated this degree of rusticness – if there was such a word.

'You'll have to send us some pictures, and as soon as you've unpacked I expect an invite,' her mum declared.

Yeah, that was what Dulcie had been afraid of. She had gone from demanding that her family come visit her as soon as was humanly possible, to wondering how long she could hold them off. She should never have crowed about winning the farm, but she hadn't been able to stop herself. If only she had held back a little, her mother, sisters and brother wouldn't be under the impression that the farm was the best thing since sliced bread. She should have waited until she'd seen it first. Maybe the place would look better with a coat of paint, and some pretty cushions.

'It's really olde-worlde,' she said, 'with beams in all the rooms, a wonderful flagstone floor in the dining room and a log burner, and an open fireplace in the sitting room. It's even got a pantry, and a shower room downstairs.'

She didn't tell her that the beams were probably dust-magnets, that there were hideous carpets in most of the rooms and that she had found a chicken in the loo.

Dulcie continued, 'The previous owner has left most of the furniture, and I'm sure one or two pieces are quite old. They might even be antiques.'

She failed to mention that old was a euphemism for decrepit. And neither did she say that she had met the former owner and his attitude had left a lot to be desired.

'It sounds lovely,' her mum said, dreamily. 'I wish you'd have let me or Maisie come with you to help you move in. She's at a loose end today.'

'Loose end?' Dulcie narrowed her eyes. 'Don't tell me she's lost yet another job?'

Her mum hesitated. 'She didn't lose it. She walked out.'

'When was this?'

'Last night. Shifts don't agree with her.'

Dulcie thought that it wasn't shift work that didn't agree with her younger sister – it was work itself. In the five years since Maisie had left college, she had flitted from job to job and from boyfriend to boyfriend. She seemed unable to stick to anything, or anyone.

Their mother claimed that Maisie just hadn't found her place in the world yet.

Dulcie reckoned that Maisie never would. As the youngest of the family, her sister had been indulged and babied. She was still being indulged and babied at twenty-four. When Dulcie was Maisie's age, she had a flat of her own (albeit rented) and had held down a decent job for a couple of years.

'Er, that's okay. Mum,' she said. She could do without Maisie's brand of helping – which consisted of getting in the way, whilst not doing a lot. Her sister was an expert at it.

Anyway, Dulcie had wanted her first view of the farm to be when she was alone, undiluted by the opinions of her mum or her siblings. And now, she was glad that she hadn't brought any of them with her.

She chatted with her mum for a while longer, and after saying goodbye she made a few calls to some broadband providers, and to British Telecom to ask how she could get the landline working. It was imperative that she had access to the internet, because her job depended on it.

There was one advantage to living in the middle of nowhere she decided, brightening up when she was told that she would be online by the end of the week, and that was there should be little risk of interruption, so she could work in peace. Her job as a customer services advisor for an energy provider, meant that she often dealt with things of a sensitive nature, and the last thing customers wanted to hear was the sound of a police siren in the road outside, or loud music blaring from the inconsiderate moron who had lived in the flat above hers. And neither did they want to hear next door's toddler having a meltdown, or a car alarm going off in the street below her window.

Look on the positive side, she told herself: she owned the farm outright, and although it mightn't be how she'd imagined it, it was nevertheless hers.

In fact, she was looking forward to the peace and quiet.

CHAPTER THREE

For once in her life, Dulcie was glad to roll out of bed. She'd had one of the worst night's sleep ever, and she would have got up earlier but she wanted to wait until it was light so she didn't feel as though she was getting up in the middle of the night.

She had gotten up a couple of times, though. Fear had driven her from her bed to stand barefoot by the closed bedroom door, as she strained to work out what was making the noises and where they were coming from. Scratching, scrabbling, the patter of scurrying feet and squeaking, and once or twice an unearthly shriek had her quaking in terror and had sent her dashing back to the safety of the bed, where she'd pulled the duvet over her head, curled into a ball and clamped her hands to her ears.

Finally, at some point, she had drifted off, but her sleep had been fitful and uneasy, and she was relieved when the sun rose and she could get up.

Her bedroom didn't look much better today, she thought, as she shoved her feet into her slippers. She had spent the rest of yesterday unloading the car, cleaning, and trying to settle in, and she was already sick of scrubbing. But much of what she had thought was dirt, was just age. Torn lino, cracked tiles, peeling wallpaper. Her first impression had been right – the place needed gutting. But without having the financial means to take the farmhouse back to bare stone and start again, she was stuck with making the best of what she had.

One thing she could be thankful for, was that the house had been rewired a few years ago, so that was one less expense to worry about, although Walter York hadn't stretched to putting in a new boiler or radiators. These were so old, they were probably back in fashion once more as retro items.

That was a thought…assuming they still conducted heat and didn't leak, perhaps she could strip them and repaint them?

Thankfully the boiler worked, as she had discovered yesterday when she had run the tap and hot water had flowed from it. She didn't know what she would have done if it hadn't, but she made a note to herself to get someone out to check it anyway.

Suddenly her knees gave way and she plopped onto the mattress.

Was this going to be too much for her to handle? She knew she was vacillating between wanting to make a go of it one minute, and wanting to throw in the towel the next, but she'd never had to face anything like this before.

Should she pack up and go home? She might have been tempted if she had somewhere to go back to, but she had given up the lease on her flat and her flatmate had moved out to live with her girlfriend. The only other option was to move back in with her mother, but although she loved her mum to bits, Dulcie would prefer to dig her own eyeballs out with a blunt spoon than to live with her.

Her older sister, Nikki, didn't have a spare room, Maisie still lived at home, and Jay, their brother, was in Asia somewhere, installing acoustic sensors in treetops (something to do with conservation), so none of her siblings was an option either.

With a sigh, Dulcie trotted downstairs, still in her jammies. It was a cow onesie actually, bought in a fit of excitement when she'd learned that she had won the farm, and it was lovely and snuggly.

Despondently thinking that she had made her bed and so would have to lie in it, she suddenly noticed the sun beaming through the sitting room window and saw the view that lay beyond the glass, and her heart lifted. The scenery was magnificent – lush green fields stretching down the hillside, and a view across the valley. And when she went into the kitchen to make coffee, she saw that the view from there was just as lovely. The garden might be overgrown but it was dotted with wildflowers and beyond it must be the orchard. She wondered where the stream was, and she vowed to go exploring later. First, though, she needed some breakfast.

Thankful that she'd had the foresight to bring supplies such as bread, butter, milk and coffee with her (she had cooked herself an omelette last night, although she hadn't plucked up the courage to use the egg that the chicken had left for her), Dulcie set about making some toast.

She had just sat down to eat it, her gaze roaming around the kitchen and thinking that the room didn't look as gloomy this morning as it had yesterday, when she almost leapt out of her chair as the back door banged open and the figure of a man barged through it.

Dulcie let out a scream and dropped her toast, butter-side down, then let out another yell as a fluttery brown ball of feathers darted between the man's legs and lunged at it.

In a mad scramble, she climbed onto the chair she had been sitting on and brandished a teaspoon. She had no idea what use it would be, but it had been the nearest implement to hand and it was better than nothing. And neither did she know who to use it on first, the chicken or Walter York.

'Get that thing away from me,' she screeched, balancing on one leg to try to give the chicken less of a target should it choose to attack.

The hen ignored her. It was too busy pecking at the toast, and with every stab of its beak, Dulcie's breakfast was flung into the air, the chicken darting after it.

'That "thing" is your responsibility,' Walter yelled at her, and Dulcie blinked at him, the wind momentarily taken out of her sails.

'What?' she asked, then rallied before he could say another word. 'How dare you come barging in here as though you own the place. May I remind you that you don't!' Fury was beginning to replace her initial fear, and she let him have it with both barrels. 'Get out *now*! Or I'll call the police,' she added, then winced as she remembered that she couldn't get a mobile signal and the landline wasn't in service either.

'*I* should be the one calling the police,' he shot back. 'Or the RSPCA. You're not fit to look after a woodlouse, let alone a chicken.'

'I didn't realise they needed looking after,' Dulcie retorted crossly, getting down from her perch as that insufferable man ushered the chicken out of her kitchen. It had left several little feathers behind, as well as a blob of something disgusting on the flagstones. 'I thought they, you know, scratched around and found their own food,' she added. 'What do they eat, anyway?' She eyed the blob with distaste.

'Spiders, caterpillars, other insects, poultry feed, but that's not what I'm talking about. You left them out last night,' he accused.

'What else was I supposed to do with them? Invite them to share my bed? It was bad enough finding one in the downstairs loo.'

'You're supposed to lock them in their coop.'

'Why? Frankly, I don't care if they run away.'

'I wouldn't blame them if they did. But they're more likely to be eaten.'

'You wouldn't!'

'Not *me*, you idiot – although I've got nothing against a nice plump bird. I was referring to a fox.'

The way he looked her up and down made her think that he was calling her a plump bird, but then she realised what he'd said.

'A fox?' she repeated.

'Yeah, you know…looks a bit like a dog, russet coloured, bushy tail? Gobbles up chickens for supper?'

'Are they alright?'

'They are. No thanks to you.'

'I didn't know, did I? You should have told me. Where is the coop anyway?' She took a wet wipe out of the cupboard under the sink and cleared away the offending blob.

'If you'd like to get dressed, I'll show you.'

Dulcie became aware that she was still in her night things, and she suddenly felt incredibly self-conscious. She might think her cow onesie was cute, but from the sneering expression on his face, Walter didn't think so.

'Look, Walter,' she began, her dander rising again. If he hadn't barged into her house without knocking, then he wouldn't have had his delicate senses assaulted by the sight of her in her cow onesie.

'Walter?' He looked over his shoulder. 'Where?'

'What?'

'My dad.'

'Your dad?'

'What about him?' he asked.

'What?' Dulcie repeated, wondering what he was talking about.

'You just mentioned his name'

'I didn't.'

'You did!'

She growled in exasperation. 'I said no such thing. What I was going to say before I was so rudely interrupted, was that you had no right to enter my house. I demand you give me the key.' She held out her hand.

'I don't have a key.'

'How did you get in, then?' she cried triumphantly.

'The door wasn't locked.'

Dulcie blinked. 'It wasn't?'

He shook his head. 'No.'

Oh god, she'd forgotten to lock the back door after she'd let the chicken out yesterday. She had been upstairs *all night* with an unlocked door! Anything could have happened.

'Walter, I—' she began, but he rudely interrupted her for a second time. The man was insufferable. Grr.

'Why do you keep saying my dad's—' he began, then his frown cleared. 'Ah, now I get it. You think *I'm* Walter.' He poked himself in the chest.

Dulcie wanted to poke him in the eye. 'Aren't you?'

'I'm Otto. Walter is my father.'

Dulcie blinked again. 'Your *father*? But it was you who handed me the keys.'

'I did.'

'I see.' But Dulcie didn't see at all. If Walter was Otto's father, why had Otto allowed him to live in such a pigsty when he himself was clearly well off? It was a disgrace.

Otto pulled a face. 'Well? Are you going to get dressed, or are you coming outside in your…whatever it is you're wearing. I haven't got all day.'

It took her a second to remember what they had been talking about. 'I'm sure I can find the chicken coop by myself, thank you,' she said, haughtily. 'And I'd appreciate it if you didn't barge into my house like you still own it. You don't.'

His eyebrows shot up. She had the feeling he wasn't used to people standing up to him or answering him back. Maybe he had expected her to doff her cap or curtsey, and apologise profusely. She had a mind to tell him it was his father's fault that the chickens nearly ended up as fox food, because the contract quite clearly stated that the transaction didn't involve livestock. She might be mistaken, but surely chickens counted as livestock?

However, the birds were on her property and appeared to be her responsibility now, and although they gave her the heebie-jeebies, she didn't want to see any of them gobbled up by a hungry fox.

Otto glared at her sullenly for a moment and Dulcie glared back, determined not to be intimidated by him. The standoff ended when he shook his head, turned smartly on his heel and marched out.

To her intense irritation, he had left the door open and she hurried to close it, worried that the chicken might decide to return. It clearly liked it in the house, and she wondered whether it had been given free rein to come and go as it pleased. The thought made her shudder.

Debating whether to make herself any more toast, she realised she had lost her appetite, so she made her way upstairs to get dressed.

She had managed to unpack all her clothes yesterday, but on opening her wardrobe in the cold light of day, she realised she was woefully unprepared for this new life of hers. Cute playsuits, smart blazers and frilly blouses weren't suitable clothing for rounding chickens up, or for traipsing about muddy farmyards. She did have some loungey-type leggings and tee shirts though, which would have to do for the time being. She'd shove a fleece over the top and wear her oldest pair of boots or trainers, but what she could really do with was a pair of wellies.

Perhaps she would take a trip into the village later for some supplies, and see if any of the shops stocked Wellington boots. She wondered if Cath Kidston did wellies – she quite fancied something pretty and floral. But then again, even if she found somewhere in Picklewick that stocked that particular brand, she probably wouldn't be able to afford it. Her mum had always accused her of having champagne tastes on beer money, and she was right.

Dulcie couldn't help it if she liked nice things…

Grimacing, she dragged one of her least favourite tee shirts over her head and pulled a pair of joggers out of a drawer, then went outside to find the chicken coop.

The morning light brought her to a halt before she had taken more than a couple of steps and she gazed around in wonder. Everything was so clean and clear, and she took a deep breath of fresh air, inhaling the scent of flowers and growing things. She could also smell a faint animal aroma, and she narrowed her eyes at the horses grazing in the fields below, guessing that it was a smell she would have to get used to if she intended to stay.

The jury was still out on that one, but she had a sneaking suspicion that she was going to give it a go, surmising that she might regret it if she didn't.

Stepping gingerly because there was still a considerable amount of mud around, as well as puddles from yesterday's rain and a coating of green moss in places, Dulcie wandered around the farmyard, peering into barns and peeping around corners, trying to get her bearings.

It seemed that there was one large barn which had empty pens in it and a strong smell of something nasty, plus another one which was open-sided and contained a few pieces of rusting metal and something that looked as though it might have been a tractor in another life. Then there was a stone building that had lots of different rooms, and held stuff she didn't want to examine too closely. She did find a big sack of something called Layers Pellets, which had a picture of a chicken and an egg on the front, so she hoped she had found the bird food. She also found several stacked bales of straw and one of the chickens, which was perched on top of a bale. It was in a stand-off with a substantial ginger cat, the same one that had been in the photograph, and which was now sitting on the ground below the bale, its tail curled around its feet and studying the chicken intently.

It seemed that neither animal was backing down, and she hoped there wouldn't be a scuffle. The cat looked like it meant business, but so did the chicken. It was looking at her out of one beady eye, its beak open, and it made a burbling noise.

The cat's response was to swish its tail and ignore Dulcie, which was fine by her because she preferred dogs anyway.

Then it suddenly occurred to her that she might be responsible for *this* animal's welfare also, and she wondered whether it was eyeing the chicken as a potential breakfast item because she had failed to feed it, and her heart sank.

At least she had discovered the chicken pellets, so she could feed one of her charges. The cat would have to wait until she went into the village later.

Ripping open the bag, she was just wondering what she should use to put the pellets in, when three things happened at once. None of them good.

The chicken uttered an excited squawk and launched itself at her head.

The cat launched itself at the chicken, ending up with its claws in her fleece and its whiskery catface inches from hers, making Dulcie stagger back, and in doing so she upended the sack and pellets scattered everywhere.

Then she was butted in the backside by a sheep.

Not that she realised it was a sheep at first because all she was aware of was a thump on the behind, which sent her toppling forwards. But when she regained her balance, a huge white woolly thing with a black nose and black eyes was lining up to charge at her.

Dulcie let out a bloodcurdling scream that shocked the sheep long enough for her to get a head start on it, as she sprinted for the farmhouse door.

She didn't think she imagined its hot breath on her legs as she dashed across the yard, and she certainly didn't imagine the excited bleats it made as it almost caught her.

Reaching the door, she careened through it, and for an awful second she thought the sheep was going to come right in after her, but she managed to slam it shut on the creature's rabid nose.

Panting, her heart thumping and her knees shaking, Dulcie leant against the door and promptly burst into tears.

CHAPTER FOUR

Otto stormed down the hill in much the same way as he had stormed up it, minus a chicken under his arm.

He had discovered the poor thing early this morning, when he had let Peg out for a wee. It had been hiding in the hedge, looking disorientated and rather sorry for itself, and realising that it was one of his dad's hens, Otto guessed that Dulcie hadn't shut them in for the night.

Furious at her lack of regard for the creatures in her care, he had gathered up the hen and marched up the lane. Spying another bird dart around the side of the farmhouse, looking equally as bedraggled as the one under his arm, he had chased after it, but it had disappeared. At that point, he had found himself standing directly outside the backdoor. Totally irate by now, he had raised his fist to give the door a damned good hammering, but to his shock it had flown open under the force of his powerful knock.

Otto had stumbled inside, nearly falling flat on his face, and had dropped the chicken as he tried to remain upright. Then all hell had broken loose.

He knew it must have been a shock to have him barge into the kitchen, but Dulcie needn't have acted like he was about to attack her. And what on earth had she been thinking, hopping onto a chair and waving a spoon around? Was she going to *spoon* him to death?

Without warning, an image of the two of them in bed, his arms around her as she spooned into him had flashed across his inner eye, and he had nearly turned tail and scarpered. If it hadn't been for the hen throwing a piece of toast in the air as it tried to peck off a morsel, and reminding him of the reason for his impromptu visit, Otto might have done just that.

Instead, he had yelled at her, and she had screeched back at him, and then an odd conversation had ensued where she had thought he was his father and he had thought that she had lost the plot.

And what the hell had she been *wearing*? He knew enough about female nightwear to know that it was a onesie, but it had looked suspiciously like she was in a fancy-dress cow costume.

She had looked darned cute in it, though.

His stomping slowed as he neared the cottage and his ire began to dissipate as he was forced to acknowledge that the issue with the hens last night wasn't necessarily Dulcie's fault.

It was his.

The responsibility for re-homing the livestock had been down to him. Not his dad. He had overlooked the chickens, too wrapped up in disposing of the larger critters on the farm. They had gone to market in batches, ewes with their lambs, and he had sold all of them apart from Flossie. The process had taken more time and effort than he had anticipated, and he hadn't given finding new homes for the three hens a second thought. Apart from collecting a couple of eggs everyday and remembering to secure them in their coop at night and letting them out the following morning, they hadn't crossed his mind.

Until today.

Oh, shit, now he was starting to feel guilty about having a go at her, and shame blossomed in his chest. He shouldn't have expected a city girl like her (and she clearly *was* a city girl) to know how to care for hens. Especially since she had been informed that no animals remained on the farm. When he had seen her reaction to the chicken, he should have advised her that they would need caring for. But he had been so overwhelmed with sadness, regret and shame because he hadn't realised just how bad things had got, that—

Oh, who was he kidding? Yes, he had felt all of those things, as well as disbelief that he was about to hand over the keys to his family farm to a complete stranger, who didn't know the first thing about farming. But he had also felt something else, something which had taken him by complete surprise – and that was attraction. Attraction that he still felt and which, if anything, had grown since he had first set eyes on Dulcie yesterday.

There was nothing else for it. In order to assuage his guilt, he would have to apologise. So he may as well do it now, and get it over with. Besides, he wouldn't mind another look at her in that cute onesie...

Turning smartly on his heel, Otto headed back up the hill.

Luckily it wasn't far to walk from the cottage to the farmhouse.

Initially, he had worried that the lack of distance between the two properties would be a major issue for his dad when he had eventually managed to convince his father that the only way out of the financial mess Walter had found himself in was to get rid of everything except the cottage and the small parcel of land it stood on. He had moved into the cottage itself, and Otto had been concerned that being so near to the farm, yet no longer owning it, might prove to be the final straw for his father.

Walter had indeed found it difficult – the farm was all he knew, and the only place he had ever lived – but he seemed to be coping, and Otto was quietly hopeful that his dad would settle into a new routine and a new way of living.

Otto hoped the same applied to him, and that he, himself, would settle into a new routine: when he actually discovered what that new routine might be. It would begin if (*when*) he found a job, and he vowed to start looking in earnest later today.

He heard a cacophony of squawks coming from the barn as he rounded the corner into the yard, his sturdy boots splashing through the last of yesterday's puddles, and wondered what could be causing the racket.

When he took a look, he discovered that Puss, the unimaginatively named ginger tomcat who had flatly refused to go live in the cottage and insisted on taking up residence in one of the barns instead, was teasing the hens. A pile of poultry feed was spilling out of an upturned sack and the birds were squabbling amongst themselves as they tried to gobble up as many pellets as was chickenly possible.

Scattering the agitated hens, Otto waded through them and reached for the sack, hefted it into his arms and took it to one of the metal bins next to the stacked bales of hay, where he lifted the lid and dropped it in.

The hens looked on in dismay.

Otto frowned. 'You've got enough to be going on with,' he told them, jerking his chin at the ground where a substantial number of pellets still lay. 'You lot won't need feeding for a week. I'd better see some decent eggs from you after all this food,' he warned, before remembering that whatever they laid would now belong to Dulcie.

He wondered whether she had found the coop yet, or whether she had even bothered to look.

'Go do something useful and catch a mouse or two,' he told the cat, who was glaring at him. The animal was in a sphinx position with his tail curled around his paws, and the tip of it twitched in irritation.

There was no way Puss could be described as a lap-cat. He was the least friendly feline Otto had ever known, and the animal was as hard as nails to boot. Puss would stand his ground against a charging bull, and Otto wouldn't bet on the bull's chances of getting away unscathed.

Leaving Puss where he was, Otto headed towards the front of the house, mindful that he should knock properly this time. But as he drew nearer, he realised he could hear the insistent bleating of a sheep coming from around the back, and he guessed Flossie must have escaped again.

'Flossie,' he called, knowing that the ewe would recognise her name. Whether she would respond to it was a different matter entirely. It hadn't yet sunk into her woolly head that Walter, who had bottle-fed her from birth, no longer resided in the farmhouse, and

Otto knew she was probably demanding her breakfast. For Flossie, the usual sheep's fare of grass wasn't good enough. Despite being a year old and fully weaned, she wanted milk and was quite vociferous in making her wishes known.

Ah, there she was, standing on the step, bleating insistently and giving the door an occasional cheeky bump with her head. He was about to catch hold of her woolly shoulder and drag her away, when he paused.

Was that a shriek he could hear?

The ewe bleated again and butted the door, which rattled in its frame, and immediately another shriek followed, accompanied by Dulcie's voice yelling, 'Go away, please go away!'

'Dulcie?' he called, reaching the step. 'Are you okay?'

'Of course I'm not okay. What a stupid question! That sheep tried to kill me. Take it away!'

Otto pressed his lips together to stop himself from laughing when he saw the pale disc of her face peering through the window of the utility room.

'She just wants a bottle. But don't give her one,' he added hastily.

'I've no intention of giving her anything,' Dulcie called back. 'Am I right in thinking this thing belongs to you?'

'To my dad, yes.'

'Then if anything happens to me, I'll hold you responsible.'

'Nothing is going to happen to you,' he assured her, but at that precise moment Flossie decided to give the door an extra hard bang, and it rattled alarmingly in its frame.

Dulcie screeched and clapped her hands to her cheeks. 'Get it away from me!' she shouted.

Gosh, she was really scared, he realised, and wasn't just being a drama queen. 'Wait there,' he instructed, but as he began to walk away he heard her cry, 'Don't leave me. It might get in.'

'It won't,' he called over his shoulder. 'I'm just going to fetch a rope.'

Years ago, his dad used to show sheep, and had won a few rosettes in his time too, so there were still a couple of halters on the premises and he soon found one, plus a lead rope to clip onto it, and hurried back to the house.

Expertly, he slipped the halter onto Flossie's head, then led her away to tie her to one of the posts next to the gate to the veggie patch.

'See, she's tame,' he said. 'You can come out now.'

'I don't think so,' Dulcie retorted, her nose squashed against the glass. 'Not until you get it off my property.'

Otto held up his hands in mock surrender. 'Okay, there's no need to get upset. She's perfectly harmless.'

'In case you hadn't noticed, I am *already* upset. The horrid thing attacked me.'

'She didn't,' Otto insisted.

'How do you know? You weren't here.'

No, but he wished he had been. He had a feeling it would have been funny.

His amusement must have shown on his face, because Dulcie slapped a hand to the glass.

'Don't you dare laugh!' she cried. 'If I see that animal again, I'm going to phone the police or the RSPCA.'

Otto's amusement quickly faded as she threw his own words back in his face.

How dare she! She didn't know the first thing about caring for animals, yet she was threatening to report *him* to the authorities.

'Fine,' he said, shortly. 'I'll make sure that the new owner of Lilac Tree *Farm*—' he emphasised the last word with drawling sarcasm '—isn't bothered by a farm animal ever again. Would you like me to remove the chickens whilst I'm at it? How about the cat? Although you might like him to stay to keep the mice down. I'm afraid I can't do anything about those because they're not classed as livestock. Neither are the birds in the trees, or the insects in the garden.' He knew he was ranting, but that woman was bringing out the worst in him.

He threw his hands in the air in disgust and marched over to Flossie.

'Wait!' she shouted. 'What do you mean, *mice*? There aren't any mice.' A pause. 'Are there?'

'I'll think you'll find that there are,' he said, grimly pleased that he had managed to put a dent in her self-righteous anger.

'Like, in the fields?' she asked.

'Like, in the house,' he replied. 'You can hear them in the walls.'

Her horrified expression was to remain with him for the rest of the day.

But it was only when he was freeing Flossie from her halter and setting her loose in the paddock, did he realise that he hadn't apologised, and he was glad that he hadn't. Dulcie didn't deserve his apology. What she deserved was his contempt, and she had that in spades.

♥

Seriously, being without a phone signal was the pits, Dulcie concluded, as she dug into an early lunch in The Black Horse, her phone propped up in front of her.

After the trauma of sheepgate, Dulcie had hurried upstairs to change into something more respectable, then had fled to Picklewick, bouncing her little car over the potholes without a second thought to any damage to its suspension. She had to get away from the farm right this minute, and Picklewick was the nearest thing to civilisation.

She had parked in the high street and then remained inside the vehicle for a few minutes, drinking in the welcome sight of people going about their normal everyday activities. She would bet her last pound that none of *them* had been attacked by a sheep this morning. She was still shaking from the experience, despite Otto putting a lead on it like it was a dog, to show her how tame it was.

After a quick coffee in one of the cafes to steady her nerves, she had explored the village.

Her delight had been unfeigned. Picklewick was quaint and pretty, and she was relieved to find that her first impression yesterday hadn't been wrong. Was it only *yesterday* that she had driven along this very same street, full of dreams and unbridled excitement? It might only be twenty-four hours, but to her it felt like a lifetime.

Telling herself that things could only get better, she purchased some paint, a wallpaper scraper, brushes and anything else in the decorating department of the small hardware store that she thought she might need, then went in search of a pair of wellies and a more practical coat.

She'd found both in a shop that seemed to cater to outdoorsy farming folk, and although the Wellington boots were a dismayingly drab shade of green (not a Cath Kidston print in sight) they would do the trick.

Shopping done, she had decided to grab a bite to eat before she returned to the farm. After having her breakfast so rudely interrupted, Dulcie was starving. She didn't fancy cooking when she got back (did she *ever* fancy cooking? – she was the most reluctant and uninspiring cook she knew), and she suspected that she would want to get stuck into the decorating and not want the faff of preparing a meal, even if it was only a sandwich. If she ate something substantial now, it would set her up for the rest of the day, which was why she was currently sitting at a corner table in the pub, wielding a fork in one hand and blissfully scrolling the internet with the other.

She had missed this. Being cut off and out-of-touch didn't suit her. And after replying to messages from her mother, Nikki, Carla (who was her oldest and dearest friend), several other mates, and blocking an ex who had contacted her out of the blue because he'd heard about her good fortune, Dulcie was searching for how to care for chickens when a familiar voice made her glance up from her screen.

The pub had filled up while she had been eating, but she spotted Otto immediately and stiffened. He was at the bar, talking to the landlord, and she was close enough to hear the conversation.

Not wanting Otto to notice her, she slumped in her seat, trying to hide behind the pepper grinder, and bent her head to her plate. Pretending to concentrate on her meal, she strained to hear what was being said as she peeped at him from underneath her lashes, enjoying being able to study him without him being aware of her scrutiny.

Otto might be an insufferable jerk, but he was a very good-looking and quite charismatic insufferable jerk, and she found she couldn't take her eyes off him. He was tall, with broad shoulders which tapered down to a slim waist and a nice bum, but it wasn't his physique that held her attention – it was his profile. Aquiline nose, full lips (but not too full), dark hair curling at the nape of his neck, hazel eyes, and even from this distance she could see how ridiculously long his lashes were. He looked different now though, and it took her a moment to realise what it was – he seemed to be uncomfortable and embarrassed, and she soon understood why when she stopped ogling him and tuned into the conversation.

He was asking the landlord for a job.

'I can't afford the likes of you,' the landlord said, 'even if I was looking for a chef. Which I'm not.'

Otto pulled a face. 'I wouldn't expect London wages, Dave.'

'All the same, my customers prefer pie and mash, not bits of this and dribbles of that served on a piece of slate or a dustbin lid.'

'I can cook pie and mash, you know,' Otto said, but he must have seen that he wasn't going to get anywhere, because he added, 'Look, keep me in mind, yeah?'

'I will, but by the time anything comes up, you'll probably be long gone.'

'I doubt that.' Otto slapped a hand on the bar. 'Thanks, Dave. It was worth a shot.'

'Good luck,' the landlord called after him as he left, and Dulcie wondered what all that was about.

Why would Otto, who was obviously well off and could afford a big fancy car and expensive clothes, and who could also afford to raffle off an entire farm for charity, be wanting to work in a small village pub?

She ate the rest of her meal with all kinds of thoughts whirling around her head, and when Dave came to collect her plate and ask whether she wanted to see the dessert menu, she said, 'Did I hear you say you've got a chef's job going?'

'Eh?' He frowned, then his face cleared. 'Do you mean Otto York? No, I was telling him the exact opposite. Anyway, he's too upmarket for me.'

'In what way?' Curiosity was getting the better of her, and she knew she shouldn't be so nosey but she couldn't help it.

'He's one of those Michelin star chefs, and although I wouldn't mind a star or two, folk come here for good honest grub and plenty of it. If I started serving three peas on a plate with a splash of jus, I'd have a mutiny on my hands.'

'Otto is a *chef*?' Dulcie had assumed she must have heard wrong, but she was amazed to discover that she hadn't. She would never, in a million years, have guessed that Otto was a chef.

'He's a darned good one by all accounts, and a bit of a celebrity too,' Dave said. 'Now, can I interest you in some pudding? The special today is white chocolate cheesecake with raspberries.'

'That sounds lovely,' she said, her fingers itching to start Googling, and she reached for her phone as soon as the landlord walked away.

'Otto Yok, Otto York,' she mumbled under her breath as she typed, then sat back, astounded, when she saw the number of hits his name generated. She clicked on the first, read it eagerly, then moved onto the next, and the one after that.

Otto York was indeed a chef. A well-known, well-respected chef, who ran his own kitchen in a prominent London restaurant. One that she would never be able to afford to eat in, even if she lived to be a hundred and started saving now.

She zoomed in on one of the many photos of him and studied his face. Then she turned her attention to the woman who was draped over him. She was gorgeous. As were the other women he had been photographed with. It seemed that Otto York liked to work hard and play hard, and although he didn't appear to have settled down with any of them, speculation was rife.

She also learned that he was thirty-four and loved hiking, dogs and the cinema.

But none of what she read was able to explain why a guy like him would be touting for work in a pub like The Black Horse.

Despite not wanting anything to do with the man, Dulcie was forced to admit that she was intrigued. And attracted. Let's not forget *attracted*.

CHAPTER FIVE

Broadband, finally! It had only taken six days, Dulcie thought sarcastically, as she checked her phone and noticed with relief that it was still connected to the router which had arrived yesterday. Thank goodness she had booked a whole week off work, guessing that she would have some sorting out to do. *Some?* Huh! She might have anticipated doing a spot of redecorating to make the place feel like hers, but she hadn't expected that she would need to strip the wallpaper from every single room, or that she would need a new kitchen, bathroom, downstairs loo, and flooring. The windows weren't the best and neither was the front door, or the back, but all Dulcie could do for the time being was to make it as cosy as possible with the limited funds she had at her disposal – which meant endless painting and a great deal of elbow grease.

She had decided to tackle the room that she'd designated to be the dining room first, as she was also going to be using it as an office and would therefore be spending most of her time in there when she started back to work on Monday. But it was Friday already, and she didn't feel as though she had made a great deal of headway, despite having worked on it all day for the past few days. She was exhausted, her body ached, her hands bore an uncanny resemblance to chickens' feet because they were so dry and chapped, and she had lived in grimy paint-spattered clothes for what seemed like forever.

She was determined to have a long hot shower later, style her hair, put some make-up on and head for the bright lights of Picklewick this evening, but before she could do that she had another full day of decorating ahead, so after she'd fed the chickens and fed herself, she continued with her painting.

Aside from all the decorating, Dulcie was beginning to feel like a proper farmer because she had made a truce with the chickens. Her newly-purchased wellies were responsible for that: with a sturdy rubber barrier between her ankles and their pecky beaks, she had felt brave enough to call them into their coop each evening, a structure which she had eventually found in the orchard. Her internet research had advised her that the easiest way to get a chicken to do what you wanted it to do was to bribe it with food, and she found that she quite enjoyed rattling pellets in a tin bucket and seeing them come running for their supper. And in turn, she more often than not found three warm eggs when she went to let them out the following morning. They didn't half whiff though – the chickens, not the eggs – and she was dreading having to clean out their little house. It was a task she was putting off until she felt brave enough. Maybe she could persuade her nephew to do it, if Nikki brought him for a visit at half term.

Suddenly a pang of homesickness and loneliness twanged her insides, and she put her paintbrush down. She missed her family, damn it, even though they were often annoying and chaotic.

None of them had ever lived in each other's pockets, having their own busy lives to lead, and she sometimes went weeks without seeing any of her siblings, although she often used to call in to see her mum. But this was different, and it abruptly struck her that apart from Otto, who she hadn't seen for several days, the only people she had spoken to face-to-face were shopkeepers, the pub's landlord and the postman. It spoke volumes when the highlight of her social calendar was hearing his van trundle up the hill. Yesterday he had brought her a very welcome card from Carla, wishing her all the best in her new home. As soon as she was settled, she would invite her for a visit, Dulcie vowed.

Just as the thought of the postman crossed her mind, there was a knock on the door and she stifled a surprised squeak. She hadn't heard the sound of an engine and it was a bit early, but her spirits lifted just the same, even though Ashton (yeah, she was on first-name terms with the guy) had mostly only brought her bills or junk mail. At least she was able to enjoy a few brief seconds of contact with another human being. She had caught herself talking to the chickens yesterday, and she had even tried to befriend the aloof ginger cat. All he had done was eye her with disdain and turn his back on her.

However, when she opened the door it wasn't the postman standing on her step. It was a woman with a baby on her hip and a wicker basket on her arm. Dulcie estimated her to be a couple of years older than herself, and she thought how pretty she was.

'Er, hello,' Dulcie said hesitantly.

'I'm Petra,' the woman said, 'and this little monster is Amory. We live at the stables, and we thought we'd better come and say hello. How are you settling in? Here, this is for you.' She offered Dulcie the basket and Dulcie took it, bemused. 'We would have said hi sooner, but we're converting an old feed store into a bungalow, and what with the builders, the horses, and this guy—' she jiggled the infant '—I've not had two minutes to myself. There's a cake in there, and some chutney, as well as a loaf of homemade bread.'

'I'm Dulcie. Thank you *so* much for this. I was about to put the kettle on. Have you got time for a cup of tea? Or coffee?'

'I certainly have,' the woman said, and Dulcie showed her in, leading her through the half-decorated dining room and into the kitchen.

'Sorry about the mess,' she said, feeling embarrassed about the state of the place.

'What mess?' Petra was gazing around curiously. 'It looks fine to me.'

Dulcie guessed that the woman was simply being polite, then was certain that she was when Petra added, 'You ought to see my kitchen. At least you haven't got a couple of dogs and a cat taking up floor space. Or toys everywhere.'

'It's a bit old-fashioned,' Dulcie said, lifting a pair of mugs off the mug tree and feeling thankful that she had washed up her breakfast things.

'I think your kitchen is quaint, and quite in keeping with the age of the house. A lick of paint and some new curtains on the windows and it'll be totally Instagram worthy.'

'Do you think so?'

Petra nodded. She had taken a seat at the scarred and pitted table that Dulcie had yet to transfer to the dining room, and was bouncing the baby on her knee.

'People love this kind of thing. I think you've either got to go high-end with a place like this or stick to traditional. Besides, it's a working farm – or, it *was* – so you can't expect it to be steel, chrome and shiny white tiles. Are you planning to restock soon?'

'I'm sorry…?' Dulcie wasn't sure what she meant. She removed the tea towel which was draped over the contents of the basket and peered inside. 'This cake looks divine. Did you make it yourself?'

'I can't cook for toffee,' Petra replied cheerfully. 'Amos, my uncle, baked that. Although I dare say I'll have to learn when he moves into his bungalow. Unless I can persuade Harry, my husband, to take over kitchen duties, that is.'

'I don't like cooking much, either,' Dulcie confessed, then asked, 'What did you mean by restock?'

'Bring a new flock in. Thanks.' Petra accepted a slice of the cake which Dulcie had popped onto a plate and placed on the table, and deftly moved it out of the reach of grabbing hands. 'You can't have any of this, sunshine,' she said to the baby, who waved his plump little arms in the air and blew a raspberry.

'A flock of what? Hens? I seem to have inherited three and that's more than enough, thanks.' Three she could cope with: any more would freak her out.

'I was talking about sheep. This is prime sheep rearing country, especially with the farm having grazing rights on the hillside.'

Dulcie shook her head vehemently. 'You've got to be joking! I was attacked by one the other day. It tried to get in the house, too. Horrid things.'

Petra laughed. 'I bet that was Flossie, Walter's lamb. She keeps turning up at the stables.'

'Walter should keep it locked up,' Dulcie said. 'It could do someone a serious injury.' By someone, she was referring to herself. 'And it's not like any lamb I've ever seen – it's *huge.*'

'She's a year old now,' Petra said, 'but she still thinks she's a baby. She's very docile. I expect she wanted a bottle. Walter hand-reared her last spring. Congratulations on winning the farm, by the way. We were all shocked when we found out that's what he and Otto were planning on doing with it.'

Dulcie slid onto a chair and bit into her cake. 'Oh. My. God. This is delicious.'

'I know.' Petra beamed at her.

When she swallowed her mouthful, Dulcie said, 'What's the story behind raffling the farm off? I mean, I'm all for giving money to charity, but *a whole farm*? I'm confused – I originally thought Otto was the owner, but he said it belonged to his dad.'

'You've met the delectable Otto?'

'He handed the keys over. He also told me off for leaving the chickens out overnight, and he rescued me from the sheep.' Dulcie blushed furiously as she remembered their previous encounter when she had ordered him off her property.

She caught Petra's eye and her blush deepened when she realised the woman was gazing at her thoughtfully.

'We didn't get off on the best foot,' Dulcie explained.

'He's gorgeous though, isn't he?' Petra said.

'And he knows it,' Dulcie retorted sharply. 'He's also rude and obnoxious.'

'Is he? I hadn't noticed. But then again, I can be rude and obnoxious myself. He's had a bit of a tough time lately,' Petra added. She drank the last of her tea and put the empty mug on the table. 'Right then, we'd better get a move on,' she said, getting to her feet. 'I've got a couple of welcome baskets to prepare for tomorrow. We rent out holiday cottages and there's always something that needs doing. Good luck with the decorating. You know where we are if you need us.'

'Thanks,' Dulcie said, returning the basket to her. 'It was very kind of you.'

'It's nice to see a fresh face at Lilac Tree Farm,' Petra said. 'It was starting to look very sorry for itself.'

Dulcie walked her to the door, and just as Petra was about to leave, the woman said, 'Otto's not so bad, you know. If you give him a chance, you might find you like him.'

The problem was, Dulcie liked him already. Far too much, and not in the way Petra meant!

♥

'Come on, Peg, let's stretch our legs.' Otto clicked his fingers and the sheepdog went to him, her tail wagging. 'You must miss being out on the hillside,' he said to her, as he fetched his coat and slipped it on. It was sunny outside and relatively warm, but he knew how quickly the weather could change, and it was still too early in the year not to wear a coat. If he got too hot, he could always take it off.

'Dad, I'm taking Peg out for a couple of hours. Will you be alright on your own?'

'Silly beggar, of course I will be. I'm not an invalid.'

No, his dad wasn't, but he wasn't as well as he might be, either, and Otto continued to be concerned about him. Thankfully, Walter was a little better than he had been when Otto had paid him that surprise visit at the start of the year. The visit that had changed everything. Otto acutely recalled how appalled he had felt when he saw his father, and how worried he had been that he was going to lose him.

Otto blamed himself.

But he was here now, and he was caring for his dad to the best of his ability, even when his father seriously objected to it. Thankfully, with the awful strain he had been under now lifting, his dad was starting to look and behave more like his old self.

Unable to imagine what his dad had been going through, having to borrow from Peter to pay Paul to keep the farm afloat, Otto was still cross that Walter hadn't confided in him sooner, before the debts had escalated to such an extent that saving the farm was an impossibility.

He sighed as he started walking up the lane. It was water under the bridge. What was done, was done, and there was no point in wailing about it. All he could do was make the best of it, look to the future and not dwell on the past. However, he still felt like the worst son in the world for not realising how bad things had become.

Pushing such non-productive thoughts out of his mind, Otto turned his attention to what he could do going forward. He had been mulling it over a lot lately, but so far he had hit a brick wall.

He had approached every restaurant, pub and cafe within a realistic commuting distance from Muddypuddle Cottage, with absolutely no luck whatsoever. No one was hiring a chef, although he had seen some vacancies for bar and waiting staff. If push came to shove and his savings ran out, he might well have to go down that route, even though it would be hell being so near to a commercial kitchen, when all he would be allowed to do was serve the meals.

Deep down he was still hoping to be able to return to London at some point, because that was where most of the job opportunities lay. He had worked so incredibly hard to get where he was, yet in a few short months he was almost back to where he had started.

Not quite, because he had the experience, the skill and his reputation to fall back on, but the world of professional cheffing was a hard and cut-throat one, and out of sight often meant out of mind. And living in Picklewick was as out of sight as it was possible to get.

The view was good though, he thought glumly, as he turned to face down the hill and scanned the valley below. He had missed this, he realised, drinking in the view. Every field was emerald with new growth, and the hedgerows were lush and leaf covered. The bleat of sheep and their lambs carried on the warm air, and a pang of regret hit him. It might be a very long time indeed until their cries were heard once more on the farm on Muddypuddle Lane. If ever.

The fields were already turning into meadow, now that they were no longer being grazed, and Otto spotted the white petals of oxeye daisies with their bright yellow centres, and the pinky-purple flowers of red clover and mallow could be seeing blooming in the long grass. The bees were having a great time, and he spotted so many fat bumbles that he lost count. A red kite circled overhead, its cry wild and savage, and he realised that nature was beginning to reclaim what was rightfully hers.

It was a sight that was probably replicated all over Britain, as farms went out of business – he forgot how many farmers a year packed it in or went bankrupt, but it was a lot. And the chances of his farm ever being used again for its intended purpose were remote. The best Otto could hope for was that a family would love it and grow up in it, and that the place wouldn't undergo any drastic changes in the process. But he had his doubts that the new owner would see the character in the old beams, the beauty of the grey flagstones on the floor that had been polished to a sheen by the passage of many feet, or the history in the bare stone walls of the sitting room. No doubt she would modernise it to within an inch of its life, until it looked exactly like any other house.

He had debated whether to walk up the lane because that meant he would have to go right past the house he used to call home. He could just have easily taken the path opposite the stables which would have taken him to the top of the hill albeit in a more roundabout and less steep route. But he had to get used to the stark reality that the farm was no longer in his family.

Telling himself to toughen up, Otto plodded up the lane and turned his attention back to what he was going to do with himself for the foreseeable future.

Otto didn't do idleness. He was far too restless a person to relax and twiddle his thumbs, and there was only so much cleaning, laundry and dog walking to be done. There was also a limit to the amount of cooking he could do. Three meals a day for two people was hardly going to keep him occupied for long, especially since his dad was dropping subtle hints that a three-course breakfast wasn't strictly necessary, and please could he have something simple like eggs, beans and chips for tea one night. 'And none of those triple-cooked chips, neither,' he had added.

But without cooking, without spending his days in a kitchen and creating wonderful food, Otto was nothing.

He took a deep lungful of clean spring air, trying to blow away the sadness invading his mind, and sniffed appreciatively as a familiar smell shot up his nose.

He had forgotten that wild garlic grew on the other side of the hedge, and when he came to a gap in the foliage, he peered through it to the pretty white flowers on the other side. There were loads of them, and he breathed deeply, wondering whether he should pick any of the edible blooms to add to the meal he would make tonight.

Then his spirits sank as he thought of the expression on his father's face if he saw flowers on his plate. He wouldn't be impressed, and would no doubt refuse to even try one.

Look, there was alexander, or horse parsley as it was also known, and it too was edible. And so were the new leaves of the brambles which scrambled over the dry stone wall. If you knew where to look, spring was an amazingly abundant time for foragers, and he remembered picking all kinds of things when he was a boy and taking them home to experiment with. He had loved cooking even when he was a kid—

Otto froze.

A thought was beginning to form, and it wasn't half bad…

Absently, he picked a hawthorn blossom and held it to his nose, inhaling its almondy scent. The tree was only just coming into flower, most of the buds still tightly furled, but one or two had braved the elements and were fully open. He picked a second, before popping them both into his mouth. The taste of marzipan exploded on his tongue, and he closed his eyes with pleasure. You can't get fresher than this, he thought.

'What are you doing?' a voice asked, and he opened them to find Dulcie watching him warily.

Instead of answering her question, he asked one of his own. 'Is there any chard or kale in the veggie patch?'

Dulcie pulled a face. 'I've no idea. I don't know what either of them look like.' And from her suspicious expression, she probably wouldn't tell him if she did, he concluded.

But she surprised him. 'Do you want to take a look?'

'If you don't mind.' He suddenly remembered that he had patient gentle Peg with him. 'Are you okay with dogs?'

She narrowed her eyes. 'I like dogs. They're cute. What's his name?'

'He is a she, and her name is Peg. She belongs to my dad.'

'She's a sheepdog, isn't she?'

She is, but she's retired now, since we've not got any sheep for her to work.'

'Except the one.'

'Ah, yes, Flossie.'

Dulcie walked over to the dog and crouched down, holding out her hand for her to sniff, which Peg obediently did, her tail wagging in greeting. 'The veggie patch is rather overgrown,' she said. 'I haven't had a chance to do anything with it.'

'It's been overgrown for a long time,' Otto replied, sadly. As his dad's health began to fail, he'd had to let some things go, and the veggie patch was one of them. Still, with a bit of TLC and a lot of graft, it could look as good as it had been in its heyday, when his mum had been in charge of it and the family had eaten fresh homegrown produce most of the year round.

Dulcie gave the dog a final pat and straightened up. 'Were you eating that tree?' She was eyeing him strangely again.

'I was,' he admitted. 'Hawthorn blossom is edible.'

'I'll take your word for it.' She didn't look convinced.

He reached out and plucked another flower. 'Try it.'

'Er, no thanks. Is that what you do in your restaurant? Cook weird stuff?'

Otto was surprised. He wasn't aware that she knew he was a chef. 'I don't cook weird stuff,' he retorted.

'Eating flowers is weird,' Dulcie shot back.

'Edible flowers are being used more and more in the kitchen,' he pointed out.

'Not in mine.'

He blinked. 'Are *you* a chef?' He wondered where she worked.

'*Me?* Good lord, no! I can just about make an omelette.'

'Oh, I thought...when you said…' He trailed off.

'You do realise that most people don't plonk daffodils on their dinner?' she pointed out.

'I'm pleased to hear it. Eating daffodils can make you quite unwell. I make sure I only incorporate edible flowers into my cooking.'

'I'm not sure I fancy it.' Dulcie looked sceptical, and vaguely revolted.

'I'm sure if you tried them, you would like them,' Otto insisted. He didn't know why he was trying to convince her, but if his vague idea of a hedgerow-to-plate cookbook was to stand any chance of getting off the ground, it would need to have a wide appeal. If he could convince someone like Dulcie – who openly admitted that she wasn't much of a cook – that eating foraged foods and the edible plants growing in their gardens was a good thing, then his idea might stand a chance.

'Tell you what,' he said. 'How about I cook you a meal made with fresh ingredients picked from the garden and the hedgerows? And you can give me your verdict.'

Her eyes widened. 'Um, okay.'

'How about this evening?' he suggested, eager to get started. 'Unless you've got plans?'

'No plans.'

'Great! See you later,' he said, excitement coursing through him.

But was he excited about finally getting back into the kitchen and trying out a new recipe or two on someone who wasn't his dad, or was he excited at the thought of seeing Dulcie again?

♥

Stunned didn't begin to describe how Dulcie felt when Otto invited her to dinner. And it wasn't a going-to-the-pub dinner either – although she was sure that would have been lovely. This was a Michelin star chef, cooking a meal just for her.

How special did *she* feel right now?!

She had spotted him from the window earlier, and had stopped work to watch him as he strolled up the hill. Her heart had missed a beat and the sudden lurch of excitement in her tummy had taken her by surprise.

It hadn't been her intention to go speak to him but her curiosity had been piqued when he began rooting around in the hedge, and she simply had to see what he was doing. Especially since she was pretty sure that the hedge he was molesting belonged to her.

And now, the great Otto York was going to cook a meal for little old Dulcie Fairfax! Her friends would be well-jealous. And so would her sisters. Maisie, especially, had been almost apoplectic with envy when she had told her (rather smugly) that she knew Otto York, and that he lived in the cottage on Muddypuddle Lane. She thought she might have had to hold Maisie back with a chair and whip to stop her from jumping on the train and coming to visit.

Dulcie hurried inside the house to grab her phone, excitement making her squeal, and she was about to make a few calls when she paused.

Maisie was model-pretty, highly-strung, flighty and dreamy. She and Otto would look good together, and with Maisie simpering all over him, how would he be able to resist her?

The thought made her bristle. Not that she didn't want Maisie to be happy (she *did*) but when it came to

Otto, Dulcie felt a bit dog-in-a-manger about him. She wasn't interested in him herself – god forbid, he was too arrogant and up himself – but that wasn't the point.

Actually, she wasn't sure what the point was, but there was bound to be one.

‘

CHAPTER SIX

What to wear…? Dulcie was standing in her underwear in front of the large wardrobe and peering into its depths. She wanted to look nice, but not *too* nice. She was fairly sure this wasn't a date, so she didn't want to appear as though she was trying too hard, but she also didn't want to look as though she'd not made any effort at all. Because, let's face it, apart from the day when he'd handed her the keys to the farmhouse, Otto hadn't seen her looking her best. A cow onesie and scruffy paint-spattered work clothes didn't project the sort of image she would have liked.

Eventually, she settled on a pair of skinny black jeans, a top in the loveliest shade of aqua, a jacket in case it got chilly later, and a pair of ballet pumps. Although… maybe wearing such delicate shoes to walk down the lane wasn't the best idea.

She wished she had a bottle of wine to take with her, but having not gone shopping for a few days, there wasn't any left. Dulcie had drunk it all. She had taken to having a glass or two with her supper after she had downed tools for the day.

The thought of food made her tummy rumble. Apart from that one meal in The Black Horse, she had been living on soup, sandwiches and whatever ready meals she had in the freezer. And eggs, of course: she had plenty of eggs.

That was a thought! She could take him some eggs, and maybe pick some flowers. Her garden had an abundance of tulips, she had noticed, and although it was more traditional for a man to give a woman flowers, considering he was going to feed her some of the damned things, she didn't think he would mind.

As she picked them, she did wonder if tulips were edible, and she was briefly tempted to eat one. She had even got as far as putting a brilliant orange-coloured flower to her lips before common sense slapped her on the cheek. Otto knew what he was doing – hopefully. Dulcie didn't. She hadn't even recognised spinach when Otto had pointed it out to her earlier, and she loved spinach. It had been a common ingredient in the food boxes which she had occasionally resorted to buying, during those times when she had vowed to become a better and more consistent cook, and not live off takeaways and ready meals.

After picking an armful of brightly coloured blooms, Dulcie stopped for a moment to enjoy the beauty of her new garden, and she took a deep breath of flower-scented air. There were no formal beds as such, just a riot of spring colour – the tulips were accompanied by a few late daffodils (although most of them were past their prime now), and she also recognised pansies, peonies and iris, and there was even a splendid lilac tree at the far end, marking the boundary between the garden and the vegetable plot. She guessed the farm must have been named after it, and even from this distance she could smell the sweet fragrance of its blossoms.

Dulcie suddenly realised how lucky she was to live in such a wonderful place. Of all the competitions she had entered over the years (and there had been many) she'd never won anything – but for her to have won not only a house, but a house in such a gorgeous location…

She felt very blessed indeed.

♥

'Hi,' Otto said when he opened the door, and as he did so Dulcie handed him the flowers.

'These are for you,' she explained, feeling embarrassed and apologetic. 'I didn't have any wine, and I couldn't come empty-handed.'

'That's very thoughtful,' he said, taking them from her and burying his nose in the petals.

Dulcie's nose was far more concerned with the mouth-watering aroma of onions and garlic. And was that roast chicken she could smell? Her tummy rumbled loudly and she winced, hoping he hadn't heard.

'I brought some eggs, too,' she said. She had wrapped them in a tea towel, and she passed it to him. 'I'm getting a bit fed up of eggs,' she admitted. 'I feel I should use them, but I've run out of ideas of what to do with them. I suppose I could do some baking, but I've not got the time and neither am I very good at it.' She halted abruptly, realising that she was wittering. Not only that, she sounded as though she was dropping great big hints.

'I can give you a few ideas, if you like,' Otto offered.

'He's full of them,' a voice called from inside the cottage.

Otto grimaced. 'Sorry, where are my manners? Please, come in. I hope you like chicken? I forgot to ask if you're vegetarian.' He looked worried, as he caught his bottom lip between his teeth.

Dulcie's attention was drawn to his mouth, and she hastily dragged it away. 'I love chicken,' she enthused as he gestured for her to walk ahead of him, but disappointment bit her sharply on the backside when she realised they weren't to dine alone. An elderly gentleman was sitting in an armchair and peering at her over the top of his glasses.

'This is my dad, Walter. Dad, this is Dulcie. I'll put these in water,' Otto said, jerking his chin at the flowers. He had a nice chin…to go with his nice mouth.

Gah! What was wrong with her? She was here for a meal, nothing more. Clearly.

'So, you're the girl who won the farm,' Walter said.

Dulcie nodded and made a face, unsure what to say. She had a feeling there was more to raffling off the farm than she knew. She had asked Petra outright, but her neighbour hadn't given her an answer and Dulcie realised that she had deftly changed the subject, turning the conversation away from the farm and onto Otto himself.

'I trust you'll take good care of it.' Walter scowled at her.

'She will, Dad.' Otto had appeared in the doorway. 'Sit down Dulcie, you're making the place look untidy. Can I get you something to drink? Wine?'

'Wine would be lovely.'

'Will white be okay? It'll go better with the chicken.'

'Thanks.'

He went back into the kitchen, leaving Dulcie to smile awkwardly at his father.

'I used to have sheep. And chooks.' Walter was staring into the unlit fireplace with a wistful expression. She guessed him to be in his mid-seventies, and he looked frail and careworn, despite a weather-beaten face and rough calloused hands. He was rubbing them together, and she wondered if she was making him uncomfortable.

'The hens are still there,' she said.

Walter perked up. 'I thought Otto had got rid of all the livestock. How is Mable? She can be a bit flighty.'

'I've no idea, sorry.'

'No idea about what?' Otto appeared at her side. He was holding a large glass with a couple of inches of wine in the bottom.

'Which of the hens is which,' she said. 'I didn't even know my hens had names. I mean, Walter's hens.' Oh dear, she thought: she was in danger of putting her foot in it. 'Would you like them back?'

She would be more than happy for someone to take them off her hands. She might have come to accept them, but that didn't mean to say she *liked* them. Even the novelty of fresh eggs every morning had quickly worn off.

'They're better off staying at the farm for the time being,' Otto said. 'Maybe when we're a bit more sorted.' He shot his father a concerned glance. 'We've got enough with Flossie and Peg, haven't we, Dad?'

Walter didn't look convinced.

'You can come and visit them if you want,' Dulcie offered. 'And you can tell me their names.'

He scratched his chin. 'Their names are Mable, Dolly and Lucky. They probably saw the sheep being rounded up and thought they were for the chop, so they gave my son the slip.'

Dulcie was horrified. 'They weren't…' She hesitated to say it, and suddenly the smell of roast chicken didn't seem quite so appetising.

'Nah, they were good layers. You don't give a good layer the chop unless it stops laying. How many eggs are you getting?'

'Three a day, every day,' Dulcie said.

'They must like you. Chickens can be a bit pernickety.'

Despite not being all that keen on them, being told that the hens must like her gave Dulcie a warm glow, and she felt an urge to know which was which. Mind you, even if Walter did point out Mabel from Dolly, Dulcie still didn't think she would be able to tell one from the other. All three were brown, clucky and feathery.

'If you'd like to take a seat at the table,' Otto called, 'dinner is served.

Dulcie hadn't known what she had been expecting – a kitchen very much like her own, perhaps – but when she entered this one it was very different. Although small and galley-shaped, it had two rows of sleek glossy cabinets on either side, and a large oven that seemed to be the focal point. At the far end, near the door to the garden, was a small round table with four chairs. It had been laid with a pristine white tablecloth and gleaming cutlery.

'What are you trying to poison us with today?' Walter asked, as he shuffled into his seat. 'He's a chef, you know. Likes drizzles of this and soupçons of that.'

Otto shot his father an amused look. 'Dad is getting fed up with my fancy cooking,' he said. 'I think he has a hankering for simpler things, like beans on toast.' Otto shuddered.

'Don't knock it,' Dulcie said. 'There's a time and a place for beans on toast.'

'Not you as well.' Otto sighed dramatically, but there was an indulgent look in his eye and Dulcie couldn't help wondering whether this was the same grumpy, unfriendly man who she had met on her first day, the same one who had told her off about the chickens.

She rather liked this new updated version. He was just as handsome, but he was now beginning to develop the personality to complement his good looks. Or maybe that personality had been there all along, but she had brought out the worst in him?

Otto placed a bowl of soup in front of her. It was green, with a swirl of what she thought might be cream on top. A small roll sat on her side plate, warm to the touch, and curls of yellow butter lay on a dish in the centre of the table.

'Sorrel soup,' Otto said, serving his dad before he sat down himself, then he picked up his spoon. He made no move to dip it in the soup, though. He was too busy watching her.

She took a cautious sip.

A burst of flavour exploded on her tongue, delicate, fresh and considerably moreish. She ate another spoonful.

Otto continued to study her.

'Well?' he asked eventually. He still hadn't touched his. Walter, on the other hand, was hoovering his up, despite his insistence that he didn't want any more fancy food.

'It's really, really nice,' Dulcie enthused. 'Sorrell, you said? Did you pick it from my garden?'

She winced as she saw a shadow flit across his face, and she realised how hard it must be for him to accept that his dad's property now belonged to her. Dulcie pursed her lips, but they didn't stay pursed for long because she simply had to eat the rest of her soup.

'Yep, freshly picked today,' he said, his voice light, making Dulcie wonder if she'd imagined it.

She tore into her roll, releasing a warm bready smell, and reached for the butter, wanting to taste everything Otto had to offer.

The bread was just as delicious as the soup.

'Did you get these rolls from the village?' she asked, thinking she would buy some the next time she was in Picklewick.

Otto gave her a bemused look. 'I baked them myself.'

Of course he did, she thought. 'Don't tell me you made the butter as well?'

He chuckled, a sound that sent a delicious shiver through her. It was throaty and sexy, and abruptly she didn't want to taste any more of his food – she wanted to taste *him*.

Dulcie put down the roll she was nibbling on, her appetite for food suddenly gone, replaced with an altogether different kind of appetite.

My, my, she had better put a stop to this unwanted desire: nothing good would come of it.

'I didn't make the butter,' Otto admitted, 'although I will make some next time, if you like.'

Next time?

Dulcie resisted the urge to fan herself with her hands. Did he mean that he wanted to see her again, or that he wanted to try out some more dishes on her? Either way, sexy man plus sexy food was a heady combination. No wonder women were attracted to him.

Was he as passionate in bed as he was about his cooking?

The thought made her head spin.

Oh, man, she needed to get out more. A week on the farm with only herself and three chickens for company was taking its toll. She needed to start making some new friends – fast.

Dulcie realised she had finished the soup and the roll, her hands and mouth on automatic pilot whilst her mind had been otherwise engaged.

'Not bad, that,' Walter announced, dropping his spoon into his bowl with a clatter. 'Mind, you can't beat a tin of Heinz tomato,' he added.

Dulcie's eyes widened, and then she noticed the twinkle in the elderly man's eye.

Otto shook his head, an indulgent smile on those gorgeous lips of his.

'Just pulling your leg, son,' Walter said. He turned to Dulcie and winked.

'Ready for your mains?' Otto asked, rolling his eyes and making Dulcie giggle.

'Definitely. What is it?' she asked.

'Roast chicken with wild-garlic potatoes, and a salad of chickweed, spinach, hawthorn buds and leaves, lime leaves, and red clover to garnish.'

'What's that?' Walter asked, pointing at the deep red liquid that Otto was pouring sparingly over the crispy golden chicken. 'See, drizzle this, jus that,' the old man grumbled.

'Blackberry ju— *sauce*,' Otto replied. 'I didn't pick those today, obviously, but I thought the chicken needed a little something. In an ideal world, I would have picked them last autumn and frozen them, but I bought them from the greengrocer in the village instead.'

'I don't care where you got them,' Dulcie told him when she tasted it, and she closed her eyes in bliss as she chewed. She had expected him to be a damned good cook, but not *this* good.

She opened them again to find him gazing at her and she blushed, hastily swallowing her mouthful.

Her mouth suddenly dry, she sipped at her wine. For a moment there, she thought she had seen something in his eyes…

Shaking the thought off, she tried to concentrate on her food, but as she ate, her gaze kept returning to Otto, and each time it did she found him looking at her. And each time he would give a little smile and look away.

By the time dessert was ready to be served, Dulcie was completely out of sorts. She didn't think she had ever been so acutely aware of a man. The way he'd rolled up his sleeves to reveal the dark hairs on his forearms. His long fingers with their neatly trimmed nails. The muscles in his upper arms. The way his hair curled ever so slightly at the back of his neck. She wanted to touch it, to see if those curls were as soft as they looked.

As he stirred something in a pan, she studied the outline of his jaw, the slope of his nose, the shape of his mouth when he quickly dipped a teaspoon in the pan and tasted what he was making. He licked his lips, and her insides fizzed as she imagined what it would be like to be kissed by him.

Take a breath, lady, she told herself: it's not you he's interested in, it's your opinion of his food that he's after.

And this was borne out when he watched her tuck into a generous slice of dandelion cake with gorse flower syrup. It was divine, and her appreciation must have shown on her face because he beamed when he saw her reaction.

'Would you eat it again?' he asked.

'Definitely!' Dulcie was emphatic.

'Is there anything about this menu that you didn't like?'

'Nothing. I enjoyed every mouthful. Who knew weeds could be so delicious?'

Otto sat back. 'That's a relief.'

She narrowed her eyes. 'Why?' Something in his tone made her think there had been more to this meal than simply trying to justify his hedgerow nibbling.

'I'm thinking of writing a book of foraging recipes,' Otto announced.

Walter said, 'You are? Since when?'

'Since this morning. I miss being in the kitchen and I've got to do something with my time, so...'

'So, go back to London,' Walter said. 'Now the farm has been sorted, there's no need for you to stay here. I can manage on my own.'

'I know you can,' Otto said, getting to his feet and collecting up the empty plates. 'But I thought I would stick around for a bit longer. I've been wanting to write a cookbook for a while, but I wanted it to be different. I just didn't know how.'

'Until today?' Walter said.

'Until today,' Otto agreed. 'You can blame Dulcie.'

'*Me?*' Dulcie gasped.

Otto chuckled. 'She caught me eating hawthorn blossom earlier. You ought to have seen the look on her face.'

'Is *that* why you invited her to dinner?' Walter asked. 'I thought it might be because—'

'Can I top up your glass?' Otto interrupted, looking at Dulcie.

'Go on, then,' she said, holding it out to him.

'Would you like some more wine, Dad?'

'Not for me. I'd love a nice cup of tea, though.'

'Go into the sitting room and I'll bring you one in,' Otto instructed.

He watched his dad leave and there was silence for a moment. Dulcie could see the concern in his eyes, and she wondered whether he was worried about his father and if that was the reason why he was staying in Picklewick. She also recalled him touting for work, and she guessed he must be desperate for a job. Why else would such a fantastic chef want to work in a small village out in the sticks? She shook her head as she remembered her initial thoughts on the first day. He might have a big car, and he might dress well, but he didn't appear to be any better off financially than she was.

Her heart went out to him. No wonder he had been so grumpy – he had a lot on his plate.

Ah, plates…

'Let me help with the washing up,' she offered.

'Not a chance. You're a guest.'

'And a sounding board?' she asked.

'That, too,' he admitted, plunging his hands into hot soapy water.

'Are you really going to write a book?'

'I'm thinking about it.'

'I'm no food critic, but if you want a guinea pig I'll give you my honest opinion. And what you cooked this evening was heavenly.' She realised she wasn't making this offer solely because he served wonderful food: it was because it would be an excuse to see him again.

'Eating flowers and leaves wasn't that bad, was it?' he teased.

She noticed that he hadn't said he would take her up on her offer. 'They were just about edible,' she smirked.

'Would you cook any of the dishes you ate this evening?' he asked.

'No way!'

'Oh. Too complicated? Too radical?' His face fell, and Dulcie felt sorry for him.

'Too…cooky. I don't cook much, to be honest.'

'When you do, what do you like to cook?'

Dulcie shrugged. 'Omelette, mac-n-cheese, soup.' She was also a fan of Pot Noodles, but she wasn't going to admit that to a top-notch chef.

'Making soup is cooking,' he pointed out.

'Not when it comes out of a tin or a plastic tub,' she said ruefully. She occasionally treated herself to a soup out of the supermarket chiller section, rather than open a tin, and that was the closest she came to home-made soup.

They chatted about food as Otto cleaned up, Dulcie sipping her wine, and when the kitchen was tidy and the only reminder of the fabulous meal she had just eaten was a faint aroma in the air, Dulcie thanked him and prepared to leave.

'I'll walk you back up the hill,' Otto said.

'There's no need. I can find my own way home.' Although she would love him to, she didn't want him to feel obliged.

'I want to.' He gazed into her eyes and her heart fluttered.

Oh my, he wanted to escort her back to the farm. Maybe he didn't want the evening to end just yet, either.

But she was quickly brought back to earth when he added, 'It's dark out and I don't want you twisting an ankle in one of those potholes.'

Oh. That's what he meant. He was just being chivalrous.

'They are rather impressive,' she said lightly, to cover her disappointment as she walked through the living room and headed towards the door. 'Bye, Walter. It was lovely meeting you.'

'You, too. Be careful going up the lane.'

'I'm going with her,' Otto said.

Dulcie almost missed the satisfaction on the old man's face and the warning look on Otto's, and she wondered what that was all about, but when they stepped outside, she forgot about it as she turned her face up to the sky.

'I've never seen so many stars!' she exclaimed.

'It helps that there isn't a moon tonight,' Otto said. 'Which is another reason I wanted to escort you home. I bet you didn't think to bring a torch with you.'

'I don't actually own one. I'd better add it to my shopping list.'

'There's one in the feed store,' he said. 'It might still work.'

'Your dad left quite a bit of stuff behind when he moved out.'

They began to walk up the hill, their pace little more than a dawdle. It was very quiet, she realised. There was hardly a breath of air to stir the leaves in the hedgerow, although she could hear the occasional rustle of an animal in the undergrowth, and she was glad Otto had insisted on accompanying her.

Otto sighed. 'You've seen how small Muddypuddle Cottage is. He couldn't bring much with him. I did think of emptying the place, but you know what farmers are like – they never get rid of anything in case it might come in handy, and there was just so much of it. I suppose I could have called in a company to clear the house, but as for the barns and the sheds…' He trailed off.

'If you don't mind me asking, why didn't you sell the farm? Why did you raffle it?' She couldn't shake the feeling that his finances were little better than her own. The cottage was much smaller than the farmhouse, although she could tell that it had recently had work done on it, especially the kitchen. And if he was as well off as she had initially assumed, why had he asked the landlord of The Black Horse for a job?

'I tried, but…' He shrugged. 'I might as well tell you because everyone in the village knows – my dad was up to his neck in debt. We had no choice but to raffle it.'

Dulcie was even more confused. 'I don't understand.'

'What he would have got if he had sold it, wouldn't have covered his debts. No one wants to buy a hill farm these days. Farming is bloody hard work and farms are going out of business left, right and centre. There's no money in it. That's why you see so many of them diversifying. We did consider alternatives such as glamping, but we couldn't afford the initial outlay.'

'But you just *gave* it away?' Dulcie had a sudden terrifying thought that as the new owner of the farm *she* might be responsible for those debts.

'It wasn't a raffle, as such. It was a lottery, and the money raised from selling tickets was enough to pay off my dad's debts, with a decent amount left over to give to charity.'

'You gave the rest to *charity*?' Gosh, what a hero. Dulcie didn't think she would have been as generous.

'That was one of the conditions for running the lottery – all proceeds have to go to charity, less certain expenses. For other companies who run this kind of thing, that would usually include the purchase of the property itself. In Dad's case, we were able to pay off the mortgage and everything else.' Otto tilted his head back to look at the heavens. 'It was a shame it had to end like this, but I couldn't see any other way out. Anyway, Dad's health isn't the best, so he couldn't have continued to run the farm for much longer.'

'Did you not want to run it yourself?' They had almost reached the entrance to the farmyard, and she slowed, not wanting the conversation to end.

'Cheffing is my thing,' he said. 'It always has been. I've never wanted to do anything else, and you can't be a chef the way I wanted to be a chef, and run a farm at the same time.'

They came to a halt outside her front door. Should she ask him in? She wanted to, but what if he declined? She would feel like a proper idiot. But on the other hand, if he agreed, he might get the wrong idea. She didn't want the evening to end, but neither did she have any intention of jumping into bed with him, not after seeing the women he had been photographed with. Although she might fancy him like crazy, Dulcie had more self-respect than to become another notch on his bedpost. Saying that though, he hadn't shown the slightest interest in her in that way, so she was probably overthinking things.

'Thanks for walking me up the hill,' she said, turning to face him and digging around in her jacket pocket for her keys.

'You're welcome.'

'And thanks for a lovely meal. It was astounding.'

'I'm so pleased you enjoyed it.'

Otto smiled, and Dulcie hastily averted her gaze from his gorgeous lips, and nibbled at her own, catching the bottom one between her teeth as she resisted the urge to stand on tiptoe and kiss him.

She cleared her throat. 'Thanks again, and if you want a guinea pig for any more recipes, I'm your gal!' she reminded him.

'You might regret saying that,' he joked. 'Goodnight.'

'Goodnight,' Dulcie replied, but he had already begun to walk away and he raised his hand, waving without turning around.

Yep, it was as she had surmised – he was only interested in her for her tastebuds.

CHAPTER SEVEN

'There's something sexy about a man cooking for you,' Nikki observed, when Dulcie phoned her the following morning. She simply couldn't keep it to herself, and her sensible, level-headed sister was the person she chose to call.

She could have had a chat with any number of her friends, and Carla should have been the obvious choice, but Dulcie wanted to keep her growing feelings for this man in-house, so to speak. Carla was flighty and flirty, and didn't believe in love or relationships, and as Dulcie had never seen her fall for a guy, she wasn't sure Carla would understand how Dulcie was feeling. Heck, Dulcie herself didn't understand.

She'd had relationships in the past, some of them fairly serious, but none of them had amounted to more than a few wasted months of her life and a bruised heart.

But this felt different. More grown up.

It might be because she was rapidly approaching thirty (she had a year or so to go yet, but she was aware it was looming) or it might be because she was finally a homeowner. It might even be because she had no family or friends in her immediate vicinity to fall back on. But whatever the reason, she had never felt like this before. And the daft thing was, she hardly knew him.

Dulcie wasn't an insta-love kind of girl. She took her time to get to know a fella before she let her emotions loose on him. She might be ditzy in other ways (not as ditzy as Maisie, thankfully – but then *no one* was as ditzy as her younger sister). In ways such as freaking out over a chicken, for instance, but when it came to matters of the heart she was cautious to the point of being accused of not having a heart at all.

She definitely did have one, but having seen the way Maisie fell in and out of love at the drop of a hat, Dulcie had no intention of doing the same. Maisie lived her life on a roller-coaster of emotions, either madly in love, or in floods of tears and heartbroken. It must be exhausting.

On the other side of the coin was Nikki – divorced with an eleven-year-old son. She had only ever loved one man and look how that had turned out! Dulcie had been serious when she had offered to beat Nikki's lying, cheating husband over the head with a shovel, then use that same shovel to bury him.

Okay, maybe not really serious, because she never would have gone through with it, but imagining doing away with her rotten brother-in-law had helped her cope with Nikki's distress, during her sister's darker moments.

'Dulcie, are you still there?' Nikki asked.

'Huh? Oh, yeah, sorry.' Dulcie refocused. 'It *was* sexy, despite his dad being there.'

'His *dad?*' Nikki spluttered, her laughter carrying over the airwaves.

'Yeah, he lives with him in a cottage down the lane. It was originally part of the farm, but they hung on to it.'

'You're going gaga over a guy who still lives at home with his *dad*?'

'It's not like that,' Dulcie protested and she went on to explain the situation.

Nikki said in a more sober voice, 'What did you say his name was?'

'Otto York.'

'*The* Otto York? The chef? Why didn't you say so! He's famous. When can I come for a visit? Do you think he'll cook for me, too?'

'You sound like Maisie,' Dulcie grumbled. 'This is why I didn't say anything sooner. I know what you lot are like. Don't tell Mum or Maisie,' she warned. 'They'll be here in a flash, and I've got loads of decorating to do.'

'Mum could help with that,' Nikki said. 'And I'm definitely coming to visit you at half term. I'm dying to see the place. It looks idyllic.'

Dulcie had sent loads of pictures to her family – carefully crafted photos which displayed the farm in the best possible light. The reality was rather different, but she was hoping that by the time her family descended on her, the interior of the house would look the best she could make it with the resources and funds she had available.

'Sorry,' she said, hearing a knock. 'I've got to go, there's someone at the door.'

Dulcie hurried to the front door, her heart pitter-pattering in the hope that it might be Otto. She had to hide her disappointment when she realised her visitor was Petra.

'Hi,' Dulcie greeted her, warmly. 'Come in.'

'I'd love to, but I can't stop. I just wondered if you'd like to come to The Black Horse tonight? It's Lena's birthday.'

'Um…'

'Sorry, you don't have any idea who Lena is, do you? She's my uncle's girlfriend – soon to be partner when they move in together. I just thought it might be nice for you to pop along and meet some people. We don't bite, honest. If you didn't want to drive, you can come in the Land Rover with us.' Petra's eyes flickered sideways to Dulcie's game little hatchback.

'That would be lovely,' Dulcie said. 'Thanks.'

Her spirits soared as she thought about the evening ahead. It was so nice of Petra to invite her, and she wondered what to take as a gift, because she couldn't arrive empty-handed.

Skipping the decorating for today, Dulcie decided to subject her poor car to the perils of Muddypuddle Lane, and pop into the village. After all, it was Saturday and she had earned a day off, and with the prospect of an evening in the pub, she was in no mood to do any more damned painting!

♥

'This is Charity and her partner, Timothy. He's Harry's brother and one of the vets at Picklewick Veterinary Practice. She works at the care home in the village and also helps out at the stables. She's got a twin sister Faith, who—'

Dulcie's eyes glazed over. The girl waving at her was the umpteenth person she had been introduced to so far this evening, and there was no way she was going to remember all their names, let alone figure out who was connected to who. She was okay with Harry, Petra's husband, because he had driven them to the pub, and she also remembered the baby's name. She thought Amos might be the old guy, who was sitting next to the lady whose birthday it was, but as for the rest…there were just too many of them.

Everyone was gathered around several tables that had been pushed together, and all of them seemed to be talking at once.

Dulcie smiled politely and said 'Hi' at each introduction, feeling rather dazed, and when there wasn't anyone left to be introduced to, she sat back and sipped her drink, her gaze flitting around the room.

Snippets of conversation reached her ears, but she couldn't follow any of them so she let it flow over her, just happy at the prospect of making new friends. She knew it was going to take time to fit in, but it was something she would have to put some effort into if she wanted to make a new life for herself in Picklewick.

After about half an hour or so she began to relax, and although she still felt like a newbie, people were very kind, going out of their way to talk to her and include her in the conversation. She was particularly drawn to Charity, who was only a couple of years younger than her, and although Dulcie got the impression the girl was quite shy, she was very friendly and had a dry sense of humour. Dulcie was a little concerned when Charity suggested that she popped down to the stables for a riding lesson, but hopefully a love of horses wasn't a prerequisite for a

92

growing friendship, because Dulcie had no intention of going anywhere near a horse.

Dulcie was halfway through telling Megan, an older lady who owned a cake decorating business, about her run-in with Walter's tame sheep, when a familiar voice made her ears prick up. Swivelling around in her chair, she spotted Otto and Walter at the bar.

Hastily she turned back, a blush creeping into her cheeks. For some reason she hadn't expected to see Otto in The Black Horse this evening, although this was his local too, and the sight of him unsettled her. Her heart did that trippety-trip thing again, and her stomach seemed to tie itself in knots. She licked her lips nervously and took a gulp of her drink, spluttering when it went down the wrong way.

By the time she had finished coughing, people had shuffled around to make way for Otto and Walter to pull up a chair. Otto was now seated next to her, with Petra on her left.

Walter was next to Amos, and the two old gents immediately fell into conversation, leaving Otto to say hello on both their behalf.

Dulcie was watching him carefully as he made his way around everyone, and when he came to her his eyes widened for a second as he noticed her studying him.

'I didn't expect to see you here,' he said, leaving Dulcie to ponder whether he was wishing she wasn't.

'Petra invited me.'

He smiled politely, his gaze glancing around the room before coming back to rest on her. He looked uncomfortable, and she wondered why, hoping it had nothing to do with her.

But why should it? She was reading too much into things, second guessing herself as she so often did, and she could almost hear her mother say, "the world doesn't revolve around you, you know."

'Nice to see you,' Petra said to Otto. 'We were beginning to think you'd turned into a hermit.'

'Dad fancied a pint,' Otto said, making Dulcie think that if his dad hadn't, Otto would have been quite happy to have stayed at home.

'How are you settling into the cottage?' Petra's husband asked.

'It's okay.' Otto shot Walter a look and his expression relaxed when he saw that his father wasn't taking any notice of the conversation. 'It's not been easy,' he admitted, lowering his voice. 'For either of us.'

'Your dad looks better than the last time I saw him,' Petra observed. 'Not so frail. It must be all that good food you're feeding him.'

'I don't know about that,' Otto chuckled. 'He keeps complaining that it's too fancy – although he was happy enough to gobble up a three-course meal last night.'

'*Three* courses!' Petra exclaimed. 'I can tell you're a chef. We're lucky if we get one course and a slice of cake afterwards. What did you have? Not that I would cook it myself, you understand…although Harry is becoming a dab hand in the kitchen.'

'What is it with you women not wanting to cook?' Otto joked. 'Dulcie tells me she doesn't like cooking much either. She doesn't mind eating, though. There wasn't a scrap left.'

Petra raised her eyebrows. 'A scrap of what?' She looked from Otto to Dulcie, then back again.

Dulcie blushed. 'Otto invited me for dinner at his place last night.'

Petra cocked her head. 'I see.'

'It's not like that,' Dulcie blustered.

'Like what?' Her new friend was grinning broadly.

'Otto was just….' Dulcie didn't feel it was her place to go into details. If Otto wanted to share his recipe book idea, that was up to him. But she hadn't wanted Petra to get the wrong end of the stick and think there was something going on between her and Otto when there wasn't.

'Being friendly?' Petra drawled.

'Exactly!'

Otto, Dulcie noticed, had failed to say anything, and when someone asked Petra a question and her attention was otherwise engaged, Dulcie whispered, 'I hope I didn't speak out of turn?'

'You didn't,' he assured her in an equally quiet voice. 'Although I am grateful you didn't mention my cookbook idea.'

'Eaten any more of the hedgerow recently?' she murmured.

'Not today. Dad was very pleased to have an old-fashioned cottage pie for dinner.'

'It sounds lovely. I had egg on toast.'

'Oh, dear…You could have eaten with us if I'd—'

'God, sorry! I wasn't angling for an invite—Honest!' Dulcie could feel her already warm cheeks burst into flame.

Amusement shone in his eyes. 'I didn't think you were. But I've got a habit of making too much, and there is loads left over. I could drop a portion up to the farm later, if you like?'

'Please don't trouble yourself.'

'It isn't any trouble, honestly. In fact, why don't you stop off on the way home, and pick it up?'

'I didn't drive – Petra brought me in her car.'

'How about if I take you back later? I'm sure Petra won't mind.'

Petra heard her name being mentioned and asked, 'What won't I mind?'

'If I drive Dulcie home,' Otto said.

Dulcie caught her eye. Petra was grinning at her again.

'I don't mind at all,' the woman chortled.

'Excuse me, I'll be back in a sec,' Dulcie said, getting to her feet and grabbing her bag. She didn't need to go to the loo, but it was a good excuse to be on her own for a few minutes to calm her furiously beating heart.

But when she got there, all the cubicles were taken. Dithering about whether to wait, she settled for washing her hands and redoing her lipstick.

'I never thought we'd see Otto York in Picklewick,' a voice from one of the cubicles said, and for a second Dulcie thought the comment was aimed at her, until another voice piped up.

'Neither did I. Do you think he's got a girlfriend?'

'Why? Are you volunteering for the position?' the first woman asked.

'I wouldn't mind trying. He's a bit of a dish. Did you see the way he was looking at that woman sitting next to him? Like he wanted to eat her up? Do you think they're together?'

'I don't believe so. She arrived with Petra.'

'Huh! It's a wonder *she's* not after him herself.'

'Sour grapes, Cher. Just because Harry was interested in her and not you.'

One of the toilets flushed, then the other.

Not wanting to be caught eavesdropping, Dulcie beat a hasty retreat, her ears burning. What was all that about? *Had* Otto been looking at her in that way?

She wasn't ready to return to the others just yet, and she definitely wasn't ready to face Otto, so to give herself some breathing space she headed outside to the beer garden.

There was no escaping him, though.

Otto was already out there, a drink in his hand and a thoughtful expression on his face.

But if she hoped she could slip back inside without him noticing her, she was sorely mistaken. He clapped eyes on her as soon as she stepped outside, and unless she wanted to be rude, she had no choice other than to keep going as he beckoned her over.

'Too much?' he asked, as she slid onto the bench opposite.

'A bit,' she admitted. 'Everyone seems to know everyone else.'

'That's Picklewick for you.'

'Hi, Otto.'

Dulcie and Otto looked up. Dulcie recognised the voice as belonging to Cher, one of the women in the ladies' toilets, and her heart sank

The woman was gorgeous, as Dulcie's quick head-to-toe scan showed. Glossy dark hair bounced on her shoulders, her make-up was skilfully not-there, she had long deep-red nails, and her clothes looked as though she had just stepped off a catwalk.

Dulcie had an immediate attack of envy. No matter how hard she tried, she would never be able to achieve Cher's level of chic sophistication.

'Uh, hi. Do I know you?' Otto asked politely.

'No, but don't let that stop us from being friends.' The woman simpered, and Dulcie scowled. 'I'm Cher. I heard you were living in Picklewick. Are you putting down roots here, or is this a pit stop?'

'I'm from here, actually,' he said.

'Scoot over.' The woman shoved her bum onto the bench, nearly sitting on his lap in the process.

Otto scooted, but Cher was still too close for Dulcie's liking, although Otto didn't seem to mind that her thigh was touching his. Or that she had placed a proprietary hand on his arm and was gazing at him adoringly.

'I'd best get back to the others,' Dulcie said. 'They'll be wondering where I've got to.'

Otto made to get up, but Cher pulled him back down, saying, 'Tell me, where are you working at the moment? I'd love to book a table and sample your…' she paused suggestively '… food.'

The woman was a man-eater. Dulcie wanted to gag, and as she hurried away Otto's reply faded as she headed inside.

She was tempted to walk straight through the pub and out into the street, but she didn't think it fair to Petra if she disappeared without giving her some explanation. Petra had been kind enough to invite her, and Dulcie didn't want to throw that back in her face.

So she went over to her and whispered in her ear.

'I'll drive you home,' Petra offered, on hearing Dulcie's flimsy excuse that she had a headache.

'Nonsense! You stay and enjoy the evening. I can find my own way back, and the fresh air will do me good.'

'Are you sure?'

'Absolutely. Thank you for inviting me this evening, it was fun. Could you pass on my apologies to the others? I'm sorry to sneak off, but I think it must be all the paint fumes I've inhaled over the past week.'

'Let me give you my mobile number. Text me when you get home. And if I haven't heard from you in an hour, I'll be sending out a search party.'

'Thanks, Petra.' Impulsively Dulcie gave her a peck on the cheek, then slipped quietly away.

'Oi! Otto! Have you got a minute?' Otto saw Petra waving at him from the door to the bar, and relief at the interruption washed over him.

He hadn't wanted to be rude, but he was getting to the point where he was seriously considering telling Cher to back off. Talk about coming on too strong! The woman didn't know the meaning of subtlety.

To be fair, she was exactly the type he was usually attracted to, and maybe she sensed it. In his other life, he would have flirted with her as hard as she was flirting with him, enjoying her confidence and her "I know what I want and I know how to get it" attitude. They would have understood each other – she would have wanted to be with him for his minor celebrity status and the opportunity to be photographed with him, and he would have been happy to spend time with an attractive woman. He wouldn't have taken it seriously, and neither would she: especially when she realised that being a chef was not as glamorous as it appeared. Long hours, hard work and a determination to be the best in the business didn't make good boyfriend material. Which was probably why he was still single at thirty-four. That, and the fact that he had yet to meet anyone he wanted to have more than a few dates with.

Until, that is, he had met Dulcie. But he was pretty sure she didn't think of him in that way, which was a shame.

'Excuse me,' he said to Cher, who was scowling worse than a five-year-old child. 'I had better see what Petra wants.' He got to his feet and Cher's scowl immediately turned into a sexy pout.

'Promise me you'll come back?' she drawled.

'Er, I don't think I'll be able to. I'm with my father, you see.'

'Perhaps we could catch up another time?'

'Perhaps. Nice meeting you,' he said, and made his escape before she could suggest swapping phone numbers. Or, god forbid, try to pin him down to a time and a place.

'Is it my dad?' Otto asked as soon as he reached Petra, a worm of worry uncoiling in his stomach.

'Your dad?' Petra looked puzzled, then her face cleared. 'Your dad is fine. He's reminiscing with Amos. I didn't know Walter had a brother?'

'Uh, yeah, Uncle Emrys. He emigrated to Australia thirty-odd years ago. Died last year. I never met him. What was it you wanted to have a word about?'

Petra blinked. 'Oh, right. It's about Dulcie. She's gone home.'

Otto frowned. 'Why?'

'A headache, she said, but I don't believe her.' Petra looked into the garden and wrinkled her nose when she spotted Cher.

Otto was disappointed; he had been looking forward to spending a couple more hours with Dulcie this evening and he had been hoping to drive her home.

'Why don't you believe her?' he asked, as Petra's words sank in.

'Because she refused a lift. Said she'd walk back.'

'So?'

Petra rolled her eyes, her exasperation evident. 'It's getting dark and Dulcie doesn't strike me as the type of woman who does much walking along lonely country lanes at night.'

'You're right!' Otto could have slapped himself for not realising. 'Why do you think she decided to leave?'

Petra gave him a pointed look and glanced into the garden again, before meeting his gaze. 'Why do you think?' she countered.

'Cher?' He hazarded a guess.

'Give the man a gold star. Oops, I forgot, you already have one,' Petra smirked. 'Seriously, I think someone should go after her, and as she only knows me and you, and I have the baby with me, I think it should be you. If you hurry, you can catch her up. When you find her, there's no need to come back to the pub – I'll drive Walter home.'

Otto gave her a searching look. Was Petra trying to set him up? Had she guessed that he was starting to have feelings for Dulcie?

It didn't matter. The only thing he was concerned about right now was Dulcie's safety.

'Thanks, Petra. Tell Dad I'll see him later,' he said.

He thought he heard Petra mutter, 'Or in the morning,' but he was sure he must have misheard.

Putting it out of his mind, he hurried out of the pub and into the deepening twilight.

♥

Stupidly, Dulcie hadn't expected dusk to be quite so dark.

She had left the village and the comfort of the streetlights behind (which had only just come on) and was now walking along the road leading to Muddypuddle Lane. The problem was, it was getting dark faster than she had anticipated, and the turning into Muddypuddle Lane was further than she thought. The distance seemed much shorter in a car.

And to make matters worse, she had a feeling she was being followed.

Dulcie glanced behind nervously and her stomach churned when she saw a silhouette pass under the last streetlight, heading in her direction.

She pursed her lips and carried on walking.

Although the outskirts of the village were unlit, the road had a couple of houses on it, so whoever it was probably lived in one of those and wasn't following her at all, she reasoned.

But as the last house faded into the distance, she looked over her shoulder to see a dark figure still following her and she began to worry.

Her concern deepened as she realised the person was catching her up, and Dulcie's palms grew clammy and her pulse quickened in fear.

Why had she been so silly? If she had accepted the offer of a lift, she could have been at home by now, making herself a cup of cocoa to cry into. Better still, she should have shoved her jealousy to the back of her mind and concentrated on enjoying the evening and making new friends.

She already knew that a man like Otto was out of her league, and he'd given her no indication that he fancied her, so she shouldn't have felt put out when he had shown an interest in a woman who was more his type.

The scuff of a shoe on tarmac made her flinch.

The pavement had petered out several metres ago, and the road had abruptly become a dangerous and threatening one.

Trying not to be obvious about it, Dulcie shifted her bag to the front and quietly undid the zip. If she could find her keys, she could grip one of them between her knuckles to use as a weapon.

'Dulcie.'

Oh, god, he knew her name. How did he—

'Dulcie! Wait up.'

She drew in a sharp breath, relief making her knees weak as she recognised the voice. Trembling, she slowed to a halt.

Her heart still thumped though, but now it was because of Otto himself, and not because she was frightened of being attacked.

'What are you doing here?' she asked, her voice squeaky with adrenalin.

'Making sure you get home okay. It's getting dark.'

Her eyes widened. Maybe she'd read him wrong and he was interested after all, and she was inordinately pleased that he hadn't stayed in the pub with Cher.

'Where's your car?' she asked. Although *Otto* might have walked into Picklewick, she guessed that his dad wouldn't have been up for it, so she guessed he had driven to The Black Horse.

'At the pub. I assumed you would have cut across the fields, and if I'd driven I would have missed you.'

'Why would I cut across the fields?'

'Because it's quicker. There's a public footpath leading from the edge of the village, past the stables, and up onto the hillside.'

'I didn't realise.' But Dulcie was fairly certain that she wouldn't have taken it, even if she had known about it.

'Remind me to show you,' he said, falling into step beside her. 'How are you feeling?'

'Eh?'

'Your headache?'

'Er, better thanks. Fresh air helped.' She hoped he couldn't hear the fib in her voice. If it had been light enough to see her face, he definitely would have realised she wasn't telling the truth, because she'd never been good at lying.

They walked in companionable silence for a while before Otto said, 'I hope you weren't too intimidated.' And for a second, Dulcie thought he was referring to Cher, before he added, 'Not like I was. I hardly knew a soul there. The only person I know is Amos. He and my dad go way back. He's lived at the stables for about forty years.'

Dulcie was surprised. She had assumed Otto was friends with everyone at their table this evening.

He continued, 'I was already in college by the time Petra moved in with Amos, so although I've bumped into her over the years, I can't say I really know her.'

'She seems nice,' Dulcie said. It was strange to think that even though Otto had grown up on Lilac

Tree Farm, he was almost as much a stranger here as she.

'Yes, she is,' Otto agreed. 'She was the one who told me you'd gone home, and suggested I come after you.'

'Oh. I see.' Dulcie felt disheartened. It hadn't been his idea after all. It had been Petra's. He had probably felt obliged.

She didn't say anything more, pretending to have to save her breath for the hike up the hill. Muddypuddle Lane was quite steep when you had to walk up it from the bottom, she realised. It was bad enough plodding up it from Otto's cottage. Coming from the bottom was quite a trek and Dulcie was puffing by the time they reached the entrance to the farmyard.

She fully expected Otto to say goodnight to her at this point, and was surprised when he escorted her right to her door.

'Thanks,' she said. 'I'm glad Petra made you come after me. It's twice as long on foot as it is by car and I didn't realise how scary it would be.'

'She didn't *make* me. I would have followed you anyway.'

He would have? She inhaled slowly, hoping the reason was that he liked her and not just because he was a considerate guy.

Otto hesitated and she wondered what he was going to say, but he didn't say anything. Instead, what he did next thrilled, shocked, and excited her in equal measure.

He *kissed* her.

His lips were soft and warm, and for the briefest of moments she froze. Then she was kissing him back with an ardour she hadn't felt in a very long time. If ever…

Her mouth opened and his tongue slipped inside. His arms wrapped around her, his embrace tight and urgent, and she was swept away by the passion he evoked, until she was breathless and dizzy. Every nerve ending burned and sizzled, until she thought she might burst into flames.

When they eventually broke apart, she was left with trembling knees, a racing pulse, and a surge of desire so strong that it was all she could do not to drag him inside and take him to bed.

He still held her, and she could feel the tension in his arms and hear his ragged breathing, and she knew he wanted her as much as she wanted him.

His voice was hoarse when he spoke. 'I'm so glad it was you who won the farm.'

'So am I,' she murmured. Then she let out a nervous giggle as she added raggedly, 'If the new owner had been a man, I couldn't imagine you kissing *him.*'

'I've been imagining kissing you since the day we met.'

The words blazed a path through her mind, and her heart soared.

'You can do it again if you like,' she suggested, thinking *please do it again*, before asking, 'Do you want to come in?' knowing full well what it would lead to if he did. And from the hunger in his eyes, she didn't think he'd refuse.

He smiled, a slow seductive upturn of his lips that made her tummy tighten in anticipation, turning her into a pool of liquid heat. His growl of, 'Hell, yes,' made her quiver, desire swamping her until all she could think of was this gorgeous, delectable man.

Her heart thudding, Dulcie unlocked the door and pushed it open. 'Do you want a coffee?' she asked in an attempt to slow things down.

But it was a futile gesture.

'I want *you*,' he said, and she drew in a sharp breath.

He inched closer and she leant towards him, the lift of her chin and the tilt of her head an unmistakable invitation, as anticipation sent every cell of her body into overdrive.

Suddenly she was in his arms, and he was holding her so tightly and kissing her so thoroughly that she couldn't breathe. Her head swam and her legs trembled as she kissed him back, her tongue slipping into his mouth. His groan of desire fuelled her own hunger, and her arms wrapped around his neck as their bodies pressed together.

She felt his firm fingers digging into her hair, and he deepened the kiss until all she could think about was his lips, his tongue, his hand cupping her breast, and the fire he had ignited.

She would have made love to him then and there, in her hall, but he dragged his mouth away and she almost sobbed in frustration as his eyes found hers and he gazed into her soul, stripping her bare.

Whatever he was searching for, he seemed to find it. Then his lips were on hers once more, and she forgot who she was and where she was, for a very long time indeed.

♥

'Did you get much sleep?' Otto asked as Dulcie stirred and opened her eyes. He was propped on his elbow, the sheet around his waist, their legs entwined.

'A little,' she said, her cheeks blooming as she recalled the reason why she had only managed a couple of hours. And how wonderful and magical it had been. This morning she felt both energised and delightfully languid. Her whole body felt as though it had turned to liquid, each limb loose and heavy. She had never felt so relaxed.

But as he continued to gaze at her, her body began to spark into life once more, and when his lips curled into a slow, seductive smile, every synapse tingled and fizzed with renewed longing.

Dear god, she couldn't get enough of this man. Nor he her, to her delight and surprise.

But finally, they were sated, and Dulcie felt the lure of tea and toast. All that exercise had made her hungry.

Kissing him on the shoulder, she slipped out from underneath his arm and reached for her onesie.

'How am I supposed to get at you when you're wearing that?' he asked, a playful frown furrowing his brow.

'I'm sure you'll find a way,' she said primly. 'But not yet. I'm starving.'

'Now you come to mention it, I could probably do with something to eat.' He rolled out of bed, allowing her a glimpse of his perfect behind and slim hips.

Oh, my…

Giving herself a mental shake – not only was she hungry but the chickens needed to be let out of the henhouse – she promised herself she would drag him back to bed after breakfast. Maybe they could share a shower?

Her pulse leapt at the thought, but she told herself to behave. Food first, love later. Not too much later though, she hoped.

Leaving him to get dressed, Dulcie went downstairs to put the kettle on. Whilst it was coming to the boil, she dashed outside to let the chickens out, scattering some poultry feed on the ground as she did so, smiling at the flurry of feathers and squawks as the three hens squabbled over their breakfast.

Otto was in the kitchen when she returned. He was fully dressed, much to her dismay, and he was also wearing his shoes.

'Tea and toast?' she asked.

'I'd prefer coffee, if you've got it. But if not, tea is fine. Then I'd better go check on my dad,' he said.

'Oh. Okay.' She busied herself by popping some bread in the toaster, so he wouldn't see how disappointed she was. 'I've only got coffee bags. I expect you're used to grinding your own beans and stuff.'

He laughed. 'I'll have you know that I'm quite partial to a coffee bag. So much more convenient.'

'Milk and sugar?'

'Black, please.'

Of course he takes it black, she thought – he looks like a black-coffee kind of guy. She realised how little she knew about him, and how exciting it was going to be to find out. She couldn't wait!

Taking a couple of mugs off the stand, she sneaked glances at him out of the corner of her eye.

Never mind his cooking, Otto himself looked good enough to eat this morning. His hair was tousled where she had repeatedly run her fingers through it, he had a shadow of stubble covering his jaw, and as he leant against the doorway his eyes smouldered when he caught her staring.

His pupils grew large and his lips parted, and with a soft growl he opened his arms. 'Dad can wait a while longer. Come here.'

Dulcie was more than happy to oblige.

CHAPTER EIGHT

'Well, well, well,' his dad drawled as Otto sheepishly slipped into the house sometime later. 'I don't need to ask where you spent the night.'

Heat crept into Ottos' cheeks. 'I like her.'

'I should hope so!'

'A lot,' Otto added, for good measure.

'Enough to keep you in Picklewick?'

Otto turned shocked eyes on his father. 'I've no intention of going anywhere.'

'Because of me?' Walter asked. 'And what happens when I'm fighting fit again? Will you go back to London?'

'I don't know.'

'You don't think I'm able to take care of myself, do you?'

Otto decided to be truthful. 'No, Dad; you're getting better, but you're not quite there yet.'

'But I'll get there, son. I'll get there.'

Otto wasn't sure whether the words were a promise or a warning. He also wasn't sure whether he would ever be able to go back to London and leave his elderly father to cope on his own again. Otto was under no illusion that a return to the city would mean a return to his former frantic way of life, with little time to pop back to Muddypuddle Lane to check on his dad.

No, he had to accept that his home was in Picklewick for the foreseeable future, and that he should concentrate on writing his book.

To be honest, he was looking forward to this new challenge in his life. If Dulcie, who by her own admission was no foodie, loved the dishes he had prepared for her the other night, then other people surely would. He had done his research and knew that there were plenty of books on cooking foraged ingredients already on the market, but he was hoping his would be easily accessible to everyone, no matter how poor a cook they believed themselves to be. And with that in mind, he vowed to try to persuade Dulcie to have a go at cooking one of his recipes – even if it was as basic as picking fresh clover from her garden and mixing it up with salad leaves and a tangy fresh dressing.

Otto had a quick shower, then made some breakfast (although according to his dad, it was more like brunch) then he got to work on preparing Sunday lunch: roast beef with all the trimmings.

Should he ask Dulcie to join them?

He wanted to, and not just because he guessed she probably wouldn't be cooking a proper meal for herself. It had only been a couple of hours since he'd kissed her goodbye, but he already longed to see her again.

As he swiftly sliced carrots into batons, he chuckled wryly. Who would have guessed that he would become besotted with the new owner of Lilac Tree Farm? And besotted was definitely the right word. He hadn't been able to stop thinking about her since the very first time they'd met, and last night had compounded the problem. Every time he blinked, her image flashed across his inner eye, and he could still feel the softness of her in his arms, taste her lips, smell her vanilla-scented skin…

In all his thirty-four years he had never experienced such a thing. No woman had touched him as deeply as Dulcie, and it was rather worrying. What if she didn't feel the same way? What if last night hadn't meant as much to her as it had to him?

The stupid thing was, he had known her for less than a week!

Take it slow, he cautioned. Although…having spent the night with her, he did wonder if it was far too late for that kind of advice.

♥

The last thing Dulcie felt like doing today was picking up a paintbrush, but she couldn't sit around all day mooning over Otto, and she had to do something to take her mind off the events of last night – and this morning. He had finally left after another energetic session of lovemaking, and she had watched him jog down the lane, feeling silly that she was missing him already.

The house felt empty without him; so much so that she even tried to tempt Puss inside to keep her company. She could see the ginger tom lying in the planter, basking in the sun, but when she opened a pouch of cat food and called him, all he did was stretch, yawn and turn his back on her, waving his tail in the air to give her a look at his backside as he sauntered off.

As she prised open a tin of white gloss and gave the pot a stir, she decided it wouldn't do her any good to think about Otto all day. And neither did she want to think about work: tomorrow was Monday, her first day in work since she had taken possession of the farm. So she resorted to what had rapidly become a favourite pastime – imagining what could be done with the farm if only she had the funds.

Structurally, she would leave the sitting room as it was, because it was a lovely-sized square room and the fireplace was to die for, although it was in dire need of a new ceiling (Artex? ugh) and she would like to replace the carpet. New curtains wouldn't go amiss either, and neither would new furniture.

The dining room was a different proposition, though. She was currently using it as an office, but in an ideal world she would like to separate her living space from her working space and install an office in one of the outbuildings – the large stone shed with lots of rooms would be perfect. One of those would make an excellent office. Mind you, she wasn't sure how much longer she wanted to stay in her current job, and she was dreading starting back to work tomorrow, so if she found another which didn't require her to work from home, she mightn't have need of an office at all.

Anyway, back to the house itself – which was a much more pleasurable thing to think about even if she didn't have the funds to do much of what she wanted to do. One of those things involved a major expense, because she would dearly love to knock down the wall between the kitchen and the dining room, to make it into one large space. She would have an island where the wall used to be, and a huge window at the front to let in lots of light, as well as to make the most of that fabulous view.

Then she snorted. Who was she kidding? She could barely afford the paint and wallpaper she had bought, let alone plan any major structural work. Anyway, before she did all that, she desperately needed a new bathroom.

Dulcie picked up the tin of paint, then put it back down again as a feeling of defeat swept over her. All this decorating was akin to sticking a plaster on a broken leg. She might make it look better on the surface, but the improvement was only marginal.

Maybe she should just sell up and be done with it?

It was a thought…

Instead of resuming her painting, Dulcie made a cup of coffee and took it outside to enjoy the sunshine. And think.

She didn't want to do anything drastic, however she was torn between wanting to stay on the farm, and not wanting the expense or the hassle to make the house into the place she would call her forever home. She simply didn't have the money and probably never would, so perhaps it was better to cut her losses now, before she spent any more on it.

Walter and Otto mightn't have been able to sell the farm, but that was because it had been laden down with debt. She had no such restriction. However, any money she got for the sale would be hers and hers alone, to do with as she wished. She could use the proceeds to buy a house in the village, somewhere that didn't need a vast amount spent on it, somewhere she could happily invite her family to visit and not worry that they would think she had won a pig in a poke.

She would be sorry to leave the farm though, because she could see its potential, and she still hadn't fully let go of her dreams of wandering barefoot through the meadow or picking apples straight from the tree.

If only there was some way of raising money—

Dulcie gasped as a thought struck her. Maybe there was!

Abandoning her half-drunk coffee, she hurried inside. She had some research to do!

'Can I ask you a favour?' Otto said, a week or so later. He nuzzled Dulcie's neck, making her squirm in delight.

'It depends,' she replied, warily.

'Will you try out a recipe for me?'

'You know I will! You can cook for me anytime.' She wriggled around to kiss him properly, moving one of the cushions out of the way.

They were snuggled together on the sofa in the living room of the farmhouse, supposedly watching a film, but there was far more kissing going on than watching tv.

It was all very domesticated and quite lovely. In fact, the whole week had been quite lovely, with Otto popping up to the farm in the evenings, often – but not always – spending the night. He sometimes brought food with him, and other times he would cook for her. She would watch him potter around in her kitchen and wonder if he found it strange. After all, he had taught himself to cook in it when he was a boy and here he was cooking in it again; however, it didn't belong to his dad anymore – it belonged to her – and according to Otto it hadn't altered much over the years either, which probably made it even more of an odd experience for him.

Hopefully, if her plans came to fruition, that might change when the kitchen and dining room became one large spacious room, with a state-of-the-art kitchen for him to enjoy.

It wouldn't be just for Otto, of course, because who knew if their relationship would last. It was still very early days and although they couldn't keep their hand off each other, the L-word hadn't been mentioned yet. Dulcie was falling for him badly, but she wasn't sure he felt the same. She hoped he did, but…

'That's not quite what I meant,' he said, chuckling. 'I want *you* to cook for *me*.'

Dulcie laughed disbelievingly. 'Will beans on toast do you?'

'I'm serious. I want to check whether someone who doesn't like to cook can actually follow one of my recipes and make a decent job of it. I'm hoping my dishes will be easy enough for everyone.'

'You're serious?'

He nodded, his expression pleading. 'Please?'

Dulcie narrowed her eyes and gazed at him slyly. 'You'll have to ask me very nicely.'

'How nicely?' His lips fluttered against the side of her mouth. 'As nicely as this?'

'I'm sure you can do better.'

He trailed kisses down her neck. 'How about this?'

'Hmm…'

'This?' His lips had reached her collarbone, but by then speech was beyond her, and it was some considerable time before she was able to utter anything coherent.

♥

Otto watched Dulcie chopping a couple of shallots and itched to take over, worried that she was about to slice a finger off.

He held back though, because this was supposed to be about a reluctant cook attempting one of his recipes, so he concentrated on making notes instead and tried not to interfere.

'What's the difference between shallots and onions?' she asked, her tongue poking out a little as she concentrated. 'Can't I use onions instead?'

'You could, but shallots are sweeter and have more flavour. Do you think I should mention in the recipe that shallots can be swapped for onions?'

'Yes. I wasn't quite sure what shallots were and it might have put me off.'

Otto wasn't convinced, but he was willing to take her advice on board, although he was fairly certain that people who knew what chickweed was, would probably be familiar with shallots.

'Done,' she announced, putting the knife down. 'Now what?'

Otto bit back a smile. 'Read the recipe.'

'It says to melt a knob of butter in a pan and fry the shallots gently for a couple of minutes. Then add the potato and fry for another five minutes.'

'Okay, then, that's what you need to do.'

'How much is a knob?' she wanted to know.

'About forty grammes.'

'I think you should say that. A knob could mean anything.'

'Agreed.' Otto made a note. See, this was why he needed a non-chef to cook the dishes he was creating. After years of practise, he instinctively knew how much butter was needed, but most people might appreciate a bit of guidance.

The aroma of frying shallots filled the kitchen and he inhaled deeply, enjoying the familiar smell. He'd make a decent cook out of Dulcie yet, he vowed.

'I've got to add the vegetable stock next and simmer for ten minutes,' she read, pouring the stock out of a jug and into the pan. As soon as she had finished, she turned to him and asked, 'Can I have a kiss now?'

'Not until we're done,' Otto protested. 'You know it won't stop at one kiss.'

Dulcie pouted and he fought the urge to gather her into his arms and whisk her off to bed.

He settled for drinking her in, instead.

The first time he had seen her he'd thought she was gorgeous, and time had only served to strengthen his initial impression. She was more than gorgeous – she was delectable. Sweet, funny, kind, playful, oddly naive in some ways…she was perfect, inside and out. Aside from being unable to keep his hands off her, Otto was also unable to keep his gaze off her. His dad had accused him of looking like a love-sick puppy whenever Dulcie was around, but he couldn't help himself.

Anyway, his dad was just as enamoured. Walter thought the world of her already, and had told him on more than one occasion that he was chuffed to bits that Otto and Dulcie were an item.

Otto was pretty chuffed too.

♥

Dulcie's face fell when she opened the email from Prodine Estates – it wasn't the news she had been hoping for, and not only that, they had also taken their own sweet time in getting back to her. But now that they had, she was flummoxed.

She had sent the estate agent an email a couple of weeks ago, asking whether they would be interested in selling a field or three for her. She had scoured the internet for hours, trying to discover what the selling price of agricultural land was in the area, but she hadn't had a great deal of luck as there were so many variables. But she reasoned that anything she got for her fields was better than nothing, and she could put the money towards renovations on the house. After all, she was hardly going to farm them herself, was she? She still disliked sheep, and she couldn't see that changing any time soon.

But this email had suggested something else entirely, and she read it again, this time aloud and more carefully.

'Blah…blah…thank you for contacting us…blah…blah.'

She paused, having come to the bit that had thrown her into a tizzy. 'After careful consideration we would be interested in securing Lilac Tree Farm ourselves and in its entirety,' she recited. 'We are aware that planning permission has been granted for the conversion of existing outbuildings on a property nearby, and we are confident that this may well be the case for conversion of your outbuildings into sympathetic dwellings. Of course, planning permission would have to be sought and granted before any sale were to take place, and with this in mind we would politely request that you make an appointment with one of our agents to visit your property for an initial and without prejudice discussion.'

Dulcie blew out her cheeks. Blimey! She hadn't been expecting that.

She was aware that Petra had converted an old cow shed into three holiday cottages, and that Amos was currently in the process of transforming a feed store into a bungalow for him and Lena, his lady friend, to live in.

But what Dulcie hadn't been aware of was the possibility that her own outbuildings might also have a new lease of life as private homes. And she certainly hadn't anticipated that Prodine Estates might want to buy the whole lot themselves – the farmhouse included.

Which meant that she would have to look for somewhere else in Picklewick to live.

But hadn't that same thought already crossed her mind, and hadn't she dismissed it because she really did like living in the farmhouse, especially since it was only a short walk from Muddypuddle Cottage and Otto?

It wouldn't hurt to speak with them though, would it? And she might be pleasantly surprised. She had no real idea what the farm was worth, but as she had previously told herself, anything she got from selling it would be pure profit – profit which she could then use to buy a nice little cottage.

No, it most definitely wouldn't hurt to speak to them.

♥

'It's our one-month anniversary soon,' Otto had said yesterday. 'I think we should celebrate.'

Dulcie's eyes lit up and she had given him a great big grin. How romantic! 'What did you have in mind?' she'd asked, delighted that he'd remembered. Not many men would.

'I thought it might be nice for you to taste someone else's cooking for a change. How about we go to The Falcon for a meal? It's not too far and I hear it's good.'

'Sounds lovely,' she'd replied, and so that was where they were heading now.

Dulcie had dressed up for the occasion and relished the feel of a skirt swirling around her legs and the sight of her painted toenails peeping out of cute sandals. Her dress was light and summery, even though it was only May and still chilly in the evenings. So with that in mind, she had slung a soft leather jacket in a dreamy vanilla colour over her shoulders. She had bought it in the sales a few years ago and it was utterly impractical – which was probably why she adored it so much and didn't wear it very often.

Otto's eyes widened when he saw her, and she wondered whether he was going to sweep her off her feet and take her to bed instead of going out for the promised meal. But he behaved like a perfect gentleman, apart from whispering in her ear that he was looking forward to seeing her without the jacket later, and without the dress…or her underwear.

Dulcie took great satisfaction in telling him that she wasn't wearing any (she was, actually) and seeing his pupils dilate and his eyes darken with hunger.

Giggling, she flounced towards the car, leaving Otto muttering something about her being the death of him.

For a while part of her wished they'd forgone the meal, but she reasoned that they had to eat and she was hungry, so making love could wait for a couple of hours. The anticipation would be exquisite, especially if they carried on flirting the way they were currently doing. She had forgotten how much fun flirting could be, and she was having a great time fluttering her eyelashes at him over the top of the menu, licking her lips suggestively, and once she had even slipped off her sandal and run her foot up and down his leg.

Seeing the strangulated look on his face had her in fits of laughter. But he soon turned the tables on her when he stroked her wrist, leant forward and whispered exactly what he wanted to do to her later.

Dulcie blushed a deeper red than the wine in her glass and had to fan her cheeks with her napkin, which wasn't at all effective, and when the waiter asked if she was alright, she nearly melted into an embarrassed puddle on the floor.

Her discomfort didn't prevent her imagination from going into overdrive though, and she could hardly contain herself all through the meal. For some reason, she sensed that this month-anniversary had marked a milestone for both of them.

Maybe tonight would be the night that he said those three little words?

♥

'I don't think I can move a muscle,' Otto groaned, much later that evening. 'I might just stay in your bed forever.'

'That's fine by me.' Dulcie draped a leg over his, enjoying the feel of his hand as he absently ran it up and down her hip. 'But I do expect food at some point in the near future.'

'You can't be hungry after the huge meal you've just eaten.'

'That was at least two hours ago,' she retorted. 'More like three. Anyway, I was referring to breakfast. I hoped we could have pancakes?' She lifted her head off his shoulder and gave him a winning smile.

'You only want me because I can cook,' he complained.

'That's not true! I want you for your body, too.' She ran her fingers through the smattering of hair on his chest.

'You'll have to wait a while. I'm exhausted.'

'No stamina, that's your problem,' she teased.

'You've worn me out.' He lay there for a moment staring at the ceiling and she wondered if he might be psyching himself up to tell her that he loved her. But she quickly deflated when he said, 'Do you know you've got a crack in the ceiling? Has it been there long?'

'Erm, not that I've noticed.' She blew out her cheeks, and hoped that the roof didn't cave in on them. She could do without this, but it strengthened her resolve to speak with the estate agents. She had an appointment with them on Monday after she'd finished work for the day. 'Oh well, hopefully it won't be my problem for much longer.'

Otto tensed. 'Why is that?' he asked, after a pause which lasted a heartbeat longer than it should have done.

'I've got someone from Prodine Estates coming to see me on Monday.'

Gently Otto extricated his arm from underneath her and sat up. She couldn't see his face properly, but from the tension in his shoulders she didn't think he was pleased.

'What?' she asked, guessing the news had upset him. It was to be expected, but he must understand that she had to do something drastic – the farm was a money-pit. If she did need a new ceiling, she didn't have the money to pay for it. And what if the problem was worse? What if she needed a new *roof*?

Slowly Otto turned to face her and she flinched.

He was staring at her with a shocked expression, which slowly darkened as she watched. His jaw hardened, his mouth narrowed into a line and his eyes grew flinty.

'What's wrong?' she repeated, dread seeping into her bones.

'You want to sell the farm to a *property developer*?' he spat out the last two words.

'Yeah…maybe…I'm not sure. I was only planning on selling a couple of fields, but they're talking about buying the whole lot.' Dulcie stared at him, and her heart plummeted. He looked seriously annoyed. And disappointed.

'You know what they'll want to do, don't you?' he snapped. 'They've got a reputation for building fast and building cheap, and they'll want to cram in as many houses as possible. They'll turn the farm into a bloody housing estate.'

'I know you're upset, but look at it from my point of view. I can't afford to keep the farm going. Not on my wages. It'll bleed me dry before too long.'

'Perhaps you should have thought about that before you bought a ticket.' He flung the duvet back, swung his feet out of bed and hunted around for his clothes.

Dulcie was stunned. She should have anticipated that he would be upset and maybe it was naïve of her not to, but his reaction was way over the top. Besides, he was being naïve too, to assume that the farm would remain the same forever. Surely he realised that whoever won it would want to do their own thing with it – which might involve selling it.

Perhaps he was right and Prodine Estates did want to build a load of houses on her land, but that was *her* business, not his. It was certainly a question she would be asking them on Monday. Because if that was the case, and they didn't want to renovate the farmhouse and the outbuildings, but wanted to knock them down and build a housing estate there instead, she needed to know.

Fully dressed now, Otto moved towards the door. His face was white, his eyes dark and glittering.

She couldn't believe he was going to walk out on her over this. 'Can we at least talk about it?' she asked.

He hesitated, and for a second she hoped he was going to stay, but instead he said, 'You don't have the slightest interest in rural life, farming, or the village.

Picklewick doesn't need characterless boxes – it needs people who respect the land and those who live on it. Over my dead body will you sell even an inch of Lilac Tree Farm to a bloody property developer.'

Shock slammed into her, and her distress turned to anger as his words sunk in. How dare he come over all high and mighty, and try to tell her what she could or couldn't do with her own property.

She hitched in a faltering breath and let it out in a rush. 'So says the man who couldn't wait to leave as soon as he got the chance. You didn't care about it either. You left your poor dad to cope on his own and look how that turned out. Get out.'

'Don't worry, I'm going. And if I so much as hear a whisper about any houses being built on Lilac Tree Farm, so help me I'll…'

She had no idea what it was that he would do, because he whirled on his heel and stormed out before he could tell her.

'Good riddance!' she yelled after him, the front door slamming hard enough to make the house rattle.

Then she promptly burst into tears.

♥

Otto wished he hadn't slammed the door, but he had been so mad that he'd yanked it shut after him as he'd marched through it and hadn't realised his own strength.

He heard Dulcie shout something, but it was lost to the bang of the door and the furious pounding in his ears.

To think he had been about to tell her he loved her!

He could kick himself, he thought, as he stomped across the yard. Dulcie was just like every other woman he had dated. They were only ever concerned about money. Although to be fair, some of them had also quite liked the prestige of being on his arm – until his dad had collapsed and he'd had to come back to the farm to live. After that none of them had wanted to know. Not a single one.

He had hoped Dulcie was different.

Trust him to have fallen in love with her. What an idiot. Despite being intensely attracted to her, he should have had enough sense and self-control, and he also should have realised that a romantic liaison with the person living in what had once been his family home wouldn't work.

She had made it abundantly clear that the farm was hers to do with as she wished, but the thought of houses being built on his fields made his blood boil, despite those fields not belonging to him anymore.

So much for his hope that the new owner of Lilac Tree Farm would actually *farm* the land.

Huh, he must have been wearing rose-tinted glasses.

But he certainly wasn't wearing them now. Dulcie had ripped them off and had trampled all over them. Just like she had trampled over his heart.

Because she owned that just as completely as she owned the farm. And he didn't know how he would be able to live without her.

CHAPTER NINE

One month, that was how long Otto had taken to wreck her life, Dulcie thought, as she sat down at the dining room table on Monday morning and reluctantly opened her laptop.

She wished she could turn the clock back to the moment just before she had bought that damned lottery ticket. If she had known then what she knew now, she would never have bought it. Trust her to enter a gazillion competitions and never win anything – but then when she did finally win something which she thought would be the greatest prize of her life, it had turned out to be a damned booby prize.

With a heavy heart she popped her headphones on and logged in.

She was seriously not in the mood for work today. The only thing she wanted to do was to crawl back into bed, burrow under the covers and pretend the world didn't exist.

Actually, it wasn't the world that was the problem. It was Otto, and her stupid feelings for him. Why did she have to fall in love?

And now he'd gone and spoilt everything.

The farm belonged to her now, and it was up to her what she did with it. If she wanted to sell it – because, let's face it, what else was she going to do with it? – it was none of his business.

But he had made it his business, and now they were over.

He obviously hadn't cared about her that much, or he wouldn't have flown off the handle like that. And what he said had been hurtful. It was unfair of him to accuse her of not having the slightest interest in rural life or farming, because how could she have? She had always lived in a city and had never experienced anything like this before, unless a week's camping holiday on a farm in Devon when she was ten counted. This was so very new to her.

Anyway, as she'd said to him, he was a fine one to talk. He had fled Picklewick and the farm the very first chance he could, so who was he to tell her that she had no interest in the farm, when he hadn't either? Just because he had been forced to return to Muddypuddle Lane, there was no need to take it out on her. Maybe if he had realised sooner that his dad was struggling financially, Otto would have considered selling a field or two himself to get him out of the mess.

Damn him for his double standards and for being so unfair and unreasonable.

With a despondent sigh, Dulcie turned her attention to her job. There would be plenty of time to nurse her broken heart after her shift ended. And she had no doubt that it was broken, because she had completely and utterly fallen in love with him.

How was she supposed to recover from that?

♥

Otto had spent the weekend alternating between seething anger and despair.

The anger was aimed at both Dulcie and himself: Dulcie for not caring about the farm or Picklewick, and himself because he cared too much.

His anger was also salted with a heavy dose of guilt. She was right: he should have come home more often; he should have realised that his father was struggling; he should have played a more active role in the farm – although how he thought he would have been able to do that whilst he was living in London, he didn't know. Mostly though, he felt guilty for being so selfish. If he hadn't left to chase his dreams, his dad wouldn't have lost the farm. And now it belonged to a woman who didn't want to work the land and who didn't care that years of tradition would be lost when she sold it.

Damn it! What had he been expecting when he'd convinced his dad that the only way to get out of his financial predicament was to get rid of the farm? His foolish hope that it would be won by someone who wanted to run a farm had been exactly that – *foolish*.

But the truth was, he hadn't thought past paying off the farm's debts. He had been far more concerned about his dad's health, both physical and mental, and he still was.

The only good thing to come out of this whole sorry mess was that now that the terrible strain his dad had been under had lifted, his father's health was slowly improving.

For a while Otto thought he was going to lose him, and although his dad wasn't yet at the point where Otto could think about returning to London to try to pick up the pieces of his career, he was beginning to hope that he might be able to do so in the future.

In the meantime, he would be forced to remain in the cottage on Muddypuddle Lane, within a stone's throw of the farm.

Which brought him to the other emotion at the forefront of his mind. His despair was fuelled by the bleak knowledge that for the first time in his life, he was in love. He had even considered telling Dulcie that last night, but thank goodness he hadn't.

'I see your mood isn't any better,' his dad said when he wandered into the kitchen and caught Otto banging pots and pans around, as he prepared to make another foraged-food dish.

This one was dandelion tart, and so far it wasn't going well. He'd not burned garlic since he was in college, and he was cross at his lack of concentration.

'I'm not in a mood,' Otto growled, scowling at the pan.

'Could have fooled me. You're like a bear with a sore head. I haven't said anything until now because I was hoping you would snap out of it, but you're getting worse.'

'I am not.' Otto flung the pan into the sink.

Walter winced at the loud clatter. 'If you behave like this in your own kitchen, I'm surprised you've got any staff left.'

Otto nearly retorted that he didn't have his own kitchen anymore because he didn't have a job, but he bit his lip. His dad felt bad enough as it was, without Otto rubbing it in.

In an effort to lighten the atmosphere and to stop his father from going on about what a bad mood he was supposed to be in, Otto said, 'I thought you realised that all head chefs were prima donnas.'

Walter gave him a disbelieving look. 'You might be a perfectionist, but as far as I know you've never resorted to throwing things. What's up, son? Is it Dulcie?'

'No,' Otto replied shortly, but he could tell from his father's expression that his father wasn't convinced.

'I thought you liked her.' Walter sucked his teeth.

Heat crept into Otto's cheeks, and it wasn't because of the flame from the gas hob. 'I did.' This reply was also short.

'But you don't now?' his dad persisted, and when Otto refused to answer, Walter continued, 'So that's the problem, is it? You like her *too* much.'

Otto's jaw tightened and he pursed his lips.

'I'm right, aren't I?'

'You don't understand.'

'I think I do.' Walter pulled out a chair and dropped into it with a groan. 'You're worried that I'll be upset because you're in love with the woman who owns my farm. Well, I'm not. I've made my peace with the farm having a new owner.'

'No, Dad, you really don't understand. Dulcie is selling Lilac Tree Farm.'

His father sat there for a moment, then rose creakily to his feet and walked slowly out of the kitchen, and Otto watched him go with a concerned expression, but didn't follow him. His dad would deal with the news in his own way and wouldn't appreciate being fussed over.

With a heavy sigh, Otto returned to his cooking, but for once, his heart wasn't in it.

♥

If she had to deal with one more stroppy caller today, Dulcie thought she would scream. Why did people think they could pick up their phone and give her a load of abuse? And didn't they realise that the louder they shouted, the less she was inclined to help them? Of course, she was always professional, and always tried to resolve the situation to the best of her ability.

After a quick comfort break, where she went to the loo, made a cup of coffee (wishing it was something stronger) and took five minutes to calm down, she sat back at the laptop and prepared to do battle once more.

She was in the middle of a call where the customer clearly wasn't right but wasn't prepared to listen to reason (in her experience customers were only right about half of the time) when a volley of bleats from outside was swiftly followed by the door rattling in its frame as a heavy object slammed into it.

Dulcie immediately guessed what it was, and her heart sank.

That damned sheep had got out again and was now trying to butt its way into her house.

'What are you going to do about it, that's what I want to know?' the man on the other end of the phone demanded. His voice had been deep and gruff at first, but it had risen an octave as he'd recounted the problem, and she sensed that his anger had risen along with it.

'I'm sorry, could you repeat that? You cut out for a minute,' she fibbed. She had been distracted by the flippin' sheep and had missed that last bit.

'Don't you give me that nonsense. You heard me the first time. You're just being awkward.'

'I can assure you I'm not, Mr Howes.'

Dulcie winced as Flossie let out a particularly loud bleat. It sounded as though the sheep had made her way to the front of the house and was now directly outside the dining room window.

'Are you making sheep noises?' Mr Howes sounded incredulous. 'You *are*! You're making sheep noises, aren't you?'

'Apologies, Mr Howes, but it's a real sheep—'

'Do you take me for an idiot?'

'Certainly not, I—'

'I want to speak to someone,' he demanded.

Another bleat. This one was even louder, and rather plaintive.

'I *am* someone, Mr Howes.' It was a pet hate of hers when customers asked to speak to *someone*, as though she was a no one, or a robot.

'Now you're being awkward and patronising, as well as rude. I will not be made fun of, do you hear me?'

Loud and clear, she thought. She would be surprised if *Petra* wasn't able to hear him. She tried again. 'I'm not making fun—'

Damn, her screen informed her that the call had been disconnected and she guessed he had hung up.

Her temper rising, Dulcie yanked the headphones off and slapped them on the table.

'Right,' she muttered grimly, getting to her feet and marching to the door. She might not like sheep, but she was in just the right frame of mind to deal with this one.

'Go away!' she yelled, opening the door. But the words had barely left Dulcie's lips when Flossie shoved her out of the way and barged into the hall, knocking her off her feet.

Landing hard on her backside, the breath whooshed out of her, and when she tried to inhale, she ended up with a faceful of woolly tail as Flossie blundered past, heading for the dining room and the kitchen beyond.

It took Dulcie several minutes of chasing the sheep around the kitchen before she managed to shepherd it out of the back door.

She was hot, even more cross, and utterly exhausted by the time she had cleaned up the little presents the sheep had left for her (yuck!) and finally returned to work. Then she wished she hadn't because the first thing she saw when she looked at the screen was a notification that a customer had made a complaint about her.

So when she heard a knock on the door, she was more than ready to give Otto York a piece of her mind – a really big piece.

♥

'Dad, do you want to be my taster for today?' Otto broke off a morsel of the tart, popped it in his mouth and chewed, before nodding to himself. It tasted fine to him, but it never hurt to get a second opinion, especially one as blunt as his father's.

He reached for a sheet of kitchen towel, broke off another portion of the tart and, holding it carefully, poked his head into the sitting room.

It was empty.

Walter wasn't in his bedroom, and neither was he in the bathroom. The tart cooling rapidly now, Otto peered into the garden.

There was no sign of his father, although Peg was sprawled out on the path, enjoying the morning sunshine.

Maybe he was in the paddock, Otto thought, but Walter was nowhere in sight.

And neither was Flossie, Otto suddenly realised.

'Don't tell me the blasted sheep has escaped again,' he grumbled, and his stomach lurched. The silly old duffer had gone looking for Flossie himself, like some ancient Bo Peep, because he hadn't wanted to bother Otto.

Since Walter had collapsed, sending Otto dashing to the farm, his dad hadn't ventured far. He hadn't been able to.

What if he had a relapse, Otto fretted. He could collapse again, and this time he wouldn't be in his own house and close enough to the phone to call for help. He would be in the lane, or worse – out on the hillside.

Otto dropped the tart on the kitchen counter as he sprinted through the cottage in search of his trainers.

Shoving his feet into them, he grabbed his mobile and his keys, and dashed outside.

There was no sign of his father.

Fairly confident that Flossie would have headed up the lane rather than down it, he began to jog towards the farm, pushing aside the worry that if Flossie hadn't gone 'home' to the farmhouse but had gone in search of her flock mates instead, she could be anywhere.

And so could his father.

♥

It was definitely a member of the York family at her door, Dulcie saw when she opened it. But it wasn't the York she had been expecting to see.

'Walter! Have you come to fetch Flossie? She's out the back, eating the flowers in the garden.'

Dulcie didn't see the point in complaining to him that the stupid animal had forced its way into her house, leaving pellets of poop over her kitchen floor. The poor chap had enough to contend with having Otto for a son. If it had been *Otto* on her step, she would have let him have it with both barrels.

Walter frowned. 'Flossie? I didn't realise she'd got out, sorry. I'll take her with me when I go.' He hesitated. 'Actually, it's you I've come to see.'

'Me?

'What's going on with you and Otto?' He held up a hand before she had a chance to say anything. 'I've asked him, but he won't tell me.'

The elderly gent was breathing heavily and Dulcie noticed that he was clutching the wall for support.

'Come in,' she said, taking his arm and guiding him inside, worried that he might keel over any moment. Otto hadn't gone into detail about his father's health, but for Otto to give up his life in London and come back to Muddypuddle Lane to live, it must have been serious.

'Just for a bit, until I get my breath back,' Walter said. 'You wouldn't happen to have a cup of tea going spare, would you?'

'I would,' she said, eying the laptop as she sidled past it. Work would just have to wait. She grabbed a chair on the way and took it into the kitchen, fearing he might keel over if he didn't sit down soon.

'The kitchen needed a lick of paint,' he said, when he had eased himself into a chair with a grunt. 'It looks all nice and fresh.' His gaze roamed around the old units, before eventually coming to rest on her. 'Well? Are you going to tell me?' he asked.

'I don't think it's my place to,' she replied hesitantly, thinking that if Otto wanted his father to know, he would have told the old man himself.

He shook his head. 'You'll understand when you have kids. All I've ever wanted was for Otto to be happy.' He grunted, 'I've made a right pig's ear of it, dragging him away from London and making him come back to look after an old man.'

'You're not that old.' She popped a couple of tea bags into a pair of mugs.

'Old enough to know better. I'm also old enough to know that my son isn't happy. Lately I thought there was a chance he might be, but these past couple of days...' Walter studied her, his gaze unwavering. 'I might be reading too much into it, but I think you're the reason.'

Dulcie was astounded.

She opened her mouth, hunted unsuccessfully for something to say, then closed it again without uttering a word. Otto had made it pretty clear that he wasn't happy with her, so yes, she *was* the reason he was upset.

But she was upset too.

She had stupidly allowed him to slip into her heart, and when he'd walked out he had left a gaping hole in it that would take time to heal.

Walter continued, 'I might not have spent as much time with my son as I would have liked in recent years, but I know him as well as he knows himself. If I may be so bold, I believe he might be in love with you. And I think you feel the same way about him.'

'We hardly know each other,' Dulcie protested, handing him his tea and nearly scolding herself when she spilt some in shock at what Walter said next.

'That hasn't stopped you from spending every waking minute together for the past few weeks.' His retort was sharp.

When she flinched, his expression softened, and he added, 'All I'm saying is, give love a chance, eh? If it doesn't work out, then so be it.'

'He's mad with me because I said I might be thinking of selling the farm,' she blurted, wringing her hands. 'I'm not a farmer. I don't have the foggiest idea what to do with it. And I need the money. This house isn't cheap to run.'

'Tell me about it,' Walter muttered.

'Sorry.' Dulcie was immediately contrite.

'You won't get much for it,' the old man continued. 'It's hardly prime arable land.'

'I'm hoping Prodine Estates will take it off my hands,' she confessed.

Walter snorted. 'They'll soon lose interest because they won't be able to get planning permission, not for the kind of houses they want to build. But another farmer might be prepared to buy an acre or two for the right price. Or you could keep it. Do something with it yourself…?'

'Like what? I'm not too keen on sheep.'

'Pity. They do well here. As do beef cattle. Dairy, not so much. The grazing is too coarse for them.'

Dulcie shuddered. Cows were even worse than sheep.

'Anyway, I'm sure a bright thing like you will think of something,' Walter said. 'Now, back to you and Otto.'

Before she could say anything, there was another bang on the door, and Dulcie sighed. To think she had imagined that this place would be peaceful. She'd had more interruptions this morning than she used to have in a whole week in her old place.

Expecting it to be the postman, her heart missed a beat when Otto shouted, 'Dulcie? Dulcie!'

'Talk of the devil,' Walter said mildly. He sipped his tea. 'You'd better let him in – he doesn't sound happy.'

With trepidation, she went to open the door.

'Have you seen my dad?' Otto demanded. He looked frantic. 'Flossie got out and I think he's gone looking for her. The daft sod.'

'You'd better come in. He's in the kitchen.'

'Is he alright?' Without waiting for an answer, Otto strode past her, calling, 'Dad? What the hell do you think you're playing at? I've been worried sick.'

Dulcie followed Otto into the kitchen and found him crouching beside his father.

Walter waved him away. 'I'm fine. Stop fussing.'

Otto shook his head in exasperation. He glanced at Dulcie, then back to Walter. 'Dad, if Flossie escapes again, tell me,' he instructed. '*I'll* find her.'

'I didn't know she'd got out until I arrived,' Walter said.

'Then why are you—?' Otto stopped. 'Dad!' He looked pained.

Walter took another mouthful of tea, put his mug down and levered himself to his feet. 'I'm going to take Flossie home,' he said. 'Otto, stay here. You and Dulcie need to have a talk. And don't come home until you've sorted things out.'

Dulcie heard the old man calling to the sheep and Flossie's answering bleat, followed by the sound of footsteps and hooves which gradually faded, leaving an uncomfortable silence in their wake.

Neither Dulcie nor Otto said a word for several minutes.

Eventually, Otto broke it. 'I'm sorry, I shouldn't have spoken to you like that.'

'No, you shouldn't have,' Dulcie agreed.

'I wasn't annoyed with you. I was annoyed with myself. It's my fault that Dad lost the farm.'

'You can't blame yourself.'

'But I do. I was selfish.'

'You were doing what was best for you, for your future.'

He pursed his lips. 'As must you. And if that means selling the farm…'

Dulcie let out a small huff. 'You know the proverb 'be careful what you wish for'? Well, I was a competition addict. I entered everything I could in the hope of winning *something*. My ultimate goal was to win enough money on the lottery to buy a house of my own.'

'Instead, you won a farm,' Otto said, his voice loaded with sympathy.

'And I've no idea what to do with it.'

'*I* do. Let me help you.'

Dulcie gasped. 'So *that* is what this was all about? You've been dating me because of the *farm*?' She could feel anger bubbling to the surface again. The cheek of the man!

'Not even close,' he shot back.

'Then why?' she demanded, her hands on her hips.

'Because I—' Otto inhaled deeply. 'Because I've fallen for you. I really am glad it was you who won the farm – whatever you decide to do with it.

Dulcie studied his face. 'Even if I sell it?'

'Yes.'

'Even though it'll break your heart? This was your home for such a long time—'

'My heart is already broken,' Otto interrupted. 'Because when you sell up you'll move away, and I've got used to you being here.'

'But you're right. I'm not cut out for this lifestyle. I'm not cut out to be a farmer.'

'You don't have to be a farmer. Sell it, if that's what you want. Buy a little place in the village instead.'

'You're serious, aren't you? You honestly don't mind if I sell your family farm?'

'It's not my farm anymore. It's *yours*. And if selling up will make you happy, then so be it. I just pray you'll stay in Picklewick.'

He moved nearer, close enough for her to smell the cologne he wore, and she breathed it in, the scent flooding her senses and making her dizzy.

But she wasn't too dizzy to know that she didn't want to sell the farm. This was part of who Otto was and she knew how much it would hurt him, despite him putting on a brave face. There must be other ways she could raise money… make the farm earn its keep. Just not with sheep. *Definitely* not with sheep.

'I'll stay,' she vowed. She would pick his brains, see what could be done that didn't cost too much, but that was a conversation that could wait for another time, because Otto was saying, 'I realise that a month shouldn't be long enough to fall in love with someone, but I have.'

He pulled a face, a dimple appearing in one cheek, and Dulcie thought how sexy he looked. And sad, too.

'I love you, Dulcie, and I know you don't feel the same way, but could you give me a chance? Give *us* a chance? You never know, in time you might begin to love me.'

'Too late,' she said, and the hope in his eyes flickered out.

He swallowed and looked away, the hurt on his face plain to see.

'It's too late because I've *already* fallen for you,' she clarified.

His gaze snapped to her, and his eyes locked onto hers. What she saw in their depths stole her breath and made her pulse race. Tenderness, love, desire, hope – his emotions mirrored her own.

Her heart soared in response, and she began to tremble with the enormity of it.

As though sensing how she felt, he cupped her face in his hand, his fingers at her temple.

'I've never felt like this before,' she murmured, as his lips slid against hers for a tentative soft kiss.

'Neither have I.' He drew back and gazed into her eyes once more. 'I'm not going to hurt you, and we can take this as fast or as slow as you want.'

'I'm scared,' she confessed.

His laugh was low, rumbling in his chest as he took her in his arms. 'So am I, my love, so am I.'

And suddenly, she wasn't so frightened anymore. This was a new beginning for both of them. A new life lay ahead, and she couldn't wait to start living it.

ESCAPE

CHAPTER ONE

Nikki Warring closed her laptop and clapped her hands.

'Settle down, people. I'm not going to let you go until I have silence. Morgan, what did I just say?' She glared at the eight-year-old boy and mimed zipping her lips up.

The child scowled, staring at her from under lowered brows. But at least he had stopped talking. Finally. He hadn't shut up all day. Mind you, the rest of the class had been just as loud and unruly, trying to see how much they could get away with.

Because Nikki was a supply teacher and not their regular one, they wrongly assumed that she was fair game.

It was the same no matter which school she taught in, but after ten years in the classroom, all of them spent flitting from school to school, she was adept at reading a class and more than capable of keeping her charges under control.

It was wearing though and it did get a little tiresome, so she was mightily relieved that it was half term next week and she could have a well-earned rest. She was also looking forward to spending time with Sammy.

Nikki's heart clenched as she thought of her son, and she hoped he'd had a good day in school.

However, the good days had become less and less frequent since he had started secondary school, and she dreaded the thought of him being upset again.

'Morgan,' she warned, seeing the child lean towards the girl sitting next to him. Nikki had already moved him twice today because he had been disruptive, and if he carried on she was tempted to have a word with whichever adult came to collect him.

The bell went and she dismissed the class, deciding not to bother. If she had been the child's regular teacher, she probably would have, but parents and carers tended to pay far less attention to supply staff.

Nikki quickly collected her things and hurried out, calling goodbye to the lady in reception. She was familiar with the school, having taught there on a number of occasions, and she guessed she would be back sooner or later.

Usually she was one of the first to leave a school when the bell went – not having any duties to delay her departure, unlike other members of staff – but on the last day of term there was always a scrum for the exit, no matter which school she happened to be in.

Getting caught up in a queue to leave the carpark, Nikki tapped her fingers impatiently on the steering wheel, anxious to be on her way. She never managed to arrive home before Sammy, but she was rarely long behind him.

The journey across Birmingham to their little terraced house in Bournville took about thirty minutes, the traffic being worse than usual because it was a bank holiday Friday, and she was hot, grumpy and tired by the time she pulled up alongside the house.

She paused for a moment, then took a deep breath and clambered out, hauling her handbag and resources bag, which also contained her laptop and looked more like a piece of carry-on luggage, with her.

The front door was unlocked, even though she kept nagging Sammy to lock it behind him as soon as he came home, and she shook her head in exasperation.

'Sammy?'

Dropping her bags at the foot of the stairs, she slung her jacket over the newel post. Sammy's school blazer had been cast aside on the bottom step, so she picked it up and hung that up also.

Nikki expected to find her son in the kitchen with his head in the fridge as he hoovered up anything remotely edible. Sammy was like a dustbin.

But to her surprise, the kitchen was empty and she checked the time. By her estimation, Sammy had only been home five minutes, so he should still be stuffing his face with the snacks she had prepared for him this morning before she'd left for work.

Unease stirred in her stomach.

'Sammy? Are you in your room?' she shouted.

No answer.

Wrinkling her brow in concern, Nikki went to the foot of the stairs.

'Sammy?' she called again.

A noise reached her, and although it was faint, she instantly knew what it was. Sammy was crying.

Nikki hastened upstairs and knocked on her son's door. 'Sammy?'

'Go away.' His voice was thick with tears.

No way was she going anywhere. He mightn't realise it, but he needed her. 'No can do. I'm coming in, okay?'

He didn't reply, so she gently pushed the door open and went inside.

Her son was on his bed, crammed into the corner, his knees up to his chest and his arms wrapped around his legs.

Her heart squeezed with pain when she saw his young face. It was streaked with tears, his eyes red, his cheeks blotchy, and his mouth was downturned.

He sniffed loudly.

Nikki sat on his bed. She desperately wanted to gather him to her and cuddle his hurt away, but she knew it was best to let him come to her in his own time.

'Do you want to tell me about it?' she asked, her voice soft. She could guess what had happened – Blake Fraser had bullied him again.

Sammy shook his head and sniffed once more, rubbing his arm across his nose.

Automatically Nikki reached into her trouser pocket and pulled out a tissue. 'Here. Blow your nose.'

Sammy did as she asked.

She tried again. 'What did Blake do this time?' It was telling that she had added 'this time.'

Her son refused to look at her so, taking a deep breath, she let it go – for now. When he had calmed down a bit, she would ask him again.

Anger tried to push its way to the surface, but she swallowed it down. Now wasn't the time nor the place. She would reserve her fury for when she spoke to her son's school. *Again.*

How many times had she contacted them to complain about Blake's treatment of her son? Ten? Eleven? But nothing was ever done, and it made her blood boil.

As a teacher she was aware of how difficult it could be to prevent and deal with bullying, but as a parent she wanted something done about it.

It had begun when Sammy transferred from primary school to high school last September. It was just little things at first, such as name-calling or taking his ruler and refusing to give it back. But over the two terms he had been there, the bullying had gradually escalated, and her son had gone from a child who liked school to one who was terrified of it.

Enough! She wasn't prepared to put up with this anymore.

It was too late to do anything today, and next week was the May half-term holiday, but as soon as school resumed, she would sort this out once and for all.

Sammy's sniffles were tapering off and he was looking at her miserably out of the corner of his eye.

Wordlessly she held her arms out and he scooted into them. As he cuddled into her, she held him as tightly as she could and kissed the top of his head.

'Shall we treat ourselves to pizza for tea?' she suggested when he pulled away. 'Then after we've eaten, we can start packing. I think both of us could do with a holiday, don't you? I bet you're looking forward to seeing Aunty Dulcie.'

So was Nikki. Not only was it a good idea for Sammy to have a change of scenery for a few days, but Nikki also couldn't wait to see her sister – or the farm she had recently won.

The lucky cow!

♥

'Does Aunty Dulcie really live on a farm now?' Sammy asked his mother doubtfully.

Nikki glanced across at him and smiled, before quickly returning her attention to the unfamiliar road.

'She does! Isn't it exciting?' Nikki was incredibly envious, even though she had been sceptical when she'd first heard the news, as she had been convinced it was a scam. Win an actual farm? Hardly!

However, it had been totally above board and legal, and Dulcie had gone from renting a tiny flat in one of the less salubrious parts of Birmingham, to being the proud, if somewhat baffled owner of a farm on the outskirts of a quaint-sounding village called Picklewick. And the farm itself was on a road called Muddypuddle Lane. How cute was that!

Nikki couldn't wait to see Dulcie and have a proper catch-up. Video messaging simply wasn't the same as seeing her sister face-to-face.

Green fields lay on either side of the road, and Nikki could see rolling hills in the distance. She wound the window down to let in some warm late-May air, and breathed deeply, thankful that the journey hadn't been a particularly trying one. The traffic had been relatively light (considering that today was the start of the bank holiday weekend), the weather was gorgeous, and Sammy seemed to be coming out of his shell a little, even going as far as to seat-dance to a song or two on the radio. The shell was a recent thing; he had been building it gradually, layer by layer, since last September, each instance of bullying adding another coating.

It was with relief that Niki saw the shadows in his eyes lessen as they grew nearer to their destination, and his gorgeous smile reappear.

'Look! There's the sign for Picklewick!' Nikki exclaimed. 'We're almost there.'

'Can I play with the chickens?' Sammy asked. He had been thrilled to hear that Dulcie was the proud (although *proud* mightn't be strictly accurate) owner of three speckly brown hens.

Sammy was fascinated by the photos of them that his aunt had sent, and he had asked Nikki an extraordinary array of questions, most of which she hadn't been able to answer.

'I'm not sure whether chickens actually play,' she told him, hoping he wasn't expecting them to play fetch or chase sticks.

'Can I play with the cat?' he asked.

Nikki pulled a face. 'Aunty Dulcie says that Puss isn't very friendly.' Dulcie had used stronger language than that, when she had told her that the miserable so-and-so had ungratefully scratched her when she had tried to stroke it.

'Do eggs come out of a chicken's bottom, like poo?' Sammy asked, his thoughts leaping around like a frog on a lily pad.

'Er...Oh, look, isn't this lovely?' Nikki tried to divert her son's attention from chickens' bottoms to the pretty street they were driving along.

Artisan shops flanked either side of the road, and she spied an old square-turreted church and a whitewashed pub. She wondered if the food there was any good: Dulcie wasn't the best cook in the world and if Nikki wanted edible meals she suspected she would have to cook them herself, or they could eat out.

She came to a stop at a zebra crossing and smiled widely. Picklewick was gorgeous. Dulcie's photos hadn't done the village justice, and Nikki couldn't wait to have a mooch around in the shops.

The last person had crossed the road and as Dulcie waited for the lights to change, she noticed a police car on the opposite side of it. The officer was smiling at her and, worried that she had done something wrong and that he was about to pull her over, she began to panic. Until, that is, she realised she had been grinning like an idiot and he must have thought she was smiling at *him*.

The lights finally changed and the traffic began to move.

When she drew abreast of the police car, Dulcie glanced into it, and catching his eye, she smiled again and was relieved to see the man smile back.

The brief glimpse was sufficient to tell her that he was rather good-looking. Or was she just a sucker for a man in a uniform…?

'Down girl,' she muttered.

'Who are you talking to, Mum?' Sammy piped up.

'I'm practising what I'll say to the chickens,' she improvised, with a giggle that was most unlike her.

Ooh, this week at the farm was going to be so much fun!

♥

Giovanni Alfonso loved Picklewick. There were a number of pretty villages on his patch, but he thought this one was the prettiest. Mind you, he was probably biased because he'd just bought a house here – and he had Megan to thank for that.

He would give her a call in a bit, to see how she was getting on. He didn't feel the need to check in on her so often these days. She had Nathan now, and although Gio would always be there for her, he didn't worry about her quite as much. Those first months after Jeremy had passed away had seen Gio obsessively checking up on her, twice and sometimes three times a day. He owed it to the man – Jeremy had been a good mate as well as a colleague, despite the ten-year age gap. And he still missed the daft bugger; even after three years he called frequently to make sure Jeremy's widow was okay.

Gio decided to take a quick break and pop into the cafe for take-out coffee, after which he would give Megan a call.

As he sat at the pedestrian crossing waiting for the lights to change, a woman driving a silver Nissan waiting on the other side of the road caught his eye. She was smiling at him, and her grin was infectious, so he couldn't help but smile back. Then he wondered if he had misread the situation and her smile had been for someone else, because when she caught him staring, her face fell.

But as the lights changed and he drove slowly past her, he noticed that she was looking at him again, and this time her smile was definitely aimed at him.

Attractive, he thought, as he returned the smile once more. Guessing her to be in her early thirties, she had lovely twinkly eyes and a generous mouth.

Then she was gone, and he snapped his attention back to the road ahead as he searched for a place to park.

After he had bought his coffee and returned to the car, he sipped the hot liquid and phoned Megan.

'Hiya, it's Fonzo,' he said. 'How are you keeping?'

'Fonzo! Hi! I'm good. *Really* good. You?'

'I'm fine. Just thought I'd touch base and make sure you're okay.'

Her voice softened. 'I'm more than okay.'

'Nathan treating you right?' he asked. 'Because if he's not…'

'Don't go all macho on me, Fonzo,' she warned, but he could hear the warmth in her voice.

'I'm a police officer, I'm supposed to be macho,' he joked.

'Don't let any female officers hear you say that. What are you doing over the bank holiday? Are you working?'

'Actually, I've got a week off.'

'A whole week?'

He slurped his coffee. 'Yep. A whole week. Go me!'

'Does that mean you're free on Monday?'

'Not necessarily,' he replied cautiously, wondering what she had in mind and not willing to commit to anything until he knew.

'Have you got a *date*?' she cried. 'Good for you!'

'Er… no, no date.'

'What, then?'

Jeremy used to tell him how tenacious his wife was, and Giovanni knew she would get the truth out of him eventually. He didn't want to lie to her, and there was only so much evasive action he could take. 'Nothing,' he admitted.

'Fantastic! That means you'll be able to come to the show,' she said.

'What show?'

'The one Petra is putting on at the stables. It's not just a gymkhana, there will be loads going on. Oh, please say you'll come! We haven't seen you in ages.'

He noticed how naturally she referred to her and Nathan as *we*, and it warmed his heart. She had been utterly devastated by Jeremy's death, and Giovanni had despaired of her finding love again. He was delighted to see how happy she now was.

With a resigned sigh he said, 'Fine, I'll come. What time?'

'It starts at eleven o'clock. I'll be there all day, manning the cake stall. Shall I save you a slice?'

'Only one?' He allowed disappointment to creep into his voice. Megan's baking had always been legendary, but since Jeremy died she had started making cakes professionally and her business was taking off.

'Okay, two slices, but no more. Since you joined Traffic, you've been sitting on your backside all day.'

'Cheeky!'

'Gotta run, I've got a cake that's about to go ping. See you on Monday. Love you, Fonz.'

'Love you, too,' he replied, laughing. He meant it: Megan was like the older sister he'd never had.

He finished his coffee, clicked his seatbelt in, and was about to start the engine when a text came through.

It was from Megan, and he chuckled as he read it.

Bring a girlfriend, indeed! Megan knew damned well that he didn't have a girlfriend, because if he had, Megan would be the first to know about it.

Unbidden, a pair of twinkly smiling eyes swam into his head, and he thought of the woman driving the silver Nissan.

Yeah, right, as if that was ever going to happen.

With a wry shake of his head, Giovanni went back to work.

CHAPTER TWO

Nikki wandered into her sister's kitchen on Monday morning, rubbing her bleary eyes and yawning. 'Have you seen Sammy?'

Dulcie was standing at the sink, her hands in a bowl of soapy water. 'Good morning, sleepy head. Or should I say, good afternoon? He's outside somewhere. With the chickens, I expect.'

'It's not that late, is it?'

'It's half-past ten. Can I make you some breakfast?'

'Just coffee, thanks.' Nikki slumped into a chair and yawned. 'I'm not used to late nights anymore.' She winced as she remembered how much wine she and Dulcie had drunk last night. They'd had a wonderful catch-up session and had chatted for hours.

They hadn't had a chance to spend time together alone on Saturday evening because Dulcie had been eager to show Otto off to her. He had cooked them the most scrumptious meal she had ever tasted, and afterwards Nikki had sprawled on the sofa in a food coma before the excitement of the day had caught up with her and she had taken herself off to bed.

Yesterday had been spent exploring the farm and, as Nikki had suspected might happen, Dulcie had roped her into doing a few chores.

She had baulked at cleaning out the chicken coop, though. Ugh! But Sammy had been well up for it, to her surprise, and she'd teased him about it, saying that she expected the same degree of enthusiasm the next time she asked him to tidy his bedroom.

Dulcie put a couple of steaming mugs on the table. 'Bees,' she said, brightly.

'Pardon?' Nikki scowled. How could Dulcie be so chirpy after all that wine? It wasn't fair.

'I've been thinking about keeping bees.'

'Why?'

'Diversification,' Dulcie said.

'Diversification from what?' Nikki blew on the scalding liquid before taking a sip.

'It's what farmers have to do these days.'

'You're not a farmer,' Nikki pointed out with a laugh.

'If I want to keep this place, I'm going to have to do something with it. And I like honey.'

Nikki's brow furrowed. 'I like wine, but I'm not about to grow grapes.'

'Hmm...there's an idea. Grapes.' Dulcie squinted as she thought.

'I love you to bits, Dulcie, but you can't keep a spider plant alive, let alone vines. You've definitely not got green fingers, and from what I can gather, vines are fussy and not very easy to cultivate.'

'Back to bees, then.' Dulcie beamed at her.

'Do you know the first thing about bees?'

'No, but I can learn. I didn't know anything about chickens until I got this place.'

Nikki sniggered as she remembered Otto's description of her sister's first encounter with a hen.

'Shut up,' Dulcie said. 'I know what you're thinking. I was surprised, that's all. I didn't expect there to be any hens.'

'Or sheep,' Nikki added. Otto had also shared the Flossie incident with her, and she'd almost split her sides laughing as Otto had recounted how his dad's tame sheep had chased Dulcie into the house and demanded to be let in because it wanted to be petted.

'That creature has got a hard head,' Dulcie protested.

'Bees sting,' Nikki pointed out.

'Only if they feel threatened. I've been looking into it.'

'I'm sure you'll work something out, and if keeping bees means that you stay afloat, then go for it.'

'Thanks, sis. I don't want to be a customer care advisor forever. I really want to make a go of this place.'

'I don't blame you for that. It's gorgeous.'

The farmhouse may be in need of renovation (seriously – that bathroom was a nightmare) but it had so much potential and Dulcie had already done a considerable amount of decorating, although there was some way to go yet and Nikki suspected she might be asked to wield a paintbrush before the week was over.

The grounds around the house – the garden, the veggie patch and the orchard – also could do with a large dose of TLC, and some of the fences needed to be repaired. The barns and the other outbuildings could do with some attention, and the fields surrounding the farmhouse had turned into meadows due to them not being grazed. They were currently full of late spring and early summer wildflowers, and

Nikki smiled as she thought that the bees would be happy.

There was even a small stream tumbling down the hillside, forming little waterfalls and pools deep enough to paddle in.

It was absolutely idyllic.

She finished her coffee and got to her feet. 'I'll find Sammy and remind him that we are going to the show at the stables today,' she said.

Dulcie laughed. 'He hasn't forgotten. It was all he could talk about at breakfast.'

'Thanks for looking after him while I was lolling about in bed.'

'You obviously needed the sleep.' Dulcie gave her a meaningful look.

Nikki had shared her concerns about Sammy, and Dulcie appreciated just how stressed she was.

Thankfully, her son seemed to have come out of his shell a little since they'd arrived at Lilac Tree Farm, and the happy fun-loving boy that he had once been was starting to show his face again.

She knew that not having to go to school for a week had a great deal to do with his improved mood, but she also suspected that not being in Birmingham also helped. It was a fair-sized city, but there was always the prospect of bumping into Blake, and Nikki had an uneasy feeling that her son was continually on edge.

This little holiday to Lilac Tree Farm was already doing him the world of good, and he was throwing himself into rural life (the bit they'd seen of it) with enthusiasm.

Now, time to prise him away from those blasted chickens, before he started clucking like one.

As Gio drove up Muddypuddle Lane, he could see that there was a hive of activity at the stables. Jumps had been set up in one of the lower fields, and in another there were stalls and vans, and the aroma of doughnuts and onions was in the air. He was surprised at how many people had turned up, and it took him a while to locate Megan after he'd parked up.

The array of cakes on her stall was amazing.

'Did you bake all these yourself?' he asked, as he hugged her and gave her a kiss on each cheek, Italian-style.

'I did,' she confirmed. 'Although, this one here and that one—' she pointed to a couple of three-tiered wedding cakes '—aren't real cakes. They are fake ones for display purposes, and I use them to showcase my decorating skills, such as they are.'

'Stop being so modest. You've got a real talent. Jeremy would have been so proud of you.'

Megan glowed. 'He would have, wouldn't he?'

Not all that long ago, Megan would have teared up at Gio saying such a thing, but although there was a momentary flash of sadness in her eyes, it was swiftly replaced by quiet pride.

'Do you want to have a slice or two now, or would you like to take your cakes home with you?' She gestured to the cakes under their see-through domes.

'I'll take them home with me, if that's okay?' He chose a couple of slices – although making a decision wasn't easy because they all looked delicious – then he left her to it, as she was busy serving customers.

He was idly watching a load of kids clambering around on a fortress constructed out of bales of straw and remembering the days when he used to love doing stuff like that, when he felt someone clap him on the back and turned to see who it was.

'Nathan, my man! How goes it?' he cried. Gio gave Megan's other half a quick once over.

The guy was looking good. Older than Megan by a couple of years, Nathan's hair was peppered with grey and he had crow's feet around his eyes. Wiry and strong, he was the stable manager, and spent most of his day wrangling horses and tractors. At least, that's what Megan said: Giovanni assumed there was a bit more to the guy's job than that.

'Fancy a pint?' Nathan asked. 'We've got a beer tent, although it's less tent and more gazebo.'

Giovanni felt honoured. Nathan was normally taciturn and definitely not a people-person, so Megan must be having a good influence on him.

'I'm driving, but I'll have a glass of something cold and non-alcoholic.' Gio narrowed his eyes at Nathan in mock displeasure. 'How are *you* getting home? Not driving, I hope?' Nathan didn't live at the stables; like Gio, he and Megan lived in Picklewick. Megan had sold the house she had lived in with Jeremy, Nathan had sold his tiny cottage, and they had bought a house together in the village – one with a decent-sized kitchen so Megan had room to bake her cakes.

'You coppers are never off duty, are you?' Nathan chuckled. 'Don't worry, Megan is driving. Anyway, I'm only having one. Come on, I've got something I want to ask you.'

'Ask away,' Giovanni said as soon as they were seated at a table, their drinks in front of them. The white plastic chair wasn't the most pleasant thing he'd ever sat on, and he shifted around to get more comfortable.

'You've known Megan a long time,' Nathan began. 'How do you think she'll react if I ask her to marry me?'

Gio was taken aback. 'Um, I'm not sure. How long have you two been an item?'

'Since a year last January. I never imagined I'd want to marry again, but this feels right, you know?'

Actually, Giovanni didn't know.

He'd had more than his fair share of relationships over the years, but he had never once felt serious enough about a woman to contemplate marriage.

'Do you love her?' he asked.

'She's my world.' Nathan's reply was heartfelt and direct.

'Does she love you?' Giovanni thought she did, but Megan had never said as much to him.

'She does.' Nathan sounded certain.

'I can't say for sure how she'll react,' Giovanni said. 'All you can do is ask her.'

'What if she says no? It might spoil everything.'

'What if she says yes?' he countered.

Giovanni didn't envy Nathan's predicament. What he *did* envy was the love Nathan shared with Megan, and he wondered whether he would ever get to experience that for himself.

He supposed he would have to meet someone for that to happen, but he was too wedded to his job. Shift work and unpredictable hours made it hard on relationships, which was why so many of his colleagues were divorced or separated.

He was better off not going down that road, he told himself, not for the first time. If he ever did meet a woman he felt serious about, he would cross that bridge when he came to it. For now, he was happy enough on his own.

Okay, not *happy*: contented.

Are you sure about that? his subconscious muttered in his ear, and at that very second he could have sworn he spotted a familiar face. A woman's face that brought a smile to his lips, an echo of the smile he had given her the other day.

But a gang of teenagers passed in front of him, and when he looked again the driver of the silver Nissan was nowhere in sight.

'Mind if I join you?' Harry, Petra's husband lowered himself into a chair. He had a pint in his hand and he took a deep draught, then smacked his lips. 'Ah, that's better. Don't tell Petra. She thinks I've popped back to the house to check on the baby. Lena and Amos are looking after him,' he added, seeing Nathan's raised eyebrows. 'He's fine. I gave Amos a quick ring to check. He's having a nap. The baby, that is, not Amos. They'll bring him down later.' He turned his attention to Giovanni. 'Fonzo, isn't it? Megan's friend?'

'And Nathan's,' Gio said. He gave Nathan an almost imperceptible nod. Nathan nodded back, and Giovanni knew his message had been received and understood. The friendship came with the proviso that Nathan didn't hurt Megan. Megan had been hurt enough.

'Petra is looking for you,' a male voice said, and Gio glanced up to see Otto York, Picklewick's celebrity chef, walking towards them. He was holding hands with a woman, and another was with them.

Giovanni was unprepared for the sudden blast of attraction when he saw who it was.

The woman noticed him at the same time, and her eyes widened.

'Please don't tell her you found me,' Harry begged, gesturing to his half-drunk pint.

'We won't. We thought we'd have a quick one ourselves. I don't know about Dulcie and Nikki, but I could murder a pint. Dulcie, what would you like?' He turned to the woman whose hand he was holding.

'I think a nice cold glass of cider would go down a treat. What do you say, Nikki?'

Giovanni had a name for her. *Nikki*.

Now that he could get a good look at her, she was even lovelier than he'd first thought. Her eyes were conker-brown, and unlike the other day when her hair was back off her face, it hung loosely about her shoulders in chestnut waves. The two women had similar features, although Dulcie's hair was darker, and he guessed they were probably related. Sisters, maybe?

'Sammy, would you like a drink?' Otto asked, and Nathan noticed a boy of around ten or eleven, hovering shyly behind her.

Nikki's son, he thought, remembering catching a glimpse of a kid in the passenger seat of her car. He hadn't taken a great deal of notice though, too caught up in staring at Nikki herself.

'Anyone else want a refill?' Otto asked, sweeping a glance at the three men. 'No? Okay. Sammy, do you want to come to the bar to help me carry them?' The boy nodded and the pair headed to the bar.

Harry grabbed a couple of chairs from a nearby table, and he, Nathan and Gio shuffled around to make room for the women to sit down.

Gio had assumed that Nathan and Harry knew both women, so he was surprised when Dulcie introduced Nikki to them.

'Harry is Petra's husband – remember me telling you about her? Petra owns the stables – and Nathan is the general manager. I'm sorry, I don't know your name...' Dulcie said to Gio.

'Fonzo. I'm a friend of Nathan's.'

'Hi, I'm Dulcie, and this is my sister, Nikki. The hunky guy at the bar is Otto, and the boy with him is Sammy, Nikki's son.'

'Hunky guy?' Harry scoffed, good-naturedly. He pulled a face, then leant towards Giovanni and said in a stage whisper, 'Not only is he a handsome fella, he's a bloody good cook too. A Michelin star chef, apparently. Of course, his head's almost too big to fit through his front door.'

Dulcie threw a beer mat at Harry, and he ducked.

However, Gio wasn't taking a great deal of notice of the banter. He was more interested in watching Nikki. She had an indulgent expression on her face, but her gaze kept slipping away to the bar, and whenever it landed on her son, worry shadowed her eyes.

He glanced at the boy, wondering why she was concerned about him, but he couldn't see anything obvious.

Otto and Sammy returned with the drinks, and Giovanni sat back, letting the others do the talking.

He noticed that Nikki didn't say much either, and her son was positively mute. Then again, why would a kid his age be interested in grown-up chatter? The boy's attention was on the various activities going on beyond the gazebo.

Giovanni's might have been too, if it wasn't for the fact that he was struggling to take his eyes off Nikki. He didn't know why, but she fascinated him.

'I'm going to take a look at that stall selling Mexican food,' Otto said, finishing his drink in record time, and Gio refocused on the conversation.

'Anywhere there is food is a busman's holiday for you,' Dulcie joked. 'I'll come with you – you can treat me to an enchilada, or something. Nikki, are you coming?'

'You go ahead, I haven't finished my drink yet.'

'Aw...' Sammy pulled a face at his mother.

'Don't tell me you're hungry?' Nikki asked, her eyebrows raised in mock disbelief.

The boy's eyes lit up and he nodded.

'Okay, then.' She picked up her cider, but before she could drink it, Dulcie made a suggestion. 'You stay here. Sammy can come with us, if you like?'

'If you don't mind?' Nikki said doubtfully.

'Why should I mind? I don't get to see as much of this little guy as I'd like. Let me spoil him.' Dulcie beamed at the boy, who grinned back.

'Alright.' Nikki subsided, and Giovanni felt a spike of pleasure that she wasn't leaving just yet.

However, Harry and Nathan were, fear of Petra's wrath making them hastily swallow the last of their pints.

'Better make a move before Petra sends out a search party,' Nathan said. 'It's alright for you, Harry, she can't sack *you*.'

'She can make my life a misery, though,' Harry grumbled, upending his glass and tipping the dregs into his mouth.

'Fair point,' Nathan conceded. 'See you, Fonzo. Nice meeting you, Nikki.'

Then they were gone, leaving Gio and Nikki alone. And for what was possibly the first time in his adult life, Giovanni was tongue-tied.

The police officer hasn't got a lot to say, Nikki thought, wondering how to breach the awkward silence after the others had left, and she wished she had gone with them. To give herself a second or two grace, she drank a mouthful of cider, and as she swallowed she caught him looking at her.

'I'm not driving,' she said, feeling instantly guilty, even though she hadn't done anything she shouldn't have.

'I'm off duty.' His voice was deep and slightly gruff. It sent a shiver down her back.

Damn, he was hot.

Did she just think he was *hot*? Hells bells, how old was she? She sounded like Maisie. That was the kind of thing her youngest sister would say. At twenty-four, Maisie was the baby of the family. She acted like one, too.

'Are coppers ever off duty?' she shot back.

He chuckled. Another shiver, this time felt right through her.

'Probably not,' he said. 'You know what I do for a living, so what do you do?'

'I'm a primary schoolteacher.'

'Do you enjoy it?'

'I love it. Most of the time. How about you?'

'I love being in the police force. Most of the time,' he added.

He smiled at her, and she smiled back. 'Fonzo? Is that short for anything?' she asked, scanning his face as he spoke.

'Alfonso.'

'Italian?'

'Got it in one.'

'First or last name?'

'Last.'

'What's the first?' she asked, enjoying the quick-fire banter.

'Giovanni.'

'Double Italian?'

'On my father's side and my mother's. What about you?'

'Double Birmingham.'

'You don't have much of an accent.'

'Neither do you,' she countered. 'Do you speak Italian?'

'Not a word. Do you speak Brummie?'

'I'm fluent.'

'Are you from around here?' he asked.

'No. Are you?'

'I live in Picklewick. Whereabouts do you live?'

'Is this a police interrogation?'

'This is a Fonzo interrogation.'

'Is that what people call you? Fonzo?'

He shrugged. 'It's easier to say than Alfonso.'

'What does your mother call you?'

He licked his lips, and she couldn't take her eyes off his mouth. 'Gio,' he said.

'Can I call you Gio? Fonzo sounds like a bear.'

'Are you referring to Fozzie Bear? I didn't think you were old enough to remember the Muppets.'

'They're still going strong, and if that's a subtle way of asking me how old I am, I'm thirty-five.'

'It wasn't, but thanks for the info. Are you here on holiday?'

'I suppose you could say that. I'm visiting my sister for a week. She owns Lilac Tree Farm.'

'I heard it had changed hands. It used to belong to Otto York's father, Walter.'

Nikki wondered if he knew the full story behind the change of ownership.

'Nice place,' he added.

'Do you know it?'

'I know of it, but I've never had any dealings with either Walter or the farm. I have been up to the stables a few times, though.'

Nikki raised an eyebrow, wondering whether it had been for work or pleasure. 'Riding?'

'Horse theft,' Gio explained. He glanced around, his eyes focusing on the world beyond the gazebo. 'Petra and Harry have done wonders with the place since I was here last.'

'I think Dulcie is planning on doing wonders with hers, but she's got a way to go yet. The house needs a complete makeover, and no doubt I'll get roped into helping while I'm here. She's already hinted that the bedrooms need decorating.'

'Sounds like it's not going to be much of a holiday. If you fancy a few hours off, how would you like to go out for a drink one evening?'

Nikki froze. Had Gio just asked her out on a date?

She wiped her suddenly damp palms on her jeans as unobtrusively as possible. 'Er...um…I can't. I've got Sammy, you see, and I can't leave him alone.'

'Who is leaving Sammy alone?' Dulcie asked, appearing at her elbow.

'I would be, if I went out for a drink with Gio,' Nikki told her.

'This *week*? While you're staying at the *farm*?' Dulcie asked. A slow, knowing smile was spreading across her face.

'Yes,' Nikki replied reluctantly. She had a feeling she knew what was coming.

'He won't be on his own, will he, you muppet. He'll be with me,' Dulcie said.

Nikki's eyes flew open, and she shot Gio a quick look.

'Muppet?' he mouthed, smirking.

Dulcie continued, 'Otto and I can babysit. It'll give me some practice.'

Nikki's eyes widened even further. 'Are you pregnant?'

'No. But one day I hope to be, and I don't get to see Sammy as much as I'd like, so I'll enjoy having him all to myself for an evening. I'll teach him how to play poker or something.'

'You wouldn't dare! Where is he, anyway?'

'Otto took him to see the show jumping. I hope you don't mind? I've only just got my head around chickens – horses are a step too far at the moment, and Otto is used to big smelly animals.'

'I don't mind,' Nikki said, trying not to. She wasn't keen on horses, either. Or cows. She was with her sister on that one, but Sammy was fascinated by any kind of animal. Look at the way he'd taken to the chickens! He had even tried to make friends with Puss, but the ginger tom hadn't been too keen and mostly kept out of Sammy's way.

'Seriously, we'll have fun,' Dulcie insisted. 'And the practice will do me good.'

Nikki knew how in love with Otto Dulcie was, and she felt a twinge of envy as she remembered when she used to be just as full of excitement for the future. These days she was considerably more jaded – getting married too young with a baby on the way, and a subsequent divorce, tended to do that to a person. She had only just completed her teacher training when Sammy had arrived, and not long after that, her husband of only a few months had disappeared out of their lives.

Gio was still waiting patiently for her answer, but Nikki continued to dither. Was going on a date with a man she had only just met and one who she was unlikely to see again after this week, a good idea?

She felt Dulcie's breath on her ear as her sister whispered, 'Go on, go out with him. It's about time you let your hair down and had some fun. What harm can it do? You're hardly likely to see him again.'

'But that's the point,' Nikki retorted quietly.

'Huh. Do you look at every date as a potential husband or long-term relationship?'

'God no! I wouldn't want to put myself through that again. I'm fine on my own.'

'You might be, but that shouldn't stop you from having fun. It's even more of a reason to enjoy a fling while you can.'

Nikki batted Dulcie away with a strained smile. This was starting to get embarrassing. What must Gio be thinking?

'Sorry, Gio, just finalising a few details. I'd love to have a drink with you one night,' she said, suddenly making her mind up and hoping she wouldn't regret it.

And that was it – Nikki was going on a date with a man she didn't want to go out with, even though he was entertaining and seriously sexy, and all because her annoying sister had embarrassed her into it.

CHAPTER THREE

Going out for the evening was becoming an increasingly pleasant prospect, Nikki decided as her date with Gio loomed larger. She hadn't been out in ages, often too knackered to want to go anywhere in the evenings, even during the school holidays, although she did manage the occasional lunch with friends. The realisation that since she and Greg had split up her world had gradually narrowed, until all she did was look after Sammy, go to work and do chores, was an unsettling one.

What had happened to the formerly exuberant, outgoing, fun loving Nikki? She had been ground down by life's disappointments, all her fizz knocked out of her, that's what.

So it was with a gently bubbling sense of excitement and a smattering of nerves that she got ready for her date with Gio.

There was another reason for her keenness to go out this evening, and that was due to a growing suspicion Dulcie and Otto could do with some time alone, without feeling they had to entertain her. For all Dulcie's insistence that she wanted to spend time with her nephew, Nikki guessed Sammy wouldn't be long to bed. All this exercise and fresh air was wearing him out.

Nikki wasn't faring much better herself, and she hoped she would be able to keep her eyes open this evening. Despite pretending not to be enthused about helping Dulcie with her never-ending decorating, Nikki had thrown herself into it with enthusiasm. It was a welcome change from lesson preparation and herding pupils.

'You look lovely,' Dulcie said, when Nikki trotted downstairs in a pair of her sister's high heels. It was lucky they were the same size shoe-wise, although borrowing anything else belonging to Dulcie had been more problematic as Nikki's taste in going-out clothes was far more conservative than her sister's.

She hadn't thought to bring much in the way of smart clothes with her, not anticipating anything more than a meal or two in a local pub, so she was relieved to be able to team a floaty blouse (Dulcie's) with a pair of capri pants (her own). The high heels and a borrowed clutch bag completed the look.

'What time will you be back?' Sammy asked. He seemed a little apprehensive about her going out without him, and as she did it so rarely, she completely understood.

She wasn't going to allow her son to guilt-trip her into calling it off, though. Anticipation at the thought of seeing Gio again swirled through her. This was so unlike her, that it made her feel positively giddy. It didn't matter that nothing could ever come of it. She intended to enjoy this evening for what it was – a date with a handsome stranger.

In fact, it was refreshing not to have to worry about whether he would ask to see her again. She wouldn't be checking her phone every five minutes, or jumping out of her skin whenever it rang, hoping it might be him. A few drinks, some (hopefully) pleasant conversation, and maybe a kiss at the end of it: although she didn't want to think about that too closely, because the thought of his lips threatened to send her into a tailspin. That was all this would be, and if she was lucky it might be just the kick up the backside she needed in order to drag her non-existent social life out of the proverbial cupboard under the stairs, blow the dust and cobwebs off it, and take it out for a drive or two.

She wasn't referring to dating, as such, because she wasn't sure she could be bothered with the hassle, and she also had Sammy to think of, but maybe she could join her friends on a couple of nights out, even if it was only for a glass of Prosecco and some overpriced tapas.

'Your fella is here,' Dulcie said, cocking her head, and Nikki heard the noise of a vehicle pulling into the yard.

Her tummy fizzed with excitement and she stamped down on the unfamiliar feeling, not wanting either her sister or her son to see just how much she was looking forward to this.

'Say ta-ra to your mum, then you can help me put the chickens to bed,' Dulcie told Sammy.

'Where are you going?' Sammy asked, his eyes on Nikki.

'I'm not sure.' She shrugged nonchalantly. 'Just out for a drink in a pub somewhere.'

'Why can't I come?'

'Because, soft lad,' Dulcie said, steering him towards the back door, 'Your mum needs some grown-up time. Anyway, you'd be bored out of your skull.'

Nikki saw Sammy stifle a yawn, and she bit back a smile. She didn't think it would be long before he was in bed.

'See you later, Sammy. I'll tuck you in when I get back.'

He seemed satisfied with that, so she blew him a kiss and hurried outside.

Gio had got out of his car and was walking towards the house, but he drew to a halt when he saw her approach.

Nikki faltered, unsure of the correct procedure these days. She was fairly sure that shaking hands wasn't the done thing, but should she go in for a quick hug, a peck on the cheek, or what?

Gio solved her dilemma.

He stepped towards her, held out his arms and drew her to him.

A light touch, a swift kiss on each cheek, then he released her.

'I thought we could go to the Black Horse in the village,' he said, opening the car door for her.

Nikki unfroze her feet and got in. She was still reeling from the brief contact. During those few seconds, she had been close enough to get an enticing whiff of his aftershave and to feel the muscles in his back as she had quickly returned the embrace.

She had also felt a hint of stubble as her mouth brushed against his cheek, and now her lips were tingling.

The rest of her wasn't faring much better, and she realised just how long it was since a man had paid her any attention.

Nikki settled herself in the passenger seat, thinking what a novelty it was not to be the one driving. But she silently cautioned herself not to get carried away and have more than one drink.

'I thought you might feel more comfortable being nearer to the farm, considering you don't know me that well,' Gio said, breaking into her thoughts.

Nikki was touched by how considerate that was. 'I don't know you at all,' she countered with a smile.

'You know I'm a police officer and I live in Picklewick.'

'That's not much, is it?'

'It's a start.' He flashed her a glance as the car moved. 'What else would you like to know? Go ahead, ask me anything.'

'You might regret saying that.' She thought for a moment, as the car trundled down the hill. 'What's the most embarrassing thing you've ever done?'

He blinked, and she could tell that he had been expecting her to ask a more mundane question.

'Aw, this isn't happening,' he groaned theatrically. 'Ask me something else.'

'Uh-uh.' Nikki shook her head. 'It can't be that bad.'

He pulled out of Muddypuddle Lane and onto the road leading to the village, and sighed. 'I once told my girlfriend's mother that I loved her.'

'*What!?*' Nikki giggled.

'I was only seventeen. We were at her place. Her parents were out and we'd been getting all kissy-kissy. Nothing heavy, but she was my first proper girlfriend and I'd had a crush on her for ages. Anyway, she went to the kitchen to fetch a drink, and her parents came home. Neither of us heard them come in – I don't know if her mum was hoping to catch us doing something we shouldn't, but she was ever so quiet. I heard someone enter the living room and naturally assumed it was my girlfriend. I'd been trying to pluck up the courage to tell her I loved her for ages. I had my back to the door, and I remember staring at the tv and just saying it. I was so embarrassed, and her mum was horrified. So was my girlfriend. She broke up with me soon after. The whole school got to hear about it, and I didn't live it down for ages.'

'It's funny what stays with you, isn't it?' Nikki sympathised. 'I threw up in assembly once, and I still cringe when I think about it. It went all over the hair and down the back of the girl in front. Amanda Couler, her name was. I was called Barfie for weeks.'

'Barfie.' Gio sniggered.

'Don't,' she groaned. 'I wish I hadn't started this.'

'We're here,' he said, pulling into a car park behind the pub. 'We can swap more embarrassing stories inside.'

'Let's not,' she said. 'My worst one involves a year three child, a school inspector and lots of pooh.'

Gio wrinkled his nose as they walked towards the entrance. 'I might just be able to trounce you on the yucky stories,' he said, holding the door open for her.

'This is cosy.' Nikki gazed around in delight. This was exactly what she imagined a village pub should look like: inglenook fireplace, old beams, whitewashed stone walls. In fact, it reminded her of Dulcie's house.

'What can I get you?' Gio asked, and after they'd got their drinks they sat down, Nikki suddenly felt shy.

It didn't last long, though. To her relief Gio was incredibly easy to talk to, and the conversation flowed between them. She discovered that he was a year younger than her, had never been married, had always wanted to join the police force, and had parents who were still together and still in love. She also found out that he was an only child, that he pretended to like footie because all his mates did, and could knit – not that he did much of it.

In turn, Nikki told him about her ex-husband, skipping over the details of their divorce. She also told him she had a sister younger than Dulcie, and a brother in the middle. She shared her love of cooking, tv dramas, and hot water bottles.

He's a nice guy, she thought, halfway through the evening, feeling glad that Dulcie had bulldozed her into going on a date with him.

Gio was the kind of man that she could fall for – if she was looking for a fella and if they didn't live so far apart.

But she *wasn't* looking, and they *did* live miles away from each other. And not only that, she fell for Greg, so that went to show what a crap judge of character she was. Trusting another man after her ex-husband was going to be hard.

Trusting her own judgement was going to be even harder.

♥

If questioned, Gio couldn't explain why he had asked Nikki on a date, but something about her had spoken to him. And it wasn't just that he fancied her, although she was very pretty.

He could see her as a primary school teacher – calm, firm, yet with a softer side, and from the (often hilarious) stories she had told, he discovered that she had a wicked sense of humour and seemed to genuinely care about her pupils.

It might have been his imagination though, but he sensed she was worried and he guessed it was to do with her son. She clearly loved the boy with all her heart and her pride was evident, but something was bothering her.

'How is Sammy enjoying his holiday?' he asked.

She looked surprised that he wanted to know. 'It's doing him the world of good,' she began, then her expression clouded.

'Don't tell me, you're worried that he might want a chicken of his own?'

'I wish! That would be the least of my problems.'

Gio stayed silent. If she wanted to tell him she would, but he wasn't going to press her.

She ran a finger around the edge of her glass, her gaze distant. 'He's really unhappy at school,' she said, 'and it breaks my heart to see it.'

'He's in the first year in secondary school, you said? Is it because he has moved up from the primary?' Gio used to love his old primary school. He couldn't say the same about secondary, though. Too big, too many kids, too many tests. In primary he had felt cared about. In secondary he had soon learnt he had been just a number, and a fairly inconsequential one at that.

'Yes and no,' Nikki replied cryptically. She took a deep breath and let it out slowly. 'I think he would have been okay with the transition, if he wasn't being bullied.' Anger flashed in her eyes but quickly faded, replaced by worry once more as she continued, 'I came home from work on Friday to find him crying his eyes out.'

Gio's heart went out to the boy. He knew from experience how awful people could be to each other, but he was dismayed at how young some of them were.

'Isn't the school doing anything?' he asked.

'It doesn't seem like it. I've spoken to them several times, but nothing changes.' She looked towards the ceiling, blinked a couple of times, then dropped her gaze to him. 'Sorry, you don't need to hear me carping on about my problems. This is supposed to be a date. Let's change the subject.'

'I'm happy to talk about whatever you want,' he said, reaching across the table to put his hand over hers. 'If talking helps, we'll talk about it.'

'Thanks, Gio, but I don't want to think about it anymore tonight. There'll be time enough for that when we're back home next week.'

A tremor of disappointment at the thought of not seeing her again passed through him, and he willed himself not to be so silly. He knew before he had asked her out that this wasn't going to be the start of anything. It was just a pleasant drink with an attractive woman.

Respecting her wishes, he changed the subject, and she was soon laughing again, the rest of the evening passing on a lighter note.

♥

'Thanks for a lovely evening,' Nikki said, as the car drew to a halt in the farmyard. It was eleven-fifteen, so not terribly late, and lights were on in the house.

'My pleasure,' Gio replied. 'I'm glad you enjoyed yourself. I had fun, too.'

Did he sound wistful?

Nikki shook herself. Unlikely. It was probably wishful thinking on her part; just because she was attracted to him and wouldn't have said no if he asked to see her again, she wanted him to feel the same way. But the distance scuppered any possibility of that happening, and both of them knew it.

There was a brief awkward silence as Nikki wondered whether he would kiss her, then she reached for the door handle.

'Nikki?'

She hesitated and looked at him. Her heart began to pound as he leant towards her.

But all he did was brush his lips against her cheek.

She closed her eyes, his mouth lingering, feeling his warm breath on her face, opening them again as he drew back.

'It was nice meeting you.' The formality of the words was lessened by a hint of regret in his voice. 'Take care of yourself, and I hope you sort things out for Sammy.'

She hoped so too, but right now her mind wasn't on her son. It was on a man who, under different circumstances, she could quite easily fall for.

Downhearted, she got out of the car, giving him a little wave as he drove off.

Then she braced herself for her sister's inevitable interrogation and went inside, pushing her melancholy to the back of her mind.

No use crying over what was never going to be. Gio was a pleasant highlight in a lovely week in the country. Nothing more.

CHAPTER FOUR

'With respect, Mrs Hardcastle, the school has had multiple opportunities to deal with this situation, yet the bullying continues. And it's getting worse. Do you intend to wait until some serious harm comes to my son before you take action?' Nikki demanded.

The headteacher's lips narrowed. 'We do not condone bullying in this school.'

'Yet, here we are. *Again.*' Nikki was trying hard to keep a lid on her anger, but this was the third time in as many weeks that she had sat across the table from this woman, and still nothing was being done. Sammy was terrified and miserable, and it broke her heart to see him like that.

The headteacher continued, 'We've placed the two boys in different classes where we can, and where this isn't possible, they are seated apart. All staff members are aware of the situation, and all do their best to keep an eye on Sammy. But you must understand that there are nearly 1200 pupils in this school and—'

'I don't care about the other 1199,' Nikki broke in. 'At this point, the only child I care about is my own. His physical and mental health is suffering, and so is his academic progress, which I'm sure will be mentioned in his school report. But how can you expect a child who is scared out of his wits, to concentrate on algebra, or write a haiku poem?'

The headteacher drew in a slow breath and Nikki prepared herself for what she knew was coming.

'Maybe this school isn't the right one for Sammy?' Mrs Hardcastle suggested.

This conversation was one that Nikki had already played out in her mind. 'I was thinking the same thing myself,' she said, noticing with annoyance the relief in the woman's eyes. 'However,' she continued firmly, 'I don't see why my son, who is the victim here, don't forget, should be the one who is forced to move schools because another child repeatedly assaults him. Despite your gross lack of duty of care where Sammy is concerned, academically this is the best state school in the area. Besides, all his friends are here. If I took him out of here, away from his friends, I would, in effect, be punishing him, when it is the other child who should be punished.'

Mrs Hardcastle glared at her. 'What do you suggest, Mrs Warring? That we permanently exclude Blake?'

'Yes.'

'Pardon?'

'That is exactly what I am suggesting. There are three weeks left until the end of the academic year. That should be enough time to either permanently exclude him, or arrange for him to be moved to another school. Or do I have to put in a formal complaint to the Chair of Governors? Oh, and any future instances of assault will lead to me involving the police.' Nikki got to her feet. 'Thank you for your time, and I look forward to hearing from you in due course.'

And with that, she marched out of the meeting room, leaving the headteacher with a shocked expression on her face.

As Nikki walked through reception, she collected a distraught-looking Sammy, who had been waiting for her, and stamped across the car park.

Furious didn't begin to describe how she felt. Yet again, she had come home this afternoon to find Sammy cowering in his room, and when she saw the bruises blossoming on his thin arms, she had bundled him into the car and driven to his school. Once there, she had demanded to speak to the headteacher, and had informed the poor receptionist that she wouldn't leave the premises until she did.

Luckily, Mrs Hardcastle hadn't left for the day, although Nikki suspected that the woman would have refused to speak to her without an appointment. Unfortunately for the headteacher though, at that very moment Nikki had seen her walking down the corridor, bag in hand. She was chatting to a colleague about looking forward to a quiet evening in front of the telly, so without the convenient excuse that she was in a meeting or that she was leaving to go to an appointment, the woman had no reason not to speak to Nikki.

Nikki wondered whether she had been too harsh, but she had meant what she'd said. She didn't want to transfer Sammy to a new school, because nothing about this situation was his fault. But she was serious about putting in a formal complaint and involving the police, if necessary.

But then again, what would all this do to Sammy? The formal complaint wouldn't affect him as such, because that would be held internally, but involving the police *would*.

They would want to speak to him at the very least, and she didn't know whether he was strong enough to cope with it.

Maybe it was for the best if she started to look for a new school for him after all.

This one might be the best school in the area, academically speaking, but Sammy was in no position to benefit from it, and she would much prefer him to be happy and settled, rather than worry about what grade he might get in any future examinations. The way he was going in his current school, he wouldn't do very well anyway.

Sammy was very quiet on the way home, and she kept shooting him worried glances. His face was pale, his eyes huge and shaded with purple. She knew he wasn't sleeping properly, his rest fitful and disturbed, and several nights he had woken from a nightmare, shaking and terrified, and it had taken her ages to settle him back to sleep.

Nicky didn't know how much longer this could go on.

When she got home, she sat him down on the sofa.

'I don't want to have to do this, but I will if the school doesn't do anything and you agree to it,' she began. 'How would you feel about not going back to that school in September?'

Sammy's eyes lit up and it was the most animated she had seen him since their visit to Dulcie's farm. 'I don't have to go to school?'

'That's not exactly what I meant,' Nikki said. 'You would still have to go to school, but what if we try to get you into another one? What do you say?'

His face fell. 'I don't want to go to another school. I don't want to go to *any* school. Not ever.'

'Sorry, Sammy, but you have to. It's the law.'

She wasn't being entirely accurate, because home-schooled children didn't. But she had to work. She had a mortgage to pay, and the bills, and she was struggling to get by on her salary as it was, without giving it up completely to live on benefits.

Nikki expected tears or anger, but all Sammy did was sit there, his eyes downcast, his face closed, and her heart broke that little bit more.

Later, as she recounted the conversation she'd had with the headteacher to Dulcie, she told her sister that she wasn't hopeful of a positive outcome.

'Bless his little cotton socks!' Dulcie cried. 'Can I do anything to help?'

'I wish you could, and thanks for offering, but we've just got to wait. And hope. He is adamant that he doesn't want to change schools, but he's also adamant that he doesn't want to stay in his current one.'

'As soon as the summer holidays start, why don't you come visit the farm again?' Dulcie suggested.

'What needs to be decorated?' Nikki asked, with a tolerant sigh.

'Nothing,' her sister replied innocently.

'Fibber. I am tempted though,' Nikki added. 'Even if you do get me painting anything that moves.'

'Please say you'll come,' her sister urged. 'It'll do Sammy good. He loved it last time. And—' she lowered her voice '—I've got more chickens.'

'How many more?' Nicki asked suspiciously.

'Another nine. Otto is getting through eggs like you wouldn't believe and I resent buying them when I've got enough space for hundreds of hens.'

Nikki smiled to herself. Was this the start of a chicken empire, she wondered. Dulcie had come a long way since her first few days on the farm if she was keeping more of them.

'How is Otto's cookbook coming along?' Nikki asked.

Dulcie laughed. 'I'm sick of eating flowers. It's got to the point where if someone sent me a bouquet, I'd probably put it in a salad. Otto is hoping to get it finished by the end of October. I suppose autumn is prime foraging season, what with all the berries, nuts and mushrooms, so he should have enough recipes by then to fill a book.'

'You sound happy,' Nikki observed.

'I am,' was Dulcie's simple reply. 'Anyway, back to the summer hols. Are you coming or not? I promise you won't have to paint anything.'

'But what about Mum and Maisie? Won't they want to come?' Nikki was well aware how hard work her mum and her sister could be, and although she loved them dearly, having them both there at the same time wouldn't make for a peaceful holiday.

'I doubt I'll be seeing them again before the autumn, so you can stay for the whole six weeks, if you want.'

Their mother and Maisie had paid Dulcie a visit back in May, but Nikki knew that her mum wasn't too keen on the great outdoors and Maisie had yet another new job and another new boyfriend to keep her occupied. Mum had had a fine old time boasting to her friends about what a fantastic place the farm was though, and how lucky Dulcie was.

Nikki made a decision. 'In that case, I'd love to come, thanks.'

'Yay! It'll be fun! Oh, and guess who I bumped into the other day? Fonzo! He asked after you.'

'He did?' Nikki's stomach turned over on hearing his name. 'That's nice of him,' she added, although she suspected he was just being polite.

Subconsciously, she touched her cheek, his kiss lingering in her mind. She had thought about him on and off since she'd got back; his face kept popping into her head at the most inopportune moments, and she would wonder whether he thought about her at all, believing it to be far more likely that he had forgotten she existed.

It was nice to think that he hadn't.

'How is he?' she asked.

'Good, I think. Still single.'

'Oh, no, you don't, Dulcie Fairfax,' Nikki warned. 'Just because you and Otto are all loved up, doesn't mean everyone else has to be.'

Dulcie chortled. 'You don't fool me. You like him.'

'What if I do? It doesn't mean I'm about to fall into bed with him, or fall in love.' Nikki's reply was firm. 'He's got his life and I've got mine. And there's also the fact that we hardly know each other. We've only been on one date!'

'Methinks, you doth protest too much.'

'If you don't stop trying to matchmake, Sammy and I won't come at all and you can look after your chickens all by yourself,' Nikki threatened.

She meant it, too. However nice the thought of seeing Gio again, there wasn't any point. She would just be teasing herself with thoughts of what could have been if circumstances were different. And that was assuming Gio was up for it, because she wasn't sure that he was, despite the connection she had felt between them.

But even though she knew she was right, a part of her hoped she wasn't.

♥

Gio's thumb hovered over the screen for the second time that day, and for the second time he slipped the mobile phone back into his pocket.

He was supposed to be keeping an eye out for a car that was being driven on false number plates, but although he was parked up in a layby in an unmarked police vehicle, waiting for it to pass him, what he was actually doing was thinking about Nikki.

She had drifted in and out of his thoughts on a regular basis since their date, a pleasant memory of a lovely evening spent with a woman he had been very much attracted to, but since he had bumped into her sister yesterday he hadn't been able to get Nikki out of his head.

It didn't help matters that he'd had a message from Dulcie via Megan, that Dulcie wanted to speak to him, and could Megan pass on his number.

He was glad Megan had asked first, as he was quite particular who he gave his private number to.

His first thought when he had seen Megan's message was that something was wrong, either with

Sammy or with Nikki herself, but Megan said she didn't think so, and was under the impression Dulcie wanted to speak to him about a social thing.

Gio took his phone out and read Megan's message yet again. A social thing could mean anything, but he had a sneaking suspicion it had something to do with Nikki, and he wasn't sure he was ready to go down that rabbit hole.

He'd had a great time and if things had been different he would have loved to see her again, but——

Damn. The car with the false plates just passed him.

Gio tossed his mobile onto the passenger seat and pulled out of the layby.

He had better stop thinking of what if, and concentrate on his job.

♥

The false number plates turned out to be a false alarm, and after first dealing with an RTC, and then with a truck with a badly secured load, Gio found himself in Picklewick and heading to his favourite cafe. Relieved that the road traffic collision had been minor and that the truck driver hadn't given him any grief, Gio wanted to get some food and caffeine inside him before he got another shout.

He had just left the vehicle and was stretching out the kinks in his back, when he spotted Dulcie. She noticed him at the same time and waved enthusiastically.

He was tempted to pretend he had an emergency and had to get back on the road PDQ, but that would be childish, so he stayed where he was.

Dulcie began talking as soon as she was close enough for him to hear what she was saying. 'Hi, Fonzo, I was hoping to speak to you. I asked Petra if she had your number, and she asked Megan, but I haven't heard back from her yet – but speaking in person is so much better, don't you think?'

'It depends on what's being spoken about,' he replied dryly,

Dulcie rolled her eyes. 'Nothing bad, obviously. Nikki is coming to stay with me for a few weeks in the summer holidays – Sammy too, of course – and I wondered if you'd like to pop up to the farm one evening for a meal? I've never held a dinner party, but Otto wants to try out some new recipes, and he was hoping for some fresh victims.'

From the way Dulcie was staring wide-eyed and earnestly at him, Gio guessed there was more to the story than she was letting on, and he had an inkling what that might be.

'Are you matchmaking?' he asked, and a blush crept into her cheeks.

'No…?' Her reply was hesitant, almost a question, which was why he didn't believe her. But he let it go.

He wasn't sure it was a good idea to go to the farm for a meal. He would be putting himself in a situation where the only logical outcome was that he would get hurt. He was a far cry from making a fool of himself where Nikki was concerned, but that was only because he had neither seen nor spoken to her since their date.

It was best if it stayed that way, because he had a feeling that she was a woman he could easily lose his heart to.

So he had no idea why he said, 'Sounds great,' and proceeded to give Dulcie his number.

Then he spent the rest of the day wondering how he could get out of it.

CHAPTER FIVE

As soon as she entered the farmhouse Nikki eased her trainers off with a sigh of relief and wiggled her aching toes. It wasn't only her toes that were aching; her calf and thigh muscles were too, and she eyed Sammy with resentment. Despite the long walk they'd been on, he was still fizzing around like a can of pop that had been shaken to within an inch of its life. Where did he get his energy from, and please could she have some of it!

All Nikki wanted to do was collapse onto the settee and not move for at least a week.

'Fancy a cuppa?' Dulcie called from the kitchen, as Nikki hobbled into the utility room.

'I'd love one.'

Dulcie stuck her head around the door. 'I was about to ask if you'd had a good time, but you look knackered. How far did you go?'

Nikki went into the downstairs loo to wash her hands, leaving the door open. 'Up to the top. We found an old disused cottage or barn. Sammy had a whale of a time poking around in it, making up stories of who might have lived there. The favourite seems to be a knight who was hiding out from a wicked king. Oh, and there was a wizard and a dragon in there somewhere.' She followed Dulcie into the kitchen.

'Hi, Otto.' She glanced around, noticing all the cooking activity. 'Are you practising a recipe?'

She dropped into a chair with a groan and rubbed her ankles. Bed was calling to her already, but with the best will in the world, five o'clock in the afternoon was a little early.

Otto shot Dulcie a look, and Dulcie smiled sheepishly.

Nikki's radar jolted into action. 'What?' she asked suspiciously.

'You haven't told her?' Otto tutted, shaking his head at Dulcie. He didn't seem particularly bothered though, so it couldn't be too bad.

'Told me what?' Nikki asked.

'Um, we're having someone to dinner.' Dulcie chewed her bottom lip.

Nikki guessed what the problem was. 'Do you want me and Sammy to make ourselves scarce? It's no problem, we'll go into Picklewick and grab something in the Black Horse.'

Driving into the village was the last thing she wanted to do, but it wasn't like she was only here for a couple of days. Dulcie had persuaded her to stay for at least four out of the six weeks that the kids were off school, and she was conscious that Dulcie mightn't want to entertain her all day, every day. In fact, it was Dulcie who had suggested that she and Sammy explore the hills above the farm this afternoon, and Nikki had got the feeling Dulcie had wanted her and Sammy out of her hair for a couple of hours.

Now she knew why: they were expecting visitors.

'You're eating with us, too,' Dulcie informed her. 'Do you honestly think Otto would cook a meal in my kitchen and not invite you to share it?'

Nikki shrugged. 'I wouldn't mind.'

'I know – you're the best sister ever.'

Nikki's radar pinged again. It had been finely honed by years of being able to tell when children were up to no good. And Dulcie was definitely up to no good. It was written all over her face.

Narrowing her eyes, Nikki asked, 'Are you going to tell me what's going on?' She had a feeling she wasn't going to like it. 'Who is coming to dinner?'

'Um…Fonzo?' Dulcie lowered her head and peeped up at Nikki from under her lashes.

'Stop trying to look cute and innocent. It might work on Otto, but it won't work on me.'

'I warned you,' Otto said to Dulcie. 'You should have told her sooner.'

Nikki sat up straighter. 'When you say *sooner*, when exactly did you plan this?'

'Acouplaweeksago,' Dulcie mumbled.

'Did you say *a couple of weeks*?'

'Oh, look, is that the time? I'd better…er…start getting ready.' Dulcie made a dash for the door, but Nikki caught hold of her arm.

'What time are you expecting him?' she demanded.

'Seven.'

'It's not even five-thirty yet,' Nikki pointed out. 'Why don't you stay and chat for a bit? Then you can explain why you invited Gio for dinner two whole weeks ago and didn't think to mention it until now!'

♥

Gio mopped up the remaining sauce on his plate with some sourdough bread. 'Otto, that was amazing,' he said. 'You ought to set up on your own.'

'It might be most chef's dream, but not mine,' Otto said. 'As long as I have creative control in a kitchen, I'm happy. The last thing I want is to have to worry about the accounts, insurance, staff issues, and so on.'

Dulcie said, 'Fonzo is right – you should think about opening your own place. You're such a brilliant chef.'

Otto rolled his eyes. 'Yes, you can have some more if you want, but only if you leave enough room for pudding.'

'Ha ha. I've always got room for pudding.' Dulcie patted her tummy with a laugh.

Gio glanced at Nikki. She had been subdued all evening, and he hoped nothing was wrong. Sammy seemed perky enough, though, so whatever it was, Gio didn't think her son was the cause.

She looked up from her plate to find him staring, and Gio offered her a small apologetic smile. From the moment he'd arrived he had the impression that she wasn't keen on him being there. Although she had been friendly, he sensed a reservation in her that hadn't been there the last time he'd seen her.

The pleasure he felt when she smiled back, took him by surprise.

He hadn't been convinced that seeing Nikki again was such a good idea, and sitting at the table with her this evening had increased his reservations.

However, that one smile sent him into a tizzy, and he found himself thinking that he would do anything to keep that smile on her face.

Aw, damn it! This was precisely what he feared might happen. He was getting involved, despite knowing he might end up being hurt.

He should never have asked her on a date in the first place. If he hadn't, Dulcie wouldn't have invited him to dinner. Then again, he was a sucker for punishment because he could easily have said no: no one had forced him to come here tonight.

But he had wanted to see Nikki again, and that was where the problem lay.

He should have walked away, because no good would come of this.

Inhaling slowly, he wanted to kick himself. He had been around the block enough times to know it wasn't wise to start something he couldn't finish. It wouldn't be because he didn't want to – it would be because it was impractical and unworkable.

It was no good trying to tell himself to go with the flow and just enjoy it for what it was. He wasn't interested in a casual fling, and he got the impression Nikki wasn't either. Been there, done that, got the notch on his bedpost; but that was when he had been young, reckless and carefree, and when thoughts of settling down had given him the heebie-jeebies.

He'd grown up since then. These days falling in love was an appealing prospect, and the thought of spending the rest of his life with one woman was a gift, not a curse. He wanted what Nathan had with Megan, what Harry had with Petra, and if the soppy look in Otto's eyes was any indication, what the chef had with Dulcie.

But the problem was, Gio didn't want to fall in love when the woman he gave his heart to lived so far away.

He almost snorted into his pudding! He'd only had one date with Nikki, yet here he was worrying about getting his heart broken? If the poor woman had any idea what kind of thoughts had been going through his head just now, he wouldn't blame her if she jumped in her car and hightailed it back to Birmingham.

To say that he was getting ahead of himself, was the understatement of the year.

'Which is yours, Fonzo?' Dulcie asked.

Gio froze. 'Come again?'

Dulcie poked him in the shoulder and laughed. 'You were miles away. You didn't hear a word of that, did you?'

'No, sorry.'

'We were discussing ice cream. What's your favourite flavour?'

He replied without hesitation. 'Pistachio.'

'What did you think of this one?' Dulcie used her spoon to point at the remains of her dessert. There wasn't much left, only a dribble of pale purple creaminess.

'It was very nice,' he said. He had a vague recollection of eating it, but he couldn't for the life of him remember the details.

'Blueberry,' Otto said, 'with a hint of lemongrass.'

'Very nice,' Gio repeated, then made the mistake of glancing in Nikki's direction.

There was a twinkle in her eye and she was chewing her lip, and he could tell that she was holding back a laugh. His suspicion was confirmed when she leant across the table as Otto and Dulcie began the clean-up process after refusing any help.

'You were away with the fairies for a while, weren't you?' she said.

'Yeah, I suppose I was. Work stuff,' he added, unnecessarily.

'Nothing serious, I hope?'

'Nah. Just…things.'

'Things,' she repeated, deadpan.

'How about you?' His eyes shifted to Sammy, who had left the table and was heading towards the hall. 'Are things any better at school?'

'Worse, if anything,' she said, with a sigh.

'Why don't you two take the rest of the wine into the garden?' Dulcie suggested. 'We'll be out as soon as we've regained control of the kitchen. You would think a professional chef would make less of a mess. Fonzo, would you like a low-alcohol beer seeing as you're driving?'

'Please.'

Dulcie got one out of the fridge and opened it. 'Go on, shoo. You're making the place look untidy.'

Gio went outside, Nikki following, and they headed for a wooden table and benches in the middle of a scruffy lawn.

It was still light, although the sun had set and twilight was rapidly descending. Bats swooped and dived, chasing insects, and the air was warm and still.

As soon as they were seated, Nikki said, 'I think we're being set up. I'm sorry, I don't know what's got into my sister.'

'I don't mind. If I did, I wouldn't have agreed to come. I wanted to see you again.' He could kick himself. The words just slipped out, and he couldn't even blame it on too much beer.

'And I was thinking you were only here for the food,' she joked, but her expression was solemn.

'That, too. Otto's not a bad cook, is he?'

Nikki's mouth dropped open, then she realised he was being tongue-in-cheek. 'I hope this foraging cookbook works out for him,' she said.

'Do you think he'll go back to London?'

Nikki shrugged. 'I hope not, for my sister's sake. She's head over heels in love. But Dulcie tells me that his dad is getting better, so maybe he will.' She stared across the valley, the orange-streaked sky illuminating her face. 'She'll be devastated if he does.'

There! Right there. *That* was the reason he didn't want to start a relationship with a woman who lived so far away. Birmingham was hardly the other side of the Atlantic, but what with his shifts, weekend working and frequently long hours, combined with Nikki being restricted by the school day and term times, getting to see each other would prove difficult.

'It's so peaceful here,' she said after a while, the silence only broken by the whinny of a horse in the field below and the rumble of a distant engine. 'Dulcie is so lucky,' she added.

'Would you like to live somewhere like this?'

'I'd love to.'

'Wouldn't you miss the city?'

'I doubt it. Apart from travelling through it twice a day to get to and from work, I don't have an awful lot to do with it.' She leant forward, putting her elbow on the table and resting her chin in the palm of her hand. 'Sammy loves it here. He couldn't wait to come back, especially when he found out that Dulcie had added to her flock of chickens.'

'She seems to have settled in well,' he observed. 'At least she's got over her fear of them.'

Nikki giggled, a sound that melted his heart. 'She has! She's still not keen on sheep, though. I don't think she'll turn into a shepherdess any time soon.'

'What about you? Could you see yourself herding sheep?'

'Not on your nelly! Herding a class of pupils is enough. A dog to round them up might come in handy, though.' Her shoulders sagged. 'Sammy would love a dog, but it simply isn't possible. Otto says he can borrow Peg, but it's not the same. Sammy was hoping that the farm's resident cat would be amenable but he's a right grumpy so-and-so. Do you have any pets?'

'No, although I'm with Sammy on this – I'd love a dog. But it wouldn't be fair on the pooch. I hardly work regular hours and I often have to work late if the situation calls for it.'

'You live in Picklewick, you said?'

'That's right. Just bought a house here.'

'Lucky you!'

Giovanni agreed: he was incredibly lucky. Picklewick was a gorgeous village in a lovely location. 'I don't suppose you hire your decorating services out, do you? My house could do with a lick of paint.'

'You must be joking! I keep trying to ignore Dulcie's hints. I thought I was supposed to be here for a holiday,' she added, laughing. She stood up. 'It's getting late. I'd better put Sammy to bed. If he doesn't get a full eight hours, he's as grumpy as anything.'

'I know how he feels,' Gio replied. 'I'm partial to my bed, too.'

Nikki shot him a look, one he found hard to interpret. 'Goodnight,' she said. 'I expect you'll be gone by the time I've persuaded my son to get into his pyjamas.'

That was a hint for him to leave, if ever he'd heard one. 'Nice seeing you again,' he replied mildly, disappointment pricking at him.

He watched her walk away, her hips swaying, and he picked up his bottle of beer, glared at it, then put it back on the table, untouched. He wanted a proper beer, not this alcohol-free stuff.

Dulcie wandered out to join him. 'Want another?' She gestured to his drink, and he grimaced without meaning to. 'Yeah, I know what you mean,' she said. 'If you fancy a proper drink, you could always stay the night.'

Gio blinked in surprise. 'I don't think your sister would appreciate bumping into a strange man on the landing in the wee small hours.'

Dulcie gave him a speculative look. 'Oh, I don't know…' she replied archly.

Gio did: he was pretty sure that Nikki wouldn't be happy. 'I'd better be off. Thanks for a lovely meal.'

'She won't be long. Sammy's not a baby – he can put himself to bed. She'll be back down in a minute.'

He wasn't so sure about that. He had a feeling Nikki might stay upstairs until he left. 'Thanks, but I need to get going. Early start in the morning.'

He was about to walk off, when Dulcie stopped him in his tracks.

'She's scared,' she said.

'Of what?'

'Love, relationships, being hurt again. Her ex-husband was a real shit.'

Gio slowly sat down again. 'I think I would like that beer now, if that's okay?'

'Coming right up.'

Whilst he waited for Dulcie to reappear with his drink, Gio took the opportunity to ask himself what on earth he thought he was doing.

He didn't have an answer – not one that made sense. All he knew was that he was thinking with his heart and not with his head. Nikki fascinated him: vulnerable, capable, sassy, sad, sparky, withdrawn…She was an enthralling mix wrapped up in a stunning package. He had never felt as drawn to a woman as he was to her.

He was still musing on his own stupidity when he saw his beer appear.

It wasn't in *Dulcie's* hand though. Nikki was walking towards him, and she was carrying two bottles.

'Shall we go for a stroll?' she asked, after handing him one of them and drinking deeply from the other.

The bottle was slick with beaded moisture and deliciously cold. He took it and wrapped his lips around the top, swigging back a couple of mouthfuls. The liquid slipped down his throat a treat, and he wiped his mouth with his fingers.

'If you like.'

She left her bottle on the table and began walking. He quickly finished his and popped his next to it, then followed her, his pulse quickening at the thought of being alone with her.

A yellow moon had risen above the hill behind them, the light from it just bright enough to see where they were putting their feet. Beyond the garden lay the orchard and they made their way over to the gate, the tree trunks ahead dark, the shadows between them even darker. Leaves rustled in the soft breeze and the scent of honeysuckle floated in the air.

Long grass brushed against the legs of his jeans, and he trailed a hand through the nodding seedheads, following her deeper into the orchard. Soon they were surrounded by trees, the boughs laden with ripening fruit.

'These are apples and pears,' she said. 'And I think I saw plums on one, but I'm not entirely sure.' She halted and gazed around. 'We've only taken a few steps, and it's like we're in the middle of nowhere.'

Gio remained silent, not wanting to disturb her pensive mood. Lights from the farmhouse windows glowed, leaves dancing across them so they seemed to flicker, and if he peered down the hill, he could see the stables, and further afield Picklewick twinkled in the distance. An occasional sweep of headlights indicated a road, and when he looked directly overhead, stars were emerging.

It was a magical evening.

He was acutely aware of her nearness, the light scent of her perfume, the faint outline of her profile, the rustling of her feet as she shifted position.

Gio wasn't sure whether it was the location, the atmosphere, the intimacy, or all three, but he so badly wanted to kiss her, to taste those full lips, to bury his fingers in her hair and run his hands over her curves.

Instead, he took a deep breath and tried to calm his thudding heart.

Every cell in his body tingled and he felt more alive than he had ever felt – and they hadn't even touched yet.

How would he cope if they did?

He had to find out.

♥

When Nikki had realised that Gio hadn't left and was still in the garden, she had been surprised and more than a little pleased. When she had told him she had to put Sammy to bed (a lie, because Sammy was perfectly capable of putting himself to bed) she had given Gio an out.

He hadn't taken it. And Nikki wasn't sure whether that was because he wasn't interested in her, or because he *was*.

Dulcie had shoved a stubby brown bottle at her and had told her to take it out to him, and impulsively Nikki had grabbed one for herself, and then asked him if he'd wanted to go for a stroll.

The orchard was fast becoming her favourite place on the farm, and she had taken to coming here when she needed space to think. She could breathe amongst the gnarled trunks, fill her lungs with oxygen-rich air and empty her mind. And night-time was her favourite.

Nikki stared out across the valley, picking out pinpricks of light in the distance. The warmth of the day lingered in the air, and she breathed deeply, relishing the rich smell of soil and growing things. And Gio.

The scent of him was tantalisingly male, with undertones of wood and citrus, and he was standing near enough to touch, if she could only find the courage.

Then she discovered she didn't need to: he found it for her.

His eyes were on her, not the view. It felt incredibly intimate, like a virtual caress, the darkness heightening her awareness until her skin glowed as though he had stroked her face with a finger.

She turned slowly.

No longer side-by-side, they were now facing each other, and in a single fluid movement she was in his arms and his lips landed on hers.

Closing her eyes and opening her mouth, she gave herself up to the sensations swirling through her, living only in this moment, the rest of the world eclipsed as effectively as the sun obscured the moon.

He held her gently, yet she felt his strength, and she wrapped her arms around his neck, drawing him to her.

Gio kissed her softly, but she felt his hunger, and her tongue found his, deepening the kiss until all she was aware of was his mouth, his arms, his body pressed tightly against hers.

When the kiss ended, his lips sliding over hers until they drew apart, he kept hold of her and she him, not wanting to let go, wanting to keep the moment alive for a few seconds longer as they stared into each other's eyes, her pulse soaring, her heartbeat loud in her ears.

Eventually she broke the spell when she turned her head and rested her cheek against his shoulder, and he lowered his lips to her hair, brushing the top of her head. It was more intimate than any kiss, and her heart melted a little bit more.

She didn't know how long they stayed like that, wrapped in each other's arms, the night deepening and darkening around them, but she knew she didn't want it to end.

If only things were different, she could seriously fall for this man.

But as they began to walk slowly back to the house and he took her hand in his, Nikki realised it was actually too late.

She had already fallen…

CHAPTER SIX

'Sammy, I'm not sure you're allowed.' Nikki reached out to grab her son, but he was already darting across the yard towards a row of stables. Three of them were occupied, equine heads poking over the tops of their half-doors, ears flicking with curiosity.

She and Sammy had taken a walk into Picklewick earlier, and she had treated him to cake and a milkshake in one of the cafes. He had devoured his with enthusiasm, chattering continually, his lively animation a pleasure to see.

But for once, Nikki's attention hadn't been wholly on her son. Part of her had been hoping she might spot Gio, and her gaze had kept returning to the street and the cars trundling up and down it.

Last night lay heavily on her mind.

The kiss had been perfect: just the right balance of passion and tenderness. Afterwards, they had returned to the house in silence, pausing when they arrived at the back door. And without saying a word, he had kissed her again, this time a brief, gentle brush of the lips as he cupped her face in his hands. She remembered pushing her cheek into his palm, and then he'd left.

She had listened to his footsteps gradually fade, her hand lingering on the door handle, reluctant to go inside just yet.

When she had no longer been able to hear them, she had let out a slow sigh.

He was gone, and she imagined him striding down the hill, his long legs eating up the ground, knowing he would have to come back. That single beer meant that he'd had to walk home, leaving his car in the farmyard, so she would see him tomorrow.

But to her dismay, his car was gone by the time she got up this morning, and she felt cheated and strangely bereft, as though he had abandoned her.

The hope of bumping into him in the village wasn't the sole reason Nikki had suggested a stroll into Picklewick. Sammy had an abundance of excess energy to burn off, and she was too restless to potter around on the farm – but it had been part of it.

After a bit of retail therapy (she had bought a scented candle for herself and some modelling clay for Sammy) and a stop for refreshments, they had made their way back to Muddypuddle Lane, following a footpath which led from the village, through open fields, past the stables, and on up the hill towards the moorland beyond.

Nikki was hoping the walk would have taken the edge off Sammy's energy, but when they'd reached the stables, he had shot off at top speed, eager to see the horses.

'Sammy,' she called after him, but it was too late. He was already petting the nearest one and giggling.

'Its nose is all soft and hairy!' he cried. 'It tickles.'

'Her name is Mabel,' Petra said, emerging from a shed with a bridle slung over her shoulder. 'She's probably hoping you've got a treat for her.'

Sammy's eyes widened. 'What sort of treat?'

'She likes carrots and apples, and she's also partial to a banana.'

He turned to Nikki. 'Have you got a banana I can give her, Mum?'

'Not on me, no,' Nikki chuckled.

'Here, give her these.' Petra bought out a handful of brown pellets from her pocket.

'What are they?' Sammy asked, as Petra showed him the correct way to feed a horse.

'Pony nuts. No, keep your hand flat, or she might accidentally eat your fingers.'

'Sorry,' Nikki said after Mabel had crunched up her treat. 'He got away from me. Anything to do with animals, and he's there.'

'I don't blame him. I prefer animals to people, as a general rule. You know where you are with a horse or a dog. People…? Not so much.'

'Come on, Sammy, let's go. I'm sure Petra has got better things to do than entertain us.'

'You can stay, if you like,' Petra said with a shrug. 'It makes no odds to me. In fact, Sammy can help out if he wants.'

Sammy gasped. 'Can I, Mum? Please!'

Nikki wasn't sure she wanted to hang around the stables, but after seeing the pleading expression on her son's face, she agreed. After all, there wasn't anything else she needed to do, and being here meant she could avoid decorating for an hour or two longer. It was mean of her, she knew, but she wasn't in the mood for painting a wall.

'Have you ever been on a horse?' Petra asked Sammy.

He shook his head, his eyes wide.

'Would you like to?'

Biting his lip, he looked to his mother for reassurance.

Nikki nodded her permission.

'Yes, please,' he said.

'In that case, we'll get Mabel saddled up and you can have a ride. You've got to earn it first, though,' Petra warned. 'I'm going to introduce you to Gerald, the donkey. He's got to have his hooves trimmed, so I want you to help me put a halter on him, then you can lead him out of the stable and tie him up just there.' She pointed to a large circular piece of metal embedded in the wall. 'After that, we need to muck out the stall, because as sure as God made little green apples, he'll have had a pee and a poop in there.'

Nikki had just parked her backside on what she assumed must be a mounting block, hoping she wouldn't get roped in, when the mention of apples took her straight back to last night in the orchard. She tried to ignore the image of Gio with his head bent towards hers and the desire she had seen in his eyes, and concentrated on the orchard itself. Tidying that up was something she'd like to get her teeth into, she thought, rather than being stuck indoors, painting.

As she had said to Gio (she silently told herself to stop thinking about him), the trees were already full of small apples and unripe pears, and she could just imagine how it would look with the ground beneath them cleared of the scrubby bushes and the brambles that were threatening to choke the fruit trees.

It was going to be quite a task, and she wasn't sure she had the time or the skills to be able to do it. However, she would like to try, and it would be one less job for Dulcie to do around the farm. She ignored the voice in her head that told her so would painting one of the bedrooms.

Whilst she was deep in thought, Petra came to stand next to her. 'I hope I wasn't stepping out of bounds when I said Sammy could have a ride,' the woman began.

'Not at all,' Nikki assured her. 'I'm very grateful. It's extremely kind of you.'

'He's doing me a favour. Mucking out isn't my favourite job. I'd much prefer to chat with you.'

'Despite me being a mere human?'

Petra barked out a laugh. 'I tolerate some people better than others. You might not believe this, but since I met Harry, I've mellowed a lot. I used to be much worse than this.'

'In that case, and while you're in a chatty mood, can I pick your brains?'

'There's not that many to pick, but go ahead.'

'I know you're not a farmer as such, but can you give me any advice on how to go about clearing the orchard up at the farm? It's badly overgrown and the brambles are threatening to take over. Although, saying that, they've got loads of berries on them.'

'If I were you, I'd pick them before I cut them back. Or let Otto loose on them. I'm sure he could do something wonderful with them.'

'Blackberry ice cream,' Nikki murmured, remembering the mouth-watering meal she had eaten last night. The meal wasn't the only thing to make her mouth water though, as she thought of Gio.

'Sounds nice. Not that I'd ever make any. But if there was some on offer...?' Petra cocked an eyebrow.

Hmm…that was a thought, Nikki mused. Home-made ice cream in unusual flavours.

'Seriously,' Petra continued. 'What you need is a goat. Or two.'

'A goat?'

'Goats are the best things for clearing the land, and they'll fertilise it for you at the same time.'

Nikki wrinkled her nose. 'Where on earth would I get a goat from?'

'Leave it to me,' Petra said with a smirk. 'Just leave it to me!'

♥

Gio walked slowly away from the scene of the accident, thanking god that no one had been seriously injured. Or worse.

He had lost count of the number of road traffic accidents he had attended over the years, and although he tried to maintain an emotional distance, it wasn't always easy. And this one had touched him more than others, despite there being only minor injuries.

Getting back in his car and leaving the clean-up to the tow truck companies and Highway Patrol, he snapped his seatbelt on and started the engine. Then he rested his head against the back of the seat and took a steadying breath.

The driver of one of the cars had had a very narrow escape indeed. An improperly secured load of metal poles had slid off the rear of a truck when it had suddenly braked. The driver of the car behind hadn't been able to avoid the poles as they smashed into the front of his car, and one of them had missed his chest by a hair's breadth. A centimetre more, and the man would be dead.

It wasn't the first time Gio had attended a similar accident and it wouldn't be the last, but this one had abruptly brought home to him how fragile and uncertain life could be. The man was roughly the same age as him, facially they were fairly similar, and both had dark hair and dark eyes.

After Gio had quickly checked with the paramedics that the driver's injuries weren't life-threatening or life-changing, he'd had the sudden thought that it could have been him in that car. But maybe he wouldn't have been as lucky.

It wasn't a sense of his own mortality that kept him sitting there: it was the realisation that there were still so many things he wanted to do in life.

A trite saying popped into his mind – live every day as though it was your last. The sentiment was admirable, but unachievable for the vast majority of people. Like him, they probably had to work for a living, would have chores to do, and a million things that wouldn't be on top of anyone's bucket list but nevertheless still had to be done.

But sitting in his car and staring at the mangled vehicles in front of him made Giovanni realise that he wasn't living life to the full. He was holding back in many ways, and what was at the forefront of his mind at this very moment was Nikki.

He wasn't sure who had kissed whom yesterday evening. Had he initiated it, or had she?

Did it matter?

He'd thoroughly enjoyed it. Heck, he'd more than enjoyed it, he had been blown away.

As he walked home last night, he had told himself that it was because of the ambience of the night…strolling through an orchard, under the stars, with the scent of flowers in the air and a beautiful woman at his side, had been enchanting.

But it wasn't because of that, as nice as it had been.

It was because of Nikki herself.

He'd been all set to leave once he'd thanked Dulcie for the meal, but something she'd said had made him stay.

And it was possibly one of the best decisions of his life, despite the very real possibility that he might get his heart broken.

Because it was high time he started living – *really* living – and he knew just what he needed to do to make that happen.

♥

'Apparently, she's more of a diva than a princess,' Nikki told Dulcie, handing the animal's lead rope to her son, so he was now holding both goats. 'That's her name, Princess. And the other one is called Toffee. Isn't she the most gorgeous colour?'

Dulcie didn't look convinced. 'What did you say I'm supposed to be doing with them?'

Nikki had told her once, but her sister hadn't taken it in. Dulcie had been too busy trying to avoid the curious creatures, dancing out of the way whenever they came too close.

'You don't have to do anything,' Nikki repeated. 'Sammy will be looking after them: under my supervision, of course.'

'But what will happen when you go back home? Who will look after them then?'

'Hopefully they'll have done their job of clearing all the brambles and other weeds from the orchard, so they'll return to the stables. And you never know, you might take a shine to them.'

'Nope. Not gonna happen. They've got horns,' she added in a low hiss.

Nikki grinned. Did Dulcie think the goats could understand her? And if they could, that they hadn't realised they had horns?

'Here's the plan. Sammy will tie them up in a different part of the orchard every day. Petra said that if they aren't tethered Princess will probably escape, and even if she doesn't, they'll eat all the fruit they can reach. Then Sammy will bring them into the barn at night. I might need some help to get set it up, though.'

Dulcie seemed dazed. 'Goats,' she repeated.

'Petra reckons they'll do a much better job of clearing the ground than we could ourselves, and in far less time. Oh, and I've been thinking about selling ice cream.'

'You're a teacher. Why do you want to sell ice cream?'

'Not *me*. You.'

Dulcie's brows lowered. 'I can't see me driving around the streets in a van, playing *Greensleeves* and asking people if they want a flake with that, can you?'

'Actually, you and Otto,' Nikki amended.

'Oh, I don't think Otto would—'

'I'm talking about selling ice cream from the farm!' Nikki broke in triumphantly. 'New, unusual flavours created by Otto, that people could buy tubs of to take home to eat.'

Dulcie looked stunned. 'Um…it's certainly something to consider.'

Nikki could see she wasn't convinced. 'It was just a thought,' she said, deflating quicker than a soggy soufflé. Oh, well, she said to herself, at least thinking about orchards, goats and ice cream had taken her mind off Gio for a while.

'Come on, Sammy, let's get Princess and Toffee settled,' she said.

Sammy walked towards the orchard, importantly leading both goats, and Nikkii was about to follow him, when she turned back to Dulcie. Another idea to help bring in some much-needed cash for the farm had bubbled to the surface, and she was just about to suggest that once the orchard was cleared it might be possible to open it up to the public so they could pick their own apples and pears, when a flash of yellow and blue caught her eye.

A police car was turning into the yard.

Nikki squinted at it, and her tummy did a slow roll as she recognised the officer behind the wheel.

'Gio,' she whispered, and her fingers went to her lips, remembering the taste of him and the feel of his mouth on hers.

His gaze was on her face as he pulled up, got out of the car and slammed the door, then strode purposefully towards her, his eyes never leaving hers.

'Ooh,' Dulcie murmured. 'Look at him.'

Nikki looked. She couldn't tear her gaze away as he rapidly covered the ground between them, and she licked her lips nervously. Was this a formal visit or a—

'Eek!' she cried as he swept her into his arms, the sound cut off as his mouth descended on hers.

She froze, then she was frantically kissing him back, ignoring her sister's incredulous stare and excited squeal.

When Gio finally put her down and she could catch her breath, Dulcie cried, 'Richard Gere, eat your heart out!'

Nikki blinked. 'Who?'

'From *An Officer and a Gentleman*? The film where…never mind.'

Gio stared at Dulcie, but he quickly turned his attention back to Nikki. 'I just had to,' he said, by way of an explanation. 'Sorry.'

'You don't look it,' Nikki retorted.

'I'm not really.'

Dulcie clapped, and Nikki and Gio shot her a look.

'I'm sure you've got things to do,' Nikki said to her sister.

'I don't think so.'

'*Yes, you have,*' Nikki hissed.

'Oh, yeah, right. I've…um…got to… er…' Dulcie grinned. 'Bye, Gio.'

He waved absently.

As soon as her sister was out of earshot, Nikki said, 'That was unexpected.'

'Nasty unexpected, or nice unexpected?'

'Couldn't you tell?'

He wrinkled his nose. 'Nice?' he guessed.

'Very nice.' She glanced in the direction of the orchard. 'I would prefer a bit of warning next time, though,' she said, adding, 'Sammy.'

Gio closed his eyes. When he opened them again, he looked contrite. 'Sorry, I didn't think. Where is he? He didn't see, did he?'

'He's in the orchard with a couple of goats. Long story.' She waved a hand in the air and shook her head. 'I'll tell you another time.'

'I'll hold you to that,' he said. 'Um…look, I'd love to see you again, but I understand if you don't want to. You've got Sammy to think about, and you live there, and I live here, and then there's my job and—'

'Yes,' she interrupted. 'I do want to see you again.'

The sudden pleasure on his face made her giggle.

'That's great!' he exclaimed, then there was a crackle from his radio and his face fell. 'Excuse me a sec.' He turned away. 'Go ahead,' she heard him say as he moved off a few paces. When he turned back to her, he said, 'I've got to go. Can I see you tonight?'

'I can ask Dulcie if she would babysit.'

'You can bring Sammy along.'

Nikki gave him a level look. 'Not yet.'

Probably not ever, she thought. This relationship would only ever be a short-term one, so there would be no need for Sammy to get to know him. As far as her son was concerned, Gio was a friend of Dulcie and Otto. Nothing more.

But even as she was thinking this, she wished it could be much, much more than what was essentially a mere holiday fling.

♥

Gio tasted of hops, the beer he had recently drunk lingering on his lips as Nikki's tongue eagerly sought his.

Her arms were wrapped around his neck, pulling him into her, and she couldn't seem to get enough of him. He filled her senses so completely that nothing else mattered

'Excuse me,' a gruff male voice said, and Nikki was abruptly brought back to earth.

Feeling like a teenager caught necking behind the bike shed by one of her teachers, she muttered, 'Sorry,' as they shuffled to one side to allow an old gent to get to the pub's door.

'I think we'd better make a move,' she told Gio, feeling the heat of a blush sweep into her cheeks. Standing on the pavement outside the Black Horse in full view of everyone with her mouth clamped on Gio's, wasn't the most appropriate thing to do. But as soon as they had stepped outside, she hadn't been able to keep her hands off him.

To be fair, Gio had been just as eager, and he was now looking dazed and dishevelled, his hair sticking up at odd angles and his breathing ragged.

'I think we better had,' he agreed, his eyes shooting towards the pub's windows, his expression one of embarrassment, and she realised that it probably wasn't a good idea for the local copper to be seen snogging in the street.

Nikki giggled.

'What's so funny?' he asked, slipping a hand into hers as they began to walk along the high street. His fingers caressed the back of her hand, sending shivers of longing through her.

'Us. We're behaving like a couple of teenagers.' She leant into him as they strolled down the pavement, feeling the solidity of his shoulder against hers.

'I suppose we are,' he agreed. 'It's fun, though.'

It was, but she hoped Gio didn't just see her as a bit of fun, as nothing more than a summer fling and a fleeting romance. Yet she knew it couldn't be anything else.

She pushed the thought away, not wanting to think of the future. It wasn't as though she didn't know what she was doing, and she was aware of the risks she might be taking with her heart if she was silly enough to fall in love with him.

Ignoring the little voice cautioning her that she was halfway there already (how could she be when she had only known him five minutes, she reasoned) she let go of his hand and wrapped an arm around his waist.

He did the same, holding her close, and they continued on their way, pausing every so often to kiss.

'Are you sure you want to walk?' Gio asked. 'It's not too late to call for a taxi.'

'I want to,' she assured him. It had been her suggestion to walk to the farm from the pub in the first place, although she had immediately felt guilty when she realised it meant he would have to walk all the way back to Picklewick after he said goodbye. But he had insisted that he didn't mind, claiming that the exercise would do him good.

In Nikki's opinion, Gio looked as though he got plenty of exercise anyway. He hadn't got that flat hard stomach and muscular chest from sitting behind the wheel of a car all day, and she guessed he must work out.

It was rather romantic strolling back to the farm in the twilight, especially when it was imperative that they had to stop every once in a while to kiss and cuddle.

Nikki didn't want the evening to end, but she knew it had to. Even if she didn't have Sammy to consider, it was far too soon to hop into bed with Gio, however tempting the thought. And she was forced to admit that she *was* sorely tempted. There was something quite liberating about the insular nature of a summer fling, and she felt like Sandy in *Grease*: summer lovin' was indeed a blast, and it was happening much faster than she could have anticipated, but that was all right, wasn't it, because it would come to a natural end soon enough – a summer fling that didn't mean a thing.

However, she had the feeling this wouldn't be a sweet romance, not with the heat sparking between them, and the thought of getting passionate with Gio sent waves of desire cascading through her.

Down girl, she admonished, and tried to tell herself that sleeping with him wasn't inevitable, even though she suspected that it probably was. There was nothing to hold her back. They were single consenting adults, and as long as they were going into this with their eyes open, no one would get hurt.

Something had definitely begun and that something would definitely end, but in between there was nothing stopping them from sharing several long, hot, summer nights.

Being impulsive was a trait Gio thought he had grown out of, but clearly not, as his actions earlier today had illustrated.

But he couldn't bring himself to regret turning up at Lilac Tree Farm and kissing Nikki in front of her sister, and neither did he regret asking her out. The evening would have been lovely, even without any kissing. With it, it had been *wonderful*.

It still was, because they hadn't reached the farm yet, and he found he was dragging his feet, not wanting the night to end.

But eventually the lights of the farmhouse came into view, and he had to let her go.

He wanted a few more kisses before he did though, and when she melted into his arms as though she was meant to be there, he held her tightly as his mouth sought hers and he lost himself in her embrace.

'You do realise I'm going to have stubble rash on my face tomorrow,' she said when they broke apart for the final time. She was smiling, so he didn't think she was overly concerned about having a red chin.

'I'll shave closer next time,' he promised.

'No, I like it. Not the rash, the designer stubble.'

'It's not designer,' he protested. 'I can't help it if my beard grows fast and it's really dark. Blame my Italian heritage.'

'I think it's sexy,' she declared, stroking his face, her touch making every nerve ending zing with longing.

He would give anything to take her to bed right now and make slow glorious love to her, but although he was hopeful it might happen in the future, it certainly wasn't going to happen right now.

'When can I see you again?' he asked.

'I'm not sure. There's Sammy to consider. I don't want to keep dumping him on Dulcie.'

Gio was disappointed but he understood. Her son came first, and that was only to be expected. 'What if I let you have my shift pattern for the next two weeks? If you can work something out, great. If not…' He left the sentence hanging.

'I'm sure I'll think of something,' she said. 'Petra at the stables has kindly offered to give him a riding lesson or two in exchange for him helping out, so what with that and Dulcie commandeering him for farm duties, I'm sure I'll have some time to myself.'

'I hope so. And I honestly don't mind if you want to bring him with you – we can do something together, something he might enjoy.'

'I'll think about it,' she said. 'He loves being at the farm, but this is supposed to be a holiday, so I don't want him to spend all his time mucking out the chicken coop and herding goats.'

'How about we go for a picnic? Or to the zoo?'

'I suppose wild animals will make a change from farm animals,' she replied thoughtfully. 'It's ages since we've been to one.' She seemed to come to a decision. 'Okay, we'll go on your next day off, if you like? But I warn you, there'll be strictly no kissing or canoodling.'

'Agreed. Now, can I have one more kiss before I say goodnight?'

Nikki lifted her chin. 'You may,' she replied primly, but the way she kissed him back was anything but prim, and when she finally pushed him away and went inside, Gio was glad of the long walk home – he needed it to cool his not-inconsiderable ardour!

CHAPTER SEVEN

'Remember, no kissing,' Nikki hissed at Gio, as she walked around to the passenger side of his car after making sure Sammy had buckled in his seatbelt.

Gio fake-pouted. 'I haven't forgotten. I promise I won't hold your hand, either. Or even look at you, if you don't want me to.'

'You're being facetious.' She pulled a face at him over the car roof, before getting in.

He was still grinning when he started the engine and drove out of the farmyard. 'You okay in the back, mate?' he called, and Nikki glanced over her shoulder

Sammy beamed back at her. 'I think he is more than okay,' she replied, on her son's behalf. 'He hasn't stopped talking about this since he got up this morning.'

Nikki had been tempted to do the same herself – not because she was excited to be going to the zoo, but because she was excited to see Gio again. It had been a couple of days and she was surprised at how much she had missed him. She hadn't been able to get him out of her mind, and Dulcie had teased her mercilessly, saying that she was mooning over him like a love-sick calf.

Nikki had hotly refuted it, but even she had to admit that she had caught herself daydreaming, and on more than one occasion she had realised that she had a soppy smile on her face.

Dulcie had smirked and suggested that it might be better for Nikki and Gio to spend his day off doing something else, and had offered to look after Sammy. But Nikki wasn't ready to take that step: after all, she'd only known him for a few weeks, and they'd only been on two dates so far.

It was a tempting thought, though...

However, she wasn't entirely sure that allowing Sammy to spend time with him was a good idea, because she didn't want to risk her son becoming attached. But as long as Sammy viewed Gio in the same light that he viewed Otto, she didn't see the harm in it. It wasn't as though she was introducing Gio as her boyfriend. As far as Sammy was concerned, Gio was simply a friend who was accompanying them to the zoo.

The journey passed quickly, with Gio entertaining Sammy with stories of the funnier or stranger aspects of his job as a traffic cop.

Sammy was fascinated. 'How fast can your car go?' he asked.

'This one? I'm not sure, because this is my own car, but unmarked police cars can reach speeds of up to 155 miles per hour.'

'Wow! That's fast. How fast are we going now?'

'About sixty-seven.'

'Can you go faster?'

'Not a good idea, mate. I'm not on duty today, so I've got to stick to the speed limit, like everyone else.'

A flurry of questions later, and Sammy ended up with an offer from Gio to sit in his panda car the next time he was in the vicinity of the farm.

'Will I be able to put the siren on?' Sammy pleaded.

'Only if your Aunty Dulcie says it's okay,' Gio replied. 'We don't want to scare the animals.'

'Princess doesn't get scared,' Sammy informed him solemnly. 'Toffee might, but she's only one year old, so she's still quite young, but she'll take her lead from Princess. Princess is her mum,' he added.

Nikki bit back a grin: her son sounded just like Petra, repeating word for word what the stable's owner had told him.

'What about the chickens?' she asked.

'They'll be fine,' Sammy replied confidently. 'They don't care about sirens. They only care about food and laying eggs. He paused. 'And foxes. They don't like foxes. Have you ever seen a fox, Gio?'

'A few times. Do you think they'll have any at the zoo?'

Sammy screwed up his face. 'Maybe. I want to see a tiger or a lion. They're better than foxes.'

'They're certainly bigger and fiercer,' Gio agreed. 'But do you know what I'm hoping will be there?'

'No, what?'

'Baboons.'

'Why? What are they?'

'A kind of monkey. They've got bright red butts and blue faces.'

Nikki rolled her eyes. Was Gio really talking about monkey's bottoms? But when Sammy sniggered, she realised that Gio had hit exactly the right note with her son, because there was nothing more amusing to an eleven-year-old boy than bottoms. And in that instant she lost another little piece of her heart to the man who already possessed far too much of it.

♥

Nikki smiled indulgently at her son as he waved his fork in the air, and chatted animatedly as he ate.

They had been in the restaurant for half an hour, and Sammy had yet to stop talking.

She didn't mind though, and Gio didn't seem bothered, either. She kept catching his eye and the amused smile in their depths made her heart sing. Going to the zoo had been a brilliant idea, and Gio had been fabulous with Sammy.

Her son had had simply the best time ever, and was now reliving every animal he had seen in technicolour detail.

True to his word, Gio hadn't attempted even one sneaky kiss. He'd not even held her hand. Instead, his attention had been on Sammy, and ensuring that her son enjoyed himself.

On seeing Sammy's face and listening to his excited chatter, Nikki could safely say that he had.

'Can you please stop talking long enough to eat your food?' Nikki begged.

Sammy's plate was still half full, whilst Nikki had almost cleared hers. Stopping off on the way home to have a meal had been another of Gio's suggestions.

'But I'm telling Gio about Princess and Toffee,' Sammy protested. 'It's important.'

Gio nodded. 'It is,' he agreed. 'Looking after two goats is a big responsibility.'

Sammy speared a chip and shoved it into his mouth, hastily eating before saying, 'I take them into the orchard every morning to a different part, and

Mum helps me tie them up so they don't wander off, and they eat all the brambles and other stuff, and then I bring them in after tea.'

'Bring them in the house?' Gio asked, wide-eyed.

Sammy gave him a withering hook. 'The *barn.*'

'Oh, I see. *The barn.*' Gio nodded sagely.

'I've got my very own chicken.'

'You have?'

'Yes, Aunty Dulcie gave it to me. She's called Kevin.'

Gio's lips twitched. 'That's an unusual name for a chicken.'

'Kevin de Bayne. He's a footballer,' Sammy informed him.

'I see. I take it you like football?'

'Sammy,' Nikki interrupted. 'Eat your meal. You can talk about football later. Or not at all,' she muttered under her breath.

'Not a footie fan?' Gio asked her, as Sammy obediently popped another forkful of food into his mouth and chewed vigorously.

'Not so much.'

'I've made a friend called Mason,' Sammy announced, his butterfly mind darting to another subject. 'He goes to the stables. Petra says I'm almost as good at riding as he is and he's been doing it for ages. It was only my first go.'

Nikki smiled at the pride in her son's voice. 'Petra is letting him have a lesson or two in exchange for helping out,' she reminded Gio. She wasn't entirely sure how much help Sammy was giving Petra, but she was grateful to the woman for her generosity, nevertheless.

'Next time he has a lesson, I'm going to show him my chicken and the goats. Can I have another lemonade, please?'

Gio caught the waiter's attention and ordered fresh drinks.

'Can Gio come to my birthday party?' Sammy asked. 'I'm going to be twelve.'

Nikki panicked. What party? She hadn't planned on Sammy having a party! She had assumed that a takeaway pizza, a birthday cake, and an evening spent playing the new video game she had bought him, would suffice. He didn't know anyone his own age here, apart from Mason, and he'd only met the boy once.

'Um...we'll see. You do know that it'll only be you, me, Dulcie and Otto, don't you?'

'Walter can come, and Petra,' Sammy added. 'And Gio.'

Nikki sighed. 'I'm sorry, kiddo, there won't be a party as such. Unless...do you want to go home to Birmingham and you can have a proper party? Maybe go to the cinema with a couple of friends? Or how about a paint-balling session, and a pizza afterwards?'

Sammy froze, then he seemed to close in on himself and his eyes grew fearful. 'I don't want to go home. I want to stay here.'

'Then we'll stay,' Nikki said, relief washing over her. She wasn't ready to go home yet, either. 'As long as you don't mind spending your birthday with us grown-ups,' she said.

However, her relief that they were staying a while was tempered by her worry that Sammy was starting to put down roots in Picklewick.

Actually, not Picklewick as such, but Muddypuddle Lane. Between the farm and the stables, Sammy was making himself very much at home, and it was going to be a wrench when they finally did have to leave.

Perhaps staying here for the whole of the summer wasn't the wisest thing she had ever done, but Sammy seemed so happy and was having such a brilliant time that there was no way she could bring herself to cut their holiday short. If he had agreed to go home early to spend his birthday with his friends, that would have been different. But she had seen the way he'd shut down when she suggested it, and had seen the misery that had flashed across his face, and she couldn't do that to him. It would be difficult enough for him when it was time for them to leave at the end of the summer.

It would be difficult for her too, and not solely because of Sammy. She now had her growing feelings for Gio to contend with.

♥

Nikki kissed her son's forehead then tucked the bed covers around his shoulders as Sammy screwed up his face and emitted a huge yawn.

'We had fun today, didn't we?' she said, getting up off the bed.

'I like Gio,' he replied.

So do I, Nikki thought. She smiled vaguely. 'That's good.'

'Do you like him?' her son asked.

'He's nice.'

'Is he your boyfriend?'

Nikki inhaled sharply. 'Whatever gave you that idea?'

'You go gooey when he talks to you.'

'I do not!'

'Mum, you *do*. It's okay, I don't mind.' He yawned again.

'Night, Sammykins.'

'Night, Mum. Tell Aunty Dulcie thank you for bringing Princess and Toffee in.'

'I will.' She switched off the bedside light but left the bedroom door slightly ajar.

He didn't need a light at night, but since he'd started secondary school, he had insisted on one, and it broke her heart to think how fearful he had become over the past academic year.

'Wine?' Dulcie asked, when Nikki walked into the sitting room and plopped down into a chair. The smell of paint lingered in the air, not quite masked by the scented candle her sister had lit.

'I'd love one, please.'

Dulcie poured her a glass of Chardonnay and handed it to her.

'Thanks.' Nikki took it gratefully and sipped at it. 'Mmm, nice.'

'So?' Dulcie leant forward. 'Did you have a good time?'

'It was lovely.'

'How did Sammy get on with Gio?'

'Surprisingly well. Gio's really good with him.' Nikki snorted. 'When I was putting Sammy to bed, he asked if Gio is my boyfriend.'

'It's a legitimate question. Is he?'

'I wouldn't call him a boyfriend as such,' Nikki objected.

'What would you call him? Your lover?'

'No! We haven't— I mean— *No.*'

'Why not?'

Nikki shrugged. 'I don't know him well enough, for one thing.' She smiled wryly. 'And there's the lack of opportunity, for another.'

'Ah-ha! So, if you had the chance you *would* jump into bed with him!'

'Not necessarily.'

'Liar.'

'Okay, I might.'

'Now we're getting somewhere.'

Nikki put her glass on the coffee table. 'I hate to break it to you, sis, but this...whatever it is—' she waved a hand in the air '—isn't going to go anywhere. He lives here and I live in Birmingham, so…' She didn't need to finish the sentence.

'Remember what I said about letting your hair down and having fun?' Dulcie reminded her. 'This doesn't have to be the love affair to end all love affairs. Just enjoy it for what it is – a holiday romance.'

'I'm not sure I'm cut out for holiday romances. I'm the sort to get too involved.'

'Are you too involved already?'

'I don't know,' she replied honestly. 'Maybe.'

Her phone ringing made her jump, and she scrambled to answer it, worry why someone was calling her at this time of night surging through her. From the look on Dulcie's face, her sister was equally as concerned.

'It's Gio,' she said, with relief, heaving herself out of the chair and going into the hall for some privacy.

'Hi, Gio.'

241

'Hi, you. Sorry, I know it's late, but we didn't have chance to say a proper goodnight.'

'Goodnight,' she replied softly. 'Is that better?'

'No.'

'I didn't think it would be.'

'Can you sneak away? Just for a few minutes?'

Intrigued, Nikki said, 'I might be able to. Why?'

'I was thinking I could drive up to the farm and meet you at the top of Muddypuddle Lane. Then I can say goodnight to you properly. I can be there in five minutes.'

'Make it ten, and you've got a deal.'

Nikki hurried into the sitting room, picked up her glass and downed the contents.

'What's wrong?' Dulcie asked.

'Nothing. Can you listen out for Sammy? I'm...er...just popping outside for a minute.'

Her sister's eyebrows shot up. 'Booty call?'

'Definitely not. I...um...left something in his car and he's popping it up.'

Dulcie bit her lip. Her eyes were twinkling when she asked, 'What is so important that it can't wait until the next time you see him?'

Nikki thought furiously, but her mind was a blank

Laughing, Dulcie said, 'Take as long as you need.'

Pulse racing, Nikki hot-footed it into the downstairs loo to freshen up, but after raking her fingers through her hair, she studied her reflection in dismay. If anything, she looked worse now than she had two minutes ago. Her cheeks were pink, and her hair was all over the place.

Drat! She didn't have time to renew her make-up or tame her hair – Gio would have to take her as he found her. And she'd no sooner thought it than the sound of an engine could be heard coming up the lane and she hurried outside.

The car came to a halt, and Nikki almost sprinted across the yard in her haste.

Gio got out and came towards her. He didn't say a word. All he did was hold out his arms and she fell into them. Then his mouth found hers and for several long delectable minutes she lost herself in their embrace.

As delightful as it was to be held by him, as they kissed Nikki had become aware of another feeling – that this was where she was meant to be, as though she had found her home – and the knowledge rocked her to her core.

♥

A final kiss, this time a far more gentle peck than the kisses they had just shared, and Nikki was gone, disappearing into the shadows as she headed back to the house. Gio watched her go, the taste of her on his lips, the scent of her in his nose. And although she had only just stepped out of his arms, he longed to hold her again.

It had been a mistake to come back to the farm tonight, he realised, but he hadn't been able to resist. Now he would spend the next few hours thinking about her.

Oh, hell, who was he kidding? He would have thought about her anyway – because since she had returned to Picklewick, he had thought of little else.

Gio had the frightening yet scarily wonderful feeling that he was besotted with her.

He still couldn't fathom how he had got himself into this position. One minute he had been happily living his life and minding his own business, and the next he had smiled at a gorgeous woman whilst he had been waiting at the pedestrian crossing for the lights to change.

And that might have been the end of it, but for a trip to the stables on Muddypuddle Lane on a bank holiday Monday in May.

Even then, he hadn't anticipated seeing her again until he'd bumped into Dulcie Fairfax…

And the rest, they say, was history.

Today had been fun though, and he wasn't just referring to the last twenty minutes. He had enjoyed the visit to the zoo immensely, and he had enjoyed spending time with her son. Sammy was a good kid and a credit to her. He was polite, funny, inquisitive, and friendly, with a hint of pre-teenage sass. Gio had sensed sadness and anxiety too, just below the surface, and he guessed it was because of the bullying. Even if it had been resolved to Nikki's satisfaction, it was bound to leave a scar. But it hadn't as yet, she had informed him, although she was hoping for a resolution before the new term started next month, so the child's anxiety was probably through the roof. Thank goodness Sammy was here for the summer, because it was taking his mind off his problems for a while.

Gio's heart went out to the poor kid and he wished it was in his power to do something to help, but there was nothing he *could* do. Just make any time they were together as enjoyable as possible. For Nikki, too, because he could tell how much it hurt her to know her son was so unhappy.

His thoughts turned to Sammy's forthcoming birthday, and how the child preferred to spend it with a bunch of old fogies rather than return home and have a party with his friends, and he wondered if there was something he could do to make the day special.

He had no idea what kind of things kids Sammy's age were into, but many of his colleagues had children, so perhaps he could pick their brains.

♥

'I've got an idea for Sammy's birthday,' Gio said, several days later. 'If it's okay with you.'

Nikki knew that when she agreed to go to Gio's house for a meal this evening that it wouldn't just be food she would be hungry for, and after he'd invited her in, she had fully expected him to whisk her off to bed, especially after the passionate welcome he had just given her. What she hadn't expected was to talk about Sammy's birthday.

'What is it?' she asked, breathless and trembling, as he led her into the lounge.

'A car driving experience.'

'Er…right.' She tilted her face up to his to be kissed again, which he did, but immediately afterwards he was back on the subject of Sammy's birthday again, much to her disappointment.

'Before you say anything, it's not the sort of driving experience you can buy online. And it won't cost you a penny, either,' he told her.

'How come?' Her interest was piqued, despite wishing he would shut up and make love to her.

She had arranged for a cake to be made by Megan, but that was as far as she'd got. Which was unfortunate, considering Sammy's birthday was fast approaching, and although she had batted some ideas around, such as camping on top of the mountain and cooking sausages on an open fire, or a visit to a theme park followed by a birthday tea, which would naturally consist of pizza (Sammy's favourite), she had yet to make a decision. It was very unlike her to be so disorganised, but being at the farm had thrown her a bit.

'I've had a word with the owner of a private airfield nearby, and he's agreed to let me use the airstrip for a couple of hours,' Gio was saying.

Nikki wasn't sure she understood. 'I don't follow…?'

'I've called in a favour from someone in the DTU – sorry, Driver Training Agency – and he has agreed to sign out one of the training vehicles so Sammy can have a go in it. He won't be allowed to drive it, but he will be able to sit in it whilst Dean takes the car through its paces. It's all perfectly safe – Dean is a police driving instructor and he knows what he's doing. Then, if Sammy wants, and you are happy for him to do so, he can have a go at driving my car around the airfield.'

Nikki blinked. 'Gosh, I don't know what to say. He'll love that. Thank you.'

Gio grinned. 'I was hoping you'd say that.'

'I suppose I'd better thank you properly,' she said, and abruptly the atmosphere changed.

'What were you thinking of?' His voice was hoarse, and the sound of it made her go all tingly.

'This,' she said, kissing him briefly on the lips. 'And this…' She trailed kisses down his neck. 'Maybe this.' She nibbled her way along his collarbone, drawing his shirt to one side. 'How am I doing so far?'

'You're getting there,' he murmured.

She felt a shiver go through him as his arms came around her, and she looked into his eyes. Her stomach clenched at the hunger she saw in them, and her breath caught as she waited for him to act, her excitement building with each beat of her heart.

Finally, finally, his head lowered.

His mouth hard on hers, the kiss deep and desperate, she frantically reached for the buttons on his shirt, her fingers trembling as she scrabbled to undo them, feeling his hands slide underneath her blouse, sensing his urgency as he met her passion with equal ardour.

'Not here,' he growled.

Then he scooped her up and carried her to his bed.

♥

Nikki's breathing was slow and deep, and every so often she would make a cute little whimpering noise in her sleep. And whenever she did, Gio held her closer until she settled again.

He knew he would have to wake her soon, but not yet, not when he was enjoying watching her sleep and luxuriating in the feel of her body against his. She was curled into him, her cheek on his shoulder, one hand resting on his chest, one leg entwined in his. Her hair tickled his nose, but he didn't want to brush it away and risk disturbing her. She looked so peaceful. There was even a small smile on her lips, and he hoped he was responsible for it being there.

She had certainly put a smile on his face. And not just because they'd made love – although that had been one of the most heady experiences of his life. He loved being with her. He felt alive when he was with her, as though the time spent before he'd met her had been lived in a shadow that he hadn't known he was under until now.

He wanted to make love to her again, but he didn't move a muscle, wanting to freeze this moment, to capture it forever, and never let her go.

This woman had taken his breath away, and if he had suspected that he might be half in love with her before this, he realised he was fully in love with her now.

Craning his neck, he checked the time. It was late, or should he say 'early'? Dawn wasn't far off, and he knew Nikki wanted to be home before Sammy woke.

Home…

He snorted softly. The farm wasn't her home, Picklewick wasn't her village. All too soon she would be going home for real, and he didn't know how he was going to deal with that.

Was this how it was always going to be, this relationship of theirs? Her always having to leave, him always having to say goodbye?

You're a fool, Gio, he said to himself. But it was too late now, the damage was done. He had already lost his heart to her, and he was terrified she might break it.

There was no *might* about it – she *would* break it, through no fault of her own.

If it was anyone's fault, it was his, for falling in love with her in the first place, despite vowing that he wouldn't get too involved. And what had happened to his new philosophy of living for the moment and not dwelling on the future?

Heartache would be the cost, so all he could do was follow his own advice and concentrate on the present and how happy she made him.

And with that, Gio woke her gently, with the softest of kisses, and when they had made love again, it was with a heavy heart that he watched her leave, knowing that all too soon he would be forced to watch her leave for good.

CHAPTER EIGHT

'This is the best birthday ever!' Sammy declared, as he shovelled the rest of his pizza into his mouth. 'Kaneyavagog.'

'Don't speak with your mouth full,' Nikki told him. 'Would you like to repeat that?' she suggested, after he hastily swallowed what he was eating.

'I said, can I have a dog?' He smiled hopefully.

'Don't push your luck, buster,' she warned. 'You've got a chicken.'

'Yes, but Kevin lives *here*, not with us.'

'You're at school all day and I'm at work, so if we did have a dog, who would take care of it?'

Sammy scowled. 'I don't *have* to go to school. I could stay home and look after it.'

Nikki clamped down on the sigh that threatened to escape. Why did he have to bring this up now? They'd had such a lovely day, and now Sammy was threatening to end his birthday on a sour note.

She had been aware for a couple of days that as the date for returning home loomed ever larger, Sammy was beginning to withdraw into his shell again. He had been his old self today, full of bubbling energy and wide-eyed delight, the opportunity to drive Gio's car being the highlight, even surpassing the high-speed rally-type driving that Dean had done, which had Sammy shrieking and screaming with pretend terror and a great deal of glee.

They had stopped off at a traditional ice cream parlour afterwards, for a sandwich and a knickerbocker glory, accompanied by a large glass of fizzy red pop, then it was back to the farm for a kickabout with the football Gio had bought him, followed by a session playing his new game, which had ended up being a hard-fought competition between him and Gio. Sammy had won and had been jubilant (and Nikki had quietly thanked Gio for letting him win). After that, they had ordered pizza with sides.

They – and by 'they' she meant Sammy, Gio, Dulcie, Otto, Otto's dad Walter, and herself – were just finishing the meal, with the intention of bringing the birthday cake out, when Sammy's mood had abruptly soured.

Nikki winced apologetically as her son sat back in his seat and folded his arms.

'We've discussed this, Sammy,' she said. 'I have to go to work, and you have to go to school.' And when he opened his mouth to argue, she shook her head in warning and he subsided sullenly.

'Cake time?' Dulcie mouthed.

'Good idea.' Nikki started clearing away the pizza boxes and the rest of the debris, to make room on the table.

'Let me help,' Gio offered, getting to his feet, and picking up the haphazardly stacked cartons.

Nikki trotted into the kitchen, anxious to light the sparkler on top of the cake, which would hopefully take her son's mind off his problems for a while longer. Gio followed her out, and as soon as he had divested himself of the rubbish he was carrying, he gathered her to him.

It felt good being in his arms, hearing the steady throb of his heart, feeling the solidity of his chest against her cheek. If only she could stay there forever, but she had to go home in a matter of days, and, like her son, she was dreading it. Not only was she having to leave a man she was fairly sure she had fallen in love with, but Sammy's misery would be almost impossible to bear.

She had tried phoning the school again yesterday, without any luck, because the call had gone unanswered even though she knew that staff would have been on site because that was the day the exam results were out. So she had been forced to send an email instead. She was still waiting for a response, but she guessed that she wouldn't get one until the middle of next week, because Monday was a bank holiday.

Unable to contain her worry, she let out a sob. 'He's so unhappy,' she cried.

'It'll be okay,' Gio murmured into her hair.

'You can't know that,' she snapped. Then said, 'Sorry. I shouldn't take my frustration out on you.'

'I don't mind. And you're right – platitudes don't help.'

Nikki lifted her head. 'What if the bullying carries on? He's adamant that he doesn't want to go to another school, but for his own sake I can't let him remain in this one. I'm beginning to wonder if I *should* give up work and home school him. After all, money isn't everything.' She screwed up her face. 'We would end up losing the house, though.'

'Maybe the school is in the middle of arranging for this other kid to go somewhere else, but it hasn't been finalised yet and they don't want to contact you until they've got some definite news?'

Nikki appreciated that Gio was trying to rationalise the delay, but she didn't believe it for one second. 'I'll just have to hope that's the case, won't I?'

'Come on, wipe your eyes. It won't do Sammy any good to see you upset.'

Nikki knew Gio was right. Grabbing a piece of kitchen towel, she dabbed her eyes, then blew her nose. Getting upset wasn't going to help, and there was a birthday cake to cut.

She opened the lid of the box and was just about to take the cake out, when she felt Gio's arms slide around her waist, and she squirmed around to face him, her lips meeting his for the briefest of kisses.

'Mum, what are——? *Oh…*'

Nikki and Gio leapt apart, Nikki's cheeks flaming. How stupid of her! To be caught kissing Gio, and by Sammy no less! What must he think of her?

'Er…Sammy, Gio was just…um…' she began, before she ran out of words.

Sammy gave her the kind of look that told her he knew exactly what she and Gio had been doing.

'Go back into the dining room, I'll be out in a second,' she said.

'Come on, mate.' Gio ushered Sammy out of the kitchen. 'It's time to sing happy birthday.'

Sammy glanced over his shoulder at her, but his expression was unreadable, and her heart sank.

Plastering a smile on her face, she lit the sparkler, picked up the cake, and walked slowly into the dining room, bursting into a rather wobbly rendition of *Happy Birthday to You* as she did so.

Everyone joined in and clapped when the cake was cut, but Nikki's attention was firmly on her son, wondering what was going through his mind.

She felt mortified, and guilty, too. The poor boy didn't need to have seen that. Two minutes previously he had been telling her just how much he didn't want to go to school, and then he catches her making out with a man who was only supposed to be a friend.

Sammy must think that she wasn't taking his concerns and feelings seriously.

As soon as she got him on his own, she would make sure that he knew he was the most important person in her life and that his happiness was the only thing that mattered.

To her astonishment though, she needn't have worried.

After saying a subdued and low-key goodnight to Gio, Nikki went in search of her son, who was saying his own goodnight to a couple of goats.

She found him in the barn, sitting on a pile of straw, staring at Princess. Puss was also there, but as usual the cat kept its distance.

'Sammy…' she began.

He looked around. 'Hi, Mum.'

She sat down next to him. 'About Gio…' She was about to tell him 'It isn't what you think' but she didn't want to insult his intelligence. So instead, she said, 'I'm sorry you had to see that.'

'You were kissing him.'

'I was.'

'You said he isn't your boyfriend.'

She took a deep breath. 'To be honest, I'm not sure what he is.'

'Will you be sad when we go home?'

'A bit,' she admitted. 'It's been fun here, hasn't it?'

'I don't want to leave.'

'I know you don't, Sammykins.'

For once, he didn't object to the endearment, and she put an arm around his shoulders and hugged him to her.

'I promise you, that one way or another we'll get it sorted, but before we do anything drastic, let's see what the school has to say first, eh?'

He scooted around to face her. 'Will Gio come to visit us?'

'I doubt it. We live too far away, but I expect we'll bump into him the next time we come to the farm.'

'When?'

'I don't know. We can't descend on Aunty Dulcie every holiday.'

His mouth turned down and his expression grew even more troubled. 'I like Gio. He's cool.'

'So do I, Sammy, so do I.'

'What if we never see him again? Will you be sad?'

'Yes, I will,' she replied honestly. She would be sadder than she ever thought possible.

♥

Determined to make the most of their final day together, Gio suggested going for a picnic on the mountain: all three of them, because he'd miss the little guy almost as much as he would miss the boy's mother.

The day was a glorious one, the air warm and clear, and to give themselves a breather (because it was a bit of a hike to the top) they had stopped to pick some of the blueberries that grew wild on the slopes above the farm.

'Can you really eat these?' Sammy asked, as he held up a fat berry. He was sitting amongst the heather and the blueberry bushes, looking incredulous. His fingers were already stained purple, and they had only started picking a few minutes ago.

'You really can,' Gio said, popping one in his mouth. 'Mmm, sweet and juicy. Try one.'

Sammy looked to his mother for confirmation that it was okay, and Nikki nodded.

She was looking even more gorgeous than usual, in a red sleeveless dress and a matching red sunhat. Her shoulders were bare, the skin lightly tanned, and so were her legs. She looked fresh and summery, and Gio couldn't believe that the summer holidays were nearly at an end. She and Sammy were going home tomorrow, and he wasn't ready to let her go.

He didn't think he ever would be.

But leave she would, and he had to accept it.

To add insult to injury, the weather today was absolutely glorious, the summer not done with them yet, despite the first of September being only three days away. The new academic year would start on Monday, Sammy would be back in school, and for Gio life would go back to the way it had been before he had met Nikki.

Except…it wouldn't be the same at all. She had changed him irrevocably, and it was both a sadness and a joy.

At the moment, sadness was winning, as he glanced at her to find her gazing back at him. His heart clenched, the pain of her loss already piercing his heart and she hadn't even left yet.

Sammy soon ran out of the patience that was needed to pick enough blueberries to make it worthwhile, but the three of them combined their efforts into one tub, and probably had enough to make a few muffins. Or rather, Otto would make the muffins, but that wouldn't be until after Nikki and Sammy had left.

There it was again: *left.* It kept popping into his mind, however hard he tried to pretend it wasn't happening.

Gio straightened up, his back aching from bending over to reach the berries. 'Shall we wash our hands in the stream, then we can have our picnic?' He waggled fingers that were covered in sticky blueberry juice.

The stream trickled down the hillside in the little valley it had carved out for itself over the course of hundreds of years, and the tinkling call of the water proved irresistible to Sammy. The boy was soon racing leaves, twigs and anything else he could get his hands on down it, before he turned his attention to building a small dam.

'This is perfect, thank you,' Nikki said as she sank down into the springy grass.

Gio sat next to her, watching the child's antics. 'I'm going to miss you,' he said.

'Don't, please don't. Can we just enjoy today and not think about tomorrow?' Her eyes glittered with unshed tears, and he felt like crying too.

'I'll try. It's not easy.'

'No, it's not.' She plucked a blade of grass and began shredding it, peeling it apart down the length of its stem, her gaze on Sammy.

'Let's eat,' Gio suggested. Although he didn't feel in the least bit hungry, he guessed that Sammy probably was.

And whilst the adults nibbled and picked at their food, Sammy wolfed down the selection of sandwiches and savoury pastries that Gio had bought from the delicatessen in the village, followed by a couple of slices of birthday cake that was left over from the other day.

After they'd eaten, the three of them carried on up the hillside until they reached the top, where they took in the view.

'Look, Sammy.' Nikki pointed to some specks far below. 'Is that Petra taking people out on a hack?'

'I'm a really good rider now, aren't I, Mum?' Sammy announced proudly.

'You are!' she enthused.

'I'm surprised Sammy didn't persuade you to have a go,' Gio laughed.

Nikki pulled a face. 'I can just about cope with the goats. Horses are a bit too big for my liking. Maybe next time.'

She turned stricken eyes to him, and pain lanced his chest when he realised that it had been a slip of the tongue, and that there probably wouldn't be a next time. Not like this.

When she did return to Muddypuddle Lane, they wouldn't simply pick up where they left off.

This was it, the end. Once today was over, their relationship would be, too. And his heart would be well and truly broken.

♥

Never had anything felt more bitter-sweet, Nikki thought.

Her head lay on Gio's chest, and their limbs were entangled, the sheets bunched and crumpled from their lovemaking.

Wild, frantic and desperate love had been peppered with tender softness, until she had sobbed with the joy and the sadness of it.

If she had known that saying goodbye would hurt this much, she would never have given in to her desire. But then, she would never have got to know this remarkable man. She would have denied herself the ecstasy that loving him had brought her. And there was no getting away from the reality that she loved him.

Love had crept up on her, sneakily insidious, until she had been well and truly caught.

So much for this only being a no-strings summer fling.

Technically, that was all it was, but emotionally it was much, much more. And like Sandy from *Grease*, Nikki was totally devoted to Gio. But that was where any similarity ended. Unlike Sandy, Nikki couldn't change her whole life for Gio. This wasn't a high school teenage crush; this was real life with real responsibilities. She had a mortgage and a job, and her life wasn't in Picklewick, however much she wished it was.

She had gone into this well aware of the limitations of their romance, and now that autumn was on its way, she had to accept that in a few short minutes their relationship would be well and truly over.

Gio stirred, and she lifted her head to find him looking at her, the love and pain she felt mirrored in his eyes.

Blinking back tears – there would be plenty of time to let them fall when she was at home – she reluctantly sat up. It was time.

'Stay. *Please*.' Gio put a hand on her thigh.

'You know I can't. It'll be light soon. I've got to get back.'

'I meant, stay in Picklewick. Don't go back to Birmingham,' he pleaded.

'You know I can't,' she repeated. 'There's my house, my job, my—'

'I love you.'

Nikki hitched in a ragged breath, the tears that she had been trying so hard to hold back, spilling over and trickling down her cheeks.

Why did he have to say that? *Why?*

'I mean it. I love you,' he repeated, and she knew it was true.

'I love you too,' she croaked. Clearing her throat, her voice thick with emotion, she added, 'But it doesn't change anything. It can't.'

'I know.' He sounded as broken as she.

Unable to bear it and worried that she might totally break down, Nikki slipped out of bed and reached for her clothes.

Gio made to get up.

'Stay there,' she instructed. 'I want to remember you just like this.'

He subsided, naked, back onto the bed, and her gaze raked him as she tried to commit every detail to memory.

He watched as she pulled on her jeans and tee shirt, misery and resignation on his face. 'Is this it? Is this how it ends?' He shook his head, as though refusing to believe it.

'It has to. We can't— It's not—' She stopped abruptly.

They both knew the score. She had made no secret of the fact that she was only here for the summer. Neither had promised the other anything more.

Yet, here they were, hearts breaking.

They were old enough to know better, but they had acted like a pair of teenagers and now they had to pay the price.

'I love you,' he said, for the third time, his voice breaking.

'I love you, too.'

For long seconds they stared at each other. Tears trickled down Nikki's face, and she let them fall as Gio swiped a hand across his cheeks, his eyes wet and glistening.

Then, without another word, she turned on her heel and walked out of the room, her heart breaking with the knowledge that she would probably never see him again.

♥

'It's a bit big, but you'll grow into it,' Nikki said in the time-honoured fashion of mothers everywhere when faced with having to buy a new school blazer for their child.

Sammy modelled the blazer sullenly, his arms dangling by his sides, his shoulders drooping. Nikki tried not to react to the despair on his face, but she couldn't help feeling equally as miserable.

'How does it feel?' she asked, going behind him to check the fit at the back.

He shrugged.

'Do you think it's too big?'

He didn't respond, so she turned to the shop assistant. Nikki had left it rather late – with the autumn term starting on Monday, most parents had already kitted their kids out with new school uniform, and there wasn't a great deal left. It was either this size, or Sammy would have to make do with his old one, which was now way too small for him, she had discovered when she'd told him to try it on. Sammy had shot up over the summer. Nikki blamed it on all that fresh air

The summer...

Best not think about it. Not right now. Not if she didn't want to burst into tears in the middle of Castor's Outfitters.

'As you said,' the shop assistant replied, 'he'll grow into it. Better too big, than not big enough.'

She sounded bored, and Nikki guessed the poor woman must have repeated the same thing hundreds of times over the course of the last few weeks.

'We'll take it,' Nikki decided. She didn't want to shell out for a new blazer, but she didn't have a lot of choice. It was the only one left in this size, and if she didn't buy it on the off-chance that she might be forced to look for another school for Sammy and therefore it wouldn't be needed and he ended up staying in his current school instead, then the odds were that the blazer would be snapped up by another parent and Sammy would end up wearing his woefully too-small old one.

'Shoes,' she said, clapping her hands together with forced jollity.

Sammy glared at her balefully.

'And a new PE kit,' she added. He could probably get away with the one he had for a few more months, but she was hoping a new footie shirt might cheer him up.

No such luck.

Her son endured the uniform buying trip in silence, only speaking to her when Nikki forced him to. Even then, most of his responses were in the form of a shrug or a flattening of his lips.

'McDonald's?' she suggested as they went outside. Laden down with bags, she'd had her fill of shopping, but as Sammy still had to find a pair of shoes (Castors hadn't had his size) Nikki needed a sit down and some sustenance, before diving back into the fray once more.

Even the offer of a Big Mac and fries was met with stony silence, but she took him for one anyway.

'How would you like it if Aunty Maisie looked after you for a couple of hours tomorrow?' she asked brightly.

Sammy stared at his food. He had done little more than pick at it.

'I'm going to see Mrs Harcastle,' Nikki explained, 'and I asked Aunty Maisie if she would pop around for a couple of hours while I'm out. Or would you prefer to go to Nanny's instead?'

'Don't care,' he grunted.

It would be less hassle to have Maisie babysit Sammy in his own house, rather than trek halfway across the city to her mum's, Nikki decided.

She was disappointed not to have heard a peep from the school, and with the pupils due to start back on Monday, Nikki wanted an answer. Tomorrow was a teacher training day, when all the staff would be preparing for the new term, and Nikki was confident that the headteacher would also be there.

Having been unable to contact the school, Nikki felt she had no choice other than to turn up and refuse to leave until she had spoken to the woman. She was aware that her actions might be regarded as confrontational, but she felt she didn't have any choice.

One way or another, she was going to sort this out. Nikki mightn't be able to do anything to ease the pain in her own heart, but she would do her utmost to lighten the pain in her son's.

♥

'As a teacher yourself, I'm sure you understand that these things take time, and what with the summer holidays—'

'With the greatest respect,' Nikki interrupted the headteacher, 'I am well aware that the Department of Education continues to function throughout August, and that headteachers rarely take the full six weeks off. What I don't understand is how it can take so long to make a decision regarding this boy.'

'As I said—'

Nikki got to her feet. 'This isn't getting us anywhere. You have been unable to deal with the situation at a school level, therefore any future assault by Blake will necessitate me calling the police, and I will also be making a formal complaint about the school's failure in its duty of care regarding my son. Do I make myself clear?' She knew she sounded officious but being polite and reasonable hadn't worked.

'Perfectly.' The woman's reply was frosty.

'Good!' And with that Nikki marched out of the headteacher's office.

She was so upset she could cry, despite already guessing even before she had spoken to Mrs Hardcastle today that nothing had been done. And probably never would be. It would take another incident and for her threat of going to the police to become a reality, before the school would set the ball rolling to remove Sammy's bully from the school, because Nikki didn't believe for one second that the bullying would stop unless drastic action was taken.

And because she wasn't prepared to put her son in harm's way again, she had a decision to make. A big one. One which would have serious consequences for her financially, but one which would benefit Sammy's mental health enormously. And that decision was whether to take him out of school altogether and educate him herself, or move him to another school and hope he would settle there.

But, in her heart, she already knew what she was going to do.

As she drove home, Nikki decided not to say anything to Sammy just yet. She needed to think this through properly, because if she did pack in her job as a supply teacher in order to home educate him, she would be without an income and she wouldn't be able to pay the mortgage. Therefore it was imperative that she found work of some description. Maybe she could find a job working from home, or do private tutoring? Or evening work in a bar or a restaurant, if her mum would babysit Sammy. It was a lot to think about, and she only had the weekend in which to do it.

'How did it go?' Maisie asked, when Nikki arrived home.

Her youngest sister was curled up in a chair, reading a magazine.

Nikki pulled a face. 'Not good. Where's Sammy?'

'In his room. He's been as good as gold. You'd be proud of me: I didn't let him play on his Xbox the whole time you were out – we had a geography lesson.'

Nikki slung her bag on the sofa and dropped down next to it. 'What did he teach you?' she asked wryly.

'Ha ha. Very funny. *Not*. I did the teaching, actually. He wanted to know where Picklewick was on the map.' Maisie wrapped a lock of hair around her finger and twirled it. 'I was thinking of going to visit Dulcie again.'

Nikki closed her eyes and rested her head against the cushion. The thought of what she was about to do made her feel ill. How she wished she could turn the clock back to this time last week. Her problems had seemed smaller, less real, and although she knew it had been an illusion, she would give anything to be there and not here.

She would also give anything to be in Gio's arms, but that was a place she could never return to except in her dreams, so she pushed the thought firmly away as she felt the familiar prickle in the back of her eyes.

'I can catch the train to Thornbury, and a bus from there to Picklewick,' Maisie was saying. 'We looked it up. We also did a few distance calculations, so I squeezed in some maths, too! Maybe I should look at teaching…'

Maisie had considered several careers since she'd left college, but teaching hadn't been one of them.

'Maybe you should,' Nikkie replied, keeping her tone neutral. Maisie was a dreamer, a free-spirit, flitting from one thing to the next, and Nikki had little hope of her settling on anything any time soon.

She blamed their mother – Maisie was the youngest of the four siblings and Mum had babied her something rotten. It wouldn't have been a problem if the babying had tailed off as Maisie grew up, but it hadn't, and Nikki's sister still acted as though she was a teenager, despite being twenty-five. It didn't help that she still lived at home and partied like she was eighteen. Saying that though, Nikki couldn't remember partying as hard as Maisie did when she had been eighteen.

'Will Dulcie mind if I visit her, do you think?' Maisie asked.

'Mum wouldn't be going with you?'

'I'm not sure she can get the time off – which was why I was looking at train times.'

Nikki's spidey-senses perked up. The last time Maisie had gone to the farm, their mum had gone with her and they had driven down in Mum's car. It wasn't like Maisie to be so proactive, and Nikki guessed something was afoot. 'Talking about taking time off, how is the job going?'

'Don't ask.'

'Don't tell me you've lost another job!' Nikki cried.

'Okay, I won't.'

'You *have*, haven't you? Does Mum know?'

'No, and you can't tell her. I'll find another one soon enough.'

Nikki puffed out her cheeks in exasperation. Her sister changed jobs more frequently than most people changed their socks. Maisie seemed to have no difficulty *getting* them – her issue was holding *onto* them.

Maisie's problem was that she was easily bored, and had yet to find anything to hold her interest. She was the same with men. Although Maisie wasn't promiscuous in that she didn't sleep around, she seemed to have a different boyfriend every other week, as she grew bored of those easily, too.

'Do you want to stay for a while? Join us for tea?' Nikki offered, recognising the futility of remonstrating with her.

'No, thanks. I'm going out later, so I need to go home and have a shower.' Maisie gathered her things and as Nikki showed her out, she yelled 'Bye, Sammy!' up the stairs.

When Maisie didn't receive a reply, she shrugged. 'I bet he's got his headphones on. Tell him I said goodbye.'

'I will, and thanks for minding him.'

'It was fun. He's a good kid.'

I know, Nikki thought, closing the door behind her. And he deserved to be able to go to school without being scared out of his wits.

She checked the time before opening her laptop: she would begin tea in an hour or so, but before that she had research to do and plans to make.

♥

Flipping heck, was that the time?

Nikki closed the lid of the laptop and gathered up the notes she had made, shuffling them into a neat pile. It was nearly five-thirty and she had been so engrossed in her research that over two hours had gone by. Sammy would be clamouring for his tea soon.

Stiffly, she got to her feet and rubbed her sore eyes. Her brain was whirling and she briefly thought about resuming where she'd left off after they'd eaten, but she was too tired to concentrate any more today. She had made some headway though, which she was pleased about. On the new school front, there was one that she definitely liked the look of. It would be a struggle to get him into it because it was oversubscribed, but she would give it a go if she could convince Sammy it was a good idea.

As for home schooling, her best option financially (but the one she liked the least) was for her and Sammy to move back in with her mum and rent her house out. The rent would provide some much-needed income, and her mum would be a built-in babysitter if Nikki was forced to go out to work in the evening. Of course, she had to run that by her mum first, who mightn't be too keen on the idea, which was why she didn't intend to say anything to Sammy yet. She didn't want to get his hopes up needlessly.

Nikki wandered into the kitchen, wondering what they could have for tea instead of the tagine she had planned on cooking. It would have to be something quick and easy – the poor kid must be starving. Then after Sammy had gone to bed she intended to open a cheap bottle of plonk and stare mindlessly at the TV for a couple of hours and try not to think about Gio.

The nights were the worst, she discovered. And so far she had spent three long, interminably lonely nights thinking about him since she'd returned home, with the prospect of many more to come.

Stop thinking about him, she admonished silently. She needed to focus on her son's happiness, not her own.

Before she started cooking, she decided to pop her head around Sammy's bedroom door. Feeling guilty for letting him play video games for the biggest part of the afternoon, and realising she had been so engrossed in finding a solution to his schooling problem that she hadn't seen him since she'd returned from her meeting with the headteacher, she climbed the stairs.

'Sammy?'

He didn't answer her knock, but she didn't expect him to: if he had his headphones on, he would be oblivious even if a brass band was playing outside his window, so she pushed the door open.

He wasn't in his room and his screen was dark.

'Sammy?' she called.

He must be in the bathroom, but when she looked across the landing, the door was open and that room was empty, too.

So was her bedroom, the kitchen, the garden, and the shed.

Sammy was nowhere to be seen.

Her mouth dry and with a coil of fear beginning to unfurl in her belly, Nikki checked every room again, even looking under the beds and in the cupboard under the stairs.

And when she noticed that his backpack and coat had gone, along with his favourite trainers, she had an awful feeling she knew what had happened.

A final check of his money box confirmed her suspicion.

Sammy had run away.

CHAPTER NINE

This was too much, too soon, Gio thought as he stepped out of the shower and towelled himself dry. What had he been thinking when he'd agreed to go on a double date this evening, and a blind one at that.

He was tempted to message Harvey and cancel, but it was a bit short notice and it wouldn't be fair on either Harvey and his girlfriend, or the woman he was supposed to be meeting. He would just have to bite the bullet, don his game face and be on his best behaviour for the duration.

Harvey, the daft bloke, was doing his best to cheer Gio up, but Gio wasn't ready to be cheered. All he wanted was to wallow in misery for the foreseeable future, but Harvey could be a right naggy git when he wanted to be, and he'd kept on, and on, and on, until Gio had agreed. Honestly, after two solid days of Harvey bipping in his ear, Gio would have agreed to anything if it shut the fella up.

The choice of venue wasn't the best, either. The Black Horse was his local, which might have been why Harvey had suggested it, but the pub held far too many memories of Nikki.

Hell, *everywhere* held too many memories, and not least was his very own bed. He kept seeing her there, her hair fanned across the pillow, her eyes with that smoky, sultry hunger that drove him nuts, inviting him to make love to her again.

Jeez, it hurt! To think he would never hold her again, never kiss her, never again tell her he loved her.

So many times during the past few days, he had reached for his phone, desperate to hear her voice, only to put it down again.

It was over. No matter how hard it was to believe, he had to accept it. They were done. He had to get on with his life as best he could without her in it. He was sure that in time the ache would lessen, but for now, it was a heart-stabbing reminder of what could have been, if only their situations were different.

He had even toyed with the idea of putting his house on the market and asking for a transfer to West Midlands Police, but he was held back by the fear that for Nikki this had only been a summer romance after all, and such a grand gesture might horrify her. What if he'd read their relationship wrong? What if he had read *her* wrong?

Despondent and heartsore, he finished towelling himself off and squirted a spray of aftershave across his chest, and wondered once again why he was going out this evening.

The sound of his phone ringing lifted his spirits a little, but only because he hoped it was Harvey calling to cancel. Or it might be work? He could always live in hope…

It was neither, and when he saw who was phoning him, his heart missed a beat before catching up with itself and making him cough. His throat constricted as he answered the call, and he coughed again.

'Gio? *Gio?* Are you there?'

The familiar voice made him want to cry…but wait, was *she* crying?

'Nikki? What's wrong? What's happened?'

Her wail of anguish sent a cold shiver down his spine.

'It's Sammy,' she hiccupped. 'He has run away and it's all my fault! I should have told him I wasn't going to send him back to school and I should have realised how upset he was but I didn't, and he—'

'Shhh, my love, slow down. Start at the beginning.'

He heard her gulp back a sob before she repeated, 'Sammy has run away.'

'When?'

'Today.'

'I know this sounds patronising, but are you sure?'

'Yes.' She drew in a shuddering breath. 'He has taken all the money out of his piggy bank.'

'What time did you notice he was missing?'

'About half an hour ago.'

'How long ago do you think he left?'

'I'm not sure!' she sobbed. 'It could be as long as three or four hours. It's my fault, I should have—'

'Let's not talk about whose fault it is, let's concentrate on getting him home. Again, at the risk of being patronising, have you phoned his friends? Your mum?' He hesitated. 'How about his father?'

'My mum was the first person I called. He's not there, and he's not with his father. His father doesn't want to know, so he would never have gone to him. None of his friends have seen him. Oh god…I should call the police.'

'That's a good idea,' Gio agreed gently. She should have done that before she phoned him. 'What's your address? I'll be there as soon as I can.'

'No! You don't understand! I *know* where he's going. He is heading to *Picklewick*. Please find him for me, please, *please*…Find my son, before anything happens to him.'

'I will,' he promised. 'I'll find him and bring him back to you.'

But as Gio hurried to get dressed, he hoped with all his heart that he could keep his promise.

♥

'*Maisie?*' Nikki opened the door to see her sister standing on her step. 'Have you—?' She looked past her, hoping to see Sammy, but Maisie was alone.

'It's all my fault,' Maisie said, her voice breaking. 'I should never have told him how to get to Picklewick on the train.'

Nikki wanted to yell at her that she most definitely shouldn't have, but how could Maisie have known what Sammy would do, when the very idea of him running away hadn't crossed his own mother's mind?

'Can you stay here?' Nikki demanded. After she'd spoken to Gio, she had tried to get hold of Dulcie, but there was no answer, so she'd left a message. She had also called the stables on Muddypuddle Lane and had managed to speak to Petra, who had promised to pop up to the farm and track Dulcie down. She had been just about to phone the police when Maisie had turned up.

'You don't need to ask,' Maisie said. 'I'll stay here as long as you need me.'

'Good. Call the police, report him missing and tell them what's happened. Tell them he's making his way to Picklewick by train. They might be able to track which train he caught.' Nikki grabbed her bag and shoved her feet into her trainers.

'Why? What are you going to do? *Nikki!* Where are you going?'

'To Picklewick, to find Sammy. Don't try to stop me,' she warned.

And god help anyone else who tried – which was why she wanted Maisie to phone the police for her. Nikki had seen enough tv programmes in her time to know that they would want to keep her here, answering endless questions, when all she wanted to do was to get out there and find Sammy.

'Call me if there is any news,' she cried, dashing to the door, snatching her car keys off the table as she flew past.

'Of course, but don't you think—?'

'No, I bloody don't!' she shrieked as she ran outside. There were still a few hours of daylight left, and if she could interrogate Siri on the way, she might have an idea of how frequently the trains ran.

If she was quick – and lucky – depending on what time train he caught and if there were no road works and the traffic was light, she might, *just might*, arrive in Picklewick ahead of her son.

♥

Gio was well aware of police procedures in the case of runaway children, and he knew that even with a possible destination, they would most likely start with Sammy's home as a base and try to track his movements from there. Gio also had no doubt that his local force would also be contacted, but all this would take time.

He might be off duty but he was in Picklewick already, and the first thing he intended to do was to drive up to the farm. Nikki had told him that Sammy would most likely have caught a bus from their house to Birmingham New Street station, and depending on which train he'd caught, he might have to change once or twice, before he ended up in Thornbury. Then it would be another bus ride to Picklewick, followed by a walk from the village to the farm. Gio highly doubted that the boy would take a taxi, but as he raced towards the farm, he radioed in to ask if someone could check with the local taxi office that no one had picked up a twelve-year-old boy who was travelling alone this evening.

Gio was also fairly certain that even if Sammy had made it as far as Muddypuddle Lane, the child wouldn't make his presence known. Sammy would probably slip into the barn or one of the sheds and hope no one would find him. Gio also guessed that Sammy wouldn't have thought much beyond getting to the farm itself, and it would only be when he was cold and hungry that he would realise the predicament he was in. At which point he would most likely make his presence known. But in the meantime, the kid had to get to the farm first, and that was what concerned Gio.

Trying not to drive like a maniac, Gio slowed as he reached the turning to Muddypuddle Lane and scanned the hedgerows and fields as he drove up the track. It was too much to hope that he would spot the child, but he looked anyway.

Dulcie was already waiting for him as he pulled into the yard. She must have heard the car, and her expression was hopeful when she saw who it was.

'I've not got any news,' he said as soon as he exited his vehicle, and her face crumpled.

She swiped at her tears and nodded when he asked if he could have a look around.

'Do you mind if I come with you?' she asked. 'Otto and I have checked everywhere. Twice. But Sammy's not very big and if he's here he could be hiding anywhere.' She bit her lip. 'Petra is checking the stables and her outbuildings, just in case. Do you think he has made it to Picklewick yet?'

'He may have. It's a two-hour journey by car, but more like three-and-three-quarters door to door by public transport. But then again he might not, especially when we don't know the time he left home. There's roughly a three-to-four-hour window.'

'Oh, god…' Dulcie's hand flew to her mouth. 'Poor little guy.'

'He'll be fine,' Gio said, despite knowing it was foolish to make reassurances. Resorting to a more professional tone, he added, 'The police will do their best to find him.' He clapped his hands together. 'Right, let's search the farm again, because it wouldn't surprise me if he's already here and keeping out of sight.'

♥

An hour later, with the farm, the stables and the surrounding area thoroughly searched with the help of Otto, Nathan, Megan and everyone at the stables,

Gio admitted defeat. The lad was not here, and with the night closing in soon, he was becoming increasingly concerned.

The local force had turned up to speak to Dulcie, but his colleagues had been happy enough to let him continue searching the farm while they pursued other avenues. They had informed him that CCTV had shown Sammy boarding the four-fifty-five train at Birmingham New Street, and alighting at Thornbury station nearly two hours later. Which meant that Sammy should have been here by now…

Where the hell could he be?

Officers were checking with the bus company, and Gio was thankful that buses also carried CCTV. They would find him. He was sure of it.

It was just a matter of when.

'I'm going to walk into Picklewick across the fields,' he said. 'Maybe I can intercept him.' Assuming Sammy had arrived in Picklewick, that is. Gio hadn't received any updates for about an hour, so he was guessing that the police were still checking with the bus company. 'You stay at the farm,' he said to Dulcie, sensing that she was about to suggest she go with him. 'Nikki should be here any minute.'

He was desperate to see her, but finding Sammy took priority over his need to scoop her into his arms and tell her everything would be alright. Because, at this point, he couldn't honestly be sure it would be.

He was still hopeful of a positive outcome, though – Sammy was a bright lad with a sensible head on his shoulders, and Gio was convinced he was okay. Physically, at least. Sammy's emotional well-being was another matter entirely, and Gio's heart went out to the boy as he thought of how desperate the child must have felt in order to resort to running away to avoid returning to school on Monday.

With determination, he strode towards the row of holiday cottages belonging to the stables, heading for the public footpath which led across the fields to the edge of the village. The cottages had already been checked, whilst trying not to disturb the occupants too much. Two of them were currently rented out, although only the guests in one of them had been at home, and Petra had reluctantly gone inside the other for a quick look-see whilst they were out. Gio had entered the unoccupied third one with Petra, but there had been no sign of the boy.

As Gio hurried past, he saw two vehicles in the tiny car park and assumed that both sets of holidaymakers were now in residence. He debated whether to check with them again, but the cottages were only two-bed affairs, so the likelihood of a twelve-year-old boy hiding within their walls without the occupants noticing was slim to non-existent, so he decided not to bother and hurried past.

The grass in the fields was long, the golden stems teased by the breeze and creating waves of ripples. Gio narrowed his eyes at the movement. Sammy could be hunkered down in the grass and Gio would never see him, the constant sway of the stalks with their feathery seedheads, combined with the encroaching twilight, would serve to hide him from view.

Abruptly, Gio halted.

A nagging thought tugged at the back of his mind, and he glanced over his shoulder at the stables.

Something wasn't quite right, but he didn't know what…

Ah! Yes, he did.

He inhaled slowly, letting the memory of what he had just seen percolate through his mind. Had he imagined the twitch of a curtain at the upstairs window of the unoccupied holiday cottage? And if he hadn't imagined it, might it have been caused by the same breeze that whispered through the grass of the field he was standing in?

Probably.

It wouldn't hurt to double check, though.

And he had a hunch that there was more to this than a wind-blown curtain.

He took out his phone and dialled the number for the stables. Petra's husband, Harry, answered.

When Gio told him what he wanted him to do, Harry immediately agreed.

'Wait until you see me coming up the path,' Gio instructed. 'You can go in the front door, and I'll stake out the back. I probably imagined it, but if I haven't and Sammy *is* in there, I don't want to frighten him and risk him running out the back.'

'Gotcha,' Harry said.

Gio began walking back the way he'd come, praying he was right, hoping he wasn't wasting valuable time on a wild goose chase. If he remembered rightly, when he had searched the cottage with Petra, both the upstairs windows had been open, so it was fair to assume that a through breeze might have caused the curtains to move.

But at the same time, he knew in his gut that he was right.

Or was it just wishful thinking?

As he approached the row of cottages, he saw Harry hovering on the other side of the small car park, keeping out of sight of the cottage's windows, and Gio pointed to indicate he was heading around the back.

Holding up a hand, he mouthed, 'Five,' hoping Harry would give him enough time to get into position.

Gio didn't think Sammy would exit the building the same way he had entered it, which, if his hunch was correct, would have been by shimmying up the drainpipe and crawling in through the open bedroom window. Gio had noticed a key in the lock of the patio door, so he fully expected Sammy to leave in a more conventional manner – assuming that he *was* inside, of course.

He had only just reached the private garden at the back of the cottage and was forcing his way through the shrubbery, when Gio heard Harry shout, 'Sammy! Wait up!' and he knew he was right. Adrenaline shot through him as he scrambled to reach the door.

The boy ran to the patio doors, a panicked expression on his pale face, wrestling with the key, and had unlocked it before he noticed Gio.

Then his body sagged and his face crumpled.

Gio rushed over and grabbed hold of him, pulling him into his embrace, and as Sammy's body shuddered with deep sobs, Gio squeezed him tighter.

'I've got you,' he muttered, 'You're safe now. Everything's going to be okay.'

Releasing his grip for a second, Gio hooked his phone out of his jeans pocket, unlocking the screen with his thumb, then he tossed it to Harry, who looked as relieved as Gio felt.

'Call his mum,' Gio instructed, not wanting Nikki to have to wait another second longer to know that her son was safe. 'Tell her we'll be at the farm in five minutes.'

He turned his attention back to Sammy, who was sobbing uncontrollably. 'It's okay,' he repeated. 'Everything's going to be okay.'

'It's not!' Sammy wailed. 'Mum is going to be so mad.'

'She probably will,' Gio agreed. 'But that's only because she has been so worried about you. I'll tell you what else she'll be – relieved that you're safe. She loves you very, very much, you know.'

'I know.' Sammy's sobs were subsiding into sniffles, and Gio sensed it was time to step back to give the boy some space.

He slung an arm around his shoulders and gave him a sideways hug instead. 'Let's go see your Mum, shall we?'

Sammy nodded, but they hadn't made it as far as the lane when Nikki came tearing down it, running as though she was being chased by the devil himself.

'Sammy!' she shrieked, her face streaked with tears, and she barrelled into them, almost knocking her son off his feet as she grabbed hold of him.

Gio stood aside, his heart melting at the sight of her.

He should let his colleagues know that the boy had been found, but he stole a few seconds to drink her in.

Finally, though, he had to look away, and he used the excuse of the need to phone the station as he headed towards the farm and his car. Harry wordlessly gave him his phone back, clapping him on the shoulder as he passed and giving him a knowing look.

Then, with his heart breaking all over again, Gio walked away from the love of his life.

♥

'I honestly don't know what to do,' Nikki said to Dulcie, that same evening. It was getting late, and Nikki was exhausted but too strung up to think about going to bed.

She was wearing borrowed pyjamas, having been persuaded that staying the night at the farm was more sensible than driving back to Birmingham.

Once all the furore had died down and phone calls to the police, Nikki's mum, Maisie, and Sammy's friends had been made, Otto, bless him, had rustled up a meal for everyone, although both she and Sammy had only picked at it, then she had put Sammy to bed, staying with him until he'd fallen asleep.

Even then she had been reluctant to take her eyes off him in case he ran away again, despite him promising he wouldn't. She believed him, but…

'Is it Sammy you don't know what to do about, or is it Gio?' Dulcie asked. 'More wine?'

'No, thanks. One glass is enough. I want to keep a clear head.' She wrinkled her nose. 'Both?'

'I thought so.'

'I have decided to give up work and teach Sammy at home,' Nikki said.

Her son and his abject misery were of more immediate concern than her love life, although she couldn't help wondering why Gio had dashed off so fast. He hadn't given her a chance to thank him, and when she had tried to call him later, it had gone straight to answerphone. She had thought about sending him a message, but she wanted to thank him in person. If he hadn't realised that Sammy was hiding out in one of Petra's holiday lets…

Nikki shuddered. Sammy would have been safe enough there, but she wouldn't have known that, and it was the not-knowing that had almost driven her mad. When Harry had called to tell her that Sammy had been found and he was okay, the relief that had swept through her had almost floored her.

Nikki never, ever wanted to go through anything like that again.

Which brought her back to the reason Sammy had run away in the first place, and whether there was anything she could have done to prevent it.

Her guilt was crippling, and tears welled, spilling over to trickle down her face. With an angry hand, Nikki brushed them away.

'It's my fault,' she said. 'I'm his mother, I should have taken him out of school a long time ago.'

'Hindsight is wonderful,' Dulcie said, scooting across the sofa to put her arm around her. 'You did what you thought was right.'

'But it *wasn't* right.' Nikki sniffed loudly. 'I'm going to ask Mum if we can move in with her.'

'What about your house?'

'I'll rent it out. It will give me some income. And maybe I can find some bar work in the evenings.'

Dulcie picked up her wine, her brow furrowed. 'You'll hate it.'

'Which bit?' Nikki asked dryly, dabbing at her eyes with a tissue.

'All of it – apart from spending more time with Sammy, of course. You'll hate living at home again after having your own place for so many years.' Dulcie shuddered. 'Then there's Maisie – she'll drive you nuts. Talk about having her head in the clouds. Did you know that Mum still does all her laundry and cleans up after her?'

'I won't be doing any of that!' Nikki retorted. 'Maisie needs to grow up.'

'See, it's already getting you riled just thinking about it.'

'I know.'

'You're not going to like bar work, either,' Dulcie pointed out.

'If Maisie can do it, so can I!'

'I'm not saying you can't do it, I'm saying you won't like it. I know you – you like to be in bed by ten.'

'It's way past ten now, and I'm still up,' Nikki pointed out.

Dulcie arched an eyebrow.

'Yeah, okay, you're right,' Nikki conceded. 'I am usually in bed by ten. I'll just have to get used to staying up later, won't I?'

'What about your job? You love teaching.'

'I'll probably go back to it again at some point.'

'When Sammy is sixteen? Eighteen? When?'

'What's your point, Dulcie? I don't see I have any other option.'

Dulcie grinned at her. '*I* do. You can live here.'

Nikki stared at her. 'You mean…move in with *you?*'

'Yep.'

'But why? It's a lovely offer and thank you, but it doesn't change anything. I'll still have to rent my house out, and there are far fewer jobs up for grabs in Picklewick than there are in Birmingham.'

Dulcie was shaking her head and laughing. 'Look at the bigger picture,' she urged. 'If you and Sammy move into the farm, you can still rent your house out, but…' She paused, her grin turning into a beaming smile. 'You don't have to home educate Sammy; he can go to the school in Thornbury, and – here's the best bit – you can still teach. I don't know much about your job, but I'm guessing that the need for supply teachers isn't limited to Birmingham. And you know how much Sammy loves being here.'

Nikki knew, alright – after all, this was where he had escaped to when he'd thought he would have to return to school. To give herself time to think and to process what Dulcie had said, Nikki joked, 'You just want me to move in because of my unrivalled skills with a paintbrush.'

'That, too. You've got to admit it though, it's a brilliant idea.'

'What about Otto?' Won't us being here cramp your style?'

'Not at all. He'll understand. Anyway, I'm guessing you won't want to live with your little sister forever. You are eventually going to want to get a place of your own in Picklewick. But until then, this is the ideal solution.'

Nikki had to admit that it certainly seemed like it. As Dulcie had pointed out, Sammy would have a fresh start in a new school, and she could carry on with her supply teaching. Sammy would love living at the farm, and even if she did find somewhere of their own to live in the fullness of time, he could still pop to the farm whenever he wanted.

There was one fly in this rather appealing ointment though, and that was Gio.

How would he feel about her moving to Picklewick?

Would he be happy to have her nearby and for them to resume their relationship? Or had it been just a summer love, ripped at the seams by her return to Birmingham and never to be stitched together again?

There was only one way to find out.

♥

Nikki sat in her car, the engine still running. Now that she was here, she wasn't convinced that turning up at Gio's house at this time of night was such a good idea after all. It was incredibly late, and he mightn't even be in as there weren't any lights on. And if he was, he might not want to see her.

Maybe she should come back in the morning, but this time she would call ahead first.

She tapped her fingers on the steering wheel, torn. If she left now, she suspected she wouldn't have the courage to return. And if she didn't speak to him and ask how he would feel about her coming to Picklewick to live, then she would have to resort to plan B and move in with her mum, because visiting Picklewick would be bad enough – she couldn't even begin to imagine living here and not being with him. Her heart simply wouldn't be able to take it.

What should she do?

In some ways she wished Dulcie had never suggested it, then she wouldn't be in such a quandary. But her sister's idea was a good one – a brilliant one, even – because in one fell swoop moving to Picklewick would solve all her and Sammy's problems.

But would it work?

That depended on Gio.

Which brought her back to the reason she was sitting in her car outside his house, trying to pluck up the courage to knock on his door.

Gio solved the problem for her when he tapped on the passenger window, making her shriek and almost jump out of her skin.

Putting a hand to her chest and her frantically beating heart, she wound the window down. 'Hi.'

'Hi, you.' His voice was soft, his expression thoughtful.

She said, 'I came to thank you.'

'It's late,' he pointed out.

'Yet, here I am.'

'Here you are,' he repeated slowly.

It was now or never, she decided, her courage almost failing her as she blurted the words. 'Can I come in?'

'Of course.' He waited for her to get out of the car and his eyebrows shot up when he saw she was wearing PJs. 'Planning on staying the night?' he joked, then winced. 'Sorry, I didn't mean that to sound the way it did.'

Seeing him again, Nikki would like nothing better than to stay the night. She would like to stay *every* night, not just one.

She followed him inside, hesitating when she got as far as the end of the hall. Then she took a deep breath and walked into the kitchen. 'I'm sorry it's so late. I had to speak to you and you didn't answer your phone.'

'I went for a run, to clear my head.'

She realised he was wearing running shorts and trainers. 'Just got back?'

'Uh-huh. Would you like a drink?'

'Not for me, thanks.' She watched him pour himself a glass of water, her eyes on his throat as he drank it down. 'I came to thank you for finding Sammy,' she repeated. 'And to ask you a question.'

'You don't need to thank me. It was sheer luck that I noticed the curtain moving. I'm just glad he's okay.'

'He's fine. For now. Not so sure how fine he'll be when I take him home. Actually, that's why I'm here. I…er…wondered how you would feel if I moved here. Me and Sammy. Into the farm. With Dulcie,' she stuttered.

Gio didn't answer and his expression didn't give anything away, so she hastily explained, 'I've decided not to send him back to school. I was planning on moving back in with my mum and home educating him. But Dulcie suggested that I live with her instead. For the time being, at least. Sammy loves it here, and he could go to the school in Thornbury, and—'

'What about *you*?' Gio leapt in.

'I love it here, too. It's a brilliant idea, but…'

'But…?'

'God, this is awkward.' She raised her eyes to the ceiling and took a steadying breath, before coming to rest on him again.

'I get it,' he said, nodding slowly. 'It won't be a problem. I don't expect us to take up where we left off.' He didn't meet her gaze.

She swallowed. This was exactly what she feared he might say. He might have told her he loved her, but that was when there was no prospect of them being together. The reality of her moving to Picklewick was an altogether different thing.

Plan B it was, then. She said, 'Look, forget it. It was a daft idea. Sorry.'

'I think it's a great idea,' he said. 'Don't let my love for you prevent you from doing what's best for you and Sammy.'

Nikki froze. 'What did you say?'

'It's a great idea?'

'After that.' She made a winding-on motion with her hand.

Gio pulled a face. 'I said, don't let my love for you stop you. Don't worry, I'll stay well clear. I went into this with my eyes wide open: just because you're moving to Picklewick, doesn't mean I'll assume we are going to be a couple.'

Nikki thought her heart was going to burst out of her chest. Happiness washed over her as her face crumpled. Don't cry, she told herself.

Then she immediately burst into tears.

Gio gathered her to him. 'Shhh,' he murmured. 'It's alright, everything is alright. He's safe now.'

'I'm not crying because of Sammy,' she wept. 'I'm crying because you love me. I thought you didn't want me anymore, that this was just a summer romance to you.'

'It was never just a summer romance. I love you with all my heart, and I would like nothing more than for us to be together – a proper couple.'

Nikki lifted her head, sniffling back tears. 'How proper?'

He was smiling at her, love in his eyes. 'Proper enough that I want to be with you all day, every day. I know that isn't possible, but…'

'You'll be able to see as much of me as you want when I move to the farm.'

'It's not enough,' he insisted. 'I want *more*. I want you to come live with *me*.' He suddenly looked worried. 'Or am I going too fast for you?'

Nikki was astounded. *Move in with Gio…?*

Her heart almost stopped at the enormity of it. But her first instinct was to say yes. So that was what she did.

'I'd love that, too,' she said. 'I'll have to discuss it with Sammy, though.'

'Of course you will. He has got to be on board with it, and if he isn't, I'll have to try harder to win him round. I love you, Nikki, and I never want to let you go.'

And he didn't, not for a very long time indeed.

♥

'Where do you want this?'

Nikki was standing in Gio's bedroom (her bedroom now, too) and she glanced around to see Gio nodding his head at the box he was holding. 'Um, I'm not sure what's in it.' She had packed up the house in Birmingham in such a hurry, that she wasn't quite sure what she had shoved into which box. 'Aw, stuff it! Stick it in the shed. I'll sort it out when I can find the time.'

Gio grinned at her, walking away with the box, leaving Nikki to finish dragging clothes out of a suitcase and hastily shove them on hangers in the wardrobe.

She disliked mess and wanted to find a place for as many things as she could before the day was out, knowing that tomorrow was going to be busy. She had to take Sammy to buy his new school uniform (thankfully the trousers and shoes she had purchased for him at the end of the summer were suitable) and she had an interview with a supply agency afterwards. Although…she was secretly hoping to land herself a permanent job, and she had already begun looking.

Thinking about Sammy had her praying he was behaving himself. It had been easier to drop him at the stables whilst she got on with the unpacking, rather than trip over him every five minutes, because he was as bubbly as a bottle of fizz with the cork out at being in Picklewick. His happiness was a delight to behold.

Gio reappeared, having deposited the box in the shed along with the rest of the bits and pieces she had yet to find a home for.

Most of her furniture was in one of the barns on the farm. She had briefly considered putting everything into storage, but Dulcie had told her not to be so silly and had offered her the use of the redundant sheep shed for the duration. Her furniture was now stacked neatly under several layers of tarpaulin, until she decided what to do with it.

After all, Gio had plenty of furniture of his own and his house didn't need an additional sofa or a second washing machine – although it very definitely did need a woman's touch, and she was the woman to provide it.

'Come here,' he said, holding his arms open for her to step into his embrace. 'No regrets?'

'None, whatsoever,' her reply was emphatic. 'Mind you, I might change my mind if you leave dirty socks on the floor or I have to nag you to take the bins out,' she teased.

'I'm completely house trained,' he objected with a laugh. 'But I know someone who isn't.'

Nikki gasped. 'Sammy is a pre-teen! He's not supposed to be house trained. It says so in the 'How to be a Teenager' manual.'

'I wasn't referring to Sammy.'

'Then who? Not me, I hope?'

'Come downstairs, I've got something to show you.' He grabbed her hand and towed her out of the bedroom, across the landing and down the stairs. 'Actually, it's not some*thing*, it's some*one*.' He led her into the kitchen. 'Meet Tara. She's an eleven-week-old border collie, and she's Sammy's housewarming present. Do you think he'll like her?'

'Are you kidding!' Nikki squealed, dropping to her knees to pick up the bewildered pup. 'He'll adore her!'

'I did think about getting him a chicken, but you can't take a chicken for a walk or play ball with it, and I remembered him saying how much he wanted a dog. I hope you don't mind,' Gio added worriedly.

'Mind? Of course I don't mind! That is such a nice thing to do.' She cuddled the tiny dog to her chest, sniffing its puppy smell and stroking the fluffy fur. Tara licked her hand, squirming in her arms as she tried to reach Nikki's face.

Gently Nikki returned the puppy to its basket, straightened up and turned to face Gio.

'Thank you. Have I told you how much I love you?' she said, offering her mouth to him.

It was only meant to be a quick kiss, but as always it turned into something much longer and far more satisfying, and when she reluctantly extricated herself because the pup was whining and making a fuss, Gio's face was so woebegone that she had to laugh.

'Never mind,' she said. 'There's always later, and this time I won't have to sneak out in the early hours of the morning. I still can't believe you asked me to move in with you.'

'I still can't believe you said yes,' he countered. 'I would have put hard cash on you saying it was too soon.'

'Other people might think that, but I don't,' she said, remembering the conversation she'd had with her mum, and the one she'd had with Dulcie. But Sammy had thought it was a wonderful idea once he realised that he could pop to the farm and the stables anytime he wanted, and the way he had taken to Gio warmed her heart.

And now Gio had bought him a puppy…

The very same puppy who was pawing at her leg right now. 'I think this little one wants some attention,' she said. 'You'll have to wait.'

'I don't mind,' Gio said, his eyes so full of love it made her heart ache with the beauty of it. 'We have all the time in the world.'

He was right – they did – but Nikki didn't want to waste a second of it.

She had come to the farm on Muddypuddle Lane to escape, but she could never have anticipated being caught by the intense and unequivocal love she felt for Gio. And now that she had, she intended to relish every moment. The puppy would be fine on its own for a short while – Nikki wanted to show her wonderful man just how much she loved him!

FIREWORKS

CHAPTER ONE

Dulcie slapped her palms against the legs of her jeans to get rid of the dust on them and stood back to admire her handiwork.

The previously unkempt and uncared-for barn looked amazing, even if she did say so herself. The bales of straw that had been haphazardly thrown on one side were now stacked neatly to form pens for two goats, a donkey, a couple of Shetland ponies – all courtesy of Petra from the stables on Muddypuddle Lane – and a sheep named Flossie. Several more bales were dotted around for people to sit on, although these did have some old rugs thrown over them to make the experience more comfortable (bales of straw were *scratchy*), and there was an assortment of tables lined up against one of the walls. The tables were groaning with finger food that Otto and Walter had just brought out from the kitchen, and the appetising smell of hot chocolate and coffee hung in the air – along with the not-quite-so-enticing aroma of the animals.

Dulcie and her sister Nikki had worked hard on prettying the place up, and homemade bunting and fairy lights were strung from the beams and rafters, giving the interior of the barn a fairy grotto atmosphere.

'I think we're ready,' Dulcie announced, then cried, 'Baskets! Where are the baskets?'

Nikki said, 'You told Sammy to put them on a table near the entrance, remember?'

'So I did.' Dulcie breathed a sigh of relief. She had been so busy trying to get the farm's version of a harvest festival off the ground, that she had found herself treble checking things and often forgetting that she had already done them.

Nikki's other half, Gio, who had also been roped in to help with the event, poked his head around the open barn doors and announced, 'Your first customers have arrived.'

Dulcie panicked. 'Oh, dear, I hope they won't be disappointed. I hope we're not charging too much. What if they—?'

'Stop!' Otto commanded, leaving the food and striding over to her. He took her in his arms and kissed her on the forehead. 'It'll be fine. Take a deep breath, put a smile on your face and go say hello.'

'Okay, yeah, I can do that.' She straightened her shoulders, lifted her chin and smiled wildly.

Otto recoiled. 'Er, maybe tone the smile down a fraction?' he suggested. 'You look a little manic.'

'Sorry.' Dulcie lowered the wattage and hoped she looked more natural.

'Better.' He kissed her again, this time on the lips, then released her.

She paused for a second, drinking him in. Otto was wearing chef's whites and a cap-like covering on his head and looked as delicious as the food he had prepared. She wanted to eat him all up right now, but she would have to wait until later. Much later…

Pushing the wicked thoughts aside, Dulcie pulled herself together and went out into the farmyard to greet her first paying customers. They were paying to pick their own apples and pears from the laden fruit trees in the orchard. There were also a couple of plum trees dotted amongst them, and the hedgerows surrounding the orchard were full of blackthorn trees with their purple velvety sloes, as well as ripe hazelnuts, and rosehips, which could be made into the most delicious syrup, perfect for pouring over ice cream or pancakes. Otto had already prepared a large jug of it; he was hoping to persuade people to give it a go. The syrup went surprisingly well with savoury dishes, too.

Visitors could also help themselves to the sweet chestnut tree over the far side of the orchard, which was weighed down with nuts. And in one of the fields beyond lay a tumbling mass of brambles bearing loads of blackberries, which would need to be picked soon before they went to mush.

Sammy, bless him, had helped Dulcie make cardboard signs nailed to wooden stakes (Dulcie had done the nailing because she hadn't been sure that a twelve-year-old boy and a hammer were a good combination) and these directed visitors to the orchard, as well as indicating what was what, in case people were unsure about what could be picked and safely eaten. Although Dulcie was no expert, she now knew a sloe from an elderberry – which was also available to be picked.

Prior to meeting and falling in love with Otto, Dulcie would never have imagined that so many wild fruits, berries, nuts and seeds could be eaten. And flowers. Over the past few months she had eaten more blooms than the Chelsea Flower Show had on display.

There were even edible flowers to be had today, mostly in the cordials that Otto had prepared, or the ice creams he had made, such as the lavender and honey flavour, or the elderflower one, both of which were incredibly moreish.

Mind you, Dulcie thought as she strode up to the first of the farm's visitors, everything that came out of Otto's kitchen was rather moreish. As was the man himself!

♥

'Dad, why don't you go sit in the house?' Otto suggested some time later, noticing that his father was flagging.

Even though Walter's health had improved significantly since the start of the year, when Otto had feared he might never recover from the strain of running Lilac Tree Farm singlehandedly, his dad wasn't out of the woods yet.

However, Otto had seen a significant improvement from those dark days when Walter's beloved farm had been raffled off to raise funds to cover the business's horrendous debts. And there had been even more of an improvement since his dad had been helping Dulcie get ready for the harvest festival event. In fact, it had been his father's idea.

Dulcie had been fretting about all the apples and pears that would go to waste, and Walter knew that she was also worried about the costs of keeping the farm going. So he had suggested opening the orchard up for a PYO fruit day. And things had escalated from there, culminating in Otto offering to showcase some of the recipe ideas he'd had for the cookbook he was hoping to publish, and Petra, who owned the stables on Muddypuddle Lane, offering to lend some of her animals for the children to pet and feed.

His dad had been a great help, but Otto worried that he was overdoing things.

'I'll just sit here,' Walter groaned as he lowered himself creakily onto a bale of straw. 'And maybe you could fetch me a cuppa?'

'Coming right up,' Otto said.

'Make it a proper cup of tea,' Walter called after him. 'I don't want none of those grass sweepings you're so keen on.'

Otto grinned – 'grass sweepings' was what Walter called herbal teas, and Otto had been experimenting with making teas out of the dried leaves of the various wild plants that grew around the farm and on the hillside above Muddypuddle Lane. Some of his attempts had been successful, others not so much. But that was what his cookbook was all about, helping people make the best use of their foraged ingredients.

Today would be a milestone, as he gauged what worked well and what people liked, and what they weren't so keen on. And with only a couple of dishes left to work on, he would soon be ready to move to the next stage: finding an agent.

Otto bustled around, in his element when he saw the delighted expressions on people's faces as they bit into a chanterelle and watercress parcel made with ground hazelnut pastry, and their exclamations of pleasure as they had that first taste of spinach and cobnut ravioli. He was especially pleased at how well the cordials and ice creams were received by the children, whilst their parents tucked into blueberry scones with damson jam. He had even made a huge batch of warming roasted beetroot and apple soup, plus some sourdough bread to go with it, and that was going down a storm, because although the weather was still fairly mild for the end of September, there was a nip in the air and when the breeze blew down the valley it carried a hint of the colder months to come.

Otto gazed around the barn in satisfaction. There had been a steady stream of visitors to the farm's Harvest Festival and the barn was filled with the sounds of chatting and laughter. He hoped Dulcie was pleased and that she would earn enough from this venture to keep her going for a while. Even though she still had her day job as a customer care advisor and was lucky enough to be able to work from home, Otto knew she was struggling with the costs of running the place.

Despite not having any animals to manage, apart from a growing flock of chickens, farms like this were money pits. There was always something that needed doing or paying for, and his main worry was that she would find it all a bit too much. She had worked wonders with the interior of the house, using nothing more than paint and elbow grease, but the farmhouse was nevertheless in desperate need of renovation, especially the kitchen and bathroom, and it could also do with new windows and doors, plus the chimneys would need sweeping before the winter, and he had noticed only yesterday that a tile on the roof had slipped… And that was just for starters. The outbuildings also needed attention, as did the land itself.

Yep, small farms like this ate money. But at least he could help to put something back into the coffers by providing the food and drinks today.

Not only that, he found it an absolute joy to cook for so many people again. Otto had missed this. Cooking was what he lived for and having to give up his job as Chef de Cuisine running his own kitchen in a Michelin star restaurant in London, had devastated him. But he'd had no choice; his father had needed him. And, by moving back to Picklewick and into the cottage on Muddypuddle Lane (the only part of the farm that his dad had managed to cling on to) Otto had met Dulcie, the woman he loved with all his heart.

Isn't it amazing how things work out for the best, he mused, as he handed a customer a steaming plate of ravioli. His life was perfect. Almost – and the only reason he said 'almost' was because he needed to start earning an income. All he hoped was that this foraging cookbook he was in the middle of writing would soon be published and bring in some much-needed cash, otherwise he would have to look for a job. And, as he'd already discovered, cheffing jobs around Picklewick were as scarce as the teeth in Dulcie's hens.

♥

A day later, Dulcie put her knife and fork neatly together on the plate and leaned back in her chair.

Letting out a contented sigh, she gushed, 'That was delicious.'

Otto beamed at her. 'I hoped you would say that. It's the last dish for the book.'

'It *is*? Congratulations! That's brilliant news,' Dulcie enthused, then she paused. 'What happens now?'

'I'm going to try to get an agent.' He got to his feet and began gathering up the empty plates.

Dulcie stood, too. 'Let me do that: you did all the cooking.' She cast a quick glance towards the kitchen and the mess which she knew would be in there. Otto might be a Michelin star chef, but he was sadly lacking star quality when it came to clearing up after himself.

He subsided as Dulcie waved him back into his seat, and she didn't miss the relief on his face.

She carried the stacked plates into the kitchen and grimaced when she saw the enormity of the clean-up operation. It didn't help that her kitchen had seen better days and was a far cry from the state-of-the-art, albeit tiny, kitchen in the cottage Otto shared with his father.

'Didn't Walter want to eat with us?' Dulcie called. He often did, and Dulcie enjoyed the old man's company. But she enjoyed having Otto to herself even more.

Carefully she moved a notepad and pen out of the way. The pad held Otto's scribbled notes on the dishes he had prepared this evening.

'He's gone to The Black Horse with Amos,' Otto replied. 'Darts night.'

Dulcie donned a pair of bright yellow rubber gloves and turned on the hot water tap.

Otto appeared in the doorway and propped himself up against the frame. 'He never used to play darts. I think it's an excuse to grab a pie and a pint, rather than face eating another one of my concoctions.'

'I love your concoctions. Mostly.' She thought back to the hogweed root curry he had cooked last week. It hadn't been her favourite. It hadn't been Walter's either, judging by the look on his face. However, the food Otto had made for the grandly titled Harvest Festival yesterday had gone down a storm with the visitors, as she had known it would.

To Dulcie, calling it a Harvest Festival had seemed too pretentious for what it was – a pick-your-own event with some refreshments and a couple of tame animals for the kids to pet – but everyone had seemed to enjoy themselves and she had made a few pounds. In fact, she had been shocked and delighted by the number of people who had turned up, and she vowed to do it again next year. A couple of people had asked if there would be a spring event so they could see some newborn lambs, but she would have to think about that, the issue being that she didn't have any sheep on the premises. Flossie didn't count – the ewe belonged to Walter, and neither was she in lamb.

Dulcie *had* overheard something she was keen on pursuing though, and that was the possibility of growing pumpkins for next autumn, so along with the PYO fruit, people would have the opportunity of choosing a pumpkin, and she was also toying with the idea of holding a pumpkin-carving competition.

It was all food for thought!

Speaking of food… 'How many recipes have you got now?' she asked Otto.

'One hundred and twenty-seven altogether, but if I include the variations, it's more like a hundred and thirty-nine.'

And Dulcie had eaten every single one of them. Not that she was complaining: she had thoroughly enjoyed being Otto's guinea pig, and she hadn't heard anyone else complain, either.

Except for Walter. Otto's dad might be incredibly proud of Otto's achievements, but he still preferred a traditional cottage pie and chips, and for Dulcie the highlight of any meal which Otto cooked for them was seeing Walter's perplexed expression when faced with one of Otto's more exotic dishes.

'Your dad is so much better, isn't he?' she said, plunging her hands into hot soapy water to find the pan scourer and thinking how well the elderly chap had coped with the Harvest Festival, and what a great help he had been, even if it had meant he had been exhausted for a couple of days afterwards.

When Dulcie had first met Walter, the elderly gent had been frail and shaky, incapable of looking after himself, which was why Otto had been forced to give up his job and return to Picklewick. Otto had also been faced with the awful financial mess the farm was in. He had been unaware of the situation until then, and it had been so dire that if Otto hadn't come up with the idea of the farm being raffled off, then Walter would have had to file for bankruptcy. The only part of the farm Walter still owned was the cottage halfway down Muddypuddle Lane. The rest of it belonged to Dulcie; and when she'd won the farm, she had also won Otto's heart.

Now that the money worries had been lifted from his shoulders, Walter's health, both physical and mental, had improved considerably. Otto had confided to her that at one point he had feared his father would never recover, but Dulcie was relieved that Walter was now well enough for Otto not to have to worry about him quite as much.

Otto had picked up his notepad and was currently busy reading his notes on this evening's meal. He glanced up with a smile as he placed it back on the countertop and sauntered over to her, sliding his arms around her waist and kissing the back of her neck.

'He most definitely is better, isn't he?' Otto agreed, in answer to her question.

Dulcie squirmed with pleasure, desire surging through her. She wriggled around to face him, careful to keep her sudsy gloved hands away from his shirt. 'Do you have to pick him up from the pub later?' she asked.

'No, Amos is bringing him back.'

She kissed him, then spoke into his mouth, murmuring, 'That's good.'

Amos, Petra's uncle, had just moved into his own bungalow, a converted feed shed near the stables, and Dulcie knew Amos would make sure Walter got home safe and sound.

'I thought so, too.' Otto nibbled his way from her jaw to her collarbone. 'Leave the washing up?' he suggested.

Dulcie pretended to look horrified. 'And come down to this in the morning? No, thanks.'

'Will it be quicker if I help?'

'Theoretically, yes, but only if you stop kissing me for five minutes.'

'Five minutes is too long. Three?'

'You can wait five minutes,' she replied firmly.

'I'm not sure I can.'

His lips were on her neck again, and Dulcie gasped in delight before extricating herself. 'Washing up first,' she insisted.

Otto pouted. 'Spoilsport,' he complained, but he grabbed a tea towel and began to dry. 'What you need is a dishwasher.'

'What I need is a new kitchen,' she retorted. Despite a nice rise in her bank balance, thanks to the Harvest Festival, it would be a long while yet before she had enough funds to make that happen. Besides, there were so many other areas of the farm that needed attention, and all of them cost money.

She didn't for one second regret winning the farm, but she wished she hadn't been quite as naive. Her images of skipping through meadows with woolly lambs at her heels had been swiftly replaced by the reality of a farmhouse that was in dire need of renovation, an overgrown orchard, ambushing hens, and a sheep with a very hard head.

Thinking of hens reminded her. 'I've got to put the girls to bed before you whisk me upstairs,' she said. The 'girls' were her chickens, and they couldn't be left out all night for fear that a fox might get them.

The speed at which Otto abandoned his dish-drying duty was eye-watering. 'I'll do that,' he offered, and before she could say anything further he was stuffing his feet into a pair of wellies and hurrying out of the door.

As she finished washing the dishes, Dulcie watched him stride towards the barn and hurry inside. Two minutes later, he reappeared carrying a bucket, and she could hear him calling to the hens.

God, how she loved that man! She had lost her heart to him so completely it scared her sometimes...

But he was as much in love with her as she was with him, and he told her so several times a day. Was it too soon to take their relationship to the next level, she wondered? Now that Walter was better, there was no need for Otto to be there twenty-four-seven for his father. The old man was now more than capable of looking after himself, so maybe it was time she and Otto moved in together. Walter could remain in the cottage and Otto could move into the farmhouse with her. Otto would still be close enough to keep an eye on his dad, as the cottage was only halfway down Muddypuddle Lane, but Walter would have his independence.

And she would have Otto all to herself. The thought was a heady one.

She had just about finished tidying up the kitchen by the time he came back.

'The chickens are all safely tucked in for the night,' he announced, taking her in his arms. 'Now, where were we...?'

'You were going to carry me upstairs and make mad passionate love to me,' she reminded him.

'So I was!'

CHAPTER TWO

Otto scrubbed his face with his hand and scowled. Closing the lid of the laptop with a grunt, he flopped back on the sofa. He had spent the last few days typing up all the recipes from his scribbled notes and was now checking out the procedure for sending it to a publisher.

'What's got you all het up?' his father asked, as he put a mug of black coffee on the side table next to Otto and lowered himself slowly into the wingback chair opposite. The chair was faded and worn, bearing the scars of cat's claws, muddy paws and unidentifiable marks which were probably of spilt tea origin.

'This blasted book,' Otto muttered. 'I wish I hadn't started it.'

Walter slurped his tea and gazed at Otto over the rim of his mug.

Otto reached for his own drink, trying not to grimace when he realised his dad had made it with instant granules out of a jar, rather than attempt to use the coffee machine. Bless him, that machine baffled him, no matter how many times Otto had shown him how to use it.

'What's wrong?' Walter asked. 'I thought you had finished it?'

'I've decided which dishes to use and gathered all the recipes together, but I've yet to pitch it to an agent, and believe me, that's the hardest part. I really should have looked into the pitching side of things before I started.'

'You're going to have to explain what pitching is,' Walter said, scratching his head.

'I need an agent to get this book published, but first I've got to convince one that my idea is worth taking on. And to do that, I have to sell it to them – not sell as in money changing hands, but sell as in persuading them that the book is a commercially viable idea. Which means I must write a proposal and send them some sample recipes. That's what pitching means.' He would also have to come up with some headnotes – which were the introductions to the recipes themselves. He continued, 'Those bits I can manage, just about. It's the photography that I'm struggling with. You see, I have to send an agent some sample images as well, and I honestly didn't appreciate how difficult it would be.'

He opened the laptop again and turned it around so his dad could see the screen.

'What is it? Soup?' Walter squinted at the photo Otto had taken.

'Yes, mushroom and mugwort.'

'Hmm, I reckon I remember you making that. You served it with crackers. I forget what was in them.'

'Toasted dock seed and rye. They tasted okay, didn't they?'

Walter grudgingly admitted that they had. 'The soup was alright, too. 'I would have preferred a wholemeal loaf with it, though. Those crackers were a bit flashy, and I said at the time that I didn't think mugwort soup sounded very appealing. Anyway, the photo looks alright to me. The soup looks like I remembered it looking.'

Otto got up and carried the laptop over to his dad, placing it on his knee. 'Here, this is what I was aiming for.' He showed Walter a professional image of a bowl of soup with some sliced mushrooms clearly visible on the top, along with a swirl of cream and a scattering of chopped parsley.

Walter examined it for a moment. 'I see what you mean.'

The mushrooms in Otto's soup had sunk and had taken most of the swirl of yoghurt with them. 'It doesn't matter what I do, I can't get my soup to look as appetising as the soup in these photos. The lighting isn't right, either.'

'You need a proper camera, not that piddly little thing on your phone.'

Otto agreed. But as well as a decent camera, he could also do with someone behind the lens who knew what they were doing. And, as he had delved deeper into what an agent would expect (he really, *really* should have looked into this beforehand, although he still would have gone ahead with the book anyway) he belatedly realised he would have to employ someone to take the photographs for him.

From what Otto could see, he had gone about it all wrong. Instead of perfecting *all* of his dishes over the last few months using Dulcie and others as tasters and then pitching to an agent, he should have sent the proposal *first*, just concentrating on a few recipes and making sure the resultant dishes were photographed to perfection.

That wasn't all; apparently he also needed the services of a food stylist, which wasn't going to be cheap. But to give his book proposal the best chance, he would have to invest in one.

Doubts rose to the surface and he wondered whether he was doing the right thing, putting all his eggs in this recipe book basket. Maybe he should knock the idea on the head and get a job as a chef? It was what he was good at, what he knew how to do. He had zero experience of publishing, and after the research he had just carried out he felt even more out of his comfort zone than he had before.

However, trying to find a job as a chef came with its own set of problems.

When he had first moved back to Picklewick, Otto hadn't entertained the idea of trying to find a job because his dad had been so ill, but when Walter had begun to improve, Otto had discovered that jobs to the level he was accustomed to working at, weren't easy to come by and would have meant a long commute – something he hadn't been prepared to do. Working long hours in a commercial kitchen was bad enough, without adding a couple of hours drive on either side, because it would have meant leaving his father alone for far too long.

Now, though, with his dad so much better, Otto no longer felt he had to be there all the time. In fact, he spent more time at Dulcie's farm than he did in the cottage on Muddypuddle Lane. More, even.

Which should have made finding a job as a head chef easier.

The problem now was Dulcie – Otto wanted to spend as much time with her as he could.

Besides, he had come this far with his recipe book, it would be a shame to give up now. He had to give it his best shot, and if that meant paying a food stylist and a photographer to show his dishes in the best possible light, then so be it.

With a sigh, he returned to the sofa and his barely-touched coffee and began to search for a food stylist.

♥

'A food stylist? What's one of those when it's at home?' Nikki asked. She was sitting on the floor of Dulcie's living room and had been playing with the dog, a border collie puppy named Tara which belonged to her son, but she stopped and looked up at Dulcie.

'Yeah, that's what I said.' Dulcie held out her hand and the pup bounded over to lick it. Dulcie mightn't be too keen on sheep, but she was quite taken with the creature that was supposed to herd them. Tara was a real sweetie.

'I didn't know there was such a thing as a food stylist,' Nikki continued.

'Apparently they're essential in the food business if you want to advertise on telly or in a magazine. Or if you're writing a cookery book.' Dulcie giggled as the dog tried to clamber up her leg, and she slid off her chair to sit on the floor. 'Aw, she's sooo cute.'

'She's a nuisance! She ate my shoes the other day.'

'Both of them?'

'Only the one, but I can't wear them because she mangled the heel and tore the sole off the front.'

'Oh dear…' Dulcie snuggled the puppy closer. 'Were you a naughty girl for your mum?'

'Hopefully, she'll grow out of the chewing phase,' Nikki sighed.

'Apart from Tara, is everything else okay?' Dulcie wanted to know. She knew Nikki was concerned about Sammy starting a new school and he seemed to be settling, but she wanted to make sure as she hadn't managed to check in with her the other day.

Her sister grinned. 'Things couldn't be better, both for me and for Sammy.'

Dulcie glanced toward the kitchen and the door to the rear of the farmhouse. Sammy was outside checking on the chickens, Kevin in particular. Kevin was his own hen and was a female, despite her name. 'How has he been in school?' she asked.

Sammy was the main reason that Nikki had moved to Picklewick. Having been badly bullied in his former school, Nikki had brought him to the village at the beginning of September to make a fresh start. That she had fallen in love with a local policeman over the summer had also been a deciding factor.

'He's still loving his new school,' Nikki assured her.

Dulcie asked, 'Are you still loving yours?'

Nikki was a teacher and she had also started a permanent job in a new school, having been a supply teacher for years in Birmingham. 'It's fab. I'm working with a great bunch of people and the kids are lovely, too. Anyway, back to Otto's food stylist; what do they do exactly?'

'Make food look better than it does in real life,' Dulcie replied. 'And you wouldn't believe some of the things they get up to.'

'Such as?'

'You know when you see a lovely bowl of fresh fruit in an advert? Did you know that they use hairspray to make it look all shiny? And if you see water droplets on, say, an apple – that could very well be glycerine mixed with water and sprayed on.'

'No!'

'Uh-huh. But that's not all. Imagine seeing an advert for a roast chicken, fresh out of the oven; it's probably raw chicken that has been blasted with a blow torch to brown and crisp up the skin, then coated with shoe polish mixed with soy sauce to make it look cooked and juicy. Oh, and you know how a whole chicken can deflate when you take it out of the oven…? Shove a balloon inside it and blow it up. It makes the bird look really plump.'

'Well, I never! And Otto is going to employ someone to do that for him?'

'Yep, and a photographer.'

Nikki whistled. 'I bet that's not cheap.'

'I doubt it is.' Dulcie pulled a face and her gaze dropped to the pup in her arms. It wasn't the *cost* that was worrying her.

'What aren't you telling me?' Nikki asked.

Dulcie glowered. 'You and your spidey senses.'

'It comes from working with kids for years. My spidey senses are honed to perfection. Now, spill.'

'Otto has found a stylist. And a photographer. In London.'

'So?'

Dulcie wondered how to phrase her concerns without sounding totally pathetic. 'I'm scared he won't come back,' she finally admitted in a small voice.

Nikki burst out laughing. 'Of course he'll come back! Picklewick is his home. His dad is here – and so are you.'

'He lived in London for years, and he only came back because Walter was so ill.' She swallowed. 'But Walter is so much better now, and I know Otto misses running a kitchen. What if he realises just *how much* he misses it? What if I'm not enough to make him want to stay in Picklewick?'

'Has he said anything to that effect?'

'No, but…'

'Does he love you?'

'Yes, but…'

'There you go! You've got nothing to worry about. Now, are you going to put the kettle on, or do I have to die of thirst?'

Dulcie handed her sister the sleepy pup and scrambled to her feet, still not convinced. Even though Otto never went a day without telling her he loved her, she couldn't say why but she had a feeling that she mightn't be enough for him, and she was dreading his impending trip to London.

♥

'Are you sure this will work?' Dulcie asked Otto as they walked down the lane. He took her hand in his and gave it a squeeze.

She was looking doubtful, but Otto knew what he was doing. As did Petra, who had suggested the arrangement in the first place.

It had all come about because Walter had thought Flossie was lonely and had said as much to Amos, who, in turn, had mentioned it to Petra. Petra had pointed out that Lilac Tree Farm had more grazing than it knew what to do with, and that it might be a good idea to put Flossie in one of Dulcie's fields so the goats could keep her company. No doubt Flossie would prefer to be with other sheep, but considering Walter didn't own any others, goats were better than nothing.

Otto smirked to himself as he remembered the first time Dulcie had met Flossie – and Dulcie's reaction to the sheep. Dulcie had been petrified, locking herself in the farmhouse, convinced the ewe had been trying to attack her, when all Flossie had wanted was a cuddle. That was the problem with hand-raising lambs, they became entitled, and Flossie had very definite views of what she liked, and that consisted of being inside the house and being fussed over. Which had been cute when she was tiny, but not so cute now she weighed about sixty kilos.

Dulcie narrowed her eyes at him. 'What are you smiling about? Don't you think I can handle a goat?'

He and Dulcie were collecting the animals from the stables to bring them up to the farm. Nathan, the stable's manager, had put them in the barn ready, and that was where they were heading now.

Otto sniffed the air, noting the familiar and rather pleasant aroma of horse. He had grown up with the whiff of sheep and horses, and he knew which he preferred! Horses smelled considerably nicer: in close confines or in large numbers the aroma of sheep could be overpowering.

The stable yard was empty, but Otto knew his way around and he led Dulcie to the large neat barn that held most of the hay, straw and feed that would see

Petra's horses through the winter. It was currently full of bales, but there was a space near the huge metal doors that had been made into a pen, and this was where Princess and her daughter Toffee were held. Both goats were wearing halters, and Princess bleated a greeting.

Dulcie reached into the pen to scratch the goat's head, and Otto marvelled at how far Dulcie had come since she had won the farm. Not so long ago, she would have run screaming if a goat tried to eat her sleeve, but all she did now was push the animal away.

'If you're going to be antisocial, don't expect to be petted,' she scolded the goat, who gave her a devil-eyed stare and tried to butt her. 'You can cut that out, too,' Dulcie added. 'If you aren't going to be nice, you won't get to eat all that lovely grass in my field.'

Otto saw her flinch when she realised what she'd said, and he draped an arm around her shoulders to show that he wasn't bothered. Anyway, it *was* Dulcie's field: she had won it fair and square along with the rest of the farm. He knew she still felt awkward about it, but he wished she didn't. He didn't want her worrying that she might say the wrong thing, so he gave her a kiss on the head and said, 'You don't have to feel bad about it.'

'I know, but I can't help it. The farm has been in your family for generations.'

'But look how much better my dad is. I'd prefer him healthy, happy and farmless, rather than stressed, ill and still trying to run it. Or worse,' he added darkly.

'Would you have kept it on if… you know…?' Dulcie asked.

'If something had happened to Dad? Not a chance.' Otto might have been brought up on a farm, but farming wasn't in his blood. He had wanted to cook.

Otto blamed his mum for that. She had tended the farm's veggie plot and had delighted in making tasty and nutritious meals from what she grew. And just as his father had expected him to help on the farm, she had expected him to help around the house. Otto had quickly concluded that he preferred cooking to sorting the laundry, so that was what he had concentrated on. After his mother died when he had been in his mid-teens, Otto had taken over the role of cook and his love affair with creating glorious dishes had begun.

Catering college had been followed by the offer of a job in Thornbury, and from there he had moved to London, and his rise up the ranks in the kitchen had been steady, until he was made Chef de Cuisine shortly after his thirty-first birthday.

Three years later, he had received a phone call from Amos telling him that his father had collapsed.

The loud ring of his mobile dragged Otto out of his reverie, making him jump, and he scrambled to answer it, smiling when he recognised the number.

'Remi, my man! How the devil are you?' he cried, hooking a lead rope off a peg near the door and throwing it to Dulcie.

She caught it deftly.

Otto put his hand over the phone and said to her, 'I'll catch up with you in a minute.' He turned away, hoping his old mate had some good news for him.

'Pretty damned good.' Remi's usually faint French accent seemed more pronounced, or did it appear that way because Otto hadn't spoken to him in ages. 'I got your message – of course you can stay with me. I'll book some time off work; they owe me days and days of holiday.'

Otto guessed the reason why Remi had so many holidays to take. Remi had probably thrown himself into work after his relationship with his girlfriend had broken down. 'Sorry to hear about Steff, man.'

'Eh, it's water under the bridge. Last year's news. Now, where shall we go? Pascal Ferkin – remember him? – he has opened his own restaurant. I've heard it's good. Or do you want to go to The Fern?'

Otto pulled a face and said, 'Not really. Maybe another time.'

'Okay, you decide.'

'Let's try Pascal's place.'

'Bien. I'll book a table. When are you coming to London?'

'Next Tuesday.'

'It'll be good to see you, my friend.'

'You, too.'

Otto was still grinning when he caught up with Dulcie, who was halfway up the lane, a lead rope in each hand, attached to a goat.

She thrust one of the ropes at him as she dragged Princess's head out of the hedge. The goat's face emerged, leaves poking out of the side of her mouth as she chewed.

Otto explained, 'That was Remi. He said I can stay with him. I didn't fancy being in a hotel. After living in London for so long, I would feel like a tourist if I had to book a room.'

Dulcie gave him a sharp look but didn't say anything.

He carried on, wondering what he had said or done to warrant it. 'It's such a shame about him and

Steff. I could have sworn they were a match made in heaven. I wonder why they split up?'

'You can ask him when you see him,' Dulcie suggested, panting ever so slightly as they climbed the hill.

Otto was horrified. 'I'm not asking him that! If he wants to tell me, he will. But I suspect we'll just talk shop or chat about sport.'

'You are such a bloke!' Dulcie cried with a roll of her eyes. 'It *is* okay for a fella to show his feelings or to give a mate a cuddle, you know.'

They had reached the field which was going to be the goats' home for the foreseeable future, and Otto opened the gate. 'Nope. Not going to happen. I'm saving all my cuddles for you.'

He removed the halters and set the goats free. Princess was off like a shot, eager to say hello to Flossie, who had been nibbling at the grass over the far side, but who was now hastily trotting towards the new arrivals and loudly bleating a greeting.

'I like cuddles,' Dulcie told him, snuggling into his side and wrapping her arms around his waist.

Otto liked cuddles, too. He liked kisses even more, and he took the opportunity to lower his mouth to hers.

'I wish you were coming with me,' he murmured when they paused for breath.

'So do I, but as you pointed out, you'll be busy preparing your dishes – or rather, the food stylist will. Isn't it mad that such a thing exists! Anyway, I've got livestock to care for.'

'Listen to you – *livestock*. You sound like a proper farmer.'

Dulcie turned to look at the field where the goats and sheep had settled down to graze. 'I feel like one,' she said. 'I really love it here.'

'And I love *you*,' Otto said, emotion making his voice hoarse. He loved this woman so darned much!

He was going to miss her when he was away – but at least it would only be for a few days. Who knew that it would take falling in love with Dulcie to make him look forward to returning to Muddypuddle Lane?

♥

Dulcie wound the curly cord of the 'so-old-fashioned-it-was-retro' phone around her finger later that evening, and confessed to her friend just how much she was going to miss Otto.

'Aw, it must be love,' Carla said.

Dulcie could hear the clatter of plates and hoped she wasn't interrupting Carla's meal. 'It is,' she sighed. 'Look, I can tell that you're busy—'

'Not too busy to hear all the goss from my favourite best friend.'

'I thought I was your only best friend,' Dulcie whined.

'You are. More or less. But since you decided to bugger off and live in the wilderness, I've had to bump Vicky up a notch.'

'Vicky?' Dulcie felt quite put out and rather sad.

'I love her to bits, but she'll never replace you,' Carla soothed. 'Now, back to Otto. Is he going to London to speak to a publisher?'

'I wish! That's the step after the next one. He's got to get a proposal together first, which is why he's going to London next week so the dishes can be photographed to perfection, then he has to send the proposal to an agent or two, and if an agent takes him on, they try to sell his idea to a publisher.'

'Blinkin' heck, that's a bit involved, isn't it?'

Dulcie let out another heartfelt sigh. 'You can say that again. One minute he's all fired up about it, the next he's in the doldrums because it's becoming too much. He hasn't said anything to me, but I sometimes get the impression he wishes he hadn't started it.'

'What would he do instead? Look for a job?'

'He'll have to, I suppose.'

'You sound down in the dumps yourself,' Carla observed. 'I tell you what – how about I come for a visit? I haven't seen you since you left Birmingham.'

Dulcie had been living in Picklewick for almost six months and Carly had yet to see the farm. In the beginning Dulcie hadn't wanted anyone to visit because of the state it was in – although she had welcomed Nikki's help when she understood just how much renovation it needed. Then, later in the summer, when she deemed that the farmhouse was respectable enough to receive visitors, Carla hadn't been able to make it for one reason or another.

'That would be fab!' Dulcie cried.

She now had something to look forward to when Otto was away, and hopefully a visit from her effervescent, irascible friend would help take her mind off him – because even though he would be gone for only a few days, she was going to miss him like crazy.

CHAPTER THREE

Dulcie called to the two goats and the sheep, as she leant on the top of the gate and rattled a bucket of pellets. As soon as the animals began to run towards her, she upended the bucket and scattered the contents in a line, so all three animals had access to the food.

Petra had suggested giving the goats supplementary feed because she was thinking about breeding from Princess again this year, and she wanted her to be in the best possible condition beforehand. Toffee was too young. To Dulcie's untrained eye, although the goat looked old enough to be bred from, apparently she was still only a youngster.

It would be nice to have a baby goat around next spring, Dulcie mused as she stroked Princess's soft ears. She liked goats better than sheep, she decided, and was more than happy for this pair to remain on the farm for a while.

With those animals fed, it was time to call the chickens in for the night. They had their own little house in the orchard where they spent their days scratching around for grubs, insects and tasty green leaves, and their nights safely tucked inside the coop. Each morning she would let them out and gather the eggs they had laid, and she often had one for her breakfast.

Dulcie lingered over the task, in no rush to go inside. Otto had only left for London this morning, but she was already feeling his absence keenly. Even though he didn't spend all day, every day at the farm, knowing he was a mere short stroll away made all the difference.

She had promised him she would look in on Walter, and although it might be a bit soon (Walter would be fine on his own for tonight) she decided to take a walk down the lane and call on him anyway. It would be for her benefit just as much as his, and they would be able to keep each other company for an hour or so.

Actually, she thought, as she dawdled down the pitted, potholed track, he probably felt less lonely than she did because he had Peg for company. Walter doted on the former sheepdog. Otto had told her that when he had first returned to Picklewick, his dad had point blank refused to move into the village's lovely care home or into an assisted-living flat because he would have been unable to take his dog with him. Which was the reason why Otto had been forced to move back to Picklewick permanently.

'Dulcie! I was just thinking about you,' Walter announced when he opened the door and saw her standing on the path. 'I keep telling you, there's no need to knock. Come in.' He waved her inside and Dulcie gave him a peck on the cheek. 'Tea? Or something stronger?' he offered.

'Tea, please,' she said, but quickly changed her mind on seeing his crestfallen expression. 'On second thoughts, I'll join you in a small one.'

Walter's 'small one' turned out to be a large plum brandy, which she sipped at cautiously. Surprised to discover that it was delicious, although rather strong, she took another, larger mouthful. It trailed a warm path from her throat to her tummy, and she cautioned herself not to drink too much. Carla was arriving tomorrow and no doubt they would indulge in a bottle of wine or two, so the last thing Dulcie needed was to start the morning off with a hangover.

Like Carla, Dulcie had taken a couple of days off work and she was looking forward to it immensely. It would be great to have a proper girly natter: phone calls just weren't the same.

'Have you heard from Otto?' Walter asked, after he had lowered himself carefully into his chair. He dipped his little finger into his glass and offered it to Peg.

'Erm, are dogs supposed to drink brandy?' Dulcie raised her eyebrows.

'No, but she likes to taste whatever I'm having, and she'll keep pestering me until I give her some. See, she's not keen.'

The dog had sniffed his finger, then backed away, not liking the smell.

'Otto has arrived safely,' she said, answering Walter's question. Otto had messaged her as soon as he had parked the car, and she had imagined him unloading all the foodstuff he had taken with him ready for the shoot tomorrow.

Shoot…? She sounded as though she knew what she was talking about, when in reality she didn't have a clue. All she hoped was that it went well, and that Otto was happy with the results.

Suddenly the book seemed very real indeed. Up until this point, for Dulcie it had been a bit pie-in-the-sky, but now that he was actually in London and meeting with the food stylist and the photographer, she began to hope Otto might find a publisher. If he did, it would stop him fretting as much. He tried to hide it from her, but she knew he was concerned about finding a job. Now that he was in a position to go back to work, he was desperate to start earning again. Walter's pension only went so far, and although she knew that Otto had some savings, they were dwindling rapidly.

As though he had read her mind, Walter said, 'He needs to get himself a job. It's all well and good trying to write this recipe book of his, but what if it doesn't sell? And what will he do after it's published?'

'Write another?'

Walter harrumphed. 'I suppose, but from what I've read in the papers there's no money in it. If his mother was still alive, she'd tell him straight, but he doesn't listen to me. He never did.'

'Was he a wilful child?' Dulcie asked. She had gleaned snippets here and there about Otto's childhood, but those had been from Otto himself. It would be interesting to get Walter's take on it.

'Woefully,' Walter said. 'I wanted him to stay here and farm with me, but he was having none of it. All he ever wanted to do was cook.' He examined the contents of his glass for a while, then looked at her, and Dulcie saw the pride shining out of his eyes and heard it in his voice when he said, 'My boy has done well for himself.'

'He has,' she agreed.

'It's good that he didn't listen to me. Not everyone is cut out for this life. Don't get me wrong, he would have made a decent enough farmer, but his heart wasn't in it. I used to think it a shame that he would have sold the farm after I passed. But you're here now, and I can rest easy knowing it's in good hands.'

Dulcie wasn't sure about that. She didn't know the first thing about farming, and she wasn't sure she wanted to. According to Otto, her farm was only suited to sheep and that was mostly due to being able to graze them on the common land on the hills above. Cattle didn't do so well up there, apparently: which wasn't an issue, considering she didn't intend keeping cattle. Neither did she intend to keep sheep. She would just have to come up with some other ideas of what to do with her land.

Walter was saying, 'My brother never wanted anything to do with the farm, either. He buggered off to Australia thirty-odd years ago.'

'I didn't know Otto had an uncle in Australia; he never said.'

'Probably because he never met him, and I hardly talked about him. We got a Christmas card every year, but that was about it. Anyway, Emrys is dead now – he passed away last year.' Walter looked wistful. 'I wish I could have seen him one last time.'

He fell silent and Dulcie concentrated on her drink. The clock on the mantelpiece ticked loudly and Peg whimpered once, her paws twitching as she dreamt.

Eventually Dulcie said, 'Do you regret staying on the farm? Did you ever want to do something else, or move away?'

Walter shook his head. 'Farming is all I ever knew. I was the eldest, so I took over the farm from my father, and it was no surprise Emrys wanted to do something else. I didn't expect him to emigrate, though. Still, from what I can gather he had a good life. He got married and had kids, so I've got a sister-in-law out there and a couple of nieces. I can't even remember their names.' He made to get up. 'It's on the Christmas cards he used to send. I kept a couple.'

'Show me another time,' she suggested, noticing how tired he looked, and he sank back down. 'I'd better be off. Can I get you anything before I go?'

'No thanks, love. I'm good. Take care going up that lane.'

'I will,' she promised, and she kissed the top of his head as she left.

As she made her slow way up the hill, Dulcie thought how very different Otto's life would have been had he stayed on the farm, and how it wasn't always easy to escape one's roots. Fate had brought Otto back to the farm on Muddypuddle Lane, and fate could just as easily take him away again. She simply couldn't shake the worry that he might be seduced back to the capital and his old life.

♥

Otto gazed around the restaurant with a critical eye, noting what was working well and what he would change if the place was his.

Pascal had done a good job. The interior was slick and chic, and the vibe was intimate but also industrial – almost as though diners were eating in a friend's converted warehouse apartment rather than a restaurant, and that was what made it trendy. Other people obviously thought so too, because the place was busy.

But no matter how good the vibe, the only thing that truly mattered was the food. And so far, Otto was impressed. Pascal's menu was crisp and en pointe, and the first course had been a wonderful blend of flavours and textures, as well as being presented perfectly. Thus far, he couldn't fault it.

'Pascal is giving The Fern a run for its money,' Remi observed, his fingers curled around the stem of a glass of chilled Vouvray. The open bottle sat between them on the table, and Otto took a sip of his and swilled it around his mouth. The wine was deliciously dry.

'How is Alistair taking it?' Otto asked.

Remi snorted. 'He's threatening to sack his head chef.' His response was as dry as the wine they were drinking.

'That sounds like him,' Otto acknowledged.

'The place isn't the same without you. It only won its Michelin star because of *your* food.'

Otto felt bad. But he hadn't had any choice other than to leave. His father's health was more important than a job: no matter how much Otto had loved it.

However, he had no illusions that he was indispensable. The Fern would be okay. Alistair just didn't like change, that was all. But restaurants had to be flexible and quick to respond to the ever-changing tastes of the public, and Otto's forte was that he had been particularly effective at persuading Alistair to put new dishes on the menu.

'How about you?' he asked, keen to change the subject. He didn't want to dwell on the fortunes of his former boss, because it made him feel he should be doing something to rectify the situation.

'Eh, you know, *comme ci, comme ça*.' Remi held out his hand and rocked it from side-to-side. 'I'll get over Steff soon enough.'

Otto was reluctant to ask, but he remembered what Dulcie had said, so he asked anyway. 'What went wrong?'

'Work.' Remi's reply was short. Then he did a one-shoulder shrug and added, 'You know how it is. We chefs work in the evening and at weekends, all the time. It didn't sit well with her.'

'She knew what you did for a living before she moved in with you,' Otto pointed out.

'Maybe she was hoping it would change.'

'As in, you going to work in an office or something?'

'Perhaps.'

'I can't see you sitting behind a desk all day.'

'I can't see you milking cows all day.'

Otto barked out a laugh. 'Dad farmed sheep, not cattle. And he no longer owns the farm, remember?'

'Ah, yes… The delectable Dulcie owns it now. How goes it with you two?'

Otto couldn't prevent a beaming grin from spreading across his face. 'It's good.' He had told Remi all about Dulcie.

'I think it is more than good,' Remi replied, astutely. 'I would like to meet the woman who is keeping you away from London.' Otto opened his mouth to object, but Remi leapt in. 'Your father is well again, no? So there must be another reason you are hiding away in the countryside – and I believe *she* is it.'

'I'm not hiding,' Otto objected. 'And my father isn't back to full health yet.'

'When he is, will you come back?'

'No.'

'Then I am right.' Remi looked very satisfied with himself.

'It's early days yet.'

'But you are in love: I can tell.'

'I might be.' Otto studied his wine glass, wishing the service was quicker so that the main course would appear and put an end to this conversation. His face was growing warm, and he berated himself for going down the relationship rabbit hole in the first place.

Remi laughed. 'You had better not forget to invite me to your wedding.'

'Hang on – who said anything about a wedding?'

His friend sent him a knowing look, then Remi's expression became serious. 'Joking aside, what will you do with yourself? Please say you will continue to cook,' he begged.

'We'll see. I've got to get this book out of the way first, before I look for a new position. And I'm not sure I want to go back to those long and unsociable hours.'

'You are thinking of me and Steff?'

Otto was, but he had already been thinking about the strain that working in a restaurant kitchen would put on his relationship with Dulcie. But what else was he to do? Giving up being a chef meant that he was giving up a massive part of himself. He had sacrificed a great deal to get to where he was before his father became ill, and he knew how disappointed his dad had been when Otto had made it clear he didn't want to run the farm. Had that been all in vain?

It was this fear that had driven him to think of his recipe book for foraged ingredients in the first place, hoping it would bring in enough income to tide him over until his dad could cope on his own. After which, Otto could either find a chef's position that he could commute to from Muddypuddle Lane, or (and he had secretly been harbouring this hope) he could return to London.

Then he had fallen in love… and he was back to square one as far as his career was concerned.

Let's just hope this cookbook pans out, he prayed.

CHAPTER FOUR

'Oh. My. God!! You didn't tell me Picklewick was so cu-ute!' Carla cried as Dulcie drove through the village the following afternoon.

'I did. You probably weren't listening.' Dulcie had picked Carla up from the railway station in Thornbury and they were now heading towards Muddypuddle Lane.

'Bet there's not much nightlife, though,' Carla continued, her head swivelling from side-to-side as the car negotiated the bustling main street with its quaint artisan shops. There wasn't a single high-street chain in the village, which Dulcie found quite amazing and very charming.

'Not a lot,' Dulcie agreed, waving to Gio, who was leaning against his police car, a refillable coffee mug in his hand. He was parked outside his favourite cafe.

Carla's eyes were out on stalks. 'Wow! That copper is hot!'

'That copper is Nikki's partner,' Dulcie informed her with a smile.

Carla muttered, 'Lucky cow. I knew I should have insisted that you invite me first.'

'Even before my own sister?'

'Yep.' Carla nodded confidently. 'I could have got to him before she did.'

'Oh no, lady, you're not getting up to your old tricks in Picklewick. I've got to live here, remember?'

'What tricks?' Carla's expression was one of total innocence.

'Your love them and leave them tricks. You've had more boyfriends than I've had hot dinners.'

'You sound like my mum.'

Dulcie shot her a look. 'Don't you dare imply I'm getting all mumsy.'

'If the hat fits…' Carla teased. 'Look at you – all you need is dungarees, wellies and a flat cap.'

'That's not mumsy, that's more Farmer Giles.' Dulcie suddenly giggled. 'It's so good to have you here. I've missed you.'

'I've missed you, too. Why did you have to win a farm in the middle of nowhere? Why couldn't you have won a villa in Italy or a swish apartment in London? That would have been far more fun.'

When Dulcie had first set foot on the farm she might have agreed with Carla. But not now. Dulcie had fallen in love with the house, the village and Otto, and she couldn't imagine living anywhere else. The thought of going back to her old life in Birmingham and that pokey flat she used to rent, made her shudder. It was alright for Carla – although she was still living at home her mother was away so much with work that it felt as though Carla had her own place. And when her mum was actually there, they were like ships passing in the night. Carla's mum just let her get on with it, whereas if Dulcie were still living at home Dulcie's mum would have been in her face all the time, so she had moved out as soon as she could afford it. Unfortunately, the only flat she could afford hadn't been the best.

'If I hadn't won the farm I wouldn't have met Otto,' Dulcie pointed out as she turned the car into Muddypuddle Lane, and it bounced and juddered up the track.

'Dear god, let me out – I'll walk from here,' Carla complained. 'My teeth are rattling.'

'You get used to it.'

Carla gazed around. 'You really are out in the sticks. There are horses in those fields.'

Dulcie chuckled. 'I know. Would you like to have a go on one?'

'Me, on a horse? I don't bleedin' think so!' Her friend shuddered. 'They're huge.'

'Petra has smaller ones. Look, this is where my land starts.'

Her eyes wide, Carla let out a gasp. 'You own all this?'

'Yep.'

'I know I've seen photos, but they don't do it justice. Is that your farmhouse? It's gorgeous!'

They had just turned into the farmyard and Carla was already reaching for the door handle. 'You lucky cow. You lucky, lucky, lucky—'

'Cow? I know.' Dulcie got out. 'You would hate it though. As you said, it's in the sticks.'

'I think I could get used to it, if it means owning a house like this.'

'It's quite old-fashioned inside, remember?' Dulcie warned her, dragging Carla's overnight bag from the back seat.

'I don't care,' her friend said, but when Dulcie pushed open the front door and showed her inside, Carla's face fell.

Dulcie had been hoping for a more enthusiastic reaction, considering all the decorating she had done over the summer, but she knew the farmhouse was what influencers would call 'rustic'. It might look great on Instagram, but the reality was slightly different. The old, patterned carpet was still on the stairs because she couldn't afford to replace it yet, and the bannister had a couple of spindles missing. The original flagstone floor in the hall was a nice feature though: Dulcie had cleaned the tiles and resealed them and they looked as good as new. And although the walls would benefit from being replastered, they had been painted a light sunny yellow and she had hung some prints to brighten it up. All in all, she didn't think it looked too shabby, so Carla's reaction was rather disappointing.

'I don't think it's old-fashioned,' Carla said, her gaze darting to and fro. 'I think it's quaint. Please don't tell me you've stripped out all the period features.'

'You like it?' Dulcie asked uncertainly.

'I do! You lucky, lucky…'

'Come and see the rest of it, then I'll introduce you to my chickens. We've got goats too, but they're not mine, they're Petra's. They're only here to keep Flossie the sheep company.'

'I'd rather not, if you don't mind.'

'Chicken,' Dulcie teased. 'See what I did there?'

Carla clucked her agreement, and Dulcie let the matter drop. She had felt exactly the same way about the feathery creatures when she had first set foot on the farm, but she was quite attached to them now, and the goats had also grown on her. She rather looked forward to greeting them every morning. She still wasn't keen on Flossie, though.

'Drink?' she offered. 'I've got wine, unless you think it's too early.'

'It's never too early for wine,' Carla enthused.

Dulcie showed her to one of the guest bedrooms, the one with the nicest view over the valley, and left her friend to freshen up whilst she got the bottle out of the fridge and poured them a glass each.

'It's a pity it's too cold to sit outside,' Dulcie said, as they took their drinks into the sitting room. 'One day I'd like to put French doors in here, or full-length windows to make the most of the view.'

'That's a great idea. I wonder what it'll be like here in the winter. Do you think you'll be snowed in?'

'It's a possibility. But the village is within walking distance, so I should imagine we'll be fine.'

'We? As in… you and Otto? I wish he was here so I could meet him. Can I be a bridesmaid?'

'Gosh, it's a bit soon to be thinking about weddings,' Dulcie said, a blush spreading up her neck and into her face which had nothing to do with the temperature in the room, considering she hadn't lit the fire yet.

'But if he asked, would you say yes?'

'I might.'

Carla studied her. 'You deffo would,' she declared. 'Would you sell this place?'

Dulcie pulled a face. 'Did you notice a cottage on your left, halfway up the lane?'

'I think so. Yes, just above the sign for the stables?' Carla looked confused.

'That's where Otto and his dad live. I can't see me moving in there. If we did ever get married – and I'm not saying that we will – I think it might be more sensible for him to move in with me.'

'Live on the farm?'

'Where else?'

'Don't you miss Birmingham?'

'I did at first…' Dulcie hesitated. 'I miss my family, but not as much since Nikki and Sammy moved to Picklewick, and I've got Otto now, of course. And I miss my friends – you know you can visit anytime, don't you?'

Carla tilted her glass in Dulcie's direction in acknowledgement. 'You don't miss living in a city?'

'You mean, the noise, all those other people, the traffic?'

'The clubs, bars, shops…?'

'If I'm honest, I was getting fed up with the party lifestyle, and I couldn't really afford to go shopping much, so, no, not really. I love it here. I can't imagine living anywhere else.'

Even if she had to sell the farm tomorrow, Dulcie wouldn't dream of returning to Birmingham. She would find a little house in the village and carry on living in Picklewick.

But she had no intention of selling it. In fact, she had every intention of trying to make a go of it. She was still working the day job thankfully, which kept her head above water, but she didn't want to be a customer care advisor for the rest of her life. Ideally, she wanted the farm to pay its way, and even make a living from it so she could jack in her job. But the question was… how?

When she explained the situation to Carla, her friend was more than happy to bandy some ideas around.

'A festival site?' she suggested. 'Think Glastonbury, but smaller scale.'

'It'll have to be *much* smaller. Besides, my farm is on a hill. Anyway, don't you have to have planning permission or a licence for something like that?'

'No idea,' Carla replied, topping up their wine. 'You're probably right. The stage would roll down the hill. You could still have campers, though. I wouldn't want to *live* here, but it's a great place for a weekend – if you like that kind of thing. Personally, I'd prefer a luxury hotel and spa, but loads of people like camping. You could rent one of the fields out or put up a couple of cabins and call it glamping.'

'I like the idea of camping, but I'd have to sort out toilets and showers – and that would cost money I don't have.'

'You've got four bedrooms – how about running a B and B?'

'Maybe in the future, but not right now; no ensuite bathrooms,' she explained, pulling a face. 'We opened the orchard up to people who wanted to pick their own apples and pears the other week, and Otto tried out some of his foraged food recipes on them. It went down a storm. I just wish we could do something like that every month. I'm planning on growing pumpkins for next autumn, but that's a whole year away.'

'Lambs,' Carla said. 'Remember that city farm place we went to in year three? Or was it year four? Anyway, they had lambs.'

'A couple of people who came to the harvest festival mentioned that, but I don't like sheep. Would goats work as well, do you think?'

'I don't see why not.' Carla sat forward, excitedly. 'You could have rabbits too, and those pygmy pigs. And a donkey! I love donkeys.'

'It's the ears,' Dulcie said. 'You just want to stroke them, and the noses. Petra has one. He's called Gerald.'

'There you go! You could borrow him.'

'There's one small flaw in this petting-zoo plan,' Dulcie cautioned. 'I don't have any baby goats.'

Carla scoffed. 'You've got a *farm* – go get some!'

Easier said than done, Dulcie thought. She didn't know the first thing about breeding goats.

Suddenly she was missing Otto even more than she had been missing him already. He would know about goats, and whether Carla's idea was as daft as Dulcie suspected it might be.

As soon as he returned to Muddypuddle Lane she would ask him. After a suitably satisfying welcome home, that is!

♥

What a day, Otto thought, as he tidied away the remains of the foodstuff he had brought with him to the shoot. He hadn't known what to expect, but it had certainly been an experience and one he wouldn't forget in a hurry.

He had arrived at the studio fully prepared to cook his dishes and for them to be photographed with some additional propping and fiddling by Fergie, the food stylist. But that was the opposite of what actually happened. Fergie had done the 'cooking', with Otto advising on what the dish should look like in real life.

And as a starting point, they had explored the photographing of the infamous mushroom and mugwort soup, with Otto comparing his own efforts to those of professional shots of soups that he had found on the internet.

Fergie had shown him how it was done, and it had almost blown Otto's mind. The man had mixed agar agar with water in the bowl which was going to be used for photographing the soup, whilst Otto finely chopped a handful of mugwort leaves (he was going to have to see if the plant was known by a nicer-sounding name) and fried the mushrooms. When the agar mixture had set, the jelly-like substance almost filling the bowl completely, Fergie had piled the mushrooms on top, added a small amount of 'broth' by using a stock cube dissolved in water, to which a dash of gravy browning had been added to give it a richer look – just enough to conceal the top of the agar mixture – then he had sprinkled a pinch of chopped mugwort leaves on top for garnish. The bowl had then been artfully placed on a table, along with additional leaves, a scattering of plump mushrooms and a very shiny spoon.

Instant mashed potato and purple food colouring became Otto's bramble ice cream, with the addition of a concoction of PVA glue, and the same food colouring painted onto it so the fake ice cream looked all shiny. The only thing real about it were the blackberries, but they had been sprayed with a hair product to make them look dewy.

And that had been just the start of it! Although Otto had done his research and knew that this was what went on, it had still been a shock to see the process in action.

After a full day in the studio (it couldn't be called a kitchen as such), Otto was knackered. His wallet was also significantly lighter and he hoped it was worth it; although to be fair, the photographer had shown him image after image as she'd taken them, to ensure that he was happy with the result, although it would be several days before he received the proofs.

Finally done for the day (he had another full day tomorrow), Otto made his way back to Remi's apartment overlooking The Thames. He wanted a shower and a stiff drink, then he wanted to speak to Dulcie.

High-pitched giggles greeted him when Dulcie answered the phone and, despite his exhaustion he smiled, pleased to hear she was enjoying herself. He guessed she was tipsy, and he suspected she and her friend might have made significant inroads into the bottles of wine he had noticed in her fridge.

'I like goats,' Dulcie slurred. 'Do you like goats?'

'Um, they're okay.' He wondered what had brought this on.

'They have babies!'

'Is Princess in kid? Petra hadn't mentioned it.'

'Dunno.'

'Riiight…' That was as clear as mud, he thought, bemused.

'*We* can have babies,' Dulcie chortled.

Otto blinked. Having children wasn't something he had given much thought to, but now that Dulcie had put the idea in his head he had a sudden vision of a little girl crawling around the floor of the farmhouse. She had her mother's eyes and maybe his hair, and it brought a lump to his throat.

'Baby goats are so cute,' Dulcie was saying. 'Can we have some? *Please?*'

Ah, *that's* what she meant.

The idea of him and Dulcie having a baby lingered as he replied, 'You'll have to speak to Petra about that. Princess and Toffee belong to her.'

'I want goats of my own. Can I have some? I'll look after them, honest.'

Otto chuckled: she sounded like a kid asking for a puppy.

'And rabbits,' she added. 'People like rabbits. They've got ears and noses.'

'So they have.' He tried not to laugh. Dulcie was more than tipsy – she was three sheets to the wind. He hoped she wouldn't have too bad a hangover in the morning, and he wished he could be there to soothe her with tea and painkillers.

Missing her dreadfully, he had just put down the phone when Remi entered the apartment.

His friend threw himself into one of the leather chairs and groaned. He brought with him a faint whiff of garlic and onions. 'That was a shift from hell,' he said. 'I swear if I had the money to set up on my own, I would.'

'I thought you were taking a few days off?' Remi had still been in bed when Otto headed off to the shoot this morning.

'So did I, but I got a phone call asking me to come in.' He rolled his eyes. 'I refused to work this evening, though.'

'You could have, I wouldn't have minded.'

'And miss out on a night on the town?'

'Is that what we're doing?' Otto had to think long and hard to remember the last time he'd been 'out on the town'. At thirty-four, he had assumed that nights spent partying were behind him. Besides, he had another day of photography tomorrow, and he wasn't sure he could face it with a hangover.

He would just have to be strict and pace himself.

♥

Oh, crap, not another shot, Otto thought, as Remi plonked a small glass of clear liquid on the table. His head was spinning already, adding to the pounding beat of the music which was so loud it reverberated in his chest. He was getting too old for this...

'Cheers!' Remi cried, downing his shot in one gulp. He slammed the empty glass on the table and turned to scan the dance floor.

Whilst Remi had his back to him, Otto hastily emptied his shot into the dregs of a pint glass on the empty table next to theirs.

It was getting late and he wanted his bed, but Remi was in full throttle and Otto remembered when he used to work hard and party hard like that, too. He might miss the work bit, but he didn't miss the partying, and he realised that living in Picklewick had changed him.

Eventually he managed to persuade Remi to leave the club and go get some food. Otto was starving, having eaten very little all day, and he dragged Remi towards a burger bar that was open all night. It wasn't far from his old stomping ground near The Fern, and he used to frequent it when he craved good, simple, tasty food after cooking elaborate meals all evening.

The burger was fat, juicy and cooked to perfection, and Otto was wolfing his down with enthusiasm, leaning against a lamppost and making noises of appreciation, when a passer-by stopped and peered at him.

Otto recognised the man at once. He had forgotten that Alistair liked walking home along this street after the restaurant closed.

'Hi, Alistair,' Otto mumbled, around a mouthful of food.

'I thought it was you.' Alistair stuck out a hand.

Otto hastily wiped his fingers on a serviette, before shaking. 'Good to see you,' he said.

Alistair pumped his arm vigorously. 'You should have told me you were back in London.'

'It's only a fleeting visit.'

Alistair's face fell. 'You're not back for good then? I was hoping you wanted your old job back.'

'Unfortunately, no.' Otto tried to sound regretful, but he didn't feel it. He had forgotten just how much of an assault on the senses being in London was. When he had first moved to the capital it had been a shock, but he had embraced it with enthusiasm and had thrown himself into everything the city had to offer. He supposed he had become immune to the hordes of people, the incessant traffic, the unrelenting noise. And don't get him started on the air quality!

'How's your father?' Alistair asked.

Otto dragged himself out of his memories. 'Getting there. He's much better now that he doesn't have the farm to worry about. How are you?' He studied his former boss. The man was in his late fifties, skinny despite being an immense foodie, snappily dressed, and thinning a little on top. He looked much the same, but with the addition of another crow's foot or two.

'I'd be better if you come back to work for me,' Alistair grumbled. 'My current head chef isn't a patch on you. I hear you're publishing a cookbook?' He raised his eyebrows.

Otto might have guessed Alistair would know – there might well be hundreds of eateries in London, but the top-notch places kept a close eye on what their rivals were up to, and gossip was rife.

'I'm giving it a go,' he said.

'Foraging?' Alistair's eyebrows remained in position.

'Yeah.'

'It's on trend,' Alistair observed. 'Let me know how it goes.' He clapped Otto on the shoulder. 'And when your father is fully recovered, let me know and you can have your old job back. Or better.' He tapped the side of his nose.

Otto had no idea what that meant. 'Good to see you, Alistair,' he said and watched him walk away, feeling unsettled.

He didn't miss working for Alistair as such, but by god he missed his kitchen. He missed the creative process of combining different ingredients and flavours together. He missed the tension of ensuring hundreds of dishes were prepared to perfection every night. He missed the sounds of people enjoying his food.

Damn it! He missed being a chef.

But he missed Dulcie more, and if he could appease his appetite for cooking wonderful food by creating new dishes for a cookery book, then that's what he would do.

But... he had already created the recipes and he now had to sell the damned thing. So what was he going to do afterwards, if he did manage to find a publisher? Could he write another cookbook, or would he have to rethink his future?

♥

'They're not quite as sweet as I imagined they would be,' Carla said, eyeing Princess and Toffee with caution, after she had insisted on accompanying Dulcie when she let the goats out this morning. 'And I thought they'd be smaller.'

'You're thinking of baby goats,' Dulcie chuckled, then said, 'Ow,' as her head reminded her that she had drunk more wine than was good for her last night. 'I need a cup of tea, but first I'd better see to this lot.'

That was the problem with owning animals – they had to be cared for no matter how hungover the human was.

'Tea sounds good,' Carla said. 'I'm gasping. And a bacon buttie? I could eat a horse.'

'I'll just let the chickens out, then I'll make us breakfast.' Dulcie wished Otto was here to make it for them. She didn't think she could face cooking bacon right now. If she hadn't had so much to drink last night, she would have suggested going into the village for a fried breakfast, but her blood alcohol level would still be over the legal limit, and she didn't want to be arrested by Gio.

'I'm starving,' Carla reiterated, and Dulcie felt a stab of envy. She recalled being able to drink a skinful, and then wake up the following morning with just a mild headache and a raging hunger. She must be out of practice.

'I must say, I'm surprised to see you out of bed before midday,' she said to Carla. If it hadn't been for the animals, Dulcie would still be in bed feeling sorry for herself.

Carla narrowed her eyes. To Dulcie's annoyance they were clear and bright, unlike her own puffy, bloodshot peepers. 'Your bloody cockerel woke me up.'

Fred was another of Petra's animals, and he often paid a visit to Dulcie's chickens, clearly thinking they were as much his ladies as Petra's own hens were. Dulcie had become so accustomed to the racket he made that she didn't hear him anymore.

'Why is everything so loud?' Carla grumbled as she followed Dulcie into the orchard, towards the chicken coop. 'I thought it would be peaceful, but it's noisier here than in the Bullring on a Saturday night.'

Dulcie flinched as she unlatched the door to the coop, the clucking noises from inside quickly building to a crescendo as the hens realised that freedom and breakfast were imminent.

'You can hardly compare Muddypuddle Lane to Birmingham city centre,' Dulcie shouted above the noise. She hastily scattered some chicken feed in the grass, and left the excitable birds to it, breathing a sigh of relief as the frantic squawking diminished.

'I rest my case,' Carla said, glaring at the hens.

'They're only like that because they want their breakfast. They are quiet the rest of the time.'

Carla tutted. 'That bloody cockerel wasn't quiet. And I swear someone was being murdered in the middle of the night. The noise was horrible.' She shuddered.

'I expect you heard a fox.'

'It's so bleedin' quiet here, that every noise is amplified,' Carla complained, contradicting her earlier comment. 'At least in Birmingham it all blends into one, nothing really stands out. Here you can even hear the individual cars.' She pointed in the direction of the village. 'It's not natural.'

'That's because it's coming up the lane,' Dulcie told her, catching sight of the postman's van as it trundled into the farmyard.

Ashton, the postie, got out. He was carrying a couple of letters and a small parcel, which Dulcie hoped was the make-up she liked to use but couldn't get in Picklewick. Thank god for online shopping!

'Morning.' he called cheerily, walking towards her. When he was close enough, he handed her the post. 'Here you go.'

'Thanks. Not too keen on the brown envelope, though. You can take that away with you,' Dulcie joked.

'Sorry, no can do.'

She was aware of his gaze alighting on Carla and noticed his eyes widen. Dulcie wasn't surprised: Carla often had that effect on men. Dulcie used to feel that she lived in her vivacious friend's shadow, but not any longer. Since coming to Picklewick she had grown into her skin, so to speak, which was mostly due to Otto. He made her feel that she was the most beautiful and most special woman on earth.

With a pang, she wondered what he was doing now. Was he at the shoot yet? She had meant to ask him how it was going when she spoke to him yesterday, but she had been rather sozzled. All she could remember was wittering on about goats.

'Who was *that*?' Carla hissed as Ashton got back into his van and drove out of the farmyard.

Dulcie gave her a quizzical look. 'The postman.'

'I know that, silly. I meant, what's his name, is he married, and did you see how gorgeous he is?'

'Put your tongue away, Carla. Only yesterday you were drooling over Gio.'

'A girl can look, can't she? And you've got to admit, Gio is lush. But your postman is even lusher – if there is such a word.'

'There is now,' Dulcie said, wryly.

Carla liked to play the field. She wasn't promiscuous, in that she didn't sleep with every man she went on a date with, but she'd had more boyfriends than Dulcie could shake a stick at.

'Well? *Is* he married?'

'I've no idea.'

'You can at least tell me his name.'

'Ashton.'

'Ooh, it suits him. No wonder you like living in Picklewick if all the men look like him.'

'Remind me to introduce you to Walter and Amos.'

'Isn't Walter Otto's father?' Carla looked puzzled.

'Yes, he is.'

'That means he must be at least sixty!'

'He's in his seventies. So, no, not all men in Picklewick are lush.' To be honest, Dulcie had never looked at Ashton that way – but then, she had already met Otto, who had filled her thoughts from the very first day.

'Ashton is though,' Carla replied, dreamily.

'Down girl. Come on, let's get some breakfast inside us, then we'll take a walk into the village and mooch around the shops.' She linked arms with her best friend. 'I'll even treat you to lunch at The Black Horse.'

♥

'What was all that talk about goats?' Otto asked. He and Dulcie were snuggled up on the sofa, watching TV in Dulcie's living room. It was Sunday evening and to his amusement Dulcie wanted to watch Countryfile. It was the first time she had shown any interest in the farming programme, and it brought to mind the drunken conversation he'd had with her earlier in the week, whilst he had been in London.

Dulcie pulled a face as she said, 'Me and Carla were trying to come up with suggestions to make the farm earn its keep, and I'm not sure which of us came up with it, but we thought a petting zoo was a good idea for the spring. You know, lambs and donkeys, a couple of rabbits... The kids had so much fun stroking Princess and Toffee during the pick-your-own fruit day that I thought I might be able to do a spring version, minus the apples and pears.' She wrinkled her cute nose. 'Then I sobered up and realised it's a daft idea.'

'Is it, though?' Otto replied thoughtfully. 'Your fields are meant to have livestock on them, and I know you don't like sheep, but you seem quite taken with Petra's goats.'

'But what happens when the baby goats grow up? I'll have to have more baby goats the following year, and the year after that, and before I know it, I'll be overrun with them.'

'You can sell them or keep them for milk. Goats' milk is big business.'

'Can't say I've ever tried it.'

'It tastes very similar to cow's milk, and it makes wonderful cheese and yoghurt. You can even make ice cream and butter with it. But – and this could be a problem – you would have to pasteurise it, and that kind of set-up costs money, not to mention the bottling process. It might be worth the initial investment, though.' He paused, then said, 'Or you could use the milk to make soap.'

Dulcie stared at him, and her eyes widened. 'Soap? *Soap!* Yes!!' She clapped her hands excitedly. 'I made soap once using a kit I had for Christmas. It was fun.' She stopped abruptly. Her mouth dropped open and she reached for her phone. Thumbs flying over the screen, she studied it. 'You can also make moisturising lotions, face wash, lip balm, candles – candles! *Yes!*' She read some more, then said, 'Do you think I should keep bees, too?'

Otto laughed; her enthusiasm was infectious and very endearing. 'One step at a time, eh? Why don't you experiment first, before you invest in your own goats? Buy some milk and the rest of the ingredients, and give soap-making a go. If you enjoy doing it and you think it will be cost effective, then you can look into owning your own animals.'

Dulcie pouted. 'Stop being so sensible.' Her nose wrinkled again, and she sighed. 'I suppose you're right. Do you want to help me make the first batch?'

'Go on, then. And if there is any milk left over, I'm sure I can use it up.'

'Ice cream?' she asked, hopefully.

'What flavour?' he began, but before she could reply, he said, 'How about hazelnut, or rosehip? I could try pumpkin flavour, seeing as Halloween isn't far away.'

'That sounds delicious.'

Otto thought it did too, but what was even more delicious was Dulcie herself. Her eyes were shining with excitement and her lips were slightly parted. He simply had to kiss her.

And it was safe to say, there was absolutely no talk of goats until some considerable time later.

CHAPTER FIVE

Dulcie eyed the assembled pile of ingredients doubtfully. She'd had to order all of it, except for the milk itself, off the internet, and every time she had seen Ashton with another parcel in his hands she'd thought of Carla.

The two of them would look good together, she acknowledged, but it was a moot point: he lived in Thornbury and Carla lived in Birmingham. But that didn't prevent Dulcie from finding out a bit more about him.

After explaining that the influx of parcels was because she was trying her hand at making soap, she had not-too-subtly suggested that he might like to give some to his wife to try, as Dulcie would need an unbiased opinion. He told her he didn't have a wife, but he did have a girlfriend, and he expected she would be delighted to give it a go.

Sorry, Carla, Dulcie had thought.

And now here she was, staring at a range of items scattered across the kitchen table and wondering if making soap was a good idea after all.

As though sensing her hesitation, Otto came up behind her and slipped his arms around her waist. The kiss on the side of her neck was comforting.

'Shall we get started?' he suggested. 'I've printed out the instructions, but don't forget, if this recipe doesn't work we can always tweak it, or try another. At this stage, it'll be trial and error.'

She was glad he was here, helping, as she was suddenly assailed by doubts; she didn't doubt that she could *make* the soap, but she doubted whether anyone would actually want to *buy* it. She hoped she hadn't wasted her money, but she supposed she could always use it herself, or give some to her sisters for Christmas.

Donning safety gear (they both wore goggles and gloves because lye was caustic and could cause a chemical burn) she and Otto worked side-by-side, measuring, stirring and mixing. She had seen Otto at work in the kitchen on numerous occasions, and he generally made a mess, but today he was being ultra tidy and careful, and she kept shooting him goggly glances, captivated by the concentration on his face.

Even though he wasn't cooking food today, it was clear that his natural home was the kitchen. He was so absorbed in his task that it made her tummy clench as she recalled her conversation with Walter. She wondered anew what Otto would do with himself once this cookbook was published. Would he immediately throw himself into the next one, or would he want to return to work in a restaurant kitchen?

She had a feeling it might be the latter: she had heard the regret in his voice when he'd recounted his chat with his former boss, and she wondered whether Otto would have taken Alistair up on his job offer if Walter *had* been back to full health.

She had a horrid feeling that he might have done, because cooking was so clearly his passion.

All she hoped was that his passion didn't take him away from Muddypuddle Lane for a second time.

But even if it didn't, she was also mindful of Otto telling her that his friend's relationship had broken up because of the unsociable hours chefs often worked. It would never happen to her and Otto, of course, but she was nevertheless aware that if he did go back into a commercial kitchen then she may very well see far less of him than she would like.

♥

Every time his phone notified him he had an email, Otto jumped. It had been well over a week since the foodie photo shoot, and he had hoped to have had the proofs by now. He was desperate to move on with pitching to an agent, and everything else was good to go apart from the accompanying images.

Not feeling hopeful (he'd had too many false alarms over the past few days) he opened his email app, and his heart leapt when he saw it was from the photographer.

Wanting to view the images on a larger screen, he hurried home.

He had been taking Peg out for a stroll, too restless to stay indoors despite the fine drizzle and low mist, and he had been almost at the top of the hill when the notification came through. He debated detouring to see Dulcie, but she was working and he didn't want to interrupt her, so he dashed past the entrance to the farmyard and jogged down the lane, Peg gambolling at his side.

'Where's the fire?' his dad asked as he charged through the door.

'I've just been sent the photos,' Otto said, grabbing the laptop as he slid into a chair at the table.

Walter heaved himself to his feet and came to stand behind him as he opened the attachment. Otto scrolled rapidly through the photos, his heart in his mouth, and then he went back to the beginning and studied each one intently.

'Well?' his dad demanded. 'Are you pleased?'

'I love them,' Otto announced. They were brilliant; the photographer had captured the essence of each dish perfectly, and had sent him several shots of each one, taken from slightly different angles. The only problem…? He now had to choose which photo best represented each dish, and it wasn't going to be easy.

Two hours later, he had finalised his choices and his proposal was complete. The last thing to be done was a *final*, final check (as opposed to the final one he had just done), attach everything, and press send.

He had a 'favourite' agent, and he would email her first, then work his way down the list. He wasn't entirely sure of the protocol of pitching to more than one agent at a time but, damn it, he didn't think it realistic to wait for a reply from the first before he sent it to the next. He had read stories online of prospective authors waiting months and months to hear back, and he didn't have that kind of time to waste.

Otto hovered the cursor over the send button for a moment, then gathered his courage and clicked it.

There, it was done. All he could do now was keep his fingers crossed and hope the agent liked it.

♥

Dulcie couldn't resist checking the soap again. She had taken the soap-filled mould out of the freezer this morning and it was currently sitting on the kitchen windowsill where it would live for the next three or four days. After that, she would remove the soap from the mould and then it would need to cure for four weeks – which she hadn't realised initially, having assumed it could be used straight away.

Apparently, if it wasn't left to cure, the bars wouldn't last as long, and neither would they lather up as well as they should. It was frustrating but necessary, but she didn't know if she could wait that long before she tried it.

It looked lovely and creamy though – almost good enough to eat – and it smelt divine. She had added oatmeal and honey fragranced oils, and the scent was mouth-wateringly good.

What was also mouth-wateringly good was the fudge that Otto had made with the leftover goats' milk. She had indulged in a couple of cubes for breakfast (who wouldn't?) and she had packaged up a portion to take down to Walter.

She was popping to the cottage for her tea this evening, so she took it with her. He would enjoy a couple of pieces with a cuppa after his meal, and if he was anything like her, he wouldn't be able to stop at two. The fudge was incredibly moreish.

Knocking once on the door to announce her arrival, Dulcie stepped into the warmth of the cottage and she was immediately assaulted by the smell of cooking, the heat from the open fire in the living room, and the enthusiastic welcome of a Border collie.

Laughing at the dog, who was as interested in the contents of her coat pocket as she was in being petted, Dulcie fought her way into the kitchen, taking her coat off as she did so. Otto was doing the cooking, and as usual Walter was sitting at the table, watching.

'Hi, Walter.' She gave him a kiss on his whiskery cheek, before enfolding Otto in a brief hug. 'Anything I can do?' she asked, feeling she should offer but guessing that her boyfriend would probably refuse.

Otto batted her away after giving her a kiss on the lips. He tasted of tomatoes with a hint of garlic. 'Go sit down and keep my dad company,' he told her.

Dulcie took a seat at the table.

'I've brought you some fudge,' she said, handing Walter a lavender-patterned paper bag. She had bought a supply of bags in anticipation of wrapping her soaps in them when she came to sell them. Although she knew she was being premature, the bags had been on offer and they were so pretty. She had wanted a lilac pattern, to reflect the name of the farm but she hadn't seen any. If the soap turned out okay, and there was no reason why it shouldn't, she might invest in having stickers made. She had already checked out Etsy and they were reasonable enough, and on looking through the site, she had realised that she might be able to sell her own soap there too, despite the market being crowded. Now that she had bought the moulds and the raw ingredients, there wouldn't be any further outlay. Unless... she invested in a couple of goats.

Walter sniffed at the packet of fudge. 'Smells nice. I'll have some later.' He popped it on the worktop and said, 'Otto has sent his query off to an agent.'

'I know, he messaged me to say he'd sent it.' He'd also forwarded the photos to her so she could take a look. They were very good, but she still couldn't believe that most of the food was actually fake or covered in something inedible.

'I don't expect to hear anything for weeks,' Otto said, gloomily.

'What will you do if you don't hear back soon, or if they pass?' she wanted to know.

'Keep sending it off to agents.' He shrugged. 'In the meantime, I suppose I'd better start looking for paid employment.'

Walter gave his son a keen glance. 'Cheffing?'

'It's what I do. I don't know anything else.'

Dulcie knew that even if he did, Otto wouldn't want to do anything other than cook. 'Have you started looking?'

'A bit. There's nothing in Picklewick obviously, but I've had a quick trawl through the vacancies in Thornbury.' He didn't look happy, and she suspected he hadn't seen anything suitable.

It would be hard for a chef of his calibre to find work. He had tried earlier in the year, asking Dave, the landlord of The Black Horse in the village, if there were any jobs going in the kitchen. Dulcie had inadvertently overheard Dave say that even if he did have a position that needed filling, he would be wary of employing a Michelin star chef to fill it.

Walter, bless him, tried to lighten his son's mood. 'I keep saying, he ought to open his own place here in

Picklewick. He could please himself then and cook what he likes.'

'I'm not sure I'd want to do that, Dad. Not only is it a hell of a commitment, it's also a hell of an outlay. I haven't got the money.' He said it gently, but Walter still flinched.

'I'm sorry, Otto. If it hadn't been for my stupidity, you'd have a farm to sell.'

Otto stopped what he was doing, walked over to his dad and put an arm around his shoulders. 'Stop beating yourself up over it. What's done is done. Anyway,' he shot Dulcie a glance. It was so full of love that her heart turned to mush. 'If we hadn't raffled off the farm, I never would have met Dulcie, so you should give yourself a pat on the back for that.'

'True…' Walter said, slowly. Although Dulcie could tell that the elderly gent wasn't totally convinced, at least he didn't look as unhappy as he had a few seconds ago.

Otto went back to the hob and the pans which were bubbling away on them. Her tummy rumbled, and she couldn't wait to see what he had made. He wasn't focusing on foraged ingredients anymore, and now had the whole of the local supermarket to choose from.

Typically, he had refused to tell her, aware that she often had preconceived ideas of what she liked and what she didn't. It had only taken a couple of instances where she had turned her nose up at something because she didn't like the sound of it, only to be surprised to discover that she actually liked it, for him to not tell her what was in a dish until she had tasted it and had given her verdict.

'I hear you're thinking of keeping goats,' Walter said. 'I knew you wouldn't be able to resist having some livestock.' He looked so pleased with himself that Dulcie grinned.

'No sheep,' she warned. 'Just goats, and that's not for definite. It all depends on how well the soap making goes.'

'We'll make a farmer out of you yet,' the old man declared. 'How many chickens have you got now?'

'Nine. Do you need any more eggs?'

'We've still got some left from last week.'

'I can't use nine eggs a day, although one or two have stopped laying. Is that normal?'

'It is,' Walter informed her. 'The drop in temperature and the decreasing daylight tells them to stop laying. If you want them to carry on, you need to bring them inside and give them more heat and light.'

'Inside – as in, *in the house*?' Over Dulcie's dead body! She liked her chickens, but not enough to have them strutting around her sitting room.

Walter nearly fell off his chair with laughter. 'In the *barn* with a light bulb and plenty of feed. But you might want to give them a rest – laying eggs takes a lot out of a bird. If you do decide to rest them, don't worry about not having any eggs – just stockpile them for a few weeks beforehand. Eggs will stay fresh for up to two months in a sealed container in the fridge (just don't wash them) or you can freeze them. Not the whole egg,' he added hastily when Dulcie opened her mouth. 'You have to separate the yolks from the whites. Use ice cube trays. They work a treat.'

It seemed like an awful lot of effort, but maybe she would give it a go. However, she might just bring the hens into the barn anyway before it got much colder

– more for her sake than for theirs, because she was already shivering at the thought of traipsing out to the orchard on dark and cold December mornings.

Suddenly a lightbulb went off in her head. She could have baby chicks to go with the baby goats and the rabbits she had yet to look into keeping. She'd had a guinea pig when she was younger, so maybe rabbits weren't too dissimilar.

Dulcie hadn't quite formed a picture of what her farm would look like next year, but she had begun making an outline. So far, she'd only pencilled in a couple of things, such as a spring petting corner (she could hardly keep referring to it as a zoo) and the autumn fruit picking combined with a harvest festival and pumpkin patch, but she was getting there.

Realising it would involve a tremendous amount of hard work, Dulcie knew she had some tough months ahead – but with Walter's knowledge and experience (he *was* the farmer after all) and Otto's support and level head (he would be able to talk some sense into her if she came up with a truly ridiculous idea), she might, *just might*, be able to make this little farm of hers work.

CHAPTER SIX

This feels more like a fun day out than a business trip, Dulcie thought, as she gazed out of the window of Petra's Land Rover. She was sitting in the back, squashed between Otto and Walter, and Amos was in the passenger seat. The vehicle smelled vaguely of horse and manure – or was the niff coming from Petra, who had just confessed to mucking out a stable or two and was still wearing grubby jodhpurs and dirty boots.

Dulcie kept glancing at the space behind the rear seats and wondering if it was large enough for a goat. She was fairly certain it wouldn't be big enough for more than one, and as she was planning on purchasing at least three or four animals, she was already worrying about how she was going to transport them from the breeder they were currently on their way to see.

The suspension in the Land Rover wasn't the best, and her teeth rattled as the vehicle bounced along a track. But as they drew nearer to their destination her excitement grew when she caught her first glimpse of goats in a field.

'Look, they've got a playground!' she cried in astonishment, seeing a couple of the creatures climbing up planks of wood balanced on what looked like enormous cotton reels, which she assumed must have once held lengths of pipe or copper wire. A three-tiered lookout post had been constructed out of pallets, and there was even some kind of large swinging platform and a seesaw.

'They get bored easily, do goats,' Amos warned. 'If you don't give them something to occupy them, they'll get up to all kinds of mischief.'

'Ooh, I want a goaty playground,' she said, turning to Otto. 'Can you help me make one?'

Otto rolled his eyes and sighed. 'If I must.' He softened his words with a kiss.

'Give it a rest,' Petra muttered. 'I wouldn't have offered to bring you if I knew you were going to get all lovey-dovey.'

'Have you and Harry had a row?' Amos asked. He scooted around to speak to Dulcie. 'Those two squabble like a cat and dog. He wants to offer riding holidays by turning the old sheep shed into a kind of hostel, but Petra's having none of it.'

'I've got enough on my plate as it is,' Petra grumbled. 'And the way Harry is carrying on, we won't have a barn left for the actual horses.'

'The horses live in the stable block,' Amos pointed out.

'Yes, but I still need a barn…'

Thankfully the discussion came to an end as Petra parked the Land Rover, and everyone got out.

A man walked towards them. He was leading a goat, who had a leather collar around its neck, and Dulcie suppressed a squeal. It was very small, and at first she thought it was a baby, until Otto said in her ear, 'That's a full-grown pygmy goat, in case you're wondering.'

'The babies must be *tiny*,' Dulcie hissed back.

'They are, and they're incredibly cute.'

'I want one. Can pygmy goats be milked?'

'Dunno, but here's the man to ask.'

Petra shook hands with the guy, who introduced himself as Mike. 'I bought Princess from you,' she reminded him, 'And last year, you had her back to put to one of your billies. Got a nice little kid from her.'

'Are you thinking of breeding from her again?' he asked.

'I did consider it, but two goats are more than enough, and if Dulcie does go ahead with her plan, I can buy all the milk I need from her.'

'Okay, shall we take a look at some of the females I've got available?' He turned to Dulcie. 'Petra says you're wanting a couple of goats for milk. Have you got any particular breed in mind?'

Dulcie had done a bit of research, but she had found it rather contradictory, with some people championing one breed, and others effusing the pros of another. So, she had an open mind and was hoping that Mike would give her the benefit of his wisdom once she'd told him what she wanted.

This, he was more than happy to do, and after wandering around the pens and stroking goat after goat, Dulcie settled on three white ones of a breed renowned for their milk yield and calm temperament, and two light brown ones which were also good milkers but were more famous for the quality of the cheese.

And of course, she couldn't resist a couple of pygmy goats. Three in fact... So she ended up buying eight goats in total – more than she had anticipated, but those little ones were simply gorgeous. She had also spent far more than she had intended, but everyone would adore those pygmies, and even if there weren't any goatlings on the farm just yet (she much preferred the word 'goatling' to 'kid', when referring to baby goats, despite suspecting she might have made it up herself), these loveable little creatures looked like babies because of their small stature.

'Do you deliver?' she asked, once again wondering how she was going to transport them from here to Muddypuddle Lane.

Mike said, 'I do. But we've got plenty of time to organise that.'

'We have? Can't you deliver next week?'

'Not if you want to ensure they are in kid. These were bred only a few weeks ago, so it'll be another month or two yet before we'll know for sure whether they are pregnant or not.'

'Oh.' Dulcie was crestfallen. 'What if they're not?'

'Because you are purchasing them on the understanding that they are in kid, if one of them proves not to be pregnant, you can choose another that most definitely is.'

'I see.' She brightened. 'I suppose it will give me time to build a playground for them.'

'They'll need a shelter, too,' Walter advised. He gave Amos a look. 'Fancy giving me a hand with that?'

'Dad!' Otto glared at his father. 'You are in no fit state to do any building work.'

'It's just nailing a few planks of wood together,' Walter protested. 'I'm sure me and Amos can manage that between us.'

Otto shook his head. 'I can't believe I'm hearing this. You're supposed to be taking it easy.'

'I've taken it easy for months. If you think I'm going to vegetate in that chair until I draw my last breath, you can think again.'

'He's feeling better,' Otto said to no one in particular.

'I've been feeling better for a while, son,' Walter shot back. 'It'll do me good to have something I can get my teeth into. I'll feel useful again.' He stopped and stared at Dulcie, 'That is, if you don't mind a bit of help. I don't want to tread on your toes.'

Dulcie, feeling very much as though she was caught between a rock and a hard place, sent Otto a helpless look. She didn't want to encourage Walter if Otto didn't approve. It had taken Walter a long time to regain his health and his strength, and she didn't want to be responsible for any relapse. On the other hand, she could tell that Walter was chomping at the bit and was getting very fed up with not having much to do. It must be hard for him to go from running the farm singlehandedly, to being an invalid and dependent on Otto, so she took it as a good sign that the old man wanted to involve himself in the farm he used to own.

Otto caught her eye. He sighed and shrugged. 'It's up to you,' he said to his dad. 'Just don't overdo it. I'll help too – it'll give me something to do.'

Something to do whilst he was waiting for a response from one of the agents, Dulcie thought. And something to do whilst he was looking for a job. Because with Walter clearly so much better, Otto was now free to find a role as a head chef, doing what he loved most in the world.

♥

'The evenings are drawing in,' Otto observed a couple of days later. It was the first of November and the leaves had already tuned colour, the dramatic displays of ochre, crimson and orange clearly visible in the valley below.

Crisp, clear autumn days were great for taking long walks in the hills above the farm, and he and Dulcie had filled a flask with hot chocolate, and he had thrown together a picnic of pasties that he had baked earlier whilst waiting for Dulcie to finish work for the day, along with some individual pumpkin pies. Before much longer, it would be too dark to go walking in the hills in the evenings, so he had been determined to make the most of it. Waiting didn't suit him, and Otto found he was restless more often than not, so he had been finding things to do to keep busy.

Work had begun on the shelter in the goats' field, with Otto keeping a stern eye on Walter to make sure he wasn't exerting himself too much. But with Otto insisting that his dad and Amos take their time, they were only doing a couple of hours a day, leaving Otto trying to find something to do to fill the rest of it. Hence the baking earlier today, and the walk he and Dulcie were on now.

Anyway, it was good for both of them to get out in the fresh air. Poor Dulcie was stuck behind a desk for seven hours a day (her dining room table actually, but the principle was the same) so it was nice for her to stretch her legs.

Dulcie gazed across the valley, her hands on her hips as she caught her breath. 'That hill is always steeper than I think it's going to be,' she puffed.

'I know what you mean. I used to be able to sprint to the top of it when I was a kid. And come back down on a tea tray or a piece of cardboard. It was great fun.' He smiled wistfully then gave her a speculative look, wondering whether she would be up for doing something like that. Not today obviously, because he wasn't in the habit of carrying tea trays or large pieces of cardboard around with him. But perhaps they could come up here another time and—

She must have guessed what he was thinking, because she said, 'Oh, no, you don't! You're not talking me into sliding back down on a bit of plastic. I'll walk, thank you.'

'You're no fun,' he grumbled. He was teasing; Dulcie was a great deal of fun, especially when she was in his arms.

Dulcie must have read his mind again, because she turned to face him, snaking her hands around his waist and working them underneath his jacket until she touched the bare skin of his back. He flinched at the chill of her fingers.

'So you don't think I'm any fun, do you?' she murmured, her lips on his neck, her hands caressing their way down the small of his back towards the waistband of his jeans.

Otto closed his eyes in pleasure at her touch, wondering just how far she was going to take things. He was up for a spot of outdoor loving if she was, despite the chill in the air and their elevated position on the hillside…

Damn and blast – his phone was ringing.

Reluctantly, Otto pulled away from Dulcie with an apologetic twist of his lips, and took his phone out.

It wasn't a number he recognised and he guessed it was one of those nuisance calls everyone seemed to get at some point. If it was, he would give them a piece of his mind. But on the other hand, it could be the hospital or—

'Hello?' His voice was hesitant.

'Hi, my name is Yvette Holmes, and I'm calling from Holmes Literary Agency. Am I speaking to Otto York?'

Otto swallowed, his mouth suddenly dry. His heart was in his throat and he coughed to clear the lump that had formed there. 'Yes, this is he.' God, he sounded officious. 'I mean, yes, I'm Otto. Hi.' Now he sounded like a muppet.

'I've got your proposal in front of me, and I wondered if we could have a chat?'

'Yes, of course. What about?' Oh, for goodness sake! He was making a right idiot of himself, but she had caught him off guard, when his mind had been focused on something else entirely. 'I mean, I know what it's about, I think…' Or did he? Did agents phone to say thanks but no thanks? He closed his eyes and wished he had let the call go to answerphone, so he would have had time to prepare.

The woman chuckled. 'The possibility of my company representing you? Yes. Are you free any time this week?'

Representing me? His heart was hammering so hard, she surely must be able to hear it. He was aware of Dulcie slipping her hand into his, and he gave it a squeeze. 'Er, yes. I can be.' *Can be?* He had absolutely nothing else lined up whatsoever.

'How about Friday? Say ten-thirty? Is that good for you?'

It was perfect. Any day or time would be perfect.

The agent said, 'Fantastic! I'll email you to confirm. I'm looking forward to meeting you.'

'Me, too. Thank you.'

'By the way,' Yvette said before she ended the call. 'The images you sent were very nice. Very professional. See you Friday,' and with that she hung up.

Otto stared at the screen for a second, to make sure she really had gone, then he looked at Dulcie. 'That was Yvette Holmes, from Holmes Literary Agency. She wants to meet me on Friday.' He slapped a hand to his forehead. 'We're supposed to be going to see the Bonfire Night fireworks in the village, aren't we? Oh, heck. Sorry, I forgot.'

'This is far more important than watching the fireworks,' Dulcie said. 'I'm so proud of you.' She was beaming from ear to ear. 'What time is your meeting?'

'Ten-thirty.'

'Then stop fretting. You should be back in plenty of time. But even if you aren't, it doesn't matter.'

'Promise me you'll go anyway? I know you've been looking forward to it.' On Halloween Dulcie had been like a big kid, decorating the house with fake cobwebs and bunting, and she had insisted on buying pumpkins to carve, which she had then taken to the stables to decorate the arena because Petra had arranged a party for her younger riders – involving horses, of course.

'If you're not back by the time it starts, I'll go with Nikki and Gio,' Dulcie said. 'They're taking Sammy, so I'm sure they won't mind if I tag along. You can either meet me there or I'll see you back at the farm.' She grabbed hold of his hand and began to tug him down the hill.

Otto asked, 'Where are we going? We haven't eaten our picnic yet.'

'The pasties will keep until tomorrow. We're going out to celebrate.'

He hung back. 'I think you might be a bit premature.'

'Don't be daft! That woman isn't going to drag you all the way to London and waste her valuable time just to tell you she's not interested. Otto, my gorgeous, wonderful man – you've got yourself an agent!'

CHAPTER SEVEN

Otto hadn't been expecting to return to London quite so soon. He had assumed it would be months before he visited the city again, but here he was – on the train this time, because driving into the centre was a nightmare and he'd had enough of that the other week.

He was feeling nervous and hadn't been able to face breakfast. The early start hadn't helped, either. He'd been up well before dawn to drive to Thornbury to catch the train. Wishing he'd had enough wits about him to suggest a slightly later time to meet, he took a deep breath and told himself to stay calm.

It was easier said than done, because he'd been on edge all week. He knew it was logical to assume that Yvette Holmes was going to offer to represent him, but until he had the contract in his hand he couldn't allow himself to believe it was actually happening. He kept thinking of all the things that could go wrong – maybe the agent wouldn't like him when she met him; maybe they'd want to change significant parts of the book. Maybe… actually, he couldn't think of anything else that could go wrong, but that didn't mean to say it wouldn't.

Cross with himself, he shook his head. This nervousness and uncertainty wasn't like him at all. He was usually confident and self-assured, but he was so far out of his comfort zone that he may as well be on another planet. If he was being asked for a demonstration of his cooking, that would be a different matter entirely.

When his phone rang, his first thought was it was Yvette calling to cancel, but when he saw it was Alistair, his curiosity was piqued.

'My goodness, Alistair, I don't speak to you for months then I get to hear your dulcet voice twice in a matter of weeks,' Otto said. 'Is there anything wrong?'

'Nothing, everything is tip-top.'

'Glad to hear it,' Otto replied.

'I wondered if we could have a chat?'

Otto had a feeling of déjà vu. Alistair was the second person this week who wanted to have a 'chat' with him. 'If it's to offer me my old job back, you already did that, and I turned you down,' he said with a chuckle. He was about to say something else, but at that moment the train went through a tunnel.

When the call reconnected, he could hear Alistair grumbling, 'Otto? Otto? Damn it, he's hung up on me.'

Otto smiled and said, 'I'd never hang up on you. The train went through a tunnel. I'm on my way to London.'

'You've not been poached by Trent Manning, have you?'

'No, definitely not.' Trent and Alistair were bitter culinary rivals. Neither of them was a chef in their own right, but both of them owned a restaurant.

'Who, then?'

'No one. Not that it's any of your business, you nosey old fart, but I've got a meeting with an agent.'

'That cookbook of yours is growing wings, is it? Well done. And while I admit to being a fart, less of the old, please.'

'Did you ring for anything in particular, or just to listen to me giving you abuse?'

'I want a chat with you.'

'So you said. What about?'

'How long will you be in London?'

'Just for the day.'

'Phone me when you're out of your meeting. I'll clear my diary for the afternoon.'

'Can't you tell me what it's about now?'

'I'd rather tell you face-to-face.'

Otto agreed to call him once he was done, on the condition that Alistair took him for lunch. They arranged to eat at The Fern, although Otto knew he would feel strange going back there as a customer and not as Head Chef.

He and Alistair had a funny relationship, Otto mused as he settled back for the rest of the journey. Alistair never minded that Otto was outspoken, and he treated Otto more as an equal than an employee. When it came to food, Otto had always expected Alistair to follow his advice – why else employ a top-notch chef if you weren't prepared to bow to their skill and experience?

But when it came to the business side of running the restaurant, Otto hadn't had any say in the matter and neither had he wanted to. The arrangement had suited them both and had been a successful one – until Otto had ended it, through no fault of his or Alistair's. If Walter hadn't needed him, Otto was fairly sure he would still be Head Chef at The Fern now.

But that chapter of his life was over, and he had a whole new book to concentrate on – *literally!* And he spent the rest of the journey between worrying about his forthcoming meeting with Yvette, and trying to figure out why Alistair was being so mysterious.

♥

Dulcie was unable to settle, despite taking call after call from customers needing help. Or wanting to vent or complain. She did her best, but not all issues could be resolved, and some people just wanted to have a good old shout at anyone in the company.

After dealing with a particularly nasty customer who had hung up on her after calling her a rude word, she desperately needed to hear a friendly voice. She had sent Otto several messages whilst he was travelling, but it was so close to the time of his meeting that she didn't dare phone. Besides, he needed to concentrate on that, not be distracted by her moaning.

Nikki was the other obvious choice, and as it was half term and she wouldn't be in school, her poor sister was it.

'I'm keeping my fingers crossed for him,' Nikki said, after Dulcie had offloaded her angst and the conversation had swung around to Otto's imminent meeting.

Dulcie checked the time – he should be there now. She wondered how long it would be before she heard from him.

'Message me as soon as you've got any news,' Nikki said. 'I've got to go, I'm in the middle of doing the weekly shop. Will we see you later at the firework display?'

'I was meaning to ask – Otto should be back in time, but if he isn't, can I come with you?'

'Hopefully you'll be at home celebrating,' Nikki whispered, her tone wicked.

'I hope we *will* have something to celebrate, but I really want to go to the display. You know how much I love fireworks.'

'I would have thought you and Otto would produce plenty of sparks of your own!'

'Ha, ha! I'd better let you get on with your grocery shop, and I'd better get some work done. Before you go, have you thought about what you're going to do for Christmas? Will you be staying in Picklewick, or will you go spend it at Mum's?'

'I want to see Mum, Maisie and Jay, but Picklewick is our home now and I'm not sure whether Gio would be able to come with us. He'll probably have to work at least one shift over the festive season, and probably a lot more.'

Dulcie wasn't keen on leaving Picklewick either, because she guessed Otto would be torn between wanting to spend Christmas with her, and not wanting to leave Walter on his own. At least Mum had Maisie and Jay: if Otto went to Birmingham with her, poor Walter would have no one.

'I've got an idea!' she cried. 'I'm going to ask Mum, Maisie and Jay if they'd like to spend Christmas at the farm.'

'Fantastic! A huge family Christmas – that'll be lush! I assume Jay will be home for Christmas?'

'I don't see why not – he hasn't missed one yet. Any idea which country he's in?' Dulcie asked.

'He's still in Asia, but I'm not sure exactly where,' Nikki replied. 'Whoever knew there would be such a demand for acoustic sensors!'

Jay was passionate about the environment and worked for a company who installed listening equipment in the jungle that monitored the health of the ecosystem and listened for illegal logging activity. Dulcie was immensely proud of her brother, but wished she could see more of him. He always came home for Christmas though, and she was looking forward to his visit.

Dulcie returned to work in a lighter frame of mind. She kept telling herself that she didn't have to do this job for the rest of her working life, and that it was simply a means to bring in some income until the farm paid its own way. As long as she could blow off steam now and again, she'd be fine.

Apart from the job, her life was looking particularly rosy. She had taken the first steps to making the farm profitable (she couldn't wait to welcome the goats to their new home, but that would be several weeks away yet), she was madly in love with the most gorgeous man in the world, and she had fireworks and Christmas to look forward to.

All that was needed to put the icing on top of the cake, was for Otto to get himself an agent. And she had total faith that was happening right now!

♥

Yvette Holmes looked exactly like her photo on the company's website, although she was shorter than Otto was expecting, the top of her head only reaching to his shoulder. Her small stature aside, she had plenty of gravitas to make her presence felt, and as she walked across the foyer to greet him, he noticed several pairs of eyes following her progress.

Holmes Literary Agency had offices on the third floor of a modern building, and he hadn't expected her to come greet him herself when he had given his name to the chap on the reception desk. It was a nice touch, and he hoped it was a sign that the meeting was going to be all he prayed it would be.

'So it's you I've got to blame for the food at The Fern not being as good as it used to be,' was her opening gambit.

'Er…' Otto shook the hand she offered, wondering what he was supposed to say to that. He had included his credentials as part of the pitching process, so agents would realise he was a bona fide chef, but it hadn't occurred to him that Yvette Holmes might have dined at The Fern.

'Just teasing,' she said. 'Although I'm telling the truth when I say I was a little disappointed. The food was good, but not *as* good.'

'Thanks. I think.'

'Take it as the compliment it's meant to be.' She walked him over to the lift and pressed the button. The doors pinged open immediately, and when he gestured for her to go ahead of him, he took a moment to study her.

Wearing a black trouser suit and a cream blouse, with slicked back grey hair and pink lipstick, she looked every inch a successful businesswoman.

The company's offices were open-plan, bright, and busy, and he received a few curious glances as he followed her into a spacious office at the far end, and nervously took the seat she indicated at the conference table. A folder was waiting for her, and without preamble, she opened it. Otto caught a glimpse of a photo which he recognised as being one of his. She must have printed it out.

'I'm interested in representing you,' she began. 'But before we discuss contracts, I want to hear from you what your hopes for your book are – besides being an international bestseller.'

That *was* what he had been hoping for, even if he would never say so out loud. Wasn't that every author's dream? However, he was realistic enough to understand that a book about foraging in the British countryside wouldn't find much of a market in Australia, for instance.

'I'd like to see it on the shelves in Waterstones,' he said, after a pause. 'I'd like it to be *the* go-to recipe book for gardeners and foragers. We need to start thinking about eating what grows in our gardens, and not be so reliant on imported or mass-farmed foods.'

'I like your passion for your subject,' Yvette said, steepling her hands under her chin as she studied him.

Otto felt like a pupil sitting in front of a headteacher, and was rather unnerved. 'My passion is for cooking,' he said. 'Foraging is second to that. No matter what the ingredients are, or where they come from, taste is paramount.'

'I quite agree. Now, if this was a book on foraging, with the recipes as more of an afterthought, I would suggest going with what you just said. But as this is a cookbook, we need to focus on the recipes first and foremost. I'm only saying this, because we need to be on the same page. I have to have a clear vision of what the book is about if I'm to sell it to a publisher.' She smiled at him. 'I think it might fly, but—'

Here we go, Otto thought. There was bound to be a 'but', and he prepared himself for the worst – she liked it, but not enough to… blah, blah, blah.

She said, 'It's going to take a great deal of work on your part. Publishing a book isn't as simple as stocking it on shelves. To give it any chance of success you're going to have to actively promote it. You will be expected to do a significant amount of marketing in the form of appearances, cooking demonstrations at food festivals, persuading your peers to review it, and so on. Not only that, but the whole process, beginning with me becoming your agent to the book being bought by a reader, could take up to two years. And please don't expect much of an advance: you're not well known enough in publishing circles for that, plus it will take a while to earn out any advance before you receive a penny in royalties. Now, the reason I'm telling you this is that if I agree to take you on, I need to know you understand the process and what a publisher will expect of you.' She shuffled the contents of the folder around and brought out a document he didn't recognise. 'Are you ready to talk contracts, or do you want to think about what I've said?'

'Talk,' he said, without hesitation. He had invested a great deal of time and effort into getting this far, and to be offered a contract by his first-choice agent was a dream come true, even if she had tried her best to rain on his parade. However, he appreciated her honesty and her transparency, and realised she was doing her best to manage his expectations.

But after he had read the contract and signed on the dotted line, the euphoria he had hoped to feel was dulled by the knowledge that he couldn't afford to wait years for the book to be published. He needed an income *now*.

So it was with bitter-sweet feelings that he messaged Dulcie to tell her the 'good' news; he'd leave the not-so-good news until he spoke to her in person. Although he was proud of himself for getting this far, he was disillusioned and disheartened by the knowledge that he would have to look for a job after all. And sooner, rather than later.

He would get today out of the way, then spend the weekend scouring the various catering job sites. Something was bound to come up. It had to.

♥

Dulcie read the message, her heart swelling with pride. Otto had done it! He had been signed by an agent. Woo hoo!

She tore her headphones off, leapt from her chair and danced around the dining room, squealing at the top of her voice. This was the best news ever! They would *really* have something to celebrate tonight.

When she had calmed down, she replied to his message, telling him how much she loved him and how proud she was of him. She would have preferred to speak to him, but she didn't like to phone in case he was still at the agency, ironing out the details or whatever it was that was being discussed. She would wait for him to phone her.

What time train do you think you'll catch? she wrote. She couldn't wait to see him.

He replied immediately. ***Got a few things to wrap up. Not sure yet. I'll let you know later.***

Dulcie supposed she would have to be satisfied with that.

Unable to keep still and wanting to share the brilliant news, she phoned Nikki, who was equally as thrilled, then she called her mum.

Her mother was as pleased as punch, and even Maisie, who was at home (*no job to go to, Maisie?*), was delighted. Finally, she sent Carla a quick message, and received one back that contained nothing more than a list of emojis and a big kiss at the end. She wondered whether she should pop down the hill and tell Walter, but she guessed Otto would have already shared the good news with him.

What happens now? Dulcie wondered. Otto had been rather vague about the next stage of the publishing process, possibly because he hadn't been totally sure himself, but she was excited to find out.

It was all coming together for them, she thought. Her with the farm, Otto with the cookbook. And Walter was making steady progress health-wise. So maybe it was time to ask Otto if he would like to move in with her…?

They may have only known each other for a smidge over six months, but she knew he was the man she wanted to spend the rest of her life with. Why delay? He spent more time at the farmhouse than he did at the cottage, so living together was the next step.

She would ask him tonight, after they'd had a private celebration. Ideally, she would like *him* to ask *her*, but theirs was a weird situation. He could hardly ask her to move into the cottage with him and his dad, and she knew he would never suggest her selling the farm and getting a place together. And neither would he ask to move in with her. Therefore, it was up to her to make the first move, and tonight was the night to do it. It would be the start of their new life together, as a proper couple – and she simply couldn't wait!

♥

Otto felt bad for not speaking to Dulcie in person and explaining the realities of the situation, but he just couldn't face her. He'd have a good chat with her this evening and explain that although the news was positive in that he had an agent, there would be a long way to go yet before he would realise any income from the book – if he ever did, because there was no guarantee a publisher would want it. He would also tell her about his plans to get a job.

As far as disasters went, it wasn't a major one, but he hoped his and Dulcie's relationship wouldn't go the same way as Remi and Steff's. Still, he supposed being a chef was no worse than any other job involving shifts and other people managed just fine, so maybe he was being overly dramatic. It wasn't as though she lived miles away and he would only get to see her now and again. She lived a short walk up the lane...

Despite the pep talk, Otto was feeling rather more sorry for himself than he should considering the circumstances, as he walked into The Fern half an hour later. It was already twelve-thirty and he hoped lunch wouldn't take long as he had a three-hour train journey ahead of him. It was doubtful whether he'd get back to Picklewick before six o'clock as it was, and he was desperate to give Dulcie a hug.

There were many familiar faces amongst the serving staff, he was relieved to discover, as he stepped inside the restaurant, and as everyone flocked around to say hello a pang went through him. It felt like coming home to be back in The Fern again – little had changed, and he soaked up the atmosphere of the front of house area where he had spent many a night after the restaurant had closed, discussing the menu with Alistair.

The man himself appeared from the direction of the kitchen, his arms open in welcome, and he drew Otto into him and gave him a patted-back hug.

'How did your meeting go?' his old boss asked as he showed Otto to the best table in the house.

'I've got an agent,' Otto said, putting on a big smile.

'Congratulations! This calls for champagne!' Alistair clapped his hands.

'No, really, I don't—'

'Bernard, open a bottle of Louis Roederer Cristal,' he instructed the maitre'd.

Like the professional that he was, Bernard didn't even flinch at the exorbitant gesture: he simply nodded, leaving Otto bemused.

'It's not that big a deal,' he said when Bernard was out of earshot, and he went on to tell Alistair about the realities of the situation.

'Nonsense! You are one step closer to publication. I have heard that getting an agent is the hardest part.'

Alistair leant to the side a fraction to allow Bernard to pour the champagne, which he did with a dramatic flourish.

Otto sniffed it appreciatively, took a small mouthful and let the sparkling liquid sit on his tongue for a moment as he revelled in the flavour and the way the bubbles discretely popped in his mouth. It was delicious, and so it should be at that price.

'This is overkill,' he said, raising his glass. 'House white would have done.'

Alistair smiled. 'I have something to celebrate too.' He gently put his glass on the table, glanced around, then leant forward and said, 'I am the proud owner of two additional restaurants.' He looked incredibly pleased with himself. 'You are the first to know, and I would appreciate it if you kept it under your hat for a while.'

'Of course. Congratulations.' Otto took another sip of the wine. It was incredibly good, and he had to stop himself from gulping it down. As well as being crass, such a wine demanded to be savoured. 'Where?'

Alistair said, 'In London, obviously, but the locations are secret for the moment.'

Otto smiled. 'Why so hush-hush?'

'They are going to be sister-restaurants to The Fern, and I want only the best so I'll be poaching all the best staff.'

Uh-oh…

'That's what I wanted to talk to you about,' Alistair continued.

Otto was shaking his head. 'I've told you, I'm not coming back to London to live.'

'Not even to be my Menu Director?'

'*What?*'

'Each restaurant will have its own distinctive menu, using only the very best ingredients, prepared by the very best chefs. I need someone who I can trust to create the menus, and to make sure they are delivered to the very highest standard.' Alistair leaned forward again, his expression serious. 'Come work for me, Otto. You will have total autonomy in the kitchens, from which pans to use, to who will be the head chef in each one. You will have full control. I trust you to put each restaurant on the map. By this time next year, I fully expect all of them to have a star. After that, they will have another…' He stopped talking, but his eyes remained on Otto's face.

'I don't know what to say,' Otto murmured, after a long pause.

'Say yes. I'll even throw in an apartment to sweeten the deal, unless you still have yours?'

'I sold it.' Before Otto was aware of the full extent of the farm's debts, he had hoped that the equity from his apartment would have covered them, so he had put it on the market and had received an offer almost immediately. When it had become apparent that the money raised from the sale of his property would be nowhere near enough, it had been too late to pull out of the sale. Instead, he had used the proceeds to renovate the cottage on Muddypuddle Lane, with enough left over to keep him solvent for a while.

'There'll be a good salary, too,' Alistair said, and when he named a figure, Otto thought he must have misheard.

'Bloody hell, Alistair, that's almost three times what I earned as your head chef.'

'I know. But I've learnt that if you want the best you have to pay for it.'

'You could get Rachel Humphrey or Hugo Maitland for that.' Then Otto backtracked. 'Okay, maybe not either of those two, but you could get some serious skill for what you're offering.'

Alistair was shaking his head. 'I want *you*. I know how you operate, and I trust you. That counts for a lot.'

'My name isn't big enough, it's not enough of a draw.'

'It will be – and with this book of yours coming out…'

'It's a recipe of foraged ingredients,' Otto argued. 'There won't be any tie-in with your restaurants.'

But then Alistair said something that turned Otto's objection on its head.

'One of them will serve only foraged and locally sourced food. Would that help your book sales, hmm?'

CHAPTER EIGHT

Disappointment flooded through Dulcie as she read Otto's last message, telling her that he wouldn't be back in Picklewick until later this evening and that she should go to the firework display without him.

She wondered what was keeping him there, but when she tried to call him he didn't answer.

Feeling as though she was being clingy and needy, she tried not to phone Walter, but she couldn't help herself.

'Have you heard from Otto?' she asked.

'Not since this morning. He said he might be late back as he had bumped into Alistair – the chap who owns The Fern – and is having lunch with him.'

Dulcie knew who Alistair was, and a frisson of unease travelled through her. Why hadn't Otto phoned and told her? She would have understood. If he could find the time to call his dad, surely he could have found the time to give her a quick bell?

Telling herself not to be silly, she thought about it rationally. Walter didn't own a mobile phone and neither did he use the internet much. She didn't know whether he actually had an email address, so, apart from sending a letter, Otto had no other way of getting in contact with his dad: he *had* to phone him. Whereas he and Dulcie had already messaged each other several times today, so maybe he didn't think it was necessary to speak to her in person. He was a bloke, and in Dulcie's admittedly limited experience, blokes didn't feel the need to talk as often.

Feeling better about it (why shouldn't he meet up with Alistair? after all, he had seen Remi the last time he was in London…) Dulcie sent Nikki a quick text to tell her sister that she would meet her at the entrance to the park where the firework display was being held, then she heated a pot of hearty vegetable soup and cut off a few chunks of Otto's homemade bread to go with it for an early tea. After she'd eaten, she would dress warmly and go enjoy the fireworks. Hopefully, if Otto wasn't too late, he would be able to join her there.

♥

As far as Dulcie was concerned, Bonfire Night drew a line under autumn and ushered in winter. She loved everything about it – the leaves underfoot (but only if they were dry and crunchy), the smell of woodsmoke, the aroma of sausages and onions (because Bonfire Night wasn't the same without a hotdog), and the heat from the fire itself. But most of all, she loved the way the fireworks lit up the heavens, those fleeting bursts of magical colours in the inky black sky. Even the loud bangs were fun: although Petra didn't agree, and Dulcie hoped the horses wouldn't be too spooked. Dulcie had left a radio playing in the barn so the goats and Flossie wouldn't get too stressed, and she had also popped another into the chicken coop.

It was totally dark when she parked the car on the edge of the village and made her way to where the display was being held. She had considered walking, and if Otto had been with her they may well have done, but she didn't fancy trekking across the fields on her own in the dark, so car it was. Anyway, Otto would probably just want to get home after all that travelling and the excitement of the day, and not have a half hour walk at the end of it.

Perhaps they could go out to celebrate tomorrow? Nothing fancy, just a drink in The Black Horse and maybe a takeaway. Then, if the time was right and she felt courageous enough, she would suggest he moved in with her.

Her tummy somersaulted at the thought. What if he said no? What if he hated the idea?

Or… maybe he would think it a fabulous idea and she would have worried for no reason, she countered, as she strode towards the park.

Argh! She hated being so dithery and nervous, but it was because she loved him so very much that she felt this way. It was a big deal to put herself out there and ask him to come live with her, and she felt justified for being worried. If he wasn't ready for such a commitment, she might spoil what they had, and that would be awful.

Putting her worries to one side, she scanned the crowd near the entrance to the park and quickly spotted her sister.

Hurrying over to her, Dulcie gave her a hug, then bent to hug Sammy. 'Gosh, I swear you've grown since I saw you last. Hi, Gio.' She waved at Nikki's partner. 'Who wants a sparkler?' she cried, spotting a man selling them.

'Me! Me!' Sammy jigged on the spot, and she was pleased to see his smiling face. Back in the summer he had been so miserable it had broken her heart. But a move to a new area and a new school, away from the bully who had made his life hell, and Sammy was a different child.

After a quick catch-up whilst Dulcie played with her sparkler – drawing her name in the air, obviously – the four of them made their way towards a cordoned-off area, ready to watch the display.

Dulcie checked her phone to see if there were any new messages from Otto, but there weren't, and her heart sank. Watching Nikki and Gio being so loved-up made her feel Otto's absence more keenly than she might otherwise have done if it had just been her and her sister. But everywhere she looked there were couples holding hands or snuggled into one another to keep warm.

'What time train was he catching?' Nikki asked, slipping her arm through Dulcie's.

'Not sure. Walter said he was meeting Alistair, his old boss at The Fern, for lunch.'

'Lucky thing! I wouldn't mind a spot of lunch out. But what with Sammy's football and judo – did I tell you he's joined the class in the community centre in Thornbury? – and Gio's awful shifts, we've hardly been out together at all since I moved to Picklewick. I'm either working myself, ferrying Sammy around, or Gio is at work. You're lucky having Otto there all the time.'

'We don't go out to lunch either,' Dulcie said.

'That's only because Otto prefers eating his own cooking,' Nikki pointed out.

Her sister was right (not about the cooking part, although Dulcie was very appreciative that her boyfriend loved to cook): she was lucky to have Otto around as much as he was. He was always there when she wanted him to be, which was more-or-less all the time. It was Dulcie herself whose time was limited because of her job. She envied couples who worked together; she could just imagine spending all day every day with Otto…

Music began to play and a flash lit up the sky as the firework display kicked off. For the next fifteen wonderful minutes Dulcie stood there with her face uplifted as she lost herself in the show. Only when the last sparks fizzled out did she check her phone again.

Her squeal of delight made Nikki jump.

'What's wrong?' her sister asked, concern in her eyes.

'Nothing's wrong, everything's *fine*! Otto is back. He's by the hotdog stand, so I think we ought to join him and treat ourselves to a snack at the same time.'

But little was she to know that everything was far from fine, and that things were very wrong indeed.

♥

Otto had already decided not to tell Dulcie about Alistair's extraordinary and very tempting offer until he had made up his mind whether to accept it or not. Having three kitchens under his management, not to mention being given free rein to create mouthwatering and unusual recipes, was a dream come true.

Then there was the cherry on the top…

A restaurant dedicated to serving foraged and in-season foods that he would be in charge of, blew his mind. With this pedigree behind him, it would make finding a publisher far easier, and hopefully the book would fly off the shelves.

When Alistair had made the offer, Otto had been too shocked to respond for a moment, but after the news had sunk in, his first instinct had been to bite Alistair's hand off. And he almost had. Then Dulcie's face had swum into his mind, and he knew he had some serious thinking to do.

Telling Alistair that he needed some time and promising to get back to him early next week with an answer (Alistair understandably wanted to get the ball rolling on his new venture as soon as possible), Otto had thought about nothing else all the way home.

And that was the problem – that one little word. *Home.*

He hadn't considered Picklewick his home for many years, although he still referred to the farm as home. But the farm didn't belong to his dad anymore, it belonged to Dulcie. It was *her* home, not his. So where was home now?

In a kitchen, that's where. But at the moment he was homeless…

But Alistair had offered him not one home, but three! Four, if he counted the apartment his old boss was willing to throw in. Alistair was making it as easy as possible for Otto to say yes to the deal. And how could he forget that remarkable salary.

Alistair had gone on to outline his vision for each of the restaurants, and Otto's heart had leapt, before quickly sinking again.

If it hadn't been for Dulcie…

He sighed.

'What's up? I thought you would be bouncing with joy,' Dulcie said.

Otto blinked, then mentally shook his head to clear it. The woman he was madly in love with lifted her face to be kissed, and he swept her into his arms and lost himself in her embrace for several wonderful seconds.

Until Gio said, 'Get a room, you two,' and they broke apart sheepishly.

'Sorry,' Dulcie said, not looking in the slightest bit contrite. She looked like the cat who had stolen the cream, and Otto bit his lip as she said, 'Let's grab a hotdog and watch the bonfire being lit.'

'You go ahead. I'm not hungry.'

'Some of us didn't get to eat a Michelin star meal today,' she teased.

'Er…no. Sorry about that.' His dad must have told her he had lunched with Alistair, and he winced.

'No need to be. What did you have? Was it as good as when you were there? Better?' she joked.

'Um, I can't remember.' He knew he had eaten something, but he couldn't for the life of him remember what.

'You can't *remember*?' Dulcie was incredulous, then her gaze sharpened. 'What's wrong?' she asked.

'I'm tired, that's all. It's been a long day.'

He could tell from her expression that she didn't believe him, but thankfully Sammy tugged on her arm and she let it go.

But as soon as they were on their own, heading to the outskirts of the village to pick up Dulcie's little car, she began quizzing him about the meeting with Yvette.

'Tell me all about it,' she demanded. 'I was thinking about you all day, and when you messaged me to say she'd offered you a contract…!' She grabbed his upper arm and squeezed. 'That was the best news ever! When does she think she'll get a publisher for it? Did she say?'

'Not really,' he replied, and he went on to tell her what Yvette had told him.

'Oh, that's a bummer,' Dulcie commiserated, when he finished. 'I know how much you were depending on this. What will you do?'

He shrugged. 'Start looking for a job, I suppose.'

'In Thornbury?'

'If there is anything suitable available.'

They reached the car and Dulcie let go of him. She opened the driver's door. 'You don't think there will be?'

'I've looked previously, but you never know. Something might turn up.' Something had, but it hadn't been what he was expecting and it was miles away from Picklewick. The question was, if he were to take it, would Dulcie come with him?

There was only one thing for it – he had to find out.

♥

'Can't get to sleep?' Dulcie rolled over and looked at the clock on the bedside table in concern. It was one thirty-three. 'I thought you were tired.' It had seemed that way, because when they had made love earlier, it hadn't been with their usual passion.

'Sorry, I'm keeping you awake. I'll go back to the cottage.'

'Please don't.' She turned to face him and propped herself up on an elbow. Otto's face was a pale disk in the darkness, the only light being a faint one from the clock. She wished she could make out his expression, because she had a feeling something was bothering him. 'What aren't you telling me? Is it to do with the book?'

'No. It is what it is. I just wish I'd known more about the process before I threw myself headlong into it.'

'What then? Are you worried about finding a job? Don't be: a chef with your skill will find one easily.'

She had every faith in him, even if he didn't have much in himself. Mind you, she conceded, it did depend on what jobs were out there, so he might have to apply for roles that were beneath head chef just to earn some money until a position he really wanted came along.

She did feel for him, though. It must have been hard giving up a prestigious position in a top London restaurant.

'I'm probably going to have to look further afield than Thornbury,' he told her.

Dulcie froze. 'How far?'

There was a timbre to his voice that she mightn't have picked up if it hadn't been for the darkness, and she sensed a tension in him that she hadn't noticed before tonight. She had a feeling there was something he wasn't telling her.

'Quite a bit further.' He shifted position so he was facing her.

'London,' she stated flatly, and suddenly everything was clear. He had been offered his old job back, and that was what the meeting with Alistair was about. Otto was moving back to London and was trying to find a way of letting her down gently.

'Um, maybe,' he said.

Before he could utter another word Dulcie sat up and swung her legs out of the bed, searching blindly for her slippers, tears close to the surface.

'Where are you going? We need to talk,' he said, his fingers brushing her hip as she stood up.

Hastily, she lifted her dressing gown off the hook on the back of the door and hurried out of the room. She could hear him coming after her as she headed for the stairs. Tears pricked her eyes, threatening to spill over, and she had a lump in her throat.

'Dulcie!' he called, pounding across the landing.

Otto caught her at the top of the stairs and gathered her to him. 'It's not what you think,' he began. 'Alistair—'

'Has offered you your old job back,' she finished, the tears welling over and trickling down her face.

'No, better than that. He's bought two more restaurants and wants me to run all three kitchens.'

He sounded more excited than she had ever heard him sound, and her heart turned to ice. *She had lost him.*

Too upset to speak, she backed away, moving out of his embrace, waiting for him to tell her it was over.

But what he said next, shocked her even more.

'I want you to come to London with me. Alistair has thrown in a flat as part of the deal, so we'll have somewhere to live, and you can work from anywhere, so you don't have to give up your job if you don't want to.'

She couldn't think straight. The only thing she could focus on was that he had asked her to go with him. He wasn't dumping her after all.

It was worse than that.

He wanted her to leave Picklewick; leave the new life she had embraced wholeheartedly; leave the farm she had fallen in love with and had big dreams for. Leave all this behind so he could follow his own dreams…

Could she do that? Give all this up to move to a city where she knew no one, apart from Otto?

Perhaps… But there was one thing preventing her from saying yes. 'If I say no, will you go back to London anyway?'

His hesitation told her everything she needed to know.

♥

Dulcie had read somewhere that true love was being able to let go, to release the person you love, to set them free. And that was what she would have to do.

Otto loved her, she didn't doubt that. And she loved him, totally and utterly. Which was why she was about to let him go, to set him free to follow his dream.

It would break her heart when he left – hell, it was broken already – but that momentary pause when she asked him whether he would stay, made her mind up, despite his protests that of course he wouldn't leave if she wouldn't go with him. She could hear in his voice and see in his eyes how badly he wanted this. The half-moon shining through the landing window and illuminating the hope on his face, showed her just *how much* he wanted it.

She wished she had closed the curtains, so the darkness hid his face the way it had done in her bedroom, but even if she had, she still would have heard the hunger in his voice.

There was no way she could live with herself if she stopped him from doing what he loved.

He mightn't have said it out loud, but that brief hesitation had told her that although he loved her, he didn't love her *enough*. It had entered his head that he would go whether she went with him or not, and that is why she had to end it now.

Was she being hypocritical in that she had also hesitated when he had asked her to leave Picklewick? Could he also apply the same reasoning to her?

Probably. Definitely…

Maybe *he* could accuse *her* of not loving him enough…

But she could see no way to make this work. He wanted to live in London. She didn't. Despite having lived in a big city all her life, she had become a country girl through and through. She would suffocate in London – when she had told Carla that she didn't miss the noise, the crowds, the traffic… she had meant it. The farm on Muddypuddle Lane had wormed its way under her skin and deep into her heart, and she loved living here. She didn't think she would be able to adjust to being in a city again.

Then there was Otto's job itself… Long, unsociable hours. No worse than for anyone else who worked shifts, she acknowledged, but without the farm to occupy her what would she do with all that time on her own? There was only so much shopping or going to the gym a girl could do.

Would she and Otto go the same way as Remi and Steff?

They would tell themselves they would make it work, and maybe they could, but she knew she would eventually grow to resent him taking her away from Picklewick.

But god, this *hurt*.

'Speak to me,' he urged. 'Say something.' He was waiting for her response to his insistence that he wouldn't go unless she went with him.

'I think you should take the job,' she said. His face lit up, but when she added, 'I won't be coming with you,' his expression crumpled.

Please don't cry, she urged silently. She didn't think she could stand it if he did. As it was, she was on the cusp of giving in and telling him she would follow him to the ends of the earth: if he broke down, she was positive she would make a decision she would regret later.

Set him free, let him fly, she reminded herself.

'This job is everything you've ever wanted. You *have* to take it. You owe it to yourself,' she said. 'You would be a fool to turn it down.'

'Nuh-uh.' He was shaking his head. 'I'm not going without you. If you don't want to move to London, I'll stay here. Something tasty is bound to turn up.'

'It won't be as tasty as this,' she pointed out, and she saw by the look on his face that he agreed with her, although he tried to hide it.

She took a deep breath and willed herself to stay strong. She was doing this for *him*, because she loved him, as she said, 'You may as well take it. I wasn't going to say anything tonight, but you've kind of forced my hand – I don't think we're right for each other. We've had a lot of fun, but…'

She left the rest of the sentence hanging. Not because she was being deliberately cruel, but because she didn't think she could hold herself together for much longer.

'You can't mean that?' The disbelief in his voice was evident. 'Please say you don't mean that.'

Dulcie cleared her throat, despair washing over her. 'I do.'

He was staring at her and the hurt in his eyes was too much to bear. So she stood to the side, and dropped her gaze to the floor, hoping her intention was clear: that she wanted him to leave.

But when he moved past her, she saw the glint of tears in his eyes and she almost relented.

It's for the best, she told herself.

The best for *him*, not for *her*.

Because she had just let the only man she would ever love walk out of her door and out of her life, and she didn't know how she was supposed to carry on without him.

♥

Don't cry, don't cry. As a mantra, it sucked, but thinking those four words over and over was better than thinking about all the other words that Dulcie had said tonight. Otto still couldn't take them in, especially the ones telling him that she didn't think they were right for each other. He refused to believe it. They were *perfect* for each other, and she knew it.

So how was it possible for her to have fallen out of love with him so quickly?

Or had she been leading him on when she had told him she loved him?

That was the more likely explanation… she hadn't loved him at all.

The pain in his heart was unbearable, and he didn't know what to do with himself. He didn't want to go to the cottage in case he woke Walter, because his dad would ask questions Otto didn't want to answer. He would have to tell his father soon that he and Dulcie had split up, but not tonight. There would be time enough tomorrow. The old man would be devastated. He thought the world of Dulcie.

He would also tell him about Alistair's offer, but he wasn't sure whether his father would encourage him to take it or not.

Otto headed up the hill, away from the cottage and the farm, aiming for the open moorland above. He needed to try to come to terms with what had happened, but he guessed it would take more than a walk in the fresh air to grasp the reality that he and Dulcie were over.

And all because of that damned offer.

If he hadn't told her about it, they would still be together.

Or would they?

Had she meant it when she had said they weren't right for each other anyway?

Gah, he was going over and over it in his head, his thoughts circling like water down the plughole. An endless supply of 'what if', and 'did she mean it'. He was going over the same ground again and again, and getting nowhere.

But he still wished he hadn't told her about the job.

He'd had to though, because how else would he have known whether she would have gone with him?

Although, if she was telling the truth (and why wouldn't she be?) Alistair's job had nothing to do with her decision to end their relationship, but he couldn't shift the suspicion that it did.

At least it made his decision easier. He could take the blasted job if he only had himself to please. His dad would understand – he knew that Otto lived for cooking. It was the opportunity of a lifetime and, as Dulcie rightly said, he would be a fool to turn it down.

He would have turned it down for her, though. Dulcie meant more to him than any job, no matter how sweet. He would have stayed in Picklewick and—

Otto slapped a hand to his forehead.

The sneaky madam! The unselfish, wonderful, thoughtful *madam*!

He knew what she was playing at, and it wouldn't work. But he also knew how stubborn she could be when she got an idea in her head – so he would just have to play her at her own game and convince her that he didn't want the damned job in the first place.

And he would be telling the truth – because without Dulcie by his side, the job was meaningless.

CHAPTER NINE

From her bedroom window Dulcie could just about see the chimney belonging to the cottage on Muddypuddle Lane. Although she couldn't see anything other than that of Walter's house, she didn't seem able to prevent herself from traipsing up the stairs every so often to peer through the glass.

She had been doing it all weekend, in a vain attempt to feel closer to Otto, but it was now Monday afternoon and she hadn't caught a single glimpse of him. Neither had there been any contact from him, although why she should expect any after telling him they were over was beyond her. Except… a part of her (the unreasonable part) wanted to think that he would have at least tried to fight for her. But then again, she reasoned, why fight for someone when they didn't love you as much as you hoped? He probably thought he was on a hiding to nothing, and he would be even more hurt than he was already.

Dulcie was about to turn away from the window and go do what she was paid to do, when she heard the rumble of an engine.

Her heart leapt and began to race, but it dropped like a stone to her boots when she saw Nikki's little hatchback turn into the farmyard.

She met her sister in the hall. 'Did you see Otto's car at the cottage?' she demanded before Nikki had a chance to say anything.

Her sister pursed her lips. 'No, sorry, it wasn't there.'

Dulcie felt like crying. Sick and heartbroken, she wondered whether Otto had left for London already.

'Have you eaten anything today?' Nikki asked, pushing past her and striding through the dining room and into the kitchen. 'I bet you haven't,' she said, as Dulcie followed behind. 'Let me make you something. You've got to eat.'

'I'm not hungry.'

'That's beside the point. You'll be ill if you don't. How about an omelette, or cheese on toast? Or you could come to mine for tea? We're having tuna pasta.'

Dulcie shuddered. The mention of food made her think of Otto, and her stomach churned. 'Do you think he's left yet?' she said.

'Dulcie…' Nikki warned. 'You've got to eat.'

'I'll have something later.'

'You'll have it *now*. I'm making you an omelette and you'd better eat it.' She began rummaging in the fridge.

Dulcie ignored her. 'Do you think I should check on Walter? He's bound to be upset, especially if Otto has left already.'

'He might not have done,' Nikki said. 'Just because his car's not there…'

'Who's looking after Sammy?' Dulcie asked, suddenly realising that Nikki must have driven straight to the farm as soon as she'd finished work.

'He's at an after-school club. I'm picking him up in an hour. I wanted to check you were okay first.'

Dulcie was not okay; she didn't think she'd be okay for a very long time indeed. 'Don't worry about me, I'm fine.'

'You aren't,' Nikki retorted, cracking three eggs into a bowl, whisking them vigorously, then pouring the mixture into a hot pan. 'Aside from the puffy eyes and the dark circles, I know you inside and out Dulcie Fairfax... and you're far from fine. And no, I don't think you should go see Walter – Otto might be there.' Nikki sent her a keen look. 'Or have you changed your mind about moving to London with him?'

'It's too late for that. Even if I have, I've blown it.'

'So, *have* you changed it?'

'It's all I've been able to think about. What if I've made the biggest mistake of my life?'

'Then it's up to you to try to unmake it.'

'What if I *can't*?'

'What if you *can*?' Nikki countered. 'Here, eat this.' She slid the omelette onto a plate and placed it in front of her.

The smell made Dulcie feel nauseous, but she knew she had to eat, and Nikki had gone to all that trouble to make her the food. With a distinct lack of enthusiasm, she picked up a fork and broke a small piece off. It was similar to how she imagined dry chicken pellets might taste, but she ploughed through it, Nikki hovering over her.

'I can't eat any more,' she said finally, pushing the remains of the half-eaten omelette away.

'Hmm.' Nikki inspected it. 'I suppose it's better than nothing. I've got to go – I need to pick Sammy up. Try to get some sleep tonight, yeah?'

'If you see Otto's car outside the cottage, will you message me?'

'I will,' Nikki promised. She gave Dulcie a hug.

Dulcie watched her leave, then went back to work. But her mind wasn't on her job. How could it be, when she had lost the love of her life through her own stupidity and selfishness?

♥

Otto threw his car keys onto the mantelpiece and slumped into a chair, exhausted. These past couple of days had been a whirlwind of activity.

'Well?' Walter demanded.

'They've got to run a few financial checks and obtain references, but it's looking good.'

He rubbed a weary hand across his face. He was so tired that he didn't know what to do with himself. That was what comes of being unable to sleep for three nights, he thought. But even if he hadn't had this madcap idea, he wouldn't have been able to sleep. Being heartbroken wasn't the best recipe for restful slumber. Add to that the thoughts swirling around his head at a hundred miles an hour, and he was unlikely to get much sleep tonight either.

'Are you sure this is what you want to do?' his dad asked.

'I'm sure.' Otto had never been more sure of anything in his life – aside from his love for Dulcie. He just hoped this wasn't in vain.

His dad voiced Otto's fear. 'What if she meant it when she said you two aren't right for each other?'

'I refuse to believe it. As I said, she's doing what she thinks is right for me. But what is right for me, is *Dulcie*.'

'Have you told Alistair of your decision?'

'Not yet. I'd better phone him now.' Otto heaved himself to his feet. This wasn't a conversation he was looking forward to. He hated letting his old boss down, but if he was to have any chance of winning Dulcie back, he had no choice.

'Alistair? It's Otto,' he said, when his former boss answered. 'I'm sorry but I won't be taking you up on your incredibly generous offer. It's a fantastic job for someone... just not for me. You see, Dulcie doesn't want to move to London and I'm not prepared to move without her. I'm staying here. I intend to open a restaurant in Picklewick instead.'

♥

Sod it, I've not got anything to lose, Dulcie thought. She couldn't face one more minute of this indecision. Five days was long enough. It was time to make her mind up one way or the other. She either had to let Otto go, or she had to tell him the truth about her feelings for him.

If he hadn't already gone...

Shoving her feet into her wellies, Dulcie stuffed her arms into her padded jacket and zipped it up, then grabbed a box of eggs. She would use it as an excuse to knock on Walter's door.

Ignoring the hopeful bleats from the barn (she had already fed the goats and Flossie), Dulcie trotted across the farmyard and down the lane, praying she wasn't too late. If Otto would just give her a chance to explain why she'd said what she had said, that was all she hoped.

She still didn't want to relocate to London, but being there with him was infinitely better than being here *without* him. She would soon get used to living in a city again; she had done it once so she could do it again. And in no time at all, she would look back on her time at the farm as nothing more than an extended holiday… although she would find it hard to see a stranger living there. Just as Otto had found it hard to see her occupying the house he had grown up in. He'd got used to it, though, and so would she.

To her immense disappointment, Otto's car wasn't parked in its usual spot outside the cottage, and she tried not to panic that she was too late. He could be anywhere: shopping, getting his hair cut, having his car serviced… *anywhere.*

But when she knocked on the door there was no answer, and after waiting a moment and knocking a second time with the same lack of response, she assumed that Walter wasn't in either.

The sound of an engine coming up the lane made her freeze, hope surging through her, but when she saw it was Petra's Land Rover, she sagged with disappointment. Amos was at the wheel, and she suddenly realised that she hadn't seen either man since she and Otto had split up. Work had stalled on the goats' shelter, and she guessed she was the reason. She didn't blame Walter for not wanting to help – why should he?

She supposed she would have to try to complete it herself. Walter must hate her for hurting his son; *if,* in fact, Otto was hurting as much as she. He might not

415

be – he might be so caught up in this new job of his that he hadn't given her a second thought.

Still, she couldn't get the look on his face out of her head when she'd told him they were over. He had looked broken.

Which was exactly how she felt.

She hadn't realised how much a broken heart could hurt, or how deep the pain.

Seeing Amos, Dulcie leapt at the opportunity to pick his brains, and she flagged him down. 'Do you know if Walter is okay? I can't get any answer.' She would hate for him to have a relapse.

'I saw him yesterday and he was fine. Sorry to hear about you and Otto.'

Not as sorry as Dulcie was – and it was all her own fault. She hated herself for asking, but she simply had to know. 'Has Otto gone back to London yet?'

Amos blinked. 'I didn't know he *was* going back. I thought—'

The door to the cottage opened abruptly, and Walter cried, 'Dulcie! I thought there was someone at the door. How lovely!'

Dulcie turned around to see him on his doorstep. He beckoned her closer.

'I've brought you some eggs,' she said, handing them to him. 'And I wanted to see how you are coping now that Otto has gone back to London.'

'He hasn't left yet. There's no rush,' Walter said. He didn't sound as upset as she thought he would be, and she was glad. He also knew that Otto's heart lay elsewhere, and he had accepted it a long time ago. She knew how incredibly proud he was of his son, and she also knew that he wouldn't want to hold him back from what he loved doing.

Neither did she… which was why she was here.

'Shall I tell him you called?' Walter asked.

Dulcie bit her lip. 'Yes, please.'

'I would ask you in, but I don't know when he'll be back. He's…er…got a bit of business to attend to, and I was in the middle of…' He trailed off.

'It's okay.' She fully appreciated how awkward this must be for him, but at least he was still speaking to her – she wouldn't have blamed him if he hadn't been. After all, she had dumped his son.

Feeling defeated, she gave him a sad little smile as she said goodbye, and went home.

She would just have to try to catch Otto later.

'Have you signed on the dotted line?' Walter asked as soon as Otto switched the engine off and got out of the car. His dad had been peering through the living room window and had hurried out to greet him.

'Give me a chance,' Otto said, smiling. 'Can we go inside first?'

'Dulcie was here earlier.'

Otto froze. 'What did she want?'

'She gave me some eggs, but I don't think that was the real reason. I wasn't going to answer the door because I was worried that I might give the game away, but by sheer bad luck Amos came up the lane at that very moment. I had to head him off at the pass, before he said something he shouldn't.'

'Did she suspect anything?'

'I don't think so, but you can't afford to hang about. Word will soon get around that you've taken the lease out on the old bric-a-brac shop, and she'll get to hear about it before long.'

'I want her to hear it from me first,' Otto said. He would have told her sooner, but he had been waiting for the contract to be signed and to have the keys in his hand. Should he go up to the farm and tell her now?

Suddenly his eyes widened. He had an idea!

'How do you feel about a bit of subterfuge?' Otto asked his father. 'It's in a good cause…'

♥

Dulcie had trotted halfway down the lane a couple of times since speaking to Walter earlier in the day, in the hope of seeing Otto's car outside the cottage, but to no avail. He was still out.

Business, Walter had said, and as she popped a couple of slices of bread into the toaster, she wondered what kind of business.

Her appetite was still poor and she still didn't feel like eating, but after Nikki had practically force-fed food down her neck, Dulcie had promised her sister that she would take better care of herself and would eat a substantial meal each evening. Hoping beans on toast counted, she took a tin out of the cupboard, but before she could open it, her phone rang.

'Walter? Is everything okay?'

'Um, not really. I'm in a bit of a pickle. I hate to ask, but Otto isn't back yet, so…'

'Ask what? What do you need?'

'Can you take me to the chemist? I forgot to get my prescription filled and if I don't take my tablets…'

He left another sentence hanging, and a shiver of alarm travelled down Dulcie's spine.

Walter didn't sound good. He sounded more like the frail old man she had met when she had first moved to Picklewick, and she prayed he wasn't having a relapse. He had been doing so well; just this morning he had looked hale and hearty, but now he sounded ill and old.

And there was something else that worried her. 'Walter,' she said gently, 'it's half-past six. The chemist won't be open.'

'It will. They don't shut until seven tonight. It's to do with the doctor's surgery having evening appointments.'

'Ah, I see. I'll be there in five minutes.'

Her concern that he was starting to become confused was alleviated by knowing that the chemist was open late, but as she set off down the lane, she continued to worry how he would cope without Otto around.

Walter didn't look as bad as she feared, she saw with relief, as she jumped out of the car and raced to open the passenger door for him. He had been waiting on the step, and he got in with a groan.

She asked, 'Are you okay?'

'Aye, can't grumble. Thanks for this, Dulcie. I really appreciate it.'

'Have you got your prescription?'

He smiled and patted his jacket pocket. 'I'm not senile yet.'

'I didn't say you were.'

They reached the end of Muddypuddle Lane, and she checked for oncoming traffic, then pulled out onto the road. It was a two-minute drive from here to get to the middle of the high street at this time of the evening, so she resisted the urge to put her foot down. As long as Walter made it to the chemist before they closed, they would hardly turn him away, even if it did take a few minutes to fill the prescription.

'Stop here!' Walter commanded, and Dulcie pulled into the kerb without thinking, before realising that the chemist was at the far end of the street.

'Um,' she began, but the old man was already getting out.

She leant across the passenger seat. 'Walter, it's not here, it's down there.' She pointed down the street.

'I think you'll find it *is* here,' he said, and he shut the car door firmly.

Worriedly, she scrambled out after him. 'Walter!'

Oh, dear, he was heading for an empty shop and trying the handle.

'Walter! That's not the chem—' Dulcie stopped.

The empty shop wasn't as empty as she first thought. There was a table in the middle of it, surrounded by lit candles on the floor, and a man standing next to it.

'Otto?' Confused, she turned to Walter. He was smirking.

'Thanks, Dad,' Otto said.

'Shall I wait up?'

Otto rolled his eyes. 'Just go.'

'Good luck, son. See you later, Dulcie. Much later, I hope.' And with that the old man was gone, the door shutting behind him with a click.

Silence reigned for a moment. Dulcie was too shocked and confused to speak, and Otto seemed at a loss for words.

Eventually he asked, 'Are you hungry?'

Mutely, she shook her head.

'Me, neither. Never mind, the food will keep.'

Dulcie found her voice. 'What food? What's going on, Otto?'

'I've got wine, if you fancy a glass.'

She thought she'd better had – a drink might help with the thudding in her chest and the pulse throbbing at her temple.

He popped the cork on a bottle of red, and poured the rich dark liquid into two crystal glasses which were sitting on the table. The table itself was covered by a white cloth and laid with cutlery.

He held one of the glasses out to her and she stepped closer to take it from him.

'What's going on?' she repeated. 'Why is there a table and candles? I don't understand.'

'Welcome to The Wild Side,' he said.

Dulcie stared blankly at him. Was Walter's confusion contagious? 'I was supposed to be taking your dad to get his prescription filled.'

'Yeah, sorry about the subterfuge, but I had to get you down here somehow.'

'*Why?*'

'Can I ask you a question first? Please? Then I'll tell you everything.'

'Okaaay.'

'Did you mean it when you said you don't think we are right for each other?'

Dulcie caught her bottom lip between her teeth, hesitated, then muttered, 'No.'

'So why did you say it?'

'That's two questions.'

'Humour me?'

'Because you wouldn't have taken the job otherwise.' She might as well be honest with him – she had planned to beg him to take her back, to take her to London with him, so…

He let out a long slow breath. 'I thought as much.'

'You did?'

'I'm not taking it.'

Dulcie frowned. 'But, I thought—'

'That it's my dream job?' he interrupted.

She nodded.

'It is, but I have another dream which means far more to me. I have a dream that we will marry and have kids, that we'll have a long and happy life, and that we will grow old together. And if that means staying in Picklewick, then I'll stay in Picklewick.'

Those were the most beautiful words she had ever heard. Gulping back tears, Dulcie said, 'You don't have to. I'll go to London with you. Heck, I'll go with you to the ends of the earth, if I have to. I'm so sorry I hurt you.'

He took the glass out of her hand and placed it on the table. '*I'm* not,' he said. 'It's made me realise what I truly want – and I want *you*.'

And with that he took her in his arms, his eyes so full of love it made her cry even harder, and he gently kissed her tears away. Then his mouth found hers and she clung to him so fiercely she thought she might never let him go.

♥

'Why this elaborate set-up?' Dulcie asked later. They were sitting at the table laid for two and drinking the wine.

'Because I needed to convince you that I was serious about not taking the job with Alistair.'

'I don't follow. Why here? You could have just come to the farm and told me.'

'How was I to know you had changed your mind about coming with me to London? I believed you still thought you were stepping back so I would take the job.'

'Yes, but why *here*, in this old shop? If you didn't want to discuss it at the farm, you could have taken me to a restaurant and wined and dined…' She slowed to a halt as something he said earlier leapt into her mind. 'Is this what I *think* it is? Are you planning on opening your own restaurant?' Her voice rose an octave on the last word.

'I am. Do you mind?' Worry flitted across his face.

'Of course I don't mind! That's brilliant news.'

'It'll mean long hours setting it up, and equally long hours to establish a good reputation.'

'I don't care – you'll be doing what you love, what you were born to do.'

'But we won't see as much of each other as we're used to,' he said, regretfully. 'If I had my way I would spend every waking second with you.'

Dulcie giggled. 'Actually, I've been thinking about that. There is something I've been wanting to ask you, and it would mean that we would see each other every morning and every night. I'd like us to live together on the farm. What do you think?'

Otto looked stunned. His mouth dropped open and his eyes widened: then the biggest grin spread across his face. 'I think it is the best idea you had since buying that lottery ticket!'

And when Otto swept her into his arms again, she knew that the spark of love he had ignited in her heart all those months ago would never be extinguished.

♥

There was no way the restaurant would be open in time for Christmas, Otto knew, but that didn't stop him from planning on working flat out to get it ready to open as soon as possible in the New Year.

'Are you sure you don't mind helping?' he asked Dulcie, for what was possibly the fifth time that morning. He thought she might have wanted to spend the weekend relaxing – she did work five days a week, and this last week had been pretty fraught – but she had thrown herself into the renovations with enthusiasm. Luckily the front of house area didn't need a great deal of work, not compared to what would eventually be the kitchen. Then there was the walk-in fridge to sort out, and customer toilets to install.

Otto guestimated that the work would take at least two months, and that's if there weren't any unforeseen delays, which he sincerely hoped there wouldn't as his budget was severely stretched as it was. He was having great fun designing the place though, and he had pulled together a list of things he liked about other restaurants, as well as the things he didn't, and he had made a mood board to work from.

Meanwhile, Dulcie was researching setting up a website with an online booking system, and he was very grateful for her help because it was the admin side of the restaurant business that had put him off opening his own in the first place.

He still wasn't sure he was doing the right thing, although he was seriously looking forward to getting back into a kitchen again.

It was while he was standing in what would eventually become the kitchen, and planning out where each piece of equipment would go, that he received the first of two important phone calls of the day.

Dulcie was stripping layers of old paint off the wall in the main part of the restaurant, but she downed tools so he could hear himself speak.

'Hi, Yvette.' He was surprised to hear from his agent, having practically forgotten about his cookbook in the events of the last two weeks.

Yvette said, 'I've got some brilliant news. At least three publishers are interested – I'll email you the details of the contracts on offer, and when you've had a chance to read through them, give me a call and we'll have a chat about it.'

'*Three?* Did I hear you correctly?'

'You did. I must admit, I wasn't expecting that, but word of your new restaurant has got out. Just wait until it gains a Michelin star of its own! Publishers will be falling over you to offer you a contract on the next book.'

'The next book,' he repeated woodenly. He doubted there would be a next one, and after the call ended, he said as much to Dulcie.

'Nonsense! If this sells as well as I believe it will, you'll *have* to write another. You can try the recipes out on your diners.'

The next call was just as surprising.

It was from Alistair.

Otto got in first. 'Do I have you to thank for spreading the word about The Wild Side?' he asked, after he had told Alistair his publishing news. The man knew more people than the devil, and most of them had dined in The Fern at some point.

'I may have whispered in an ear or two,' Alistair admitted. 'But that's not why I'm calling. I still want you to be my Menu Director.'

Otto's good mood dipped. What was Alistair playing at? 'You know I can't.'

'You *can*,' Alistair insisted. 'You can work out of your own kitchen, and I'll send my chefs to you to be trained. Once a month you can pop down to London to quality-assure the dishes. It's a win-win situation for both of us.'

'It'll be bloody hard work for me.'

'It'll be bloody *lucrative* for you,' Alistair countered. 'And it'll put your name and that of your restaurant firmly on the map.'

Otto looked at Dulcie.

She was beaming at him and holding both thumbs up. 'Go for it,' she mouthed. 'You'll regret it if you don't.'

He knew she was right.

So he said yes. Just as he hoped she would say yes when he asked her to marry him.

Not now, but soon… They had a restaurant to open first, and a farm to run.

Never had Otto been so busy, and never had he been as happy; and when Dulcie threw herself into his arms, demanding kisses, he vowed that no matter how busy or how frantic life became he would always,

always put this wonderful woman first, because her love was the only thing that truly mattered.

CHRISTMAS KISSES

CHAPTER ONE

Eliza York stood to one side as the cabbie lifted her bags from the boot of the taxi and placed them on the ground next to her feet. The ground in question was a rough, asphalt carpark whose surface glistened from the sleety rain falling from a dark, misty sky. She paid him, adding a generous tip, then looked around, pulling her jacket closer as he drove away.

Abruptly she felt very alone. She was in the middle of nowhere, in a strange country, and there wasn't a soul in sight. However, lights shone from the windows of a house beyond the carpark and more lights illuminated a stable yard, so she shook off the feeling and took a deep breath. She hadn't come all this way to let second thoughts get the better of her.

As per the instructions that had been emailed to her by the owner when she'd booked the holiday cottage, Eliza headed for the house, hitching her carry-on over her shoulder and pulling her wheeled case.

Mist swirled around her, and the silence was unnerving as she hurried towards civilisation and the place she would call home for the next two weeks. But as she picked her way along the path, she was forced to wonder whether two weeks was going to be too long.

From what she had seen of Picklewick as the taxi had sped through it, there didn't appear to be much there to maintain her interest. But then again, it was ten-thirty at night, so a little English village was hardly going to be humming with activity, and she *had* spotted a pub that seemed to still be open, so she had a smidgeon of hope that there would be something to do in the evenings.

In hindsight, maybe she should have hired a car – at least she would have been able to travel around a bit – but she'd had the romantic idea that she would see more of the local area if she used public transport. However, she had swiftly changed her mind when she'd got off the train in Thornbury earlier and was informed that the last bus to Picklewick had left over two hours ago. Her journey had been going so well up to then…

Meh, she thought as she trundled her case across the cobbled stable yard; she was just tired and fed up with travelling – she would undoubtedly feel more upbeat tomorrow.

It was a shame she didn't have anyone to enjoy this trip with, but neither her mother nor her sister had wanted to come, and Eliza no longer had a significant other. It was the latter that had been responsible for her impulsive purchase of a plane ticket to the UK, together with a promise that she had made to herself after Dad died. She had originally harboured the hope that she and Archer would make the trip together, but he had decided to bugger off to Australia instead, to work on a sheep farm of all places. As if there weren't enough of the blighters in New Zealand!

When it came to men, she couldn't half pick 'em. After her disastrous marriage to Larry, she swore she would never look at another man again. Then along came Archer and she'd forgotten all about the promise she had made to herself.

Huh, she wouldn't be making *that* mistake again.

As she approached the farmhouse, she was about to knock when she heard a dog bark and the door flew open.

A woman, whom Eliza estimated to be in her early thirties, smiled warmly at her. 'You must be Eliza. Hi, I'm Petra. Come in. Would you like a cup of tea? Coffee? How was your journey?'

A black spaniel darted out from between the woman's legs, its tail wagging furiously, and Eliza bent to ruffle its ears.

'Sorry, Queenie thinks everyone loves her,' Petra said, clicking her fingers. The dog slunk back to its mistress.

'That's okay, I like dogs. Er, yeah, I'm Eliza. Nothing for me, thanks. I just want to settle in, have a shower and get my head down.' She had been travelling for nearly forty-eight hours, and although she had managed to get some sleep on the plane, she was buggered.

'Of course. I'll take you to your cottage. There's a couple staying in the one next to yours, but they'll be gone tomorrow and I haven't got anyone booked in until after the New Year, so if you start to feel a little isolated, feel free to pop up to the house. There's always someone around.' Petra reached for a key sitting on a chunky hall table and picked up a torch.

Eliza gazed at it doubtfully, and Petra noticed her concern. 'Don't worry, there are torches in the cottage if you need them, and there's a welcome pack, too. I've popped in some extra bits and pieces, seeing as you'll be staying over Christmas.'

'Thanks, that's very kind of you.' Eliza hoped milk and tea bags were included, because she couldn't get going without a cup of tea in the morning and she wasn't sure how far it was to the nearest shop. According to her research, it was less than two kilometres, but she wanted to get her bearings first before she ventured further than the immediate vicinity of the cottage.

Petra led Eliza back the way she had just come, but turned off down a little track before they reached the carpark, saying, 'If you want to move your car in the morning, the cottages have their own parking area and it'll save you trekking up to the stables whenever you want to go out.'

'I haven't got a car, but maybe I should think about hiring one? I took a taxi from the train station.'

The woman wrinkled her nose. 'No worries, you can get to Picklewick easily on foot. But if you did want to explore more of the local area, a car would come in handy. At least we drive on the same side of the road as you,' Petra added with a laugh. 'I bet the weather here is a bit different though.'

'You can say that again!' Eliza's reply was heartfelt. She had swapped a balmy New Zealand summer for a freezing English winter, and she wished she was wearing more layers.

As they rounded a corner, a row of three cottages emerged out of the mist. Petra halted outside the middle one and unlocked the door, indicating for Eliza to go first.

A lamp was shining inside, and Eliza stepped into a cosy lounge and gazed around in delight. It was small (she had been expecting that) but a first glance it seemed to have everything she would need. There was a fireplace with a log burner that was kicking out a lovely amount of heat, and there were even Christmas decorations and a sparkly tree in the corner. It all looked very festive, and Eliza suddenly felt homesick. She would be spending this Christmas without seeing her family, and once again she wondered whether she had made the right decision in coming all this way.

Petra was saying, 'There's a booklet in the kitchen with information on the local area, plus my mobile number – although I must warn you that the mobile signal here is dire. If you need anything, it might be easier if you just pop up to the stables.' She handed Eliza the key. 'I hope you enjoy your stay.'

'I'm sure I will.'

Eliza waited for the woman to leave, then she wearily eased the bag off her shoulder.

Knowing that she would be arriving quite late, she had packed a pair of pyjamas in her carry-on, as well as a few toiletries, which meant she could hit the sack without having to unpack her suitcase.

But before she went upstairs, she had a quick look in the kitchen and was touched to find that the fridge contained milk, butter, cheese, and a bottle of Devil's Creek Sauvignon Blanc. Providing her with a taste of home was incredibly thoughtful, and she looked forward to having a glass. A wicker hamper on the countertop held chocolates, a box of mince pies that appeared to be homemade, tea, coffee, bread, jam, and a few other bits and pieces that she was too tired to examine right now.

Yawning hugely, Eliza fished her night things out of her bag and went upstairs, to fall asleep seconds after her head hit the very comfy pillow.

♥

Jay Fairfax peered out at the drizzly night through his sister's living room window and said, 'I hope it will clear up by tomorrow.'

'Snowflake,' Dulcie teased. 'I assumed you would be used to rain, what with spending all your time in a rainforest.'

'Yeah, a *warm* rainforest.' As Jay returned to the sofa and sat down, he continued, 'I don't mind the cold and I don't mind the wet, but not the two together.'

'How about snow?' Dulcie asked. 'It's forecast for later in the week. We might even have a white Christmas.'

Maisie squealed and clapped her hands, and Jay winced. At twenty-five, she was the youngest of his three sisters, and she acted it, too. Jay had forgotten how childlike she could be. Well, he would, wouldn't he, considering he only came back to the UK once or twice a year, so he hardly ever saw her. Although, that might be about to change. If he didn't get another contract, he would be staying in the UK for a while, and that meant moving back in with his mum and Maisie, in the family home in Birmingham.

Dulcie pulled a face. 'I hope it holds off until Thursday because I'm having goats delivered on Wednesday.'

'It's amazing what you can buy on the internet,' their mother said, and Jay raised his eyebrows.

'Please tell me Mum is joking,' he pleaded.

Dulcie laughed. 'I suppose I *could* have bought them online, but I wanted to see them first. The breeder has confirmed that they're all in kid, so in a few months there'll be lots of baby goats running around.'

'I love goats!' Maisie cried. Her expression became dreamy. 'Can I help with them when they have their babies?'

'Maybe – *if* you've not found another job by then,' Dulcie said, and Maisie pulled a face.

Jay caught the look Dulcie gave her, and he guessed the reason. Maisie was notorious for the number of jobs she'd had since leaving school. He had lost track. Whenever he spoke to his mum on the phone, Maisie had either just walked out of a job because it 'wasn't for her,' or she had been 'let go'. He was totally in favour of people trying different careers until they found one that inspired them, but all Maisie did was flit from job to job, sticking at none.

She was nothing like him or her sisters, or Mum for that matter, and if it wasn't for the fact that she had the Fairfax eyes, he might have thought Maisie was adopted.

'Are you going to breed goats?' he asked Dulcie. She was turning into a proper farmer.

'I'll have to see how I get on first. I'm hoping to make soap and other lotions from their milk. And

Otto will also use the milk in the restaurant once we get the pasteurisation shed up and running.'

'I can't wait to have a look around this farm of yours,' he said. It had been dark when he'd arrived, the December day having already turned to dreary evening, so he hadn't had a chance to see it yet.

Jay was delighted that his middle sister was doing so well for herself. Not only had she won the farm in some kind of lottery (how had she managed *that!?*) she was also in love with a man who could cook so incredibly well that he had earned himself a Michelin star.

Otto had made the family a fabulous meal this evening, and was now poring over a laptop and scribbling notes on a pad. The fella was opening his own restaurant in Picklewick shortly, and according to Dulcie, he was working flat-out all day every day to get it ready for early January.

During dinner, Dulcie had made Otto promise to take some time off over Christmas, and Jay had seen the reluctance in the man's eyes when he'd agreed. Otto was clearly driven, and Jay hoped his restaurant would be successful. If his cooking tonight was any indication, it should do very well indeed.

'And I can't wait to show you around,' Dulcie said, pride evident in her voice.

From what he had seen so far, which was only the inside of the house, Jay was impressed. Dulcie had worked hard to make it look nice, and although the farmhouse wasn't modern, it was rustic and cosy. She had painted the plastered walls white, but had left the exposed stone ones as they were. There were thick rugs on the flagstones downstairs and the floorboards upstairs, fires burned in the dining room and the living room, and the place was festively decorated to within an inch of its life.

Dulcie had a large (very large) Christmas tree in the living room, and a smaller one in the dining room, and he had even found a miniature tree in his bedroom. Then there were the garlands, the bunting, the candles, the… He could go on, but there was just so much. Still, it was very festive and she had gone to a great deal of trouble, which he appreciated. He was looking forward to spending Christmas with his family. Good food, plenty of alcohol, slobbing about in his scruffs, and perhaps a party game or two whilst watching a cheesy film on the telly… for Jay, that's what Christmas was all about.

Plus seeing his old mates, of course.

But this year would be different.

In the past, he had always stayed with their mum, sleeping in the little box room that used to be his bedroom when he was a child. For the first few years after he had begun working abroad, visits home had invariably involved catching up with his old mates. But lately, those boozy blokey sessions had become fewer as, one by one, the lads who he had gone to school and college with, had settled down. He still saw them occasionally whenever he came back to the UK, but he was more likely to be invited to a dinner party with their wives or partners, than go for a fun night out in a bar or a club. And over this past year, it seemed as though everyone else had raced ahead relationship-wise, leaving him in the starting blocks.

He wasn't sure whether he envied them, or whether he had dodged a bullet.

He felt a tad envious seeing his sisters so loved up and happy, and a part of him wanted what they had.

But was that just FOMO, or did he genuinely want to fall in love and settle down?

He supposed he might find out, now that his contract had ended and it looked as though he would be staying in the UK for a while until he landed another. He wasn't sure how long he could take living with his mum and little sister though, so the sooner he found another job, the better.

Dulcie, sounding remarkably like Maisie, brought him out of his reverie when she cried, 'Ooh, this is going to be the best Christmas ever!'

Jay seconded that. He also had a feeling it was going to be a Christmas to remember.

♥

Eliza slept for a full eleven hours, and when she woke she felt considerably more refreshed than she had expected. No doubt jet lag would kick in later, but for now she was keen to explore.

Eager to see what the weather was doing, she peeped through the curtains and was delighted to discover that yesterday's mist had lifted and the rain had stopped. The view from the bedroom window across the valley was stunning. Despite it being the middle of winter and most of the trees being bare, the overwhelming colour was green, and it was easy to imagine how lush the place would be in summer. Her dad hadn't been exaggerating when he'd told her how verdant and vibrant his homeland was.

A pang shot through her as Eliza thought of her father, and she wondered how much longer it would be before she could think of him without feeling as though she was being stabbed in the heart. He had died two years ago, but it felt like it was only yesterday when she'd had that awful phone call.

She wished she had been able to persuade her mum to come with her to the UK (it might have helped Mum with her crushing grief if she could see where Dad had lived before he'd emigrated) but she claimed she couldn't face such a long journey. Neither had she been too enamoured of Eliza's desire to fly halfway around the world alone, and had tried to talk her out of it, but Eliza had been adamant. If she didn't do it now, she probably never would. Plus, she had an uncle she had never met and at least one cousin in Picklewick, so if she could track them down she wouldn't be on her own, would she?

Eliza popped downstairs to grab her case and took it back to the bedroom, where she unpacked and dressed hastily, then she made herself some breakfast.

After a sterling meal of eggs, toast, butter and jam, washed down with two cups of tea brewed in an old-fashioned teapot with a cute horsey themed tea cosy, Eliza was ready to go exploring.

Donning a pair of sturdy boots, bought especially for the trip, and putting on a thick padded jacket with a hood, she wound a scarf around her neck, plonked a bobble hat on her head and was ready to go.

She decided she would start by walking up the lane first and see how close she could get to the farm where her dad had grown up. It irked her that she had been unable to discover who lived there now, and she wondered whether it was still in the family. Her dad's brother, Walter, had lived there up until a couple of years ago – she knew because Dad used to send a Christmas card every year – but for the past two

Christmases, especially the first one without Dad, no one had felt like sending cards. For Eliza, her sister, and mum, the festive season had been a very low-key and subdued affair.

Although she was tempted to knock on the door and introduce herself, Eliza didn't feel entirely comfortable with that, so she elected to take a brisk walk-by instead. Maybe she would pop into the stables on the way back and ask for directions to Picklewick: and at the same time, she could subtly enquire whether Walter still lived there.

At the last second, Eliza dashed back inside to grab her little sketch pad, the one that fitted in her pocket, and her pencil set. One never knew when the mood might strike!

♥

'What time do you call this?' Beth demanded as Jay staggered down the stairs and into the kitchen.

It always amazed him how sitting in an aeroplane could wear him out so much. He was knackered, as usual, and he knew it would take him a couple of days to get over the jet lag.

'Morning, Mum,' he greeted her, rather tongue-in-cheek considering it was almost noon.

'Only just. Dulcie has been up for hours. Even our Maisie managed to get up at a reasonable time.'

He scratched his beard and wished she would at least give him time to wake up properly before she started nagging. He set about making a coffee, using the flashy machine in the corner. It was a smart piece of kit and looked out of place in Dulcie's very rustic kitchen.

'Where is everyone?' he wondered.

'Dulcie and Maisie have gone into Picklewick, and Otto is at the restaurant.'

'Why didn't you go with them?' he asked, thinking that if she had, he might have had five minutes peace to get his head together.

'I wanted to see you. You're not home often.'

Drat, now he felt awful. Mum was right, though… he *hadn't* visited the UK very often these past few years, and she must miss him. He missed her too, but he had become so used to answering to no one (apart from his boss) that it was always a shock to find himself under his mother's beady and inquisitive eye.

Feeling incredibly guilty, he walked over to her and gave her a hug. She hugged him back fiercely, and he hoped she wasn't about to cry. He hated seeing her upset, and every time he left she would shed a few tears. It made him feel bad for days; but what could he do? His job used to take him to far-flung places, and he had loved his job. He hadn't told her that he might be home for a while, in case he landed another contract in yet another far-flung country, as he didn't want to get her hopes up only to dash them again. Thankfully she hadn't yet twigged that he had more luggage than usual, because it wasn't a great deal more as he didn't own a lot, having learnt that it was easier if he didn't have to haul too much around every time he was relocated.

'Tea?' he asked, and his mum nodded. He made her a cup while his coffee brewed, then sat down at the table with her. 'Do you fancy showing me around the farm?' he asked, taking a gulp of the hot liquid.

'Not on your nelly! It's bitter out there. If you're that desperate to see it, you can go on your own. Otherwise, you'll have to wait for Dulcie to come back.'

Now that he had some caffeine in his system, Jay was starting to get restless. He wasn't used to sitting on his backside for long periods, so he decided to take a stroll and stretch his legs. He'd go up the hill aways – the tarmacked lane petering out beyond the farmyard and becoming a dirt track – and take in the view. Dulcie would probably want to show him around the actual farm herself, but he was sure she wouldn't mind if he hiked up the mountain a bit. The fresh air would do him good.

Leaving his mum with a crossword book and the telly, he dressed warmly and headed outside.

In direct contrast to yesterday, today was crisp and bright, with a weak yellow sun hanging in a pale blue sky.

Jay shivered. He wasn't used to such low temperatures and he wondered whether Dulcie was right when she'd said it would snow later in the week. He hadn't seen snow for a long time, and he felt almost as excited as Maisie – although he would never let on.

His boots ate up the ground as he made his way up the steep hill and onto the moorland above. The air was fresh, and he filled his lungs, marvelling at the crisp clean smell. It was quiet up here, too. The only noise was the wind sighing through the brown bracken and the savage call of a buzzard overhead. There weren't any insects either, and for that he was truly grateful. Buzzy flying things found him irresistible, and they irritated the hell out of him.

The hill above the farm wasn't particularly high, but the mountain seemed to roll ever upwards until he despaired of reaching the top, so when he spotted the remains of an old stone building in the distance, he gave up his quest for the top and walked towards that instead.

As it grew closer, he was able to make out that it had probably been an old farmhouse or a shepherd's hut. It was quite small, but it did have a chimney on the outside although the roof had long since gone, and he guessed it might have been rather cosy once.

The ruined, moss-covered walls looked safe enough, so he decided to go inside.

Treading carefully, he was gazing up to admire the craftsmanship that went into the stonework above the doorway, and didn't see the figure perched on a pile of rubble in the corner until it cleared its throat.

Jay let out a yell, staggered back and nearly fell.

It took him a moment to regain his balance and his equilibrium, and when he did, he realised several things simultaneously. The figure who was perched on a pile of mossy rubble was female, around his age, and very pretty.

'Sorry, I... um... didn't realise anyone would be in here,' he stuttered.

The woman gazed at him, her dark eyes inscrutable, and he wondered whether he should leave, but then she spoke.

'Am I trespassing?'

Jay thought for a second, and he recalled Dulcie saying that the land above the fields was common grazing. 'I don't believe so,' he replied, trying to get a fix on her accent.

She had only spoken three words, but he could have sworn there was a definite Antipodean twang to them. He had met loads of Kiwis and Aussies over the years, so he was fairly certain she was from that part of the world.

His gaze dropped from her face to her hands, and he saw she had a pad balanced on her knees and was holding a pencil.

'Sketching?' he hazarded a guess, scanning her face again. She had a golden tan, large eyes and plump lips that begged to be kissed. A mass of dark hair poked out from underneath a red bobble hat, fanning out over her shoulders. Long legs encased in faded jeans and ending in a pair of chunky black boots, completed the picture. God, she was cute; sexy, too, as she caught her bottom lip between her teeth.

Embarrassed to be having such thoughts and hoping they didn't show on his face, he cleared his throat.

'Yeah, I'm an artist,' she said with a shrug. From her expression he got the feeling she hadn't wanted to admit it, and he wondered if he was making her feel awkward. He was acutely aware that she was a lone female in the middle of nowhere and that she might be concerned about his presence. Perhaps he should leave and let her get on with it, but he didn't want to go, not just yet.

Trying to put her at ease, he said, 'Cool. Watercolour?'

'Mostly, but I dabble in all kinds. Whatever takes my fancy at the time.' Her eyes left him and she scanned the walls. 'Watercolour for this, I think. I love the way the stones fit together and how moss and ferns grow between the cracks. How old is it, do you know?'

Okay, so she wasn't wholly *uncomfortable* in his presence if she wanted to keep talking. He looked around and took an educated guess. 'Early last century, maybe older. Possibly nineteenth. Well over a hundred years old, I should think.'

'Crikey, I'm surprised there's anything left of it.'

'We've got way older buildings than this in the UK,' he teased.

'It's that obvious, huh?'

'That you're not from these parts? A bit. Australia?'

'New Zealand.'

'Whereabouts?'

'You won't know it – Ruakaka? It's about a hundred and thirty kilometres north of Aukland?'

He liked the way her voice lifted at the end of each sentence, so it sounded like a question. It was a common trait amongst Kiwis, and he found it endearing. On *her*, that is: not so much on his former colleagues who had all happened to be guys. He hadn't found them endearing at all.

'Have you been in the UK long?' he asked.

'I arrived last night.'

He blinked in surprise. Just a day in the country and she'd already found her way to Picklewick? He guessed she must have family or friends in the village. 'I take it you flew into Heathrow? Weren't you tempted to explore London, see the sights?'

'No, I don't like cities much. Too many people. This,' she gestured around her, 'is more my scene. I like nature.'

'So do I.' Jay beamed at her. 'I'm Jay, by the way.'

'Eliza. Nice to meet you.' She glanced down at the drawing pad and Jay took the hint.

'I'll, er, leave you to it. Nice meeting you.'

'You, too.'

He turned on his heel, but before he left, he said over his shoulder, 'Maybe I'll see you around?'

Her smile seemed genuine. 'Maybe…'

Guessing he probably wouldn't see her again, he gave her one last look, then left. But out of sight didn't mean out of mind, and she stayed in his head all the way back to the farm and then some.

CHAPTER TWO

Eliza watched the guy walk away and kept her eyes on him until he was out of sight. He'd seemed harmless enough, but he had given her a scare when he'd appeared in the doorway, and suddenly she had been acutely aware that she was on her own on this mountain and not a soul in the world knew she was here.

'Stupid, Eliza, really stupid,' she muttered, taking her mobile out of her pocket. Relieved to discover that she had a signal (Petra had been right about the coverage being patchy), Eliza pinged off a quick message to her mum and sister on the group chat to let them know she had arrived safe and sound, and that she was planning to explore the local area today. She also attached a photo of the sketch she'd just done, in the vain hope that one or the other of them might be interested.

Getting stiffly to her feet (it was too cold to be sitting on blocks of stone and she had begun to seize up), Eliza took a final look at the ruins, then retraced her steps down the hill, keeping a close eye out for Jay. The guy had seemed nice enough, but she didn't particularly want to bump into him again when she was on her own on a bleak hillside.

He was rather cute though, although cute was probably not the best way to describe him. Sexy was better, but sexy had got her into trouble in the past. Archer had been sexy. He had been a charmer, too. She had a feeling this fella might be equally as charming, so if she did happen to see him again, she would make sure to keep her distance.

There was one thing she was kicking herself for though, and that was not asking him about Lilac Tree Farm. As a local, he might have known whether Walter still lived there. Despite her internet digging, she'd not been able to determine whether or not her uncle still owned the place. Or whether he was even alive. Dad had been younger than him, and Dad had been dead for two years, so it was entirely possible that Walter had also passed away.

Eliza paused, her foot raised, slowly lowering it as a thought occurred to her. Might the fella she had just met be her cousin? She knew Walter had a son in his mid-thirties, and she estimated that the chap with the green-blue eyes was around that age.

But for some reason she hadn't got the impression Jay was a farmer. Although his light tan indicated that he spent time outdoors, he looked more like someone who had just returned from a winter holiday in the sun rather than a windswept weather-beaten farmer.

Meh, why was she wasting time thinking about him and wishing she had picked his brains, when she could pay a visit to the stables and pick the brains of someone there instead. The stables were just down the lane from the farm, so Petra must surely be able to give her some information about it.

Just as she had on the way up the mountain, Eliza slowed as she passed the entrance to the farm on her way back down, and tried not to look as though she was looking. Which was difficult, because she most definitely *was* looking, and it would be obvious to anyone who saw her.

However, despite her nosing as she sauntered past, there wasn't a soul in sight. The yard was empty of people, cars and animals, and she slowed even more as she studied it. She could just imagine her father walking across those very cobbles from the farmhouse to the barns, and she closed her eyes briefly as a wave of grief crashed over her.

Every so often it would catch her unawares, and the resulting sadness was overwhelming. Those instances were becoming less frequent and not as intense, but she suspected they would never totally leave her.

A bleating coming from inside one of the barns brought her out of her thoughts, and she gave herself a shake. It was too cold to be standing around daydreaming, and she hurried off down the lane. If she discovered that her uncle did still live on the farm, she would go and introduce herself properly. Even if he was no longer there, she might knock on the door anyway and ask if she could have a look around. The worst they could do was say no, and if she didn't ask, she wouldn't get.

The stable yard was a far different beast today to the way it had looked last night, and the doors to all the stalls were either fully open, or half-open. A couple of the half-open ones had equine heads poking over the tops, the animals' ears flicking back and forth at her approach.

She was stroking one of the soft noses when a voice said, 'Can I help you?' and she glanced around to see an elderly gentleman walking across the yard. He was carrying something wrapped in what appeared to be a red and white checked tea towel.

'Hi, my name's Eliza. I'm staying in one of the cottages.'

'Ah yes, pleased to meet you, Eliza. You met my niece last night – Petra. Is the cottage to your satisfaction?'

'It's lovely,' Eliza enthused. 'And the welcome basket was a nice touch. I've already tucked into it – eggs, bread and jam for breakfast.' She spied a chicken pecking about on the cobbles. 'I see you've got chooks, so I'm guessing the eggs are from here?'

'Name's Amos,' the old gent said. 'The eggs are indeed from our hens, and I also made the jam and the bread.' He held up the tea towel. 'I've just baked Petra a loaf, in fact.'

'It was delicious. I wish I could bake.' She hesitated, aware of his expectant expression. He was clearly wondering what she wanted. 'Petra said she would give me directions to the village,' she continued. 'I've already been up the lane for a walk. That was okay, wasn't it? There's a track just past the farm leading into the hill and I didn't see any keep-out signs.'

'You won't, either,' Amos said. 'It's a public right of way, a footpath, although not many people come walking up here in the depths of winter.'

'I was going to ask at the farm, but...' Eliza wrinkled her nose. 'It isn't part of the stables, is it?' Subtle, *not*, but if it got her the answer she was looking for...

'No, it's owned by Dulcie Fairfax. You'll probably meet her at some point. She's about the same age as you. Nice girl. Wants to keep goats.'

'Right. I see. Thanks. And thank Petra for me, for the wine? It was very thoughtful.'

'I will. Now, those directions you wanted… Go back to the old cowshed, then—'

'Sorry, what old cowshed?' she interrupted. Surely he didn't mean the derelict building she had just sketched?

Amos tutted to himself. 'The cottages you are staying in have been up over a year, and I still refer to them as the old cowshed. It used to be a cowshed, see, until Harry – that's Petra's husband – had the idea of turning it into holiday lets.'

'Do you keep cows?' she asked. She hadn't seen any this morning, just horses in the fields below the stables and the occasional sheep on the hill.

'No, just horses. And a donkey. And two goats, but they're up at the farm with Dulcie at the moment. And chickens, of course, and a dog and a cat. This used to be a farm, many years ago when my wife's parents owned it, but not now. Mags, my wife, preferred horses. And so do I.' Amos shuddered. 'Cows get this look about them and you can't tell what they're thinking most of the time.'

A shiver travelled down Eliza's spine. Surely not, she thought; if there had been two farms on Muddypuddle Lane, maybe she had got it wrong and *this one* was the farm she was looking for? 'This used to be a *farm*?' she squeaked.

'Yes, but as I said, that was years ago.'

'It wasn't called *Lilac Tree* Farm, was it?'

'No, Lilac Tree Farm is the one further up the lane.'

Eliza sagged. 'I thought it was, but for a second there…' Amos was looking at her curiously and she knew she had to explain. 'My dad used to live there,' she said. 'Many years ago, before he emigrated to New Zealand.'

'Your *dad*? That was Walter York's old place. He lived there all his life. Your dad couldn't have—' Amos broke off, and realisation flared in his eyes. 'Walter had a *brother*, younger than him. He moved to New Zealand… You aren't… you *are*! You're Walter's niece!'

'I am!' Tears pricked at the back of Eliza's eyes. She had found someone who knew Walter. 'Do you know where he moved to? You said a woman called Dulcie owns it now.' She froze and her heart sank as her fears resurfaced. 'Is he dead?' she asked in a small voice.

'He most definitely is not.'

Relief cascaded through her. 'Can you give me his address?'

'I can go one better. I can take you to him!'

♥

Eliza expected Amos to drive her to Walter, so she was surprised when, after he had taken the newly baked loaf into the house, Amos had ushered her out of the stables on foot, and at that point she assumed they must be walking to the village.

But when he turned left to go up the hill and came to a halt outside a small cottage about halfway between the stables and the farm, she did a double take. It had fairy lights around the porch and a Christmas wreath on the door, and her heart leapt into her mouth when Amos lifted the knocker.

Time seemed to stand still as the door slowly opened and she caught her first look at her uncle… Her breath caught in her throat, her heart thudded wildly and she must have let out a small sound, because she was aware of Amos staring at her.

She didn't look at him, though – her attention was fixed on the man standing in front of her. With a strange sense of déjà vu, and for the second time that day, Eliza was shocked by a man in a doorway. But this was no stranger: this man looked so much like her dad that it was only with great restraint Eliza didn't throw herself at him.

Walter was staring at her too, but there was only mild curiosity on his face and no recognition. How could there be when she was the spit of her mother?

Amos spoke first. 'Walter, this is Eliza York.'

Then she studied her uncle's expression as curiosity turned to bewilderment and incomprehension.

'York? I don't understand.' Walter's gaze shifted from her to Amos, and back again.

'Emrys was my father,' she said, and dawning understanding spread across his face before the colour drained from his cheeks and he grasped the doorframe for support.

Seeing him so shocked, Eliza had a terrible feeling that she had made the biggest mistake of her life in coming here. Had her dad and Walter parted on bad terms? She hadn't thought so, but who knew what had happened all those years ago? Her father had spoken about his childhood on the farm, but he had been very reticent about his latter years in the UK. And Walter's reaction convinced her that something bad must have taken place. Why else did the old chap look as though he was about to collapse?

Thankfully Amos took charge, because all Eliza could do was stand there and wish she'd stayed at home. She should have listened to her mother. Mum had told her that nothing good ever came of digging up the past. Eliza wouldn't have come if she'd realised – she had just assumed that her mum hadn't wanted her to fly halfway across the world and meet her extended family in case Eliza had liked the UK so much that she wouldn't want to come back. That very same thing had happened when a son of one of her mother's good friends had tracked down his Irish roots. Barry Skomer was now living in a tiny hamlet near Galway, fishing for lobster and crab.

Then there was the letter Eliza had found when she had been going through her dad's documents, and although it wasn't the sole reason why Eliza was here in Picklewick, it had piqued her curiosity about her dad's past before he had emigrated to New Zealand. The heartbroken reaction of Julie Richards, the woman who Eliza had contacted as per the request in her dad's letter, had made her realise just how little she knew about her father's earlier life. What had this woman been to her dad, for him to want her to be contacted and informed of his death?

Without a word, Amos hustled Walter inside and sat him down in a straight-backed armchair. A dog wandered in and lay on its master's feet, as though it knew something was amiss.

'Come in,' Amos said to her, seeing her hovering uncertainly in the tiny hall. 'Walter will be alright. It's the shock of seeing you, that's all. It's my fault, I should have warned him.'

'No, it's mine,' she replied, miserably.

'Nonsense. Put the kettle on and make him a cup of tea. Strong, mind you, none of this dishwater stuff. Milk and two sugars. Make one for yourself, too. I'll be off – I expect you've got a lot of catching up to do. Chop chop,' he added, when she didn't move.

Eliza bit her lip and sidled past the old man, heading for the expanse of gleaming steel and chrome she could see through an open door beyond the lounge. Once in the kitchen, she hunted ineffectually for the kettle, until she realised that the curved tap arching over the sink spat out boiling water as well as cold.

Seeing a teapot on a nearby benchtop, she soon found the tea bags and filled the pot with hot water. While it brewed, she searched out a couple of mugs and tried to listen to the conversation in the next room, but she couldn't make out what they were saying.

Taking the milk out of a very impressive fridge that was stocked to the rafters with all kinds of foodstuffs, she marvelled that the old gent had such an impressive kitchen, and guessed he must really love to cook. It looked more like the kitchen of a bistro she used to work in when she was a teenager, than the sort of set-up usually seen in a house as small as this.

When she returned to the lounge, a mug in each hand, she was relieved to find Walter looking more robust. For a while, she had been terrified he was going to collapse.

'Put the mugs on the coffee table,' he instructed, and she did as she was asked, trying not to let his voice get to her; he sounded so much like her dad, it made her heart ache.

'So, you're Emrys's daughter? The eldest one?' he asked, reaching for his tea and grasping the mug with both hands to lift it to his mouth.

'Yes. I'm Eliza.'

'Are your mother and sister with you?'

'No, it's just me.'

He slurped his tea then nodded slowly, his eyes searching her face. 'You don't look much like him.'

'I take after my mum. You look like my dad, though.'

'We both followed our dad, your grandfather. In looks, that is. I was more like him in my ways, but your dad, not so much.'

'After Dad died, I wanted to see where he grew up,' she said, trying to explain why she had turned up out of the blue, unannounced. 'This is…' She grappled to find the right words. 'A kind of pilgrimage, I suppose.'

'You must miss him.' Walter had regained the colour in his cheeks, and his shocked expression had mellowed into a sympathetic one. He was gazing at her with kindly eyes.

'I do.' She bit her lip, as much to stop herself from bursting into tears as from asking Walter whether he missed his brother.

'Were you close?' Walter asked.

'Very. I was a proper daddy's girl. Cathy, my sister, is more of a mummy's girl, so we kind of had a parent each.'

'Then you lost yours?'

'Yeah…'

'How is your mother? Is she well?'

Eliza nodded. 'She misses my dad, though.'

'I expect she does.' Walter lapsed into silence and Eliza felt awkward. She should have asked Amos to alert her uncle that she was here, and not spring it on him like this. It had clearly been a big shock, but for some reason she had hoped for more emotion from him. Not gushing displays of affection as such, but *some* indication that he was pleased to see her would be nice.

'When did you sell the farm?' she asked. 'Before I arrived, I tried to find out if you were still there, but I couldn't, otherwise I'd have got in contact beforehand.'

'I moved out earlier in the year. Dulcie Fairfax owns it now.' He smiled wearily. 'It hasn't changed much since I was a boy. Dulcie's got plans for it, though.'

'Is Dulcie a relation?' she asked. She knew Walter had a son, Otto, but she hadn't heard of anyone called Dulcie until Amos mentioned her a few minutes ago.

'She's my son's girlfriend. They live together at the farm, but she owns it. It's a long story.' He paused, and she could see him struggling with something. 'Did your dad have a good life?' he blurted.

Eliza blinked. 'I think so. He seemed happy.'

Walter's smile was tinged with sadness. 'That's good. I'm glad he found love again.'

She drew in a slow breath, willing herself to stay calm. '*Again?*'

He winced. 'Ah. Right. You didn't know. That was the reason he left. Not all of it, but some of it. Mind

459

you, he wasn't living at the farm by then, or even in Picklewick. He was living in Thornbury.' He stopped and studied her. 'Are you sure you want to hear this?'

'Yes.' Eliza was emphatic. 'I want to know all about Dad; the good and the bad.'

His expression was compassionate. 'There is plenty of good, but not much bad, you'll be pleased to hear. You mightn't believe it, but I miss him too, even though I haven't clapped eyes on him for over thirty years. It's strange to think he's gone. He was younger than me.' Without warning a huge smile lit up his face. 'I'm so happy you're here. I never thought I'd get to meet one of Emrys's daughters. We've got such a lot of catching up to do.'

He's right, Eliza thought. She and Walter had a lifetime to catch up on, so that was exactly what they did.

CHAPTER THREE

Jay was in the living room, enjoying the warmth from a hearty fire and wondering what time dinner would be, when the front door opened. He looked up from the book he was reading when he heard Otto's voice, then the sound of an older man, Walter. He had met Otto's dad when Walter joined them for dinner last night, and Jay guessed he must be eating with them again this evening. Otto had insisted on cooking once more (he did that a lot, apparently) and Jay was looking forward to it. The meal yesterday had been exceptional, and so was the soup he'd eaten for lunch, which Otto had prepared this morning and had left on the stove so everyone could help themselves. Jay had helped himself to two portions – all that walking had given him an appetite.

His eldest sister, Nikki, had rocked up half an hour earlier with her son, Sammy, saying that Gio (her partner, who Jay had yet to meet) was working, and that she had also been invited to dinner. Jay thought it would be great having the whole family together – something that hadn't happened since last Christmas. He had seen so little of his nephew over the years, that it would be fun getting to know him. Sammy had brought his puppy with him, and Jay wondered whether Nikki would allow him to take Sammy and the dog for a walk tomorrow. He had enjoyed his hike up the hillside today, but it would have been more fun if he'd had company. Perhaps he could also persuade his sisters to come with him? If everyone carried on eating the way they had last night, they would need all the exercise they could get!

Dulcie, who had been sitting on the floor playing with Sammy and the dog, leapt to her feet as soon as she heard Otto's voice, her face glowing with happiness, and she rushed into the hall. Sammy followed her, with the pup hot on his heels, and Nikki and his mum also got up, leaving Jay alone.

He decided to remain where he was, relishing the (very) brief moment of peace. His family was rather loud, and he wasn't used to being around so many people, no matter how much he loved them, and he had to admit it was rather overwhelming. If it hadn't already been dark, he might have considered a quick stroll before dinner to recharge his depleted social battery.

An image of the ruined farmhouse on the hillside above swam into his mind, and Jay rested the book on his stomach and dropped his head back against the cushion, his thoughts filled with the woman he'd met earlier today. He had been thinking about her on and off since he'd returned to the farm, but he couldn't work out why. She had been pretty, but he had seen pretty women before. He'd even dated a few. What was so memorable about this one?

Perhaps it was because he hadn't been expecting to hear an accent like hers in Picklewick, and especially not on top of a mountain on a cold December day. It had made him feel slightly homesick for warmer climes; so much so that he could practically hear her voice in his head.

Hang on a sec… he *was* hearing her voice. Really *hearing*, not imagining!

Book forgotten, Jay leapt to his feet and went to join the rest of the family in the kitchen, where everyone had congregated.

And came face-to-face with the woman from this morning.

She was standing in his sister's kitchen and gazing around intently, then she turned her head a fraction, caught sight of him, and her intense expression turned to one of surprised recognition. 'Jay?'

'Eliza. Hi.'

Dulcie's mouth dropped open. 'Do you two know each other?'

'We met this morning,' Jay explained, a million questions flying around in his head. 'She was out for a walk and so was I.'

'Did she tell you that she's Walter's niece?' his sister asked. 'Her dad and Walter grew up on this farm.'

Eliza, who had been looking rather shell-shocked, found her voice. 'I wanted to see where Dad was born.'

That explained why she was in Picklewick, Jay thought. But he was surprised no one had mentioned her last night, and he wondered why she hadn't joined them for dinner considering Walter had been there. But perhaps that was why Walter had left as soon as he'd eaten his pudding, Jay mused, remembering that she had told him she had arrived last night.

Walter said, 'She's staying at one of the cottages at the stables. I told her she could stay with me, but Eliza is adamant she wants to remain where she is.'

'I don't blame her,' Otto laughed. 'This lot are a bit much to take in all at once, and considering you're here almost as much as you're in your own house, Dad, she'll not know what's hit her. At least she'll get a bit of peace at Petras's place.'

'Oi!' Dulcie elbowed him and Beth waved her fist. Maisie poked her tongue out as she came into the kitchen, catching the tail end of the conversation, the arrival of visitors having flushed her out of her bedroom.

Otto said to Eliza, 'See what I mean? Not only are they rowdy, but they can be violent.' He danced out of the way of jabby elbows. 'You can't hit me, I'm cooking dinner.' He laughed at Dulcie, then turned to Eliza. 'If they haven't put you off, do you still want to join us for dinner?'

She bit her lip and glanced at Walter, who nodded encouragingly. 'If that's okay?' she replied, shyly.

Otto grinned. 'Right!' He clapped his hands. 'Everyone out, unless you are keen on helping.'

There was a mad scramble for the door, Dulcie grabbing hold of Eliza's hand and tugging her out of the kitchen.

Jay watched them go, remaining where he was.

He caught Otto giving him an amused look. 'It's just me and you,' the chef said, 'and a meal for nine to prepare.'

'Er, okay.' Jay didn't mind cooking, but he wasn't terribly good at it. However, he could follow instructions and prepare veg, so as long as he left the actual cooking to Otto, it should be fine. Besides, he may as well make himself useful if he was going to stay in the kitchen and not join the others.

Raucous laughter drifted from the living room, and Jay surreptitiously nudged the kitchen door closed. He had been utterly shocked to see Eliza, and he needed time to process it, having gone from assuming he would never see her again, to eating dinner with her in the blink of an eye. To say he was surprised would be an understatement.

Otto set him to work chopping onions for a ragu sauce, while Otto made pappardelle – from scratch, no less! Jay had never heard of it; his pasta always came out of a packet and was the usual kind, such as spaghetti, tagliatelle, or the one that looked like little shells. He had once bought fresh ravioli, though…

Otto chatted whilst he worked. 'I got the shock of my life when I called into Dad's to bring him up the farm for dinner and was introduced to a long-lost cousin,' he was saying.

'Didn't you know about her?' Jay was curious.

'I kind of forgot I had any relatives in New Zealand. It has been me and Dad for such a long time. Mum died when I was in my teens,' he added. 'I remember seeing envelopes with New Zealand stamps on them at Christmas, but I honestly didn't take much notice.'

Jay said, 'She seems nice.' She seemed more than nice, if he was honest. He was quite taken with her. She was an attractive woman and one he would like to get to know better.

He hoped she would be around for a while, because if she was, the relaxing Christmas he had been anticipating was about to get a lot more exciting.

♥

Eliza had assumed that the stranger on the hill was a local, but she hadn't expected to see him in the farm's kitchen this evening.

Confused as to who all these people were (when Walter's son, Otto, had arrived at Walter's house to take him to dinner at the farm, she had expected to share the meal with just Walter, Otto and Dulcie) Eliza been taken aback when faced with three women, a boy of around twelve or thirteen, plus a puppy who had bounded around like an idiot until Walter's dog Peg had told it off by growling at it. Then Jay had put in an appearance, as well as a fourth woman, and Eliza had been completely thrown.

So many questions were whirling around in her head. Was he married to one of the women? Which one was Dulcie? Who was the older woman? Dulcie's mother? Not Otto's, because she knew that his mum – her aunt – had died years ago. Or was she Jay's mum?

Walter came to her rescue after Dulcie had dragged her into a spacious sitting room and gestured for her to take a seat. Eliza sank into the squashy armchair, feeling somewhat overwhelmed.

'Let me introduce you to everyone. This is Dulcie.' Walter gave one of the women a squeeze. 'She's Otto's girlfriend, and she owns the farm. This is Nikki and her son Sammy. Nikki is Dulcie's older sister, and the other one is Maisie, the baby of the family. This lovely lady is Beth, their mother. And you've already met Jay.'

Eliza had, but all he had told her was his name – and she was still none the wiser as to which sister he belonged to, Nikki or Maisie.

'You must tell us all about your life down under,' Dulcie said.

'What do you want to know?' Eliza asked uncertainly.

'Leave her be,' Walter leapt in. 'She doesn't leave until the second of January, so you'll have plenty of time to quiz her. Let her get used to you first.'

'It's okay,' Eliza said, but she was glad he'd intervened. She still couldn't believe she was sitting in the same room which her father had sat in all those years ago, and she wondered if it had changed much.

With the room full of people and dogs, it was hard to envisage him here. If it had just been her and Walter, she might have found it easier. But the farm didn't belong to her uncle anymore and she could hardly ask everyone to leave just so she could soak up the atmosphere of the past.

'Stop being a fusspot, Walter,' Beth, the oldest of the four women, said. 'You make us sound scary.'

'If the cap fits…' Walter muttered.

'I heard that!' Beth was indignant.

'You were meant to.'

'Take that back.'

Walter stuck his tongue out at her, and Eliza burst out laughing.

'Don't take his side,' Beth warned. 'Blood isn't always thicker than water – not if you want any dinner.'

'Mum, stop it.' Nikki frowned at her mother, then turned to Eliza. 'She isn't always like this.'

'Yes, she is,' Walter retorted. 'She's a right pain in the ar—'

'Walter!' Dulcie cried. 'Why do you act like a pair of kids every time you're in the same room?'

'I behaved myself yesterday,' Beth objected.

'So did I.' That was from Walter. 'I was as nice as pie at dinner.'

'Only because you ate and ran,' Beth snapped. 'He gobbled his meal down then buggered off home.'

'That's because there's only a certain amount of you I can take.'

'Well!' Beth pressed her lips together and folded her arms across her chest, her expression stony.

'If you can't play nice, *neither* of you will have any dinner,' Nikki said in a commanding voice.

Walter leant towards Eliza and hissed, 'Spot the primary school teacher.'

'Nikki?' she guessed.

'Got it in one. I wonder if she speaks to Gio like a naughty schoolboy when he does something she doesn't like.'

'Gio?'

'Her other half. He's a copper. They've got a house in the village.'

Ah, so Jay must be with Maisie, Eliza concluded. But as her gaze slid across Maisie's face, she couldn't see those two as a couple for some reason, even though they would look good together.

All three sisters were attractive women. They had got their looks from their mother, she realised. Despite her grumpy demeanour and downturned mouth, Beth had good cheekbones and lovely blue-green eyes. Jay had nice blue-green eyes too—

Eliza's mouth dropped open as a thought struck her. Quickly closing it again and hoping no one had spotted her gormless expression, Eliza shuffled closer to Walter and said out of the corner of her mouth, 'Is Jay Beth's son?'

Walter blinked. 'Yes, why?'

'No reason, just trying to get everyone straight in my head. Are there any other brothers or sisters I should know about?' she asked lightly.

'Why are you two whispering?' Beth demanded. 'It's rude to whisper.'

'I was just explaining to my niece—' he puffed out his chest at the word '—that Jay is your son. The poor boy.'

Beth glared at him, and Dulcie rolled her eyes.

'Dulcie is getting goats tomorrow,' Sammy announced. The child had been sitting on the floor playing with the puppy, but he suddenly leapt to his feet, put his index fingers to his head like horns and began bleating.

'Stop being silly, Sammy,' his mother said, and the boy subsided.

'Do they have goats in New Zealand?' he asked Eliza. 'I like goats.'

'So do I.' That was from Maisie – the first words Eliza had heard the woman speak. Until now, she had been focused on her phone, her thumbs flying across the screen.

'Yes, there are goats in New Zealand,' Eliza said with a smile. 'And sheep.'

'Aunty Dulcie hates sheep,' Sammy sniggered. 'Otto had to rescue her from Flossie. Dulcie was hiding in the house, screaming that it was going to eat her.'

'Flossie is a sheep,' Walter explained. 'She's as tame as my dog, Peg. I hand reared her, you see.'

'I was not screaming,' Dulcie objected.

'Uncle Otto said you were.' Sammy sniggered again.

'Uncle Otto was exaggerating.'

'What was I exaggerating about?' Otto asked. His head had appeared around the living room door, and he brought with him the enticing smell of cooking. Eliza's tummy rumbled.

'Flossie,' Sammy and Maisie chorused.

Otto grinned, and said to Eliza, 'Have they been telling you about sheepgate? You wait until you hear how she screeched when she came face-to-face with her first chicken. It was so loud that the dogs in the next county must have heard.'

Dulcie huffed. 'How long is dinner going to be?'

'It's ready, my sweet, so if everyone would like to take their seats? Jay has laid the table. Eliza, I believe you will be sitting between him and Walter.' He winked at her, and Eliza wondered what that was about.

Apprehensively, she followed Walter into the dining room and sat beside him. The chair to her right was empty, but not for long, as Jay slipped into it. He was so close she could smell his cologne. The scent made the hairs on her arms stand on end.

Otto came in holding huge bowls of steaming pasta in each hand and placed them on the table. Baskets of bread, a block of Parmesan cheese and a jug of water already graced the table, and after Otto had hurried into the kitchen once more, returning with a bowl of rich red sauce and a ladle, everyone began reaching for everything at once, all of them talking at the same time.

Except for her and Jay.

Like her, Jay seemed to be waiting for the rush to abate. 'Can I pour you a glass of water?'

'Please.'

'Can I have wine?' Maisie asked.

'No,' Dulcie and Otto chorused at the same time.

Maisi pouted. 'Why not? We had wine with dinner last night.'

Jay moved one of the bowls of pasta towards Eliza and began to lift some onto her plate. 'Say when,' he told her.

'Because we drank it all,' Dulcie said. 'I'm going to have to go to the supermarket tomorrow and stock up for Christmas.'

'Can you get me a bottle of sherry?' Beth asked. 'Actually, make that two.'

'When,' Eliza said to Jay, then he ladled a large spoonful of sauce on top of her pasta, before he served himself.

'I like Prosecco,' Maisie said.

'I want beer.' This was from Sammy, and the table fell silent as everyone turned to look at him. 'What?' he asked, his chin covered in red sauce.

Eliza could see Jay struggling to hold in his mirth, and Otto was also trying not to smile.

'You're not having beer.' Sammy's mother was adamant.

Eliza ate a mouthful of pasta and almost swooned in delight. The sauce was rich and fragrant, and she thought it was the best she had ever tasted. No wonder Otto was opening his own restaurant. Walter had been so full of pride when he'd told her about his son, and she could understand why. The man was a genius in the kitchen if he could make a simple meal like pasta with tomato sauce taste so divine.

Sammy was pouting. 'You're mean.'

Nikki said, 'Yep, mean is my middle name. You are too young to drink beer. Or any other kind of alcohol, for that matter.'

Eliza mentally gave her a high five for cutting any further alcohol-related requests from her son off at the pass.

'Aunty Maisie does, and you said she's a big kid,' Sammy replied.

Silence descended once more, but this time there was no humour in it.

Nikki shook her head and glared at her son, who gazed back at her innocently. Beth was tutting, and Dulcie's head was down as she concentrated on her food.

'Is that what you think of me?' Maisie asked eventually. Her jaw was hard and her eyes flashed.

With a shake of her head at Sammy, a clear warning that she would deal with him later, Nikki replied, 'If you want the truth, yes. You flit from job to job, from boyfriend to boyfriend, and you expect Mum to do your washing and ironing, to cook you a meal every evening, and to clean up after you… If that's not behaving like a teenager, I don't know what is.'

Maisie gasped, before rallying. 'It's better than being uptight. You act like you've got a broom stuck up your backside and a face like a slapped—'

'That's enough!' Beth smacked her palm down on the table, making everyone jump and the glasses rattle. 'May I remind you we have a guest? What must she think of us? Sorry, Eliza, we're not normally like this.'

'Yes, they are,' Jay whispered in her ear, once everyone had resumed eating.

'They?' she whispered back. 'Don't you include yourself?'

'My sisters fight like ferrets in a bag. I'm sweetness and light.' He assumed an exaggeratedly virtuous expression, then sobered. 'I hope we haven't scared you off?'

'Only a bit,' she replied, smiling to show she didn't mean it.

She had to admit to being a little taken aback, though – her own family were considerably more subdued than this one. If she was feeling unkind, she might even say they were repressed. She loved her mother to pieces, but Mum would often sulk if she didn't get her own way, and if she didn't approve of something, she had a habit of giving whoever it was who had upset her the silent treatment. Out of herself and her sister, Eliza was often on the receiving end of that. It was an eye-opener to see the way this family dealt with their issues, and she wasn't sure which method she preferred.

Thankfully the little spat was soon forgotten and Eliza carried on eating her meal, quietly observing the family, but at the same time acutely aware of the man sitting beside her.

He didn't say a lot either, but now and again he would smile indulgently as the conversation swirled around them.

'So, Eliza,' Dulcie said, 'I'm dying of curiosity here. Is this your first visit to the UK?'

Eliza hastily swallowed a mouthful of food and nodded. 'It is.'

'And you go back on the second of January, is that right?'

'Yes. I'm here for two weeks.'

'When did you arrive?'

'Yesterday.'

Jay said, 'I only arrived myself last night.'

'Ah, yes, you two have already met.' Dulcie's gaze darted between them, before coming back to rest on Eliza.

Eliza felt the need to explain. 'I was out for a walk and was exploring this derelict building on the top of the hill, when I saw Jay.'

'She was inside, sketching,' Jay said. 'I think I gave her the fright of her life when I appeared in the doorway.'

'I think you were equally as surprised,' she said, remembering the way he'd almost jumped out of his skin.

'Are you an artist?' This was from Maisie.

'I am.' Eliza blushed self-consciously. She had always found it difficult to acknowledge that she earned a living from her creativity, even when her dad had been alive. Only having one person out of the family who believed in her, had made her hesitant about telling people.

'Are you online? Do you have an Instagram page?' Maisie asked, reaching for the phone next to her plate.

'I am and I do,' Eliza admitted.

'Oh, no, you don't, Maisie Fairfax,' Beth interjected. 'Put your phone down and don't be rude. You can play on it later, after we've eaten.' Beth turned to Eliza and said, 'If I had my way, I'd ban mobiles from the table.'

Maisie protested, 'I was just—'

'Shush.' Her mother arched her eyebrows and Maisie subsided, grumbling under her breath.

'Eliza is very talented,' Walter said, his voice oozing with pride. 'She showed me some of her paintings.'

And at that, Eliza felt a spark reignite in her heart – a spark she thought had been extinguished when her dad died. Would Walter be her new champion? God knows she needed one; her mother certainly wasn't, and her sister couldn't care less.

'Eliza takes after *my* mother, her grandmother,' Walter was saying. 'She also liked to sketch and paint. The picture above my fireplace is one that she did.'

'You never said,' Dulcie chimed in. 'I assumed you'd had it commissioned. It's lovely.'

Eliza hadn't known what to feel when Walter showed it to her earlier. Her dad had spoken about his mother's artistic streak with fondness, but to see something her grandmother had painted had brought a lump to her throat.

'My niece is just as good… better, I think,' he said, as Eliza's blush deepened.

And her face was positively on fire when Jay leant closer (so close that she could smell his clean-skin scent, with a light overlay of cologne) and said softly, 'Take the compliment.'

'You don't understand,' she murmured, without thinking, and wished she could take the words back when she sensed his curiosity.

'Perhaps you could explain it to me sometime?'

'Maybe.' Eliza was just being polite – she had no intention of sharing anything with a man she'd only just met. She might tell Walter, but it was honestly no biggie: all families had their issues, and her mum and sister not believing in her talent was hardly a major one. Besides, she had proved them wrong, to a point. She *was* supporting herself through her art, although it hadn't made her rich yet and probably never would.

But seeing the way this rambunctious family argued and squabbled one minute, then made up and were the best of friends the next, made her wonder whether she had been blowing things out of all proportion. Maybe her mum's opinion didn't matter as much as she thought it did.

She'd call home tomorrow, she decided. She would take a stroll into the village – she needed some groceries – and give her a bell. Mindful of the thirteen-hour time difference, as long as she didn't leave it too late, she would hopefully catch her mum before she went to bed.

Dessert followed (a wonderful molten chocolate cake) and as they finished the meal, Eliza continued to be quizzed about where she lived, what life was like 'down under' and about her family. Although she felt bombarded, their interest was friendly and she enjoyed telling them about her homeland.

Finally, after a sumptuous cheeseboard, she was stuffed, and jetlag was catching up with her.

It seemed to be catching up with Jay too, and she smiled when she caught his eye mid-yawn. Over the course of the meal, she'd found out that the tan she had noticed earlier had been acquired in Borneo, and that he worked for an organisation which installed and monitored acoustic listening devices in the jungle.

It sounded fascinating and she would have liked to have learnt more, but the conversation never seemed to linger on any one subject for long.

By the time everyone retired to the lounge with cups of tea and coffee, Eliza was bushed. She was definitely all peopled-out, and she needed sleep and time to mull over the events of the day.

'Sorry, guys,' she said, after having her offer to help clear away the dinner things turned down. 'I think I'll have to call it a night. I'm exhausted.'

'I'll walk you down the hill,' Walter said, but Eliza refused.

'You stay here and enjoy the rest of the evening,' she told him. It was only eight-thirty, and she didn't want to spoil his night.

'I don't like the idea of you walking back to the stables in the dark,' Walter said, attempting to heave himself out of his chair.

Jay waved him down. 'I'll walk her home,' he said. 'I could do with stretching my legs before I hit the sack.'

Eliza said, 'It's fine, honestly. I'll be okay.'

'No doubt you will,' Walter agreed, 'but humour an old man, eh? Dulcie, have you got a torch Jay can borrow?'

'Of course.' Dulcie went to fetch one and when she returned with it, she said to Eliza, 'Would you like to pop up to the farm tomorrow and have a proper look around? About twelvish?'

'That's very kind, thank you.' Eliza was touched by the woman's thoughtfulness.

With goodbyes said, along with a promise to call in and see Walter soon, she donned her coat and headed outside. The sudden drop in temperature made her shiver, but the cessation of noise was very welcome.

'Thank goodness for some peace and quiet,' Jay said. 'I love my family to bits, but they ain't half noisy.'

'They're lovely,' Eliza said honestly. 'Look, you don't have to walk me down the hill if you don't want to.'

'I want to, and I need to get some fresh air. I just wish it wasn't quite so fresh. I forget how chilly British winters can be.'

Eliza wrapped her scarf more firmly around her neck. 'It doesn't get cold where I live – not like this.'

'It's a shock to the system, isn't it? I'm hoping we get some snow, though. It's forecast for later this week.'

'Will we get snowed in?' she asked, suddenly mindful that Muddypuddle Lane was off the beaten track.

'Possibly. Otto says that the farm has been cut off in the past.' Jay aimed the torch's beam at the ground, and she was grateful for light. Those potholes were lethal.

'I'd better get some provisions in,' she said. 'I was planning on going to Picklewick in the morning anyway. Do you know how to get to it from here?'

'Down the lane, turn right and follow the road into the village. It's about a five-minute drive, if that.'

'I won't be driving, I'll be walking. I haven't got a car.' She should definitely think about hiring one, and she wondered where the nearest car hire centre was – Thornbury, maybe? Or further afield? Or had she left it a bit late, considering Saturday was Christmas Day, and today was Tuesday?

'Do you need to buy much?' Jay asked.

'Some,' she admitted, wondering how she was going to carry everything back.

'I'll drive you.'

'That's kind of you, but I don't want to put you out.'

'You're not. I haven't got anything planned. Which one is yours?' he asked, as they approached the row of three little cottages.

'The middle one.' Eliza halted. 'Thanks for walking me back.' Did he expect to be invited in, she wondered in alarm.

'It's no bother.' He turned away, then said, 'What time do you want me to pick you up in the morning?'

'Is eight-thirty too early? I'd like to give my mum a call and the signal here is dire.'

'No problem. See you tomorrow. G'night.'

'Night,' she said, letting herself in, but she waited until the light from the torch had disappeared before closing the door.

What a day, she thought, as she got ready for bed. She'd met her uncle and her cousin, had eaten a meal in the very house where her dad had grown up, and had been assimilated into a family she had only just met.

And then there was Jay.

Better not think about him too much, no matter how attracted she might be, she told herself, climbing into bed. If she wasn't careful, she might land in a whole heap of trouble, because she didn't think she had imagined that he was as equally attracted to her.

CHAPTER FOUR

The following morning, Jay was far more eager than he should have been when he drove down the lane towards the stables to collect Eliza. He had tried telling himself he was simply doing a friend of the family a favour, and that this was nothing more than a quick trip into the village to pick up some groceries, but he had been telling himself that since he left her at her cottage last night and it hadn't made an iota of difference – his stomach still turned over every time he thought of her.

It continued to do somersaults as he pulled into the little parking area just up from the row of cottages and saw her hurrying outside to meet him.

Bloody hell, she was gorgeous, he thought again, and a bolt of sheer lust jabbed him in the chest, making his heart skip a beat.

Maybe offering to drive her into Picklewick wasn't such a good idea after all, not if he was going to react like this every time he clapped eyes on her. But he'd offered now and could hardly retract it considering she was opening the car door and getting in.

'Thanks for this,' she said. She sounded slightly breathless, as though she'd been rushing around, and perhaps she had. Like him, she was probably still suffering from jet lag, but unlike him she might have actually had some sleep last night. For some reason, he hadn't been able to drop off, despite being so tired he would have thought he could have fallen asleep on a bed of nails. Instead, he'd tossed and turned for ages, and then when he had finally managed to get some rest, he'd woken far too early. He blamed it on the blasted cockerel, who seemed to have taken a liking to the spot directly beneath his bedroom window to announce the start of a new day.

Jay was sure he looked as rough as he felt.

Eliza, on the other hand, looked as fresh as a proverbial daisy, and he guessed (rather enviously) that she must have had at least eight hours of blissful slumber.

The journey to the village took less than five minutes, and soon they were driving along a road with houses on either side.

Jay glanced around curiously. It was picture-postcard lovely, and he could see why his sister had fallen in love with the place. *Two* of his sisters actually, because Nikki had moved to the village a few months after Dulcie. Mind you, she had also fallen in love with a local chap, so that might have had something to do with it.

The main street was quaint and old-fashioned, and looked like a scene out of *A Christmas Carol*, minus the snow. Every shop window sported trees laden with baubles, reindeer, and beautifully wrapped presents, and there were festive lights draped across the lamp-posts high above. If it looked pretty now, it would look even lovelier when it was dark and all those fairy lights came to life.

'Do you mind if we go for a coffee first, so I can phone my mum?' Eliza asked. 'Or if you've got things to do, we can arrange to meet somewhere?'

'I could murder a coffee, so I'll come with you, if that's alright,' he said. 'If you don't want me listening in, we can sit at separate tables.'

She shot him a look. 'I don't mind. You'll be bored to death, though.' She caught her lip between her teeth, and he had a mad urge to kiss her.

Shaking his head at his stupidity, he concentrated on finding somewhere to park, which proved to be more difficult than he thought; but he caught lucky when a police car pulled away from the kerb and Jay shot into the resulting space. Handily, it was directly in front of a café.

Once inside, he lingered over placing their order to allow Eliza to make her call, but she was still on the phone when he carried the tray to the table where she was sitting.

Eliza smiled her thanks as he placed a mug of coffee in front of her, and as he sipped his, he scrolled through a news channel on his phone and tried not to listen to her conversation.

'You'd like it, Mum,' Eliza was saying. 'I wish you were here… It's quaint… Yeah, really small, but it's got everything I need. Did you get the sketch? I sent it to you yesterday. No…? Check your— never mind… Walter sends his regards. He looks so much like Dad. Sounds like him, too. Otto is nice… Yeah, I will. As I said, the signal is poor. Give my love to Cathy… Hmm… Right. I'll ring you when I can. Love you, Mum.' Eliza ended the call, took a sip of her coffee, and said, 'That was my mother.'

'I thought as much.'

'She didn't want to come on this trip, but I wish she had.'

Jay, selfishly, was pleased Eliza's mother hadn't, because if she had, he probably wouldn't be sitting here with Eliza right now. Then he felt awful for putting himself before what was best for Eliza. She was clearly missing her mum and was no doubt homesick – not ideal at the best of times, but worse around the festive season.

Vowing to try to make her feel as included as possible, he made a mental note to ask Dulcie to invite Eliza for Christmas lunch. Walter was coming to them for the day anyway, so Dulcie would most likely have already thought of inviting Eliza, but just in case she hadn't, he would mention it.

'I'm hungry,' she announced. 'Can I treat you to one of those famed English breakfasts as a thank you for bringing me shopping?'

Jay beamed. 'You can. But only on the understanding that I buy the next one.'

'Will there be a next one?'

'I don't see why not. You'll probably have to go shopping more than once. And while we're here, do you think you can help me pick out some gifts for my daft family? I've brought a few things with me from Borneo, but I need some more. Take Sammy, for instance – what do you get a twelve-year-old boy for Christmas?'

'Don't look at me, I haven't got a clue. I don't have much to do with kids. Cathy, my sister, is pregnant with her first, so I dare say I'll find out in due course.'

'That's nice. Are you and she close?'

'Not really. She doesn't approve of me.'

Jay was taken aback. What was there not to approve of?

When he raised his eyebrows, Eliza said, 'I live in a bach on the beach.' She pulled a face. 'It isn't up to her or Mum's standards, but it's mine, I own it outright and I love it.'

Jay heard the defensiveness in her voice. 'What is a… what did you call it… a *batch?*'

'Yeah, it's spelt b-a-c-h,' she spelt it out, 'but it's pronounced *batch*, rhyming with hatch. They are what us Kiwis call holiday homes, and are usually near a beach or lake, or even in the forest. Mine's on the beach.'

'It sounds idyllic.'

'The setting is – the bach not so much. When I told Mum I was planning on buying one, she had visions of something a bit more upmarket; the sort of property that well-off people buy as a second home. Not the wooden shack I live in. The light is fantastic, though.'

'Do you have a studio?'

She nodded. 'It's built on the side of the house, with views of the ocean and scrubland all around. It's so calm and peaceful.'

'I can imagine.'

Eliza stared at him. Yeah, he probably could. 'What about you? Where do you live?' she asked, and over breakfast Jay told her about the rather rustic accommodation that used to be his base in Borneo, and how he had been moving around quite a bit over the years, installing acoustic sensors and training people how to use and maintain them.

'I love being outdoors,' he said. 'I love exploring and seeing the wildlife.'

'Me, too. Wildlife and landscapes are my two favourite things to paint, the sea especially.'

'Would you show me some of your work?' he asked, and when he saw how talented she was, he let out a low whistle. 'Walter said you were good, and he wasn't exaggerating.'

Her use of colour was extraordinary, and he could see why she loved painting seascapes – she was incredibly good at them. Then he came across the drawing she'd done of the ruins above the farm, and he smiled.

'I was hoping to see the end result,' he said.

'It's not finished. It's only a rough sketch.'

'It looks finished to me. Have you brought any paints with you?'

'Some, but I couldn't bring much. Just a small watercolour palette and a few brushes. Don't tell Petra, but I'm going to use her wooden chopping board to stretch my paper.'

Jay was puzzled for a moment, then he recalled his school art classes. 'That's when you pre-wet the paper and stretch it out to let it dry before you paint on it, isn't it?'

'That's right. If you don't prepare paper properly, it tends to ripple. Do you paint?'

'Nah, was hopeless at it. Can't draw either, but I can whittle.'

Eliza was laughing. 'Whittle?'

'You know, carve bits of wood.'

'What do you carve?'

'Animals, mostly.'

'Got any photos?'

'I might have.'

'Can I see?'

Jay found one on his phone and showed it to her.

'What is it?' she asked.

'It's a tapir.' He saw her blank expression. 'A creature from South America that looks a bit like a large pig, but isn't.'

'Sorry,' she said, with a pained expression. 'I don't mean to diss your tapir, but I don't know what a tapir is supposed to look like.'

Jay scrolled through his phone for another photo. 'How about this?'

'Ah, that I *do* recognise. It's an Indian elephant.'

'Thank goodness for that!' he chuckled.

'You're good,' she said.

Jay shrugged. He didn't think he was that good, but he enjoyed doing it, and that was all that mattered. Seeing that they'd finished their meal, he said, 'Shall we make a move?'

As they made their way outside and into the bitter December air, Jay shoved his hands into his coat pockets. He'd had to borrow it from Otto, because any winter gear he owned was at his mother's house in Birmingham. Luckily, he and Otto were of a similar build, although Jay was a little leaner, so the coat fitted just fine.

Speak of the devil – there was the man in question. Otto was heading into a building on the opposite side of the road, and Jay pointed him out to Eliza.

'That's where Otto is opening his restaurant,' he said.

'That's The Wild Side?'

'Yeah; has Walter told you Otto specialises in foraged ingredients?'

She nodded, her eyes on the restaurant. 'He also told me he's got a book deal. I'm not surprised – the meal he cooked last night was delicious.'

'It was, wasn't it? If he keeps feeding me like that, I'll be ten kilos heavier by the time I leave,' Jay joked. He glanced over at Eliza to find her studying the street.

She said, 'Picklewick is so pretty – exactly what I imagined a typical English village to look like. And it's so Christmassy.' Her eyes roamed over the shops. 'Gift shopping first, grocery shopping last?'

The tip of her nose had turned pink, and for a moment Jay imagined kissing it. He coughed to cover his embarrassment at having such thoughts. 'Er, okay. I'm easy.'

'Let's try here.' Eliza pushed open the door of the nearest shop and an old-fashioned bell tinkled above their heads.

It was warm and cosy inside, and smelt of waxed candles and cinnamon. Fairy lights were festooned along the shelves and carols played softly in the background. The interior of the shop was a jewel box of gold, silver, red and green, with a smattering of other colours thrown in.

'I don't think they'll have anything here for Sammy,' Eliza said, 'but who else do you need to buy for?'

You, he thought, as a vision of her on her own on Christmas morning without even a single present to open, swam into his head.

He shelved the thought for consideration later, but he couldn't help making a note of anything that caught her eye.

Eliza wandered around the shop, picking things up and putting them down again, but not lingering on any specific item. 'You say you've already bought a few things – so who do you need to buy for today?' she asked again, gazing at him expectantly.

'I've got Mum's and Maisie's gifts sorted, and a little something for Otto – authentic Asian spices – but Dulcie isn't easy to buy for, and neither is Nikki. Then there's Sammy, as I said, plus Walter and Gio.' *And you*, the voice in his head repeated.

'Let's start with Dulcie. What sort of thing does she like?'

'If you had asked me that question last Christmas, I'd have said anything sparkly and girly, but since she won the farm—'

'Excuse me,' Eliza interjected. 'Did you just say *won the farm*?'

Jay laughed. Her expression was kitten-cute. 'I did. It's a long story to do with Walter not being able to cope and running into some financial difficulties, but the result was that the farm was kind of raffled off, and Dulcie won it.'

'Blinking heck!'

'I know, right? It's unbelievable. I would never have put 'my sister' and 'owning a farm' in the same sentence, yet eight months on, she's not only loving rural life, she's trying to make a go of it.'

'So that's why Otto was teasing her about sheep and chickens? I did wonder.'

'Until she won the farm, the nearest she'd come to a chicken was a McNugget,' Jay said wryly.

'And now she's buying goats?'

'Wild, isn't it? Good luck to her, I say. She's found her niche.' *And she's found Otto*, he thought, but didn't say, not wanting to sound cheesy. But he hadn't been able to help notice how in love his sister and her man were, and if jealousy was a green-eyed monster, envy must be its emerald cousin because Jay abruptly realised that someday he hoped to have what they had.

That was the second time since he'd arrived in Picklewick that he'd had that thought, and he found it troubling.

'Essential oils!' Eliza cried, startling him.

'You what?'

'For Dulcie, for her soap making. There's a gift box here with lots of different scents. She's probably already got some, but she mightn't have all of them.'

Jay took the box of oils from her and examined it. 'Perfect. Now for Nikki.'

'I know I've only met her once, and I haven't met Gio at all, but what about something they can do together? Like a couple's spa day, or theatre tickets?'

'You're a genius. I'll have a look online later. So that just leaves Sammy and Walter.'

'I might have an idea about Sammy's present,' she said. 'Why don't you whittle him a dog? As for Walter...' Eliza shrugged.

Jay was impressed with the suggestion. 'That's a brilliant idea! I'll have to pull my finger out and get a move on, but it might be doable in two days. There's bound to be a suitable piece of wood in the huge log store in the barn.' His excitement mounting, he said, 'I'll take a look as soon as I get back.' He didn't have a clue what to get Walter though, so he said, 'I'll ask Otto about Walter. Let me pay for this, and I'm done.' He indicated the box in his hand.

That was painless, he thought. He generally disliked gift buying, but this had been enjoyable – possibly because it had been quick, and definitely because Eliza was with him. And he was looking forward to doing some whittling, too.

But as he accompanied her around the village whilst she bought her groceries, he realised he was enjoying this little shopping trip far too much, and considering Eliza would be leaving in a couple of weeks, that wasn't good, was it?

♥

Eliza hadn't expected to see the whole of Jay's family, plus several people who worked at the stables, to be there for the Grand Goat Delivery (as she had begun to think of it) later that day. The only person missing was Otto, who she suspected was still at the restaurant. She and Jay had spotted him going into The Wild Side earlier, but they hadn't tried to attract his attention because he'd looked rather preoccupied.

After being introduced to Gio (Nikki's other half), Harry (Petra's husband), a woman about her own age who worked at the stables (but Eliza couldn't for the life of her remember her name), and Amos's partner, Eliza retreated to the back of the crowd and waited for the goats to arrive.

Dulcie and her mum were making an occasion out of it, and had made mugs of hot chocolate for everyone, and were now handing out Christmas cookies that Otto had baked. They were delicious and Eliza wondered whether she could filch another.

Glancing around in the hope of seeing an unattended plate of the gorgeous goodies, she caught Jay's eye and her own widened at the fleeting expression on his face. She could have sworn she spotted desire there, but it was swiftly replaced by a friendly smile.

'Jay seems nice,' Walter said, and she turned to see her uncle standing at her elbow. He was clutching a mug of steaming hot chocolate in one hand and a cookie in the other.

Eliza eyed it enviously. 'Yeah, he does,' she agreed. 'He gave me a lift into the village this morning.'

'So I heard.'

She shot him a keen glance. 'Who told you?'

Walter tapped the side of his nose. 'Never you mind. But what you may want to mind, is that you can't keep anything secret around here. This lot,' he jerked his head towards Beth and her daughters, 'are worse than four old biddies nattering over a garden fence.'

'I've got nothing to hide,' Eliza said with a chuckle, but she was a little ruffled to discover that Walter knew about her trip to the village, and she wondered whether he felt put out that she hadn't asked him for a lift instead.

'Did you get what you wanted?' he asked.

Eliza had got slightly *more* than she'd bargained for, namely an increased liking of, and attraction to Jay. Not only was he good-looking, but he was also fun to be with and easy to talk to, and warning bells kept going off in her head. A quick jump in the sack wasn't her cup of tea, but considering that this was all it could be, she wasn't prepared to allow anything to develop between them.

She forced herself to look anywhere except at Jay, and saw Dulcie heading their way, as she replied, 'I did, thanks. I might have to pop back for some bread and milk later in the week, but for now I'm good.'

'I hope you've not bought a turkey,' Dulcie warned, drawing alongside.

Eliza hadn't. Not even a breast of one. She would have steak and veggies instead.

When she shook her head, Dulcie said, 'Good, because you're officially invited to Lilac Tree Farm for Christmas dinner.'

'I couldn't possibly impose—' she began, but Dulcie cut her off.

'It's either that, or we come to you, and as I don't think we would all fit into your little cottage, I think it's best if you come to the farm.'

Eliza glanced at Walter, who held up his hands. 'Don't look at me,' he said. 'This isn't my doing – although I was going to ask Dulcie if she minded you joining us.'

'Jay suggested it,' Dulcie said. 'But I was going to invite you anyway.'

Eliza's gaze shot to Jay. He had his back to her, but for some reason she had a feeling he knew what was going down.

'You can't be on your own at Christmas,' Dulcie argued. 'You've come all this way to discover your roots, so whether you like it or not, you are part of our family now.'

'If you insist,' Eliza replied weakly, but deep down she was thrilled to be asked. If she was honest, she hadn't been looking forward to spending Christmas Day on her own, and it wasn't as though she could have video-called her mum to eat a festive lunch together and pretend they were in the same room. Her mum would be eating lunch at three in the morning UK time! Maybe they could open their presents at the same time though, she thought – then she remembered the abysmal phone reception, so that wouldn't work either, unless she wanted to stand on top of the hillside to open the gift her mother had thrust into her hands before she'd departed.

Gifts!

Maybe she should buy Walter something, now that she was going to be seeing him on Christmas Day. And what about everyone else? Should she get the others a little present, too?

'Good, that's sorted,' Dulcie said decisively. 'Oh, and we're off to the pub tonight, if you'd like to join us.'

Before Eliza could reply, a shout went up and she heard the sound of an engine labouring up the lane. A minute later, a truck lumbered into the yard and she saw several furry little noses poking through the bars of the trailer it was pulling. Goats were cute, and she was looking forward to seeing them, and maybe even stroking a couple of those sweet noses.

She hung back whilst the truck manoeuvred the trailer into position in front of the barn, and watched as barriers were erected to make sure the creatures went where they were meant to go.

The bleating emanating from the trailer was incessant. Eliza guessed that the animals were eager to get out, and she craned her neck to see as a collective 'Ah!' went up.

When she spotted the littlest pygmy goat tiptoeing delicately down the trailer's ramp, Eliza realised why. It was the cutest, sweetest, most adorable creature, and she had a sudden urge to paint it. Whipping out her phone, she edged closer to get a couple of photos, but as she did so, she noticed the rapture on Maisie's face.

Maisie looked like she was in love – with a goat, no less!

If Eliza hadn't already had the urge to paint, the young woman's expression would have had her reaching for her brushes in an instant.

Then Eliza smiled – she knew exactly what she was going to give this new family of hers for Christmas.

♥

Eliza put the finishing touches to her make-up and took a look at herself in the mirror.

She'd do, she decided. Not too much slap that she looked like she was trying too hard, but enough to show that she was making an effort. She had also tried not to wear every item of clothing she had brought with her, even though it was freezing outside and getting colder by the hour.

Before she'd left the farm this afternoon (after taking what felt like hundreds of photos of the goats and several of Maisie – without the woman's knowledge, but Eliza hoped she would be forgiven), Walter had insisted he could smell snow and that it would be with them by tomorrow morning. Eliza wasn't entirely convinced that he wasn't pulling her leg; she had no idea what snow was supposed to smell like, or that it had any kind of smell at all.

She might get to find out in the morning, and she was strangely excited at the prospect: Aukland didn't get much in the way of snow, although there had been a blizzard several years ago which she only vaguely remembered.

A glance at her phone informed her that it was time to leave and she hurried downstairs, hooking her coat off the peg by the front door and hastily donning it. She was being picked up by Jay again, but this time she wouldn't be on her own with him for the short drive into the village. Maisie was travelling with them, whilst Dulcie, Beth and Walter were hitching a lift with Otto. Petra and her husband would also be joining them, as would Amos and his partner, Lena. It was going to be quite a crowd, and Eliza was apprehensive. Although she'd met most of them before, she wasn't used to so many people at once, and they were still relative strangers – even the two that *were* actual relatives!

Eliza hurried towards the car, got in and buckled up, saying hello as she did so, then blushing when she caught Jay's eye as he glanced in the rear-view mirror. 'Thank you for inviting me to Christmas lunch,' she said. 'It's very kind of you.'

'Blame Walter,' he replied with a smile. 'He insisted that you be subjected to the Fairfax version of festive fun. I think he wants a buffer between him and us, and I'm sorry to say that you're it. You'll probably wish you'd stayed at the cottage by the end of it. We can be a rowdy bunch.'

Maisie huffed. 'Speak for yourself.' She swivelled around to look over her shoulder at Eliza. 'I'm the quiet one.'

'Only because you've got your head in the clouds most of the time. Maisie is a daydreamer.' he added, speaking to Eliza. 'Or maybe a butterfly, flitting from one thing to the next. You've yet to find your niche in life, eh, Maisie?'

Eliza could hear the genuine affection in his voice as he teased his sister.

'Has Nikki been moaning again?' Maisie sounded cross. 'Just because she knew she wanted to be a teacher when she was six... Did you always want to be an artist?' she asked Eliza.

Eliza laughed. 'When I was growing up I wanted to be a hairdresser.'

'What made you change your mind?'

'My dad: he encouraged me to draw and paint, and the day I sold my very first painting I decided I wanted to be an artist instead.'

'How old were you?'

'Fifteen.'

'Gosh, I'm twenty-five, and I still don't know what I want to be when I grow up!' Maisie exclaimed.

'Sis, you *are* grown up,' Jay laughed.

She moaned, 'So why does everyone still treat me like a kid?'

'Because you're the baby of the family?'

'I thought that was supposed to be Sammy,' Maisie retorted. She smirked at him. 'Do me a favour and give Mum another grandchild, so the heat's off me.'

'Hey, ask Dulcie! She's the one with a partner.'

'I did. She said she can't think about having children just yet.'

'But I *can*?' Jay sounded amused.

Eliza thought it quite informative; in just a couple of minutes she had learnt that Jay was single and childless. Not that it mattered, of course...

Her train of thought was derailed as The Black Horse, the pub she had noticed on Monday night from the backseat of the taxi, came into view, and her chest constricted when she thought of all the people who would be there, some of whom she had only just met and others who would be total strangers.

She needn't have worried, though. She was made to feel very welcome, even if most of the chat went over her head, and she was content to listen to the various conversations flowing around her, answering the occasional question that was asked of her, and generally trying to take it all in.

Amos's partner, Lena (a cheerful woman in her sixties), was in the middle of telling them about something she called 'the wedding of the year,' which involved a woman by the name of October and a guy who owned a horse and could afford a big swanky do, when a blare of noise interrupted her.

It was coming from the corner of the room where a microphone had been set up, and Eliza's heart sank as she glanced up at the TV screen on the wall above it. It had burst into life with colourful flashing images and the words 'Sing Your Heart Out'. Yippee, karaoke, her favourite – *not* – and she shuddered at the thought of hearing yet another rendition of *Riptide* by Vance Joy.

'Is that what I think it is?' Jay asked Dulcie, nodding towards the setup in the corner.

Dulcie beamed. 'It is.'

'Why didn't you tell me it was karaoke night?' he groaned.

'Because you wouldn't have come?'

'Damn right, I wouldn't have.' He caught Eliza's eye, and she bit her lip. He looked as dismayed as she felt, and for some reason, she was pleased to discover that they had a dislike of karaoke in common.

'The Black Horse doesn't usually do karaoke,' his sister was saying. 'This is an exception. We get to sing along to Christmas songs, so think of it as a kind of carol service, but with wine and better music.'

Jay rolled his eyes and Eliza giggled. Maybe this wouldn't be so bad, she mused. She rather enjoyed a carol service.

With only three days to go until Christmas Day, the pub was very festive, and she particularly liked the log burner that pumped out lovely warmth from its home in the chimney breast. She had yet to find the courage to light the one in the cottage after it had gone out sometime during the early hours of Tuesday morning, but perhaps she would give it a go tomorrow. She planned on having a lie-in, doing some sketching and perhaps reading one of the books on the shelves in the cottage's living room. After two days of travelling followed by two days of meeting her uncle and his new family and being engulfed in their hectic lives, Eliza could do with a quiet day to recharge her batteries and give herself time to reflect.

But right this instant there was no chance of being quiet because the karaoke machine had kicked into life with the lively tune by Wizzard, and the whole pub began to sing along to the lyrics of *I Wish It Could Be Christmas Every Day* – with the exception of herself and Jay, who looked thunderstruck at the eruption of noise. Then he saw her gazing at him, gave a reluctant smile and a shrug, and began to sing.

Not wanting to feel left out, Eliza tried a tentative warble, aware that her singing voice left a lot to be desired, but she was soon belting out the tune as enthusiastically as the rest of them.

Several songs later, there was a brief respite for drinks to be refreshed, then it was all go again as *Merry Christmas Everyone* filled the air.

By the time the sing-along was over, Eliza was hoarse but happy. She hadn't had this much fun in ages, and she was incredibly grateful to Dulcie for inviting her this evening. The alternative – watching unfamiliar TV, in an unfamiliar house, all by herself – hadn't been a particularly appealing prospect.

It took ages for everyone to say goodnight, with lots of to-ing and fro-ing, and hugs and kisses on cheeks, but eventually Eliza found herself in the back seat of Jay's car once again and bouncing slowly up Muddypuddle Lane.

Jay insisted on driving as far as the little parking area reserved for the residents of Petra's cottages instead of dropping her in the lane, and when Eliza clambered out of the vehicle, she found that he had already got out.

'I'll walk you to your door,' he said, holding his phone aloft, the beam from it illuminating the path.

'You needn't bother, I'll be fine,' she replied not wanting to put him out. No doubt he would be glad to get back to the farmhouse after such a raucous evening.

'Humour me,' he said, falling into step alongside her. He cleared his throat and she sensed he felt awkward. 'I don't know about you, but my ears are ringing.'

'Mine, too,' she giggled. 'It was fun though.'

'Yeah, it was. Er, what are you doing tomorrow?'

'I thought I'd have a quiet day, pottering around the cottage.' She came to a stop outside the front door, the glow of the lamp that she'd left on before she went out visible through the living room curtains. It was enough to illuminate Jay's face.

'In that case, would you like to come to a nativity play? Petra is holding one at the stables, and Dulcie has ordered everyone to come along to show their support.' He huffed. 'If I've got to go, I don't see why *you* shouldn't have to, considering you're one of the family now.'

One of the family… was that how Jay viewed her? The thought was as lovely as it was disappointing – for reasons she would attempt to analyse later.

'How can I resist such a charming invitation?' she teased. 'What time?'

'Three o'clock. I'll see you there. Oh, and dress warmly. It's held in the arena but apparently it's colder inside, than out. Or so Dulcie reckons. Frankly, I'd be surprised if she has ever been in it: she doesn't like horses much.'

'I do,' Eliza said. 'I used to ride when I was younger.'

'Rounding up sheep on horseback?' Jay teased.

Eliza rolled her eyes. 'Why does everyone think of sheep when they think of New Zealand?' she shot back. 'We have plenty of other animals; but they're not too keen on being herded, though.'

'Such as?'

'How about seals?'

'Now you're talking.'

'Platypuses and echidnas?' she continued.

Jay groaned, 'Stop talking dirty to me.' Then he looked horrified and winced. 'Sorry, I didn't mean that the way it sounded.'

Eliza tried unsuccessfully to stifle a giggle. 'I take it you're fond of wildlife?'

'It kinda goes with the territory,' he said. 'I don't just install listening equipment, I help analyse the results, too. I might never see the creatures who make most of the noises I hear, but when I do… oh, man. It's such a privilege.'

Eliza felt the same. 'You'll have to come visit me sometime,' she said lightly. 'I might be biased, but Ruakaka is one of the best places for wildlife.'

'I might take you up on that.' He was looking into her eyes, his expression unreadable, and Eliza had a sudden vision of him in the hammock outside her bach, a hat over his face and a tinny in his hand. In her mind's eye, he looked as though he belonged there.

The vision dissolved when Maisie called from the car, 'Jay? What are you doing?'

'I'll be there in a sec,' he shouted back, his eyes not leaving Eliza's. 'See you tomorrow?'

She nodded, not trusting herself to speak. The image had sent a shiver down the back of her neck, and desire stirred in her stomach.

His voice was soft as he said, 'Sleep tight, Eliza.' And with that, he turned on his heel and headed off up the path.

She watched until he was out of sight. Watching him as he walked away was becoming a habit.

♥

Eliza's head was bent over the drawing pad, her pencil moving in quick, decisive strokes. Every so often she would refer to the photo on her phone to ensure the angle was right, but the true essence of the delight on Maisie's face was only coming to life in the sketch she was drawing.

The living room light overhead wasn't the best, but it was bright enough to sketch by, so when Eliza had found herself strangely restless (she should have been bushed after the busy, exciting day she'd had) she'd resorted to doing the one thing guaranteed to soothe and calm her – she drew.

As well as the sketch she was currently working on, several more drawings lay scattered across the table. She had been working for a couple of hours, unable to stop until she'd got the urge to create out of her system (for the time being) but she vowed to call it a day when she finished this one. It was late – or early, depending on one's perspective – and she should try to get some sleep, else she would be fit for nothing tomorrow.

Happy with what she'd done so far, she put her pencil down and surveyed the pieces of work critically. Maisie, face-to-face with the cutest of the pygmy goats; Sammy with his pup, Tara, licking his face; and a pastiche of all four of the Fairfax siblings, which still needed a great deal of work.

She also had the beginnings of a drawing of the farmhouse and yard (similar to the one hanging in Walter's house) and a very brief sketch of what she remembered of Otto's new restaurant.

She would paint the ones she could in the morning, when the kitchen was flooded with natural daylight, and resume work on the others later. But for now, she was done.

There was one painting that she wanted to do that she had yet to begin work on though, but that would have to wait until another time.

Exhaustion overwhelmed her, and she dropped her head into her hands and tried to find the energy to take herself off to bed.

But as she sat there sleepily, she became aware of the absolute silence filling the cottage.

It was unnerving and rather eerie.

Eliza straightened up, her eyes darting around the room. There wasn't so much as the tick of a clock to break the silence, and she was acutely aware of how isolated and alone she was in this little cottage. Her neighbours had left and the nearest people were up at the farm.

There was no one she could call on for help, should anything happen.

She got to her feet, feeling silly, and told herself off. *Of course* there were people she could call on: there was Petra for one, and there was always Walter or Jay.

Jay…

Her thoughts had kept circling back to him whilst she was working tonight, and she guessed he might have played some part in her restlessness.

Gah, she needed to get some sleep, but this blanketing silence was disconcerting. She could have sworn it hadn't been this quiet last night, or the night before.

Telling herself she was being a wimp, and trying to ignore the fact that it didn't matter how many numbers she had in her phone as there was no signal anyway, she got to her feet. It was time for bed. A good night's rest was all that was needed to put such fanciful thoughts out of her head.

But when she switched off the living room light, there was a strange glow coming from outside. The room should have been in darkness, but she could see far better than she should have been able to, and she eased the curtain aside, wondering if Petra had left an outside light on.

Eliza gasped at the sight before her.

Snow!

It was falling thickly in big fat flakes, and there was already a covering on the ground and a little layer had even accumulated on the windowsill.

Mesmerised, Eliza watched the snow drift lazily out of the sky, and her heart swelled at the beauty of the scene in front of her.

At that moment, Eliza felt happier than she had felt in a very long time.

CHAPTER FIVE

'It's been snowing,' Maisie announced, as Jay bounded into the kitchen, bright-eyed and bushy-tailed, eager to go outside and play. He had planned to work on Sammy's present some more today, but how could he resist that lovely snow!

'So I see. Great, isn't it!' he cried, snatching a slice of toast off her plate and cramming it into his mouth before she could object. Sometimes, he could be as childish as his youngest sister, and the sight of the snow-covered valley when he'd opened the curtains seemed to have brought out the big kid in him.

It had been years since he'd seen snow!

'Do you think the goats will be warm enough?' Maisie asked, worriedly.

'They're in the barn with lots of hay and straw, and they've got fur coats to keep them warm,' he told her.

'Dulcie said the same thing.'

'There you go, then!'

'But Dulcie doesn't know any more than I do about keeping goats.'

'Petra does, so Dulcie can always ask her. Wanna come outside?'

'I've been outside. It's cold.'

'You're no fun.'

Maisie sent him an arched look. 'Why don't you ask Eliza? You seem really into her.'

Jay was about to retort, when he hesitated. Was it so obvious that he fancied her? But fancying someone and doing something about it was a completely different box of frogs. He might be attracted to her and he might enjoy her company, but that didn't mean he was going to proposition her, not with her being part of Walter's family, and therefore part of his by Dulcie's association with Otto. Imagine if he did and she rebuffed him? It would make the rest of her stay here awkward for both of them.

But what if she didn't? What if she was as attracted to him as he was to her? Would it be awkward then?

Maybe… Especially when it was time for them to go their separate ways.

Then again, he had been in the same situation before, several times, and it had turned out alright, with both parties knowing full well that the relationship would only last a short while.

Which was why he was never going to settle down, he said to himself. Or, not for some considerable time at least. It simply wasn't feasible unless the woman in question was happy to follow him around the world.

Putting those thoughts to one side and ignoring the fact that he no longer had a job that took him around the world (unless he landed another contract) he made a mug of coffee and went to see if there was a pair of wellies he could borrow, and some gloves. He could feel a snowman-making session coming on!

♥

Despite having had only five hours sleep, as soon as Eliza opened her eyes she was instantly alert, as the memory of sitting at the window in the middle of the night and watching the snow fall from a leaden sky popped into her head.

Pushing the covers back, she leapt out of bed and raced to the window, and when she opened the curtains the sight had her gasping and laughing in equal measures.

The world was white, a stark contrast to the clear pale blue sky and watery sun, and she couldn't wait to go outside.

Ignoring her rumbling tummy, she threw on some clothes and scampered downstairs, lamenting her lack of waterproof boots as she dragged on her coat and opened the door.

To her amazement, it wasn't as cold as she'd assumed (although it was far chillier than she was used to) so she decided to walk up to the stables to ask whether the planned nativity play was still going ahead. She also wanted to take a photo or two of the farm, in order for her to complete her drawing this evening, so she set off gingerly, hoping the snow wasn't be as slippery as it looked.

It wasn't, and neither was it particularly deep – a few centimetres at most – but it crunched underfoot in a very satisfactory way and she had great pleasure in stamping along the path and leaving her footprints in the virgin snow. She even drew a heart in the snow-covered banking, standing back to admire her handiwork and smiling broadly.

The low rumble of an engine interrupted her fun, and she glanced in the direction of the lane. A tractor was moving slowly up it, and she wondered whether it was clearing the road.

Resuming her trek up the path to the stables, Eliza found several equine heads poking over the top of their stalls, ears flicking back and forth.

A woman was walking across the yard pushing a wheelbarrow with a fork poking out of the pungent pile it contained, and she halted when she spied Eliza. 'Can I help you?'

'Hi, I'm looking for Petra? I'm staying in one of the cottages down the way.'

'You must be Eliza. I've heard all about you. I'm Charity. I help out now and again. I think she's up at the house.'

'Thanks.' Eliza stopped to stroke a nose or two, breathing in the comforting smell of horse and wondering whether she would be able to book a hack. She had always wanted to ride in the snow and today would be perfect. However, she guessed Petra probably had her hands full with the nativity play (assuming it was still going ahead) so maybe she could book it another time. It would be good to get on the back of a horse again.

She knocked at the door and when Petra yelled, 'Come in,' Eliza tentatively stepped inside. Mindful of her snow-covered boots, she slipped them off and waggled her cold damp toes. Those boots weren't meant to be worn in the snow, or the rain for that matter.

'Take your socks off and put them on the radiator,' Petra instructed, coming into the hall and seeing her predicament. Her son appeared behind her, toddling determinedly towards the door, and she scooped him up, ignoring his protests. She said, with a grin. 'Amory has just learnt to walk, and now there's no stopping him.'

Petra's pride was obvious, and after Eliza had removed her wet socks and draped them on the radiator, she chucked the child under the chin. The little boy's lip quivered, and he gazed at her petulantly.

'I don't think he's very impressed with me,' Eliza said.

'He's not impressed with me right now either, so don't take it personally,' his mother said. 'Come through; there's a pot of coffee on the go and a slice of cake, if you fancy it.'

Eliza's tummy rumbled, and she laughed. 'I'd love some, please. I didn't bother with breakfast.'

'In that case, I can furnish you with a sausage sandwich, if you like?'

Eliza was sorely tempted. 'No thanks, cake will be fine.'

'It's no bother,' Petra insisted, leading her into a large kitchen where her husband, Harry, was seated at the scrubbed pine table, along with two other people. She continued, 'Nellie and Isaac have already had one, so I've got a couple of sausages going spare. If you don't eat them, they'll end up in the dogs.'

The dogs in question, the black spaniel who Eliza had seen before, and a brown and white terrier with a patch over one eye, stared at her balefully, as though daring her to deprive them of their breakfast.

'In that case, I'd love one,' she said, sending a silent 'sorry' to the dogs.

Petra handed Amory to his father and busied herself making the sausage sandwich, talking as she did so. 'This is Nelly and Isaac. Isaac is the architect who drew up the plans for the cottage you are staying in, and Nelly owns the building firm that did the construction. They're here this morning because Harry, bless him, thinks we need to build a hostel and offer riding holidays – as if I haven't got enough on my plate already.' She jabbed a knife in Eliza's direction and said to the couple, 'This is Eliza – she's staying in the middle cottage.'

Harry grinned. 'My idea of turning the cow shed into holiday lets was a good one, wasn't it?'

'Everyone is allowed one good idea in their life,' Petra retorted, but she was smiling to show she didn't mean it.

'How do you like the cottage?' Isaac asked.

'It's lovely,' Eliza said.

Nelly laughed, 'Stop fishing for complements.'

Isaac looked affronted. 'I just wanted some feedback,' he protested.

'You had feedback from your mum and dad. They were your guinea pigs when they stayed in one.'

Petra placed the sandwich on the table in front of Eliza, who uttered her thanks then picked it up and bit into it with enthusiasm.

'How *are* Julia and Stephen?' Petra asked Isaac as she reached for the coffee pot.

Julia? Eliza's ears pricked up. Was that a coincidence, she wondered, as she chewed.

Petra was saying, 'I haven't seen them for ages – not since the wedding. Ask them if they'd like to come to the nativity play this afternoon. As you saw, Nathan has cleared and salted the lane and the car park, and I believe the main roads are clear.'

'They are,' Nelly confirmed. 'The gritters were out last night.'

'I'll ask,' Isaac said. 'They did go to the summer fete, but you must have missed them.'

'I spent most of the day organising the gymkhana,' Petra explained. She turned to Eliza. 'Sorry, this must be boring for you, prattling on about people you don't know. Julia and Stephen are Isaac's parents, and they were the very first guests to stay in the cottages.'

'How long are you here for?' Nelly asked.

'Until the second of January.'

'Is that an Australian accent, I hear?' The woman tilted her head to the side.

'Not quite,' Eliza replied, and Petra leapt in with, 'Sorry, I should have mentioned when I introduced you, that Eliza is Walter's niece, over from New Zealand.'

Isaac was frowning. 'Walter's niece? As in, *Emrys's* daughter? Goodness me!'

And suddenly Eliza knew without a shadow of a doubt that this man's mother was the same woman who her father had been in love with all those years ago.

♥

Eliza tried to concentrate on the nativity play, but she couldn't. She had arrived early and had been scooped up by Dulcie and the rest of the family, who insisted that she joined them, and she was now seated between Walter, on her right, and Jay, on her left. But instead of enjoying the experience, she was craning her neck to look for Isaac, and wondering if any of the women in the arena's viewing gallery might be Julia.

Eliza managed to laugh in all the right places, clap when everyone else did, and look suitably enchanted at the 'ahhh' moments as the youngsters recited their lines. But neither her attention nor her heart had been truly in it, and as the play drew to an end, she felt guilty for not being as invested as she should, seeing how kind Petra had been earlier. The woman had obviously put a great deal of effort into it, and it had been wasted on her.

However, Eliza couldn't help how she felt, or how distracted she was, so when she found an opportunity to speak to Petra, she took it.

'Great play. The children were wonderful,' she said, taking a hot chocolate from a tray that one of the youngsters was holding. Several children were circulating with drinks and nibbles, and the old people from the care home in Picklewick were tucking in with enthusiasm.

Petra saw the direction of her gaze. 'I do it for them, mainly,' she said. 'I did worry that William, the care home's manager, might cry off because of the roads, but he decided it was safe enough, and they look forward to it so much.'

'They seem to be having a great time,' Eliza agreed. 'Did your other guests manage to make it?'

'Which ones?'

'Um, Julia and… Stephen?' Eliza struggled to remember the man's name but the woman's was seared on her mind.

'Yes, they did.'

'I know this sounds odd, but do you mind pointing Julia out to me?'

'May I know why?'

'My dad used to know her.'

'Emrys did?' Petra pursed her lips, and understanding flared in her eyes. 'I see. I suppose it's okay. But before I do, can you promise me that you'll speak to her privately and not in front of her husband.'

'Oh?'

'Last year, her marriage went through a difficult patch. I don't know the full details and neither do I want to, but I believe it was triggered by a certain phone call from New Zealand.' Petra gave her a knowing look.

Eliza's eyes widened and her mouth fell open. She closed it slowly and took a deep breath. It was clearly *her* phone call to Julia to which Petra was referring.

Petra added, 'I'll ask her to pop along to my office. You can chat there. It's the second door on the left as you leave the gallery.'

'Thank you.'

'I'm not saying she'll want to speak to you, mind,' Petra warned, 'but if she does, I'd appreciate it if you didn't upset her.'

'I'll try not to,' Eliza replied, wondering whether she was doing the right thing. Might it be prudent to let sleeping dogs lie?

She hurried along to the office and slipped inside, closing the door behind her. Briefly, she debated whether to pop back to the arena and tell Walter, or someone, where she was, in case they were looking for her, but as she dithered there was a knock on the door.

Eliza watched the handle move as the door slowly opened, and her eyes shot to the woman coming into view.

Julia looked puzzled and a little cross. 'Petra said someone wanted to see me, but she refused to tell me who or why.' Eliza could hear irritation in the woman's voice. 'I must say, I'm not too keen on all this cloak and dagger stuff.'

'Sorry.' Eliza was immediately on the back foot. 'It's me: I wanted to see you.' Her Kiwi twang was more noticeable next to the woman's clipped English tones.

Julia narrowed her eyes. 'Why? Who are you?' But there was a hint of wariness in her face, as though she had already guessed.

Eliza drew in a deep breath. 'I'm Emrys's daughter. We spoke on the phone.'

The woman froze. She looked alarmed and Eliza stepped forward. Julia took a corresponding step back, then glanced over her shoulder. People were leaving the viewing gallery and the corridor outside the office was noisy.

Eliza said hurriedly, 'Please, let me explain.'

'Sorry, I have to go. My husband will be wondering where I am.'

'I'm not here to cause trouble.'

'Trouble?' Julia's voice was sharp.

'Petra suggested there might have been a few issues between you and your husband after I spoke to you. I'm sorry if I was the cause.'

Her face softening, Julia said, 'It wasn't your fault. Thank you for informing me of your father's death.'

'Did you love him?' Eliza blurted.

Julia hesitated, then seemed to come to a decision. 'I can't talk here, but if you want to meet for a coffee after Christmas…?'

Eliza sighed with relief. 'I fly back to New Zealand on the second of January, so it'll have to be before then.'

She didn't know why it was so imperative that she found out more about her father's and Julia's relationship – it just *was*.

Julia said, 'There's a cafe called Rossi near the town hall in Thornbury. Shall we say next Thursday at ten o'clock?'

'I'll be there,' Eliza promised.

Julia nodded once and turned to the door. But before she stepped through it, she said softly, 'I can see him in you.'

Then she was gone, leaving Eliza with tears trickling down her face.

♥

'There you are!' Jay had been sent to look for Eliza by Walter, who wanted to ask her to have tea with him this evening but was worried that she had already left.

Jay had been on his way to the cottage, hoping to catch up with her, but just as he was about to leave the gallery a woman stepped out of a room, hurrying past, and when he glanced inside he spied Eliza.

It appeared to be an office, with a desk strewn with papers and a large whiteboard covered in marker pen on one wall. On another was shelf after shelf of riding hats.

Eliza stood in the middle of the room, her shoulders hunched. Her head was bowed and she was half-turned away from the open door.

'Walter sent me to—' Jay began but broke off abruptly. Unless he was very much mistaken, Eliza was crying. She was brushing at her cheeks with her fingers and her shoulders were shaking. 'What's wrong?' Instinctively he glanced behind him but there was no sign of the woman. 'Did that woman upset you?'

'Yes. No.' Eliza's voice wobbled. 'It's not her fault.'

'Can I do anything?'

'Not really.'

'Do you want to talk about it?'

She bit her lip and stared at the floor, and he assumed she didn't, but then she nodded and said, 'Not here – at the cottage?'

'I'll just go tell Walter. He sent me to find you because he wants to know if you'll have tea with him this evening. Just you and him.'

'I'd like that.'

'He also told me to tell you he does a mean hotpot.'

That raised a smile, albeit a small one, and Jay was relieved.

'What time does he want me?' she asked.

'Six?'

'Tell him I'll be there.'

'I'll see you back at the cottage,' he said, and hurried to deliver the message to Walter.

There was no sign of the woman he had seen coming out of the office a few moments ago, and Jay wondered what she could have said or done to make Eliza cry.

After telling Walter that Eliza would love to have tea with him, Jay found Petra and thanked her, congratulating her on a successful nativity play, then he squeezed past the numerous old folks who appeared reluctant to leave, and jogged across the yard and down the path leading to the row of holiday cottages.

The door to the one Eliza was staying in was ajar, so he knocked and went inside, looking around curiously.

He had stepped straight into the sitting room, and although it was small, it had a nice squashy couch, an armchair and a telly at one end. At the other was a dining table situated in front of patio doors which led out to a small courtyard-type garden.

The room was warm, cosy, and festive, and he could tell that Petra had made an effort to make her guest feel welcome over the Christmas period.

On hearing noises coming from the kitchen, he called, 'Hello?' not wanting to startle Eliza.

'I'm making a pot of tea,' she called back. 'Would you like a cup?'

'Please.' He moved closer until she came into view, and studied her carefully as she made the tea. She looked perkier than she had a few minutes ago, he was relieved to find, and she even managed another smile when she saw him looming in the doorway.

'The cottage is nice,' he said, hunting around for something to say.

'It's lovely,' she agreed. 'Milk and sugar?'

'Just milk.' He watched her pour the tea into two mugs, from a proper teapot, then add a drop of milk.

She gave them a quick stir, then handed one to him.

'Shall we go sit down?' she suggested, and he stepped back into the living room, taking a seat on the sofa.

'I bet it's toasty in here when that's lit,' he observed, after an awkward silence where neither of them seemed to know what to say. He jerked his chin at the small log burner.

'It would be if I knew how to get it going.'

'Would you like me to show you?' Over the years, Jay had lit a fair few fires in his time. Crouching down on the floor, he opened the front of it, aware that Eliza had joined him on the rug.

She was watching intently as he scrunched up a couple of sheets of the newspapers that had been placed neatly in a basket next to the burner, along with kindling and some suitably sized logs.

She was so close that her knee was touching his thigh, and he could smell her perfume – a light, floral scent that reminded him of summer meadows. His heart skipped a beat when she leant even closer to study the way he was stacking the kindling on top of the newspaper.

'You need something that catches light quickly,' he explained. 'That's what the newspaper is for. And something that burns easily but a little slower, like these sticks. Then the logs go on one at a time, but only when the kindling has caught. If you put too many on at once, you run the risk of smothering the fire before it has a chance to get going.' He reached for the box of matches on the mantlepiece and struck one, holding the flame against the scrunched-up newspaper until it caught.

Slowly the fire ate through the paper, and he thought it had gone out, but with a little spark a piece of kindling caught, and pretty soon he had a small blaze going.

After adding some logs and watching it for a while, Jay was confident that the fire wouldn't go out. He sat back on his heels.

Eliza was gazing into the flames, a distant look on her face. Her skin glowed, and the fire flickered in her eyes. 'I guess you're wondering what all that was about?' she said.

'You don't have to tell me, if you don't want to.'

She didn't seem to have heard. 'She said she can see my dad in me.'

Jay was confused. 'Is that a bad thing?'

'No, it's a good thing.' She glanced up at him. 'No one's ever said that before. I look nothing like him, you see; I take after my mother.'

There was silence for a moment, then Jay said softly, 'Maybe she wasn't referring to your looks?'

Another silence.

Jay risked a glance in her direction and was dismayed to see Eliza crying again. Tears were trickling quietly down her face, and her expression was so sad that his heart went out to her.

Without thinking, he scooted closer and put his arm around her, pulling her into him. Resting his cheek lightly on the top of her head, he gently rubbed her arm and waited.

'I'm sorry,' she sniffed after a few minutes. 'What must you think of me?'

'Do you feel able to talk about it? Do I need to thump someone?'

She uttered a croaky laugh. 'No, no thumping needed.'

Jay felt quite bereft when she sat up to brush away the tears with her fingers, and he told himself to stop being a jerk. To his shame, he had enjoyed holding her far too much, given the circumstances.

'My dad – Walter's brother – died two years ago, and nothing's felt right since,' she began, drawing her knees into her chest and wrapping her arms around her legs as she stared into the fire. Jay put another log on it and closed the burner's door.

'He was my champion, you know?' she continued. 'He always had my back and fought my corner. When Mum tried to get me to study *something sensible*—' Eliza did air quotes '—Dad told her to let me be, that I had to tread my own path.'

'As an artist?'

She nodded. 'Mum wanted me to have a *proper job*, get married and settle down, like my sister, Cathy.' Her laugh had a bitter edge. 'I failed on both counts. My job is precarious, I live in what she calls a shack, and my marriage fell apart after a couple of years. I think I'm a big disappointment to her.'

Jay didn't know what to say to that, so he said nothing.

Eventually she carried on. 'I miss my dad so much, and I just wanted to see where he was born, where he spent the first part of his life. I suggested that we all go to the UK, as a kind of homage to him, but Mum was dead against it and Cathy wasn't interested. Mum claimed she couldn't face all the travelling, and she also said she didn't want to rake up the past. She's not happy that I'm here – and I think Julia might be the reason.'

'Julia?'

'After Dad died, I found a note in his papers, asking for a woman by the name of Julia Richards to be contacted in the event of his death.' Eliza turned her gaze on him. 'I believe they had a relationship.'

'They were lovers?'

'Walter seemed to think so.' She shrugged. 'There was definitely something between them.' After a deep sigh, she said, 'I suspect my mum's reluctance to accompany me on this trip might have more to do with Julia, rather than the travelling. Maybe Mum was right: digging up the past wasn't a good idea. Perhaps I shouldn't have come.'

'Did you come here just to find out more about your father and Julia?'

'No, I came here because I wanted to know about Dad's life before he came to New Zealand.'

'And have you?'

'A bit. Walter and I had a long chat.'

'Are you glad you met Walter? And Otto?'

'Yes.' Her reply was emphatic.

'Then you didn't make the wrong decision,' he assured her.

She gave him a rueful smile. 'I've discovered I have a whole new family.'

'Yeah, about that... You may wish you hadn't. My sisters can be very full-on. Not to mention my mum.'

'They're lovely, Dulcie especially.'

'What about me?' he joked. 'Aren't I lovely too?' He was trying to cheer her up and lighten the mood, but when he saw the solemn expression on her face as she gazed soulfully into his eyes, he realised it had backfired. Now was not the time to be making jokes, however well-intentioned.

She continued to stare at him, and he felt the tension in the air. It sizzled between them, an electric current that he was unable to name

Her eyes were large and luminous, glistening from her recent tears, and her face seemed to be growing closer. It was only when her lips parted and she lifted her chin, that he realised he was about to kiss her.

Or she, him…

Without knowing who moved first, his mouth was on hers and a jolt shot through him. Then he was kissing her deeply, his tongue delving between her lips. She entwined her arms around his neck and he sank his fingers into her hair, his other hand resting on the rug behind her as he gently lowered her down, his body covering hers.

Her soft curves lay underneath him, and all he could think of were the sensations coursing through him as the kiss carried him away.

Just as his hand slipped underneath her fleece, a loud crack from a log splitting on the fire brought him to his senses, and he froze.

What was he *doing?*

This was such a bad idea on so many levels. Not only was she a guest of his sister's (in a way), but she was also upset, and he felt as though he was taking advantage of her. Although he badly wanted to make love to her, it went against the grain to do so like this.

Reluctantly, he kissed her softly, the passion dial turned way down, then he released her and sat up.

Eliza lay sprawled on the rug, her lips rosy from his kiss and her pupils so large and deep he feared he might fall headlong into them. Her chest heaved, and when she caught her bottom lip between her teeth and blinked slowly, it took all the control he had not to throw caution to the wind.

'I'd better go,' he said. 'You'll be needing to set off to Walter's soon.' He watched her closely as her eyes regained their focus and the desire drained out of them.

'What? Er… yeah. Walter.' She sat up, adjusting her fleece, and smiled nervously. 'Thanks for listening.' Spots of colour had appeared on her cheeks, and he wondered whether they resulted from embarrassment or arousal.

'It was my pleasure,' he replied warmly.

'Mine, too.' Her voice was low, and her blush deepened.

'I didn't mean…' he began, realising how that sounded, then he trailed off.

With a wry twist of her lips, she said, 'I did.' And without waiting for a response, she scrambled to her feet.

Jay also stood up. 'Will we see you tomorrow?' He said it lightly, saying 'we' instead of 'I' because he didn't want to put any pressure on her, despite hoping she would say yes. There was something about this woman that had captured his imagination. She had fired a spark inside him that burnt brighter each time he saw her.

It did concern him that she had such an effect on him, but he didn't want to think about that now. He simply wanted to see her again – soon.

'Possibly.' Her reply was non-committal. 'I've got some shopping to do.'

'Would you like a lift into the village?'

'I think I'll have to go to Thornbury.'

'I can take you if you like?'

'Are you sure?'

'I'm sure. Ten o'clock?'

When she agreed, some of his tension eased. He told himself that he didn't like the idea of her traipsing around a strange place alone, despite realising she had travelled halfway around the world on her own and was quite capable of taking the bus to a town that was only nine miles away.

But the real reason was that since the first moment he saw her, he hadn't been able to get her out of his mind. And now that he'd kissed her, he had the disturbing feeling he wouldn't be able to get her out of his heart.

CHAPTER SIX

When Eliza woke, the first thought to enter her head was that she had kissed Jay. The second was that it was Christmas Eve and she was nearly twenty thousand kilometres from home.

It was strange to think of her mum doing some last-minute shopping in the summer sunshine to the sound of Christmas tunes in the shops and festive lights in store windows. She could imagine her strolling along Queen Street and eyeing Smith & Caughey's famous Christmas windows. The department store always had the best animated decorations, which usually included handmade puppets and light displays. Her mum would have already picked up the lamb for Christmas lunch, but she would want to buy the veggies and salad stuff fresh, as well as the seafood for the starter and the fruit for the customary pavlova.

Traditionally, Eliza had always made the trip to Aukland to spend the festive season with her parents, although the previous two Christmases had been awful without her dad.

Thinking of her father brought yesterday into sharp relief again, but rather than her mind being filled with Dad and the chat she'd had with Julia, her thoughts centred on Jay.

For a while, she'd thought that he had been about to make love to her, and never had her body craved another's touch as it had craved his. But he had pulled back, and her disappointment had been acute.

All through the delicious meal of lamb hotpot that Walter had made with his own hands (no Otto, this time) Eliza hadn't been able to get Jay out of her mind. Nevertheless, she'd had a lovely evening getting to know Walter better, and he had regaled her with stories of his and her dad's childhood, and had clearly enjoyed reminiscing. Eliza also felt that she had gotten to know her father better too, which was a comfort.

With an hour to go before Jay collected her, Eliza pottered around, getting dressed, eating breakfast, and looking over the work she had done after she'd got back from Walter's yesterday evening. She'd been forced to paint without the benefit of daylight, but she was pleased when she saw the results of her efforts this morning, as the weak winter sun shone through the window illuminating the pictures sitting on the table.

They were nowhere near her best work, but they weren't her worst either, and she decided they would do. All except one. She picked it up and examined it, trying to work out what was lacking, but it eluded her for the moment.

Irritated, she gathered up the others and took them upstairs to lay them on the mattress in the spare bedroom. They were dry, so they would be fine there until she was ready to mount and frame them. *If,* that is, she could find a shop in Thornbury that sold ready-cut mounts and frames.

Luckily, the drawing pad she used was a standard A4 size, so she shouldn't have any difficulty buying frames for the paintings and if she had to do without the cardboard mounts, then so be it.

She'd just finished getting ready when she heard Jay's car pull up. Grabbing her coat and bag, she hurried out to meet him, slipping into the passenger seat with a tentative smile, unsure how to behave after yesterday's kiss.

To her relief, he smiled back, as open and sunny as always, and she began to wonder whether he was going to pretend it had never happened.

She wished she could!

Although she didn't regret it as such (it had been far too exciting for that) she knew it had been reckless. Eliza was self-aware enough to know that she had a tendency to give her heart too freely, and that if she gave her heart to Jay she would get hurt. Not because he was a bad person, but because there was no hope of any kind of relationship beyond the short time she would spend in this country.

It didn't take long to drive to Thornbury, but it took considerably longer to find a free parking space. The town was busy, and the atmosphere was extremely festive; there was a sense of anticipation in the air, and also a sense of urgency as people hurried to and fro to finish their Christmas shopping.

'What exactly is it you need?' Jay asked as they wandered down the high street.

'I'm looking for a shop selling picture frames,' Eliza replied.

'Shall we try down here?' Jay pointed to a side street that seemed to have fewer chain stores and more independent shops.

'We can give it a go,' she said, and was surprised when Jay took hold of her hand. It was busy, and they had to dodge and sidestep elderly people, pushchairs, and groups of teenagers. Anxious not to lose him, Eliza gripped Jay's hand tightly. At least, that's what she tried to tell herself. The real reason was that she found she enjoyed the contact very much indeed.

It took her a while, but she eventually spotted a shop that seemed promising and went inside, and a short while later she emerged clutching several frames of the same size that had mounts already built into them. All she needed now was wrapping paper and greeting cards, and her shopping was done.

'Do you mind if we stop off for a coffee?' Jay asked.

'Not at all.'

'Actually, I was thinking perhaps you could have a coffee while you wait for me?'

'Why? Where are you going?'

'I've got some errands to run. I won't be long, I promise.'

A short way down the street was a cafe and she went inside, bemused, wondering what Jay was up to that he didn't want her to see. The thought briefly crossed her mind that he might want to pop into a chemist for some condoms, and the very idea made her shiver. Perhaps that was why he had stopped kissing her yesterday afternoon? Another shiver travelled down her spine, and she swiftly pushed away the heady thought of Jay making love to her.

Ordering a hot chocolate with decadent cream and fluffy marshmallows on top, she took a seat near the window to keep an eye out for him, and as she sipped her drink she wondered anew why she was taking such a risk. She was in danger of losing her peace of mind if she gave into her base desire to jump his bones.

Eliza almost snorted into her hot chocolate. Jump his bones, indeed! That was hardly romantic, was it? But that was precisely what she felt like doing. She didn't want to take it slow. She wanted to dive headlong into a mad passionate affair, regardless of how soon it might end.

Recognising how reckless those thoughts were, she concentrated on her forthcoming meeting with Julia instead. Thinking about what the woman and her father might have meant to each other certainly served to throw a bucket of cold water on her lust, and by the time Jay eventually returned (which was rather longer than she had anticipated) she was thoroughly in control of herself once more.

Jay strode into the coffee shop, breathless and apologetic. 'Sorry I took so long,' he said, but he didn't offer any further explanation of where he'd been or what he'd done. He wasn't holding any packages or any bags, so she could only assume that whatever it was could be easily concealed in a pocket. Or maybe he'd not been able to find what he wanted? Or maybe his errands hadn't had anything to do with shopping.

Hoping for a clue, she asked, 'Did you get what you wanted?'

Jay blinked. 'Yes, I did, thank you.'

Ah, so he *had* been shopping.

Before she could question him further, he asked, 'Are you done? Is there anywhere else you'd like to go?'

'I just need wrapping paper and Christmas cards,' she said, getting to her feet. He held his hand out for the bag of frames, and she hesitated before passing it to him. 'It's not heavy,' she protested.

'That's not the point. It wouldn't be right, you with your arms full and me not carrying anything. Let's get you that wrapping paper and those cards, then how about we have a quick bite to eat before we head back to Muddypuddle Lane?'

Eliza thought that was a wonderful idea, so the rest of her purchases were made very quickly and they were soon sitting across the table from one another in a small bistro just off Thornbury's main street.

Over a light lunch of hot pulled pork and apple rolls, along with a small glass of white wine for Eliza and a glass of Pepsi for Jay, he advised her that Dulcie expected Eliza to spend the rest of Christmas Eve with the Fairfax family, along with Walter and Otto. The agenda was to walk into Picklewick to attend the carol service at the church and watch the candlelight procession through the village this evening, followed by a late dinner cooked by Otto.

'Poor Otto,' Eliza said, after confirming that she would be delighted to spend the evening with them. 'It must be awful for him to have to do all this cooking and not be able to join in.'

Jay arched an eyebrow. 'I get the feeling he enjoys it,' he said with a smile. 'Otto strikes me as the sort of man who wouldn't do anything he didn't want to do. Anyway, from what I understand, he's going to prepare everything beforehand so he can come with us to the carol service.'

'I hope his restaurant is a success,' she said, taking another bite of her delicious pork roll.

'So do I. He's invested an awful lot in it,' Jay said, and went on to explain about the job offer that had been made to Otto a couple of months ago by his former boss in London which he had turned down, finishing with, 'My daft sister is still holding onto vestiges of guilt because she felt Otto has given up an awful lot for her.'

'But anyone can see how happy they are,' Eliza pointed out. The pair of them made her heart melt, they were so much in love. Then there was Nikki and Gio, who, from what Eliza had witnessed, were more reserved, especially around Sammy, but despite that, she could see how devoted they were to each other.

At that moment, she happened to glance away from her plate and up at Jay.

He was staring at her intently, as though he wanted to whisk her off to bed and make love to her until morning.

But what stole her breath and made her heart leap, was the realisation that she would happily let him.

♥

It might be dark and cold this evening, but Jay thought the walk from Muddypuddle Lane to Picklewick across the fields to the church was simply magical.

Snow still lay on the ground, covering the grass in an uneven blanket, and the sky was a clear inky black studded with diamonds. A gibbous moon lit the path to the village, and as he walked alongside Eliza, the snow crunched underfoot and their misty breath hung in the air.

Dulcie and Otto were ahead of them, but Maisie and Beth had opted to take the car into the village with Walter. To his shame, Jay wished that Dulcie and Otto had also driven, so he could have had Eliza all to himself and kissed her under the stars in the snow.

Not a good idea, mate, he admonished silently, as soon as the thought crossed his mind. He had to keep reminding himself of this, because he seemed to be rather forgetful lately. Eliza was dominating his thoughts and was in his mind constantly.

It took about twenty minutes to reach the outskirts of the village where the path leading from the stables met the road into Picklewick, and as they walked along the pavement, Eliza slowed to peer into a garden.

'Aw, isn't that pretty!' she exclaimed. The house it belonged to was draped in twinkling fairy lights and a miniature Santa's grotto sat in the middle of the lawn. 'Christmas seems so much more Christmassy here than it does in New Zealand.'

'Is that because it's summer there?'

'Probably. I've always wanted to experience a Dickensian Christmas Day, instead of spending it sweltering in the sun with a barbeque on the go.'

'Is that what you'd normally have for Christmas dinner? A barbecue?'

'No, Mum always cooks lamb. That's more traditional in New Zealand, rather than turkey or goose.'

'I don't know anyone who actually has goose. Otto is cooking turkey. He put it in the oven before we left this evening. You ought to see it – it's massive. But I suppose it has to be if it's going to feed ten. My task in the morning is to peel the spuds, Dulcie's is to tackle the carrots – Otto is insisting they are cut into batons and not round slices – and Mum is responsible for the sprouts.'

'Is there anything I can do?'

'Hide,' Jay said dryly.

'What about Maisie? Will she be hiding too?'

Jay pulled a face. 'I don't think Otto trusts her to do anything in the kitchen. Not after she burnt the milk for the hot chocolates the other day. I think she did it on purpose.'

'Surely not!'

He nodded. 'It wouldn't be the first time. Dulcie suggested that Maisie sees to the chickens and the goats, and leave the cooking to everyone else.' He leant in closer, inhaling Eliza's sweet perfume as he added in a whisper, 'I wish I'd thought of that. I'd much prefer to feed goats than peel potatoes.'

'Are you sure I can't help?'

'I'm sure. Relax and enjoy your holiday.'

'It's *your* holiday, too.'

Jay flinched. He still hadn't told anyone that he wouldn't be returning to Borneo. He had decided to leave it until the New Year, in the hope that something would have come up by then, so all he said now was, 'It's my family, therefore I'm obligated to help.'

'I thought you said I was part of it?'

'You are.'

'Well, then. I'll help with the potatoes.'

Jay found he was looking forward to it. Which was strange, because until now he hadn't been too enthused to be given such a chore.

Eliza brought him back to the present when she cried, 'Oh, how lovely!' and pointed to the lychgate.

533

The entrance to the churchyard was festooned in twinkling lights, and the path leading to the porch was lined with flickering candles inside glass lanterns. An organ was playing, and the sweet notes of *Away in a Manger* drifted on the air.

Without warning, it brought a tear to his eye, as the ethereal atmosphere enveloped him in a sense of peace and serenity.

Feeling unusually emotional, Jay's hand sought Eliza's and he wrapped his fingers around it and squeezed lightly. She returned the gesture, her eyes shining, and unable to stop himself, Jay bent his head and kissed her.

She tasted of cinnamon and honey, and her lips were warm and soft. They parted, his tongue slipped between them, seeking hers.

He was so lost in her that he forgot he was standing on the pavement outside a church, until someone pushed past him, muttering, 'Get a room.'

Jay dragged his mouth from Eliza's, his heart hammering, his breathing ragged, and he met her shocked gaze in dismay. 'Sorry,' he stammered, scrambling to turn the heat down on his super-charged emotions. This was neither the time nor the place to give in to such temptation.

'I'm not.' Her reply was soft, but the look in her eyes was anything but. They smouldered and his desire spiked again, slamming into him, making him want to throw her over his shoulder and march back up the hill to her cottage.

'Shall we go inside?' he said instead, his voice gruff.

'I think we'd better, before I suggest something I'll regret,' she replied.

Please suggest it, he almost begged, but held himself in check. Never had he wanted to take a woman to bed more than he wanted to make love with Eliza, and not giving in to his desire was killing him because he sensed she wanted it as much as he.

But this time it wasn't worry about whether it would make things awkward for the rest of their time in Picklewick that held him back; it was because he was worried that he would never want to let her go.

The rest of the Fairfax family, plus Walter, were already inside the church. Jay and Eliza slipped into the pew behind Dulcie and Otto, and for the next forty minutes Jay joined in with the hymn-singing and pretended to listen to the readings. He wasn't a church-going man, but he usually enjoyed the tradition and familiarity of the service, as well as the uplifting and expectant atmosphere. However, on this occasion, all he could concentrate on was Eliza.

The happiness on her face when she collected her Christingle orange, which had cloves inserted into it and a flickering candle on the top, made his heart swell and he couldn't take his eyes off her as she carefully walked down the aisle, shielding the flame with one hand to ensure it didn't go out.

By this point, the lights in the church had been dimmed, and it was lovely to see the procession of candles making their way towards the main door. Once there, people popped them into lanterns stacked on a table and took them outside.

When it was Jay and Eliza's turn, he heard her delighted gasp as she emerged from the church to see a snaking line of bobbing lanterns along the path to the lychgate and beyond, led by Picklewick's vicar.

'I feel like I've stepped back in time,' she said, holding her lantern aloft, her eyes shining. 'I wonder if my dad took part in a ceremony like this when he lived here.'

'He did,' Walter confirmed. 'Every year, until he left home.'

Eliza sighed in satisfaction. 'I was hoping you'd say that. I feel so much closer to him, doing the things he used to do and seeing the things he used to see.'

Jay noticed that the glimmer in her eyes was due to unshed tears, and he put an arm around her shoulder and squeezed gently.

She leant into his side and he inhaled her intoxicating perfume, his heart thudding as she gazed up at him. Never had he wanted to kiss any woman as much as he wanted to kiss Eliza right now, and it was with considerable effort that he pulled his gaze away.

He didn't let go of her, although he did drop his arm, his hand finding hers again, and they proceeded to meander through the village hand-in-hand. And in that moment, one that would be forever etched on his heart, Jay fervently wished that he could hold her hand forever.

♥

Eliza popped a morsel of honey-glazed ham in her mouth and swooned. It was so succulent and flavoursome, that she eagerly ate another mouthful.

'This is divine,' she said to Otto. 'What's your secret?'

He beamed at her. 'Pineapple juice.' Otto gazed around the dinner table, a cheeky grin on his face.

'I've got some left over, if anyone wants a Pina Colada later?'

'Ooh, yes please!' Maisie squealed, and Eliza was sorely tempted.

But when Otto gave her the choice between a Snowball, a blackberry brandy or Baileys Orange Truffle, she was spoilt for choice.

After an impressive meal of cold meats, salad, potatoes and more relishes than she had seen outside of a Pac'N'Save supermarket, Eliza was stuffed. And the salad hadn't just been a few lettuce leaves and tomatoes in a bowl, either! It had been magnificent. The main course was followed by cheese, biscuits and fruit, and Eliza was convinced she couldn't eat another morsel. However, she was certain she could manage a glass of something alcoholic and Christmassy, so she eventually opted for the Snowball, figuring that she might have a taste of the delicious-sounding Baileys later.

With Otto presiding over the drinks in the kitchen (did that man never stop?!) Eliza wandered into the living room.

Seeing the Fairfax family and Walter gathered there, laughing and chatting, sent a sudden blast of homesickness straight through her, and she abruptly realised that it was already Christmas Day in Auckland and had been for several hours.

Jay saw her hovering in the doorway and he beckoned her over. He was sitting on the floor with Sammy (who was beginning to flag) and the pup (who had already flaked out) and he gestured for her to sit next to him.

Eliza hesitated. Ever since Jay had kissed her in the snow outside the church, all she could think about was how much she wanted him, and she wasn't sure how wise it would be to cuddle up on the floor with him. She was already ankle-deep in this man, and she didn't want to sink any deeper because she guessed she might struggle to extricate herself.

Yep, she was a sucker for a handsome face and a fit body; but she had firsthand experience of what handsome could do, and there was no way she was going back to New Zealand with a broken heart simply because she had allowed Jay to have his wicked way with her. She didn't have the type of personality to enjoy a romp between the sheets and for it not to mean anything. She wished she did, because she could give in to her desire, have a thoroughly enjoyable time, and then walk away without a backward glance.

'Are you okay, Eliza?' Dulcie asked. 'You're looking rather pensive.'

'I bet she's missing her mum,' Beth said, sending Eliza a sympathetic look. 'It can't be easy being away from your family at Christmas. Why don't you give her a call? You'll feel better after you talk to her.' Beth glanced at the clock on the dining room wall. 'What time is it in New Zealand?'

'About nine-thirty,' Eliza said. It was a good idea to call her mum, and it would also give her an excuse to have a few minutes away from Jay.

'Go on, what are you waiting for?' Beth urged.

'Privacy?' Walter muttered under his breath.

He might have spoken quietly but Beth heard. 'She can have as much privacy as she wants.' She stuck out her chin and glared at him.

Dulcie got to her feet. 'Come with me. I'll give you the wifi password and you can go upstairs and talk in peace.' She raised her eyebrows at Walter, who nodded his approval.

After telling her the password, Dulcie shoved Eliza towards the stairs. 'Take as long as you need. I'll make sure you won't be disturbed.'

It was kind of Dulcie, but Eliza was already disturbed, and it was Dulcie's brother who was doing the disturbing.

She trotted upstairs, eager to speak to her mum, hoping she would be up by now.

'Where on earth are you?' were her mother's first words when the video call connected.

'Lilac Tree Farm.'

'It looks as though you're in a cave.' Her mum was peering at the screen, her face filling it. She had a dab of sunscreen on the bridge of her nose and Eliza guessed that she, along with Cathy and Toby, Cathy's husband, were out on the deck, enjoying breakfast in the sun.

'I'm at the top of the stairs,' she explained.

'Why are you at the top of the stairs?'

A burst of raucous laughter drifted up from the living room and Eliza smiled. 'That's why. It's noisy down there.'

'You appear to be having a good time,' her mother sniffed.

'I am.' She was having the best time ever, and her homesickness abruptly faded in the face of her mother's obvious disapproval.

Honestly! Her mum could at least be thankful that Eliza wasn't spending Christmas Eve on her own. But then again, it would have given her an opportunity to say 'I told you so,' and crow that Eliza should have stayed in New Zealand and not gone traipsing halfway around the world.

Eliza changed the subject to one more to her mother's liking. 'How's Cathy?'

'The morning sickness has stopped, thank God, and about time too. She's twenty-eight weeks now. Hopefully, she can enjoy her lunch.'

'Is she visiting her in-laws this year?'

Another sniff. 'She and Toby are leaving the day after tomorrow, so I'll be all alone for New Year.'

Great guilt-tripping, Mum, Eliza thought. 'Haven't you been invited to next door's party?'

Her parents used to go to their neighbours' bash every year. Last year Eliza had gone with her. The year before that, Dad's death had been too recent and too raw, and none of them had felt like going anywhere.

'I don't want to go on my own,' her mum complained.

Eliza held back a sigh. 'You won't *be* on your own. The whole street will be there.' There was more sniffing and when Eliza heard her sister calling in the background, she said with relief, 'I'll let you go,' adding softly, 'Happy Christmas, Mum.'

'Hmm, you too.' A pause followed then, 'Love you, Eliza.'

'Love you, too.' Eliza ended the call with a lump in her throat, and she took a moment to compose herself before joining the others.

When she reached the bottom of the stairs, Jay emerged from the living room and wordlessly took her in his arms. She didn't know how much, if anything, he had heard, but she didn't care if he'd heard every word, because a hug was exactly what she needed.

He held her for several seconds as she clung to him, then he kissed the top of her head, took her by the hand and led her into the bosom of her new, exuberant, and incredibly welcoming family.

CHAPTER SEVEN

Eliza carefully hoisted the bag of presents and stepped outside. It had snowed again overnight (she hadn't been awake to witness it this time) and flakes were still falling, although the cloud layer was lifting.

She thought of Sammy, and the countless other children waking up this Christmas morning to a white world, and she wondered if they felt any of the joy that was coursing through her veins right now. Their parents mightn't be as thrilled, especially if they had places to go and people to see, but Eliza couldn't help feeling thankful that she was here to experience her first, and probably her only white Christmas.

Treading carefully in her borrowed wellies – Dulcie had loaned her a pair earlier in the week – Eliza walked up the path to the farm. It meant passing through the stable yard, and she spotted Petra and Harry, who were seeing to the horses. Little Amory was with them, dressed in an all-in-one padded suit and bright yellow boots with ducks on them.

'Merry Christmas,' Petra called on seeing her. 'Off up to the farm?'

Eliza chucked the child under his chubby chin. 'Merry Christmas. Yes, I've been invited to lunch.'

'Amos told me you had, otherwise I would have asked you to join us here.'

Eliza's heart swelled. 'That's so kind of you, but I'm sorted. Is this little one pleased with his presents? He's so cute.'

'This 'little one' is a tyrant. He's had us up for hours. Not because he wanted to open his presents, you understand, but because he wanted to go outside and play in the snow. As far as he's concerned, building a snowman is the best present in the world. God help us when the weather turns and it melts. I'm bracing myself for the biggest tantrum ever.'

Eliza giggled. 'I don't blame him. I couldn't wait to play in it, either.' She would never admit it, but she had already built a small snowman of her own in the courtyard outside the cottage, and she'd had immense fun doing it too.

When she arrived at the farm, despite it being only ten o'clock, Eliza discovered that all the lunch preparations had already been done, and no potato peeling was required.

Jay held up his hands and wiggled his fingers. 'See these? Wrinkled from hours spent peeling spuds, so you don't have to,' he teased, before scooping her into a hug. 'Merry Christmas, Eliza.'

The rest of the Fairfaxes plus Walter and Otto followed suit, until she was all hugged out, and when they finally released her, she said, 'I've, um, brought a couple of little gifts,' and she held the bag aloft.

'Aw, you shouldn't have,' Dulcie said, taking it from her. 'Shall I put it under the tree? We've not opened any presents yet, as we thought we'd wait until Nikki, Gio and Sammy got here.'

'Good idea.' Eliza unzipped her coat, beginning to feel rather warm now she was indoors, but Jay stopped her.

'Keep that on, we're going outside,' he said. 'You too, Dulcie. Otto, are you coming?' Jay had a glint in his eye, and Eliza wondered what he was up to.

She soon found out.

The moment she stepped through the door, a snowball hit her on the arm, and Jay had another in his hand, armed and primed. Not to be outdone, Otto bent down to scoop up a handful of snow, and swiftly moulded it into a ball.

Dulcie shot Eliza a look and they nodded to each other. 'Game on!' Dulcie cried and Eliza gave a squeal of joy.

Leaping aside to dodge Jay's next missile, Eliza grabbed a mitten-full of snow and lobbed it at him. It hit him on the shoulder and disintegrated impact, leaving a smudge of white on his jacket. He widened his eyes, a warning that she was about to get as good as she got lurking in their depths, but before he could act on it, another snowball caught him on the chest, thrown by a gleeful Dulcie.

The next few minutes descended into a blur of flying snow and loud squeals and shrieks. At one point, Eliza was aware that Beth and Walter had joined in from the relative safety of the open living room window, but they quickly exhausted the supply of snow on the sill, so resorted to shouting encouragement from the sidelines instead.

The fight ended when Dulcie shoved an icy handful of the white stuff down the back of Otto's neck. With a growl, he picked her up, dumped her into the nearest drift and threw himself down next to her, kissing her until she begged for mercy and surrendered.

'Huh! Dulcie might have thrown in the towel, but I haven't!' Eliza cried. 'I'm still standing.'

Jay's eyes narrowed. 'Not for much longer.'

She realised his intention a fraction before he lunged at her, and she skipped out of reach, before turning with a shriek and racing for the door. He caught her just as she reached it, grabbing her around the waist and pulling her into him.

Eliza squirmed in his grasp, squeaking in mock fear, and then she abruptly froze.

Jay was focusing on a point above her head, and when she followed the direction of his gaze and saw what had caught his attention, she almost melted.

A bunch of mistletoe hung directly above them, and as her eyes dropped to his face, she inhaled sharply.

He was looking at her as though he wanted to eat her all up, and when his head bent and his lips brushed lightly against hers, she would have been more than happy to have let him devour her completely as she sank into his embrace.

Beth's chirpy cry of, 'Sherry, anyone?' broke the mood, and they leapt apart guiltily, Eliza feeling distinctly wobbly. As Dulcie and Otto stepped around them, Dulcie sent Eliza a knowing smirk and Otto lightly punched Jay on the arm and winked.

Eliza and Jay stared at each other. At least this kiss could be blamed on the mistletoe, and although she would dearly love for him to kiss her again, she knew how unwise that would be.

Feeling cold as a trickle of icy snowmelt worked its way down her neck, Eliza shivered.

'Let's get you warmed up,' Jay said, gesturing for her to go ahead of him, but as she took a step into the hall, she shivered again. This time it wasn't because she was cold. It was because of the promise in his eyes. Jay Fairfax wasn't done with her yet – and she couldn't wait.

With her head spinning, her heart racing and her emotions all over the place, Eliza was more than happy to shuck off her wet things and accept a glass of sherry from Beth. She sipped at it gratefully, feeling its rich warmth track down her throat and into her stomach, where it joined the ball of anticipation that was already there.

She avoided looking at Jay, for fear of seeing her own desire reflected back at her, and was relieved when Nikki and her family arrived, Sammy's exuberance giving her something less risky to focus on.

What followed next was an orgy of present-opening, torn wrapping paper and squeals of delight. The two dogs joined in, as they excitedly examined each gift in the hope that it might be for them, so to keep them quiet (Peg was acting like a puppy as she snuffled through the wrapping paper, tearing it to shreds) Walter dug out her and Tara's gifts, and the dogs quickly settled down to gnaw on their fake bones, whilst the humans continued with the unwrapping.

Eliza was touched to discover that the Fairfaxes had clubbed together to buy her a pretty silver necklace and earring from one of the artisan shops in the village, and she was reduced to tears when Walter handed her a small box covered in worn and faded blue velvet.

Inside it was a ring.

'It belonged to my mother, your grandmother,' he said. 'I had no idea why I've been hanging onto it all these years – until I met you.'

'Walter, it's too much. I can't accept this. What about Otto?'

'He's more than welcome to have his mother's wedding and engagement rings if he wants them.' Walter glanced at Otto, then at Dulcie, his meaning clear.

Eliza examined her gift. It was a gold band with a cushion-cut diamond in the centre, flanked by two smaller sapphires, and was absolutely exquisite.

She shook her head. 'I can't take this.'

'You *can*,' Walter insisted. 'I'm sure your father would have wanted you to have it.'

Ooh, that was a low blow, she thought, but when she looked at her uncle, she could see how much it meant to him if she were to accept.

'Thank you,' she said softly and gave him a long hug.

He clung to her, then kissed her cheek. 'I'm so glad you found us.'

'So am I.' She meant it. Being here with Walter, with her new family, in the house her father had once lived in, meant the world to her.

Beth passed Eliza the bag of presents that she had brought with her this morning. 'You'd better give these out, otherwise we'll still be opening presents as Otto is dishing up our dinner.'

Eliza took the bag from her and began handing out the little gifts she'd made. 'I didn't know what to get you,' she said nervously, 'so I hope you like them.'

'I'm sure we will,' Dulcie replied, tearing eagerly at the paper on her present, and when she saw what it was she gave a shriek. 'Look! It's the farm.' She turned the painting around for everyone to see. 'It's perfect. Thank you so much! I really, really love it.'

Eliza breathed a sigh of relief. Thank goodness one of the family liked her gift. She just hoped the rest of them did, too.

One by one, everyone held up the paintings she'd given them: a pastiche of her four children for Beth, a portrait of Otto for Walter, a painting of the boy and his dog for Sammy, a portrait of Sammy holding a chicken (apparently it was his pet chicken) for Nikki and Gio. Otto received a picture of his restaurant and Eliza could tell that he was thrilled to bits with it, and Maisie was delighted with a watercolour of herself. It showed her face-to-face with the cutest of the pygmy goats, and her rapturous expression was plain to see.

Last but not least, was Jay.

Shyly she handed him the final present. It was obviously a picture of some kind, so she couldn't hide that, but she prayed he liked it and would be able to fit it into his luggage when he returned to Borneo.

His eyes widened when he unwrapped it, and he studied the gift for such a long time that she feared he hated it.

Finally, his gaze sought hers and he smiled, a long slow smile that set her pulse soaring and made her insides melt. 'Thank you,' he mouthed, and placed it on his chest next to his heart.

'Don't keep it to yourself,' his mother said. 'Give us a look.'

Eliza didn't think she imagined his reluctance when he turned it around, although there was nothing controversial about the picture, nothing that was overly personal. It was a portrait of Jay as she had first set eyes on him.

He was standing in the doorway of the abandoned farmhouse on the mountain, and was staring straight out of the picture. It had taken her ages to get his expression right, because for a while she hadn't realised what was lacking. When she finally did, she had painted it in, and now she was fervently praying that no one else realised that she had depicted Jay with hunger in his eyes. From the very first time he'd set those gorgeous blue-green eyes on her, he had wanted her, whether he had known it then or not.

He still wanted her, that much was abundantly clear, and now Eliza wanted him just as fiercely.

The question she had to ask herself was, would she give in? And if she did, could she trust herself not to lose her heart? She knew this could never be anything more than a holiday romance, that they were like ships passing in the night. But should she live for today and enjoy whatever life gave her, or retreat and guard her emotions? She thought of a line from Casablanca, one of her father's favourite films, and realised how compelling it was when Rick had told Isla that they would always have Paris.

If Eliza continued to steel herself against her growing feelings and her undeniable desire for Jay, she would never have her own Paris. She would return to New Zealand and would forever wonder what she had missed.

It was then that she understood that she would regret *not* sharing a few stolen hours with Jay far more than she would regret sharing them. Humphrey Bogart was right...

Jay was Rick, she was Isla, and she wanted her very own Paris here on Muddypuddle Lane.

♥

Jay's emotions were all over the place. The desire on Eliza's face after he had kissed her under the mistletoe had almost sent him into orbit, and he'd had to give himself a stern talking-to. She had been as hungry for more as he, but they were about to open presents and eat lunch with the family, so he'd had to curb his urge to whisk her back to the cottage and make long, languorous love to her.

But when he'd opened the present she'd given him and saw the passion she had captured in his eyes, he had found it hard to keep a lid on things. She had read his hunger even before he'd been aware of it himself, but on looking back to the moment when he had seen her for the first time, he knew she was right. He had wanted her then, and he wanted her now. But did she want him enough to spend the remainder of her time in Muddypuddle Lane with him? After all, she was here to find out more about her father and his family. She wasn't here to be carried off to bed by a man she hardly knew.

There was also something else bothering him.

He liked her. Very much. Too much for this to be a casual roll in the hay. He wanted to get to know her far better than the brief time she had left in the country would allow. He wanted to explore all of her, not just her body – he wanted to explore her mind, too.

And that was what worried him. He had never felt like this about anyone before and he didn't know how to handle it. Should he take whatever she deigned to give and be grateful, whether it be time, friendship, or more…? And if there was more, how would he cope when she left?

He realised he was still standing there with his portrait in his hands and that everyone was staring at him. 'It's fantastic,' he said. 'I love it!' He truly did. Eliza was so incredibly talented.

He saw the relief on her face and smiled.

She smiled back, then caught her bottom lip between her teeth and dropped her gaze. When she glanced back at him from beneath those long lashes of hers, he wondered whether she was flirting with him. When she looked away and then looked back again, he was positive she was.

God! He wished she wouldn't do that. It was sending him wild.

To cover his abrupt surge of lust, he cleared his throat and beckoned her into the dining room. He had contributed to the gift the family had bought, so he didn't want to make an issue of the fact that he'd bought her a present that was purely from him. Hoping not to draw too much attention, he decided to give it to her in private. Or as private as he could get considering Lilac Tree Farm was bursting at the seams with people.

Praying that everyone would stay put in the living room for a couple of minutes, he turned to face Eliza and said huskily, 'I've got something for you,' then wished he hadn't phrased it like that when he saw the amusement in her eyes. 'It's only a little something,' he added, and realised he'd made things worse when she giggled.

He grabbed the festively wrapped package from where he'd stashed it next to the dresser and shoved it at her. 'Here.'

'What is it?'

'Open it and find out.'

Eyes wide, she took it from him and gently eased the paper aside to reveal a wooden tabletop easel with a compartment underneath for paints.

'Look inside,' he urged, and when she opened it she discovered a full array of oils and brushes. 'I asked the woman in the shop to fill it with whatever she thought you might need. I hope it's okay?'

'It's more than okay,' she breathed. 'But this must have cost a fortune.'

'Nah.' He waved a hand in the air. 'Just promise me you'll make good use of it while you're here.'

'I will! Thank you so much!'

She threw her arms around him and he staggered back, but swiftly regained his balance and hugged her to his chest, enfolding her in his arms and breathing in her sweet perfume.

'I want to paint now!' she cried.

Jay chuckled. 'I think Otto will have something to say if you're up to your armpits in paint instead of doing his Christmas dinner justice.' He released her, so she could examine the contents of the box again.

She said, 'I've got so many ideas, I don't know where to start.' Then her face fell. 'Oh…'

'What is it?'

'I'm not going to be able to take the paintings home with me.'

'Whyever not?'

'Oil paints wouldn't have hardened off in time.'

'No worries. Let me know approximately when they'll be ready and I'll ship them for you.'

'But you'll be in Borneo.'

'Um, probably not. Look, keep it to yourself for now, but my contract with the acoustics company ended a couple of weeks ago and it's yet to be renewed. So I'll be in the UK for a while.'

'Will you stay at the farm?'

'Maybe. I don't know. Dulcie and Otto would like the place to themselves, I expect. You've seen what they're like.'

'Will you go stay with your mum?'

'That's another option,' he said, guardedly. He loved his mum to the moon and back, but he couldn't face going to Birmingham.

Otto strode into the room before Jay could say anything further, and as soon Otto spied them he said, 'Come on you two, I could do with a hand in the kitchen. I need to check on the turkey, and while I'm doing that you can put the potatoes on to boil for roasties. Eliza, how good are you at making cranberry sauce?'

'Er…'

'Stuffing?'

'Um…' Eliza pulled a face.

Otto laughed. 'Just kidding. It's already made. But I'm sure Dulcie wouldn't mind you helping her lay the table.'

With an apologetic smile at Eliza, Jay followed Otto into the kitchen. To his surprise the roasties had already been par-boiled and were ready to go in the oven. He sent a questioning look to Otto.

Otto said, 'I wanted to get you on your own for a sec. Sorry, I didn't mean to eavesdrop, but did I hear you say you'd be in the UK for a while?'

'Yeah…'

'What are you going to do about a job?'

Jay shrugged. 'Try to get another contract.'

'What if you don't?'

'Something will turn up.' But the problem was, he wasn't sure whether he wanted to carry on doing what he was doing. He was thirty-four, and anchorless. Aside from a fairly healthy bank balance and a couple of kit bags stuffed with clothes and little wooden carvings, he didn't have much else to his name. Seeing Dulcie with her farm and Otto opening a restaurant, was making him think.

But what else was he equipped to do? Bioacoustics was all he knew.

♥

'I've had the loveliest Christmas Day imaginable,' Eliza announced. She was pleasantly replete, slightly tipsy and full of festive spirit.

It was late – nearly midnight – and Jay was escorting her down the hill back to the cottage. He had one arm around her shoulder and the other was clutching the easel he'd bought her. Despite the falling temperature, she felt warm and cosy (which probably had something to do with the amount of cherry brandy in her system) and she snuggled in closer, loving the feel of his hard body against hers.

'I'm glad,' he said. 'I would have hated for you to be alone on Christmas Day, so far from home.'

Eliza paused, drawing to a halt. 'So would I. If I'm honest, I hadn't really thought this through. I was so focused on getting here and finding Walter, that I hadn't fully appreciated how I might feel being all alone over Christmas. And I was being a bit petty, too.'

They carried on walking.

'In what way?' Jay hugged her into him and his warmth percolated through her jacket and into her body.

'Cathy has always been Mum's favourite, and now that my sister is pregnant, I was feeling even more left out than usual. I was dreading spending Christmas with them. Mum would have fussed over Cathy even more than usual, and what used to be such a happy season when Dad was alive would have been totally miserable. Cathy and Toby – her husband – always spend Christmas with our Mum and New Year with his parents, and Mum would have practically ignored me until they left, then she would have expected me to step into the breach as soon as they'd gone.'

She fished the key out of her pocket and opened the door. A wall of welcome heat rushed out at her. 'I don't even think she knows she's doing it,' Eliza said.

'It still hurts though,' Jay empathised.

'Yes, it does. I know she loves me in her own way, but I'll always be second fiddle to Cathy.' She eased off her coat, and when she held her hand out for Jay's jacket, she hung them side-by-side on the pegs near the door.

'Come here,' she said, pulling him closer. 'I don't want to think about Mum or home right now.' She stared into his eyes and her lips parted.

His voice was gruff as he said, 'What *do* you want to think about?'

'Nothing. I want you to take me to a place where there is no thought, only feeling. Make love to me, Jay.'

And for a long, long time afterwards, Eliza was blissfully incapable of thinking anything.

CHAPTER EIGHT

Eliza gave Jay a hesitant shake of her head from the passenger seat of his hire car as he asked, 'Are you sure you don't want me to come with you?'

She would dearly like him to accompany her but she didn't want to spook Julia, so she said, 'I'll be fine. Thanks, though.'

'Call me when you're done,' he replied, gathering her to him and kissing her.

'That might be as little as ten minutes, or it could be a couple of hours,' she warned.

'It doesn't matter. Take as long as you need.'

They were parked within sight of the cafe Julia had suggested. Steeling herself, Eliza got out of the car. Wrapping her scarf more tightly around her neck, she hunched deeper into her coat. It was bloody freezing, and she hurried along the pavement and darted into the cafe before her nerves could get the better of her.

Inside was warm, the windows steamy, and she quickly scanned the occupied tables, her disappointment acute when she realised Julia wasn't there. Eliza chose a table near the window, removed her coat and scarf, peeled off her gloves and took a seat. Then she ordered a pot of tea and settled down to wait.

Through the glass she could just make out the bonnet of Jay's car, and a warm glow filled her chest. It was five gloriously wonderful days since they'd first made love on Christmas Day, and she didn't think they'd been apart for more than an hour at a stretch. Jay had spent every night at the cottage, in her arms, and she had revelled in it.

Stubbornly, stupidly, Eliza refused to think of the future, of the undeniable reality that she only had four days left (including this), before she would board the aeroplane and fly out of his life. Four days wasn't long enough. A *lifetime* wouldn't be long enough.

But she had gone into this with her eyes wide open. She had known what she was letting herself in for, that the cost of loving Jay would be gouged out of her broken heart. And still she thought it was a price worth paying, despite the inevitable tears and the inevitable heartache. She would always have Muddypuddle Lane.

The door opened and Eliza sat up straighter as Julia cautiously stepped through it. Breathing a sigh of relief, Eliza lifted her hand in a small wave.

'Can I get you anything?' she asked as Julia took a seat.

'A latte, please.'

Eliza gave the order, then an awkward silence descended. She had no idea how or where to start in asking this woman about her father. And the longer it stretched, the more awkward she felt.

Julia must have felt awkward too, because just as Eliza didn't think she could stand it any longer, Julia blurted, 'I loved him with everything I had. I still do love him, although perhaps not as fiercely as I once did. You don't stop loving someone just because they're dead.'

Eliza gulped. Never had anyone spoken a truer word, and grief clawed at her.

'I loved him so much that I had to let him go,' Julia continued. 'I was married, you see. And pregnant.'

Eliza gasped and clapped a hand to her mouth. Did that mean she had a half-brother or sister out there?

Julia noticed her reaction. 'The baby wasn't his.' She looked up as the waitress placed a cup of steaming coffee in front of her and waited for the woman to retreat before saying, 'You would think that it isn't possible to love two men at the same time, but it is.' She stirred a cube of sugar into her drink, her eyes downcast. 'It's not something I'm proud of, but neither was it something I could control. I fell in love. End of story.'

But it wasn't the end, was it? Eliza wanted to say, but she held her tongue, hoping Julia would fill in the blanks.

Julia finally looked up and sighed. 'I suppose you want to know what happened?'

'Please, if you feel you can talk about it.'

'You deserve to know. Your father – it feels strange to think of Emrys as having children – had already been planning to emigrate to New Zealand before I met him. It was his dream, a new life in a new country. I couldn't take that away from him, but neither could I deprive my husband of his son. If I hadn't been pregnant, I'd have gone with your father in a heartbeat, but I was, so I didn't. Emrys never knew I was carrying Stephen's child. I simply told him that we'd had our fun, but it was over. I never saw or heard from him again. I broke his heart and I'm not sure he ever forgave me.'

'I think he did,' Eliza said slowly. 'Otherwise, why would he have wanted you to know that he'd died, and why did he want you to know that he'd never stopped loving you?'

A tear slid down Julia's face and she brushed it away. 'When you phoned to tell me that he was gone, you said he'd had a good life, that he'd been happy. Is that true?'

'I'd assumed he was. I never really thought about It. He was just my dad, you know? It wasn't until after he died and I found the letter asking me to contact you, that I began to wonder.' Eliza fell silent, thinking. Then she said, 'No, I'm sure he was happy. As you just said, it's possible to love two people at the same time, and I believe he truly loved my mother.'

Julia's reply was soft. 'I'm glad. I still had my husband, you see, and I worried that Emrys wouldn't find anyone to love him as much as I did.'

Eliza said, 'And I'm glad you let him go, because if you hadn't, I wouldn't be here.'

'I want to ask you about his life in New Zealand, about your mother, but I've worked hard to bury it deep, and digging it up again probably isn't a good idea.'

'Probably not,' Eliza agreed.

Julia pushed her untouched coffee away and got to her feet. 'I'm pleased I met you and I'm happy your father found love again, but don't take offence when I say I hope I never see you again.'

'I won't,' Eliza assured her. 'I'm flying back to New Zealand in a few days, so I doubt we will meet again.'

Julia stared at her for a long time, then reached out to pat her on the shoulder. 'Take care, Eliza.'

'You too.' Eliza squeezed Julia's hand, then watched her father's first love walk out of the door.

'Are you okay?' Jay asked. Eliza looked upset. Her generous mouth was downturned, and her eyes swam with unshed tears.

'I'm not sure.'

'Do you want to talk about it?'

Eliza buckled her seatbelt and crossed her arms, hugging herself. 'I've got the feeling my mother knew about Julia. I never told her about the letter Dad left asking me to contact her. I think I guessed even then that it was something I should keep from her. And when I phoned Julia and told her that Dad had died, I knew for sure. Julia was so upset that I honestly believe she loved him deeply. She was married when she and my dad fell in love, but she became pregnant and the baby was her husband's not my dad's. It's quite a sad tale. Dad had already told her it was his dream to emigrate to New Zealand, but she couldn't go with him and I think she guessed he would stay in the UK for her, so she told him she didn't love him. It must have taken a great deal of courage on her part to let him go.'

The tears trickled over, and he reached across and gently wiped them away. 'I should imagine it did.'

The thought occurred to Jay that very soon he wouldn't have to imagine it. He would know firsthand how it felt, because he would be the one to have to let Eliza go. Since that glorious night when he had made love to her for the first time, he hadn't been able to stop thinking of ways they could be together, of how he might persuade her to stay in the UK. But what could he offer her? He didn't have a home of his own and he didn't have a job. Whereas she had both in New Zealand.

It had occurred to him that he could suggest he went with her when she left on Monday (the next four days would be gone far too soon) but how could he, given his circumstances? Besides, he wasn't entirely sure that this wasn't just a flash in the pan for her, a brief fling with a Brit whilst she was on holiday. How would she take it if he suddenly suggested flying out with her? She might be horrified. If he had a job in New Zealand that might be different, but even then, she mightn't want him in her life. He would basically be inviting himself to shack up with her, and that wasn't on. His only option was to make the most of the short time they had left.

Glumly, he started the car and headed for Muddypuddle Lane.

When he arrived at her cottage, he made no move to switch the engine off, aware that Eliza needed time to process what had happened, so when she said, 'I'll see you later,' he let her go without a murmur.

She did lean across the gear stick and give him a kiss on the lips before she got out, so he was somewhat cheered by that.

He said, 'Will you be alright?'

'I'll be fine. There's just something I need to do while it's still fresh in my mind.'

He watched until she had gone inside, then he turned the car around and drove the short distance up the lane to the farm, his heart heavy.

It didn't grow any lighter when he pulled into the yard and saw that the email he'd been waiting for was sitting in his inbox.

He read it twice, then slumped back in his seat and stared into the distance. He'd never been to Belize.

And he wasn't entirely sure he wanted to.

This time last week, he would have leapt at the chance. Now though...

Oh, what the hell? He may as well take the contract. It wasn't as though he had job offers coming out of his ears. And it wasn't as though he and Eliza would be together if he *didn't* take it.

He didn't bother going into the house to change his clothes. The ones he was wearing would do just fine for what he was about to do. Whittling wasn't a particularly grubby pastime, and although the flakes of wood could cling to fabric they would soon brush off.

The goats were pleased to see him and they crowded against the bars of their pen, bleating plaintively.

'I haven't got anything for you,' he told them, stroking the nose of the nearest. She butted him on the hand, a demand for food. 'You've got hay,' he said. 'Eat that.' The creature gave him a disgusted look, as if to say '*You* eat it and see how you like it'.

She was small and white, with little horns and a round belly, and was so damned cute. He could understand how Maisie had fallen in love with her.

The others were just as sweet, and he sought out the one who he had been using as his model for the past couple of days.

Unwrapping his tools, he picked up the piece of wood and began to work. The concentration it took was welcome, because it meant he didn't have to think about how he was going to cope when Eliza left.

In some ways, he wished he was leaving first, but his contract didn't start until mid-January, and although he supposed he could fly out early, it wouldn't be early enough. Her flight was on Monday. Today was Thursday. Even if he could get a flight tomorrow, or the next day, he didn't think he would be forgiven if he missed Otto's big night. The Wild Side was due to open on New Year's Eve and Dulcie expected Jay to be there.

After a couple of hours, his sister's voice cut across his thoughts. 'There you are! I wondered where you'd got to. I saw the car in the yard. Is Eliza with you?' She scanned the barn.

'No.' He didn't look up. He was aware he might appear sullen, but he didn't want his face to give away his feelings.

'What's wrong?' Dulcie asked. 'Have you fallen out?'

'No, but it wouldn't make any difference if we had.' He made the mistake of looking at her.

She gave him a shrewd glance. 'Because she's leaving soon?'

He shrugged and carried on shaving slivers of wood off what would eventually become the goat's neck.

His sister continued, 'Why don't you go with her?'

Jay put the knife and the block of wood down, his enthusiasm for the task waning. His reply was simple. 'She hasn't asked me.'

'Ah.' Dulcie paused. She took a step closer and picked up the half-carved piece of wood. 'Goat?' she guessed.

'Uh-huh.'

'You're rather good at wood carving, aren't you?'

'Not really.'

'You *are*,' she insisted. 'The carving of Tara that you gave to Sammy is gorgeous.' She didn't say anything more for a moment, then she asked, 'Would you go with her, if she did?'

'I doubt it.'

'Why not? You love her, that's obvious, and I believe she loves you. So what's stopping you? There's nothing to keep you here. Otto told me you are between contracts at the moment.'

'I had an email this morning. I've been offered another contract.'

'Where?'

'Belize.'

'But what about you and Eliza?'

'There is no me and Eliza. At least, there won't be after Sunday. She lives on the other side of the world, if you remember?'

'She doesn't have to. She could always stay here. So could you.'

'In the UK?'

'In Picklewick. You can stay at the farm for as long as you want. Both of you.'

Jay scowled. 'Thanks, sis, but I can't see that working. For one, I doubt whether Eliza would want to stay. She's got a house, a job and a family in New

Zealand. Second, I can't impose. You and Otto need your own space. Besides, I'd want a place of my own if I was going to settle anywhere. And third, if I don't take this contract, I won't have a job.'

It was kind of Dulcie to be so concerned, and even kinder of her to offer for him and Eliza to stay at the farm, but it simply wasn't an option.

Dulcie pursed her lips. 'First, you don't know until you ask. Eliza might jump at the chance to stay here with you. Second, you wouldn't be imposing, but if you insist on having your own place, I've got an idea about that. Third, job-wise you can turn your hand to anything to tide you over, but I've got an idea about that, too.'

'It won't work, Dulcie,' he repeated. He eased his mobile out of his jacket pocket. 'I'm going to email them back and let them know I'm taking the contract.'

His sister opened her mouth, then closed it again. He waited for her to say something, but all she did was kiss him on the forehead, and when she walked out of the barn, Jay didn't think he had ever felt as alone as he did right now.

For a long time he sat on the bale of straw, turning his phone over in his hands, his thoughts a jumbled mess.

God, he was so tempted to take Dulcie up on her offer to stay in Picklewick, but it wouldn't be fair on anyone, him included. Nope, it was better all round if he took the contract. He'd soon get back into the swing of things, and Eliza would become just a fond memory of a lovely Christmas.

Without dwelling on it any further, Jay sent his acceptance. There, it was done. He would enjoy the rest of his time here and spend as much of it as possible with Eliza.

There was nothing else he could do.

♥

Otto had chosen New Year's Eve for The Wild Side to open its doors for the first time. According to Dulcie, he wasn't charging for the food, just the drinks, and was using the evening purely as an advertisement for the restaurant. Eliza had firsthand experience of how wonderful Otto's cooking was. She guessed if anyone could make a go of it, he could, and she prayed it would be a success.

She hadn't brought anything particularly partyish with her, not expecting to attend any parties, so she'd gone into Thornbury earlier today with Jay to buy something appropriate to wear.

Eliza had discovered a gorgeous little shop down a side street selling all manner of one-off clothes. It was a posh second-hand shop, and she was able to find a gold sparkly dress without a hideous price tag.

Jay had urged her to step out of the fitting room so he could see, but she had refused. She wanted his first sight of her in this dress to be when she was at the restaurant, her hair and make-up done, and she was all glammed up.

So when she shucked off her coat this evening and handed it to one of the waiting staff, the naked admiration on Jay's face gave her a warm glow.

'You look stunning,' he said, kissing her lightly on the lips, careful not to mess her make-up, and his thoughtfulness made her glow some more.

He didn't look too bad himself, dressed as he was in charcoal-coloured chinos and a plain white shirt, open at the neck and with the sleeves rolled up. He looked casual yet smart, confident and sophisticated, and she wanted to eat him all up.

Eliza was pleased to see that everyone had made an effort. Otto was in a tux and Dulcie looked gorgeous in a midnight-blue cocktail dress. Maisie wore something chiffon and floaty, and even Walter was in a suit and tie, although from the way he plucked at the knot at his neck, Eliza guessed that he didn't dress up very often, and she giggled, making a bet with herself that he would take the tie off within the hour.

There were several people Eliza recognised, such as Lena, Amos's partner, and Charity who helped out at the stables. She was here with her boyfriend Timothy, a local vet, and Eliza did a double take, fearing that the bubbly she was drinking was spiked when she saw two of her, before realising that Charity had a twin sister.

There were also many people she didn't recognise, and to Eliza it seemed as though the whole village was here to offer their support.

Jay slipped an arm around her waist. 'It's a good turn-out,' he said. 'And I don't think it's just because of the free food. Otto spent today and yesterday preparing a buffet for the opening, so he doesn't have to spend the whole evening in the kitchen.'

Eliza didn't think so either. There was a real sense of community spirit and support, and she was amazed at the way everyone rallied around, when she couldn't even get her mother or her sister to rally around her.

Jay said, 'I can't believe how well Dulcie has settled in. It's as though she's been a part of Picklewick all her life. Otto, too; even though he grew up on the farm on Muddypuddle Lane, he had lived away for many years. No wonder Nikki decided to make the village her home.'

Eliza spotted Jay's eldest sister laughing up at Gio, and she smiled. 'I think a certain policeman might also have played a part in that decision.'

Dulcie had told her about Sammy being bullied in his school in Birmingham, and how he had run away to the farm. Dulcie had also told Eliza about how Nikki had fallen in love with Gio last summer, but Dulcie hadn't imagined anything would come of it considering Nikki lived in the city and Gio lived in Picklewick. But then Gio had asked Nikki and her son to move in with him and the rest, they say, is history.

Eliza couldn't fail to compare Nikki's situation to her own – minus the child, of course. Her and Jay's relationship was also a holiday romance, but the biggest difference was, she lived on the other side of the world. It was going to break her heart when she had to say goodbye to him.

But what if he asked her to stay in Picklewick? Would she? *Could* she?

Eliza thought of her little bach near the beach, of the sunlight flooding into her studio, of the beauty of the bay and the peace she enjoyed, and her slowly growing reputation as an artist. Could she give up everything she had fought so hard for, for love?

And suddenly she knew, without any doubt, that she could, that if Jay asked her to stay, she would.

Then she glanced down at her glass and thought the alcohol must have gone to her head, because what she was thinking was absolute nonsense. Jay wouldn't be staying here either; he was off to Belize at the end of next week, which was roughly eleven thousand kilometres from New Zealand. She knew because she'd looked it up.

She also knew something else – that she was in love with him. She had lost her heart to Jay as she suspected she might. And when midnight came and everyone cried 'Happy New Year!' Eliza wondered just how happy this new year could possibly be without the man she had fallen in love with.

CHAPTER NINE

'A picnic? Won't it be chilly?' Eliza looked doubtful.

'Humour me?' Jay urged. This was their final day together and he wanted to pay homage to the first time he met her. He wanted to take her back to the abandoned farmhouse high on the mountain above, because even though he hadn't realised it at the time, that was where he had fallen in love with her.

Eliza said, 'I suppose we can't stay in bed *all* day. But isn't Dulcie expecting us for lunch?'

On hearing those words, Jay nearly changed his mind. All day in bed sounded wonderful, and he briefly debated suggesting that they hide under the duvet and refuse to answer the door. Dulcie was insisting that everyone enjoyed a final meal together, a New Year's Day lunch to rival the Christmas Day feast, and Jay and Eliza were expected to attend.

But Jay wanted Eliza all to himself for as long as possible, and the only way to ensure that had been to tell Dulcie that he and Eliza were going out for the day. Dulcie had reluctantly pushed lunch back to dinnertime, and had told him that if he didn't show up, he would have their mother to answer to. Her final piece of guilt-tripping had been to tell him that Eliza needed to say a proper goodbye to Walter and the rest of her new-found family, because not only was Eliza going home tomorrow, but so were Beth and Maisie.

'Lunch is at 6 o'clock now, so we've got plenty of time to go for a walk,' he told her.

'I need to pack,' she said, glancing around the bedroom.

Jay swallowed. 'How about you make a start on that, and I'll pop back to the farm to change, and I can rustle up a picnic while I'm there.'

He had already asked Otto to pack up some of the leftover buffet food from last night and bring it home with him, so it shouldn't take more than a few minutes. He hated being away from her for even that short length of time.

How he was going to cope when he would be away from her permanently, was something he didn't want to think about.

Jay hurried up the track to the farm and barrelled in through the door, almost sending Dulcie flying in his haste to get to the kitchen.

'Whoops, sorry.' His hand shot out to steady her.

She said, 'I was hoping to catch you. Are you in a hurry? I'd like to run something by you.'

'A bit. I'm taking Eliza for a picnic, remember? Do you have any hot water bottles?'

'Um, I think so. Try the pantry. Top shelf.'

Jay trotted into the kitchen, Dulcie following.

He said, 'Can you put the kettle on and fill them up for me, while I sort the food out? Oh, and I'll need to borrow a couple of blankets, if I can.'

Dulcie shook her head but flipped the switch on the kettle and rummaged around in the pantry, yelling, 'Ta-dah!' when she emerged with a pair of hot water bottles.

'What do you want to run by me?' Jay asked, his head in the fridge as he sorted through various Tupperware boxes of buffet food. There hadn't been much left over, but there was enough for him and Eliza to have a nice picnic.

Dulcie put a hand on his arm, and he looked over his shoulder. Her expression was serious. 'You don't have to go to Belize, you know. You don't *have* to take that contract if you don't want to.'

Jay stifled a sigh. 'We've been through this,' he began, but his sister said, 'Hear me out,' so he subsided and turned to face her.

She continued, 'I've been thinking... What if you had a place of your own in Picklewick? Would you stay?'

'It's a moot point. I *don't* have a place of my own, and even if I did, I don't have a job remember?'

'You can make things and sell them,' Dulcie said.

'Like what?'

'Your carvings. Don't get annoyed, but I've made some enquiries at the shop in the village that sells lots of little handmade crafty stuff, and they said they'd be happy to stock some of yours on a commission basis.'

Jay was taken aback. 'I can't see that working. I'd have to shift an awful lot of carvings to afford to pay the rent on even an outhouse in Picklewick, and before you suggest it again, I'm not going to move in with you and Otto.'

'I'm going to need help on the farm,' she persisted, 'and I'd prefer to employ you than a stranger. Otto wants to turn one of the outbuildings into a pasteurisation shed, and that's not going to be cheap. He suggested that you could help in exchange for board and lodge.'

'I'd still be living with you.'

'Would that be so bad? Anyway, it mightn't be for long.' Dulcie took a breath and stared him in the eye. 'You know that old abandoned farmhouse on the top of the mountain?'

Jay blinked at the sudden change of topic. 'That's where me and Eliza are going for our picnic. Has the kettle boiled yet?'

Dulcie didn't so much as glance at it. She continued to stare at him, her expression serious. 'It's yours if you want it.'

'Hurry up, Dulcie. I want to get up there before it gets dark,' he said, taking a couple of plastic tubs out of the fridge and checking the contents. Then he froze. 'What did you say?'

'It's yours, if you want it,' she repeated. 'It'll be a lot of work and I don't even know if it's doable, or if you need planning permission, and there's no electricity so you'll have to be off-grid, but there is water and I'm sure you can—'

'Stop there.' Jay held up his hand. 'What do you mean *it's mine if I want it?* How can it be mine?'

'I own it. It's part of the farm, but if you want it, you can have it.'

Jay slumped against the worktop in shock. '*Mine?* As in, you're *giving* it to me?'

She pulled a face. 'I'm never going to use it. It needs too much work.'

'I should say so – it's practically a ruin. You'd be better off knocking it down and starting again.'

'That's for you to decide.'

He gazed at her incredulously. 'You're serious.'

'Yes, I am.'

'But…'

'Think about it. The offer is there.' She bit her lip. 'I'm not sure what Eliza would make of it though. It's a bit… rustic.'

'It's a bit derelict.' Jay puffed out his cheeks. 'It's a lovely offer, sis, and I appreciate it, but there's no point in me staying in the UK.'

'Because Eliza won't be here?'

'You've got it in one.'

♥

Eliza was amazed to see how much snow remained on the hillside. It hadn't quite disappeared from the lower slopes yet, but it was all slushy and the roads were totally clear, yet up here it was ankle-deep on the track and had drifted to knee-deep in places. It had also started to snow again, large flakes falling from a cloud-filled sky, and part of her was praying that the flakes would turn into a blizzard and she would be snowed in and unable to get to the airport tomorrow.

But then, would it be worse if she had to psych herself up to leave all over again in a few days?

Tears pricked behind her eyes at the thought of leaving, and she hurriedly blinked them away, hoping Jay didn't spot them. If he did, she'd blame her watery eyes on the cold.

Surprisingly, she didn't feel particularly cold right now. The hike up the hill was keeping the blood pumping, and if it hadn't been snowing she might have considered taking a layer off.

It was a different matter when they reached the abandoned building though, because as soon as she stopped moving, she could feel the chill settling into her bones.

'First things first, let me get a fire started,' Jay said, and her mouth dropped open when he retrieved kindling, newspaper and several briquettes from the rucksack he was carrying.

She watched, bemused, as he pulled a blanket out of the large rucksack he was carrying, along with a couple of hot water bottles. He gave one to her, then spread the blanket on the stones for her to sit on.

As soon as she was settled and had assured him that she was warm enough, he set about making the fire, and before long flames were crackling in the little makeshift hearth he had created, and was kicking out a surprising amount of heat.

Jay joined her on the blanket. 'Are you hungry?'

She wasn't, but she said she was because he had gone to so much effort and she didn't want to disappoint him by not eating.

He passed her a tub of goodies, and she opened them and popped a tiny tartlet in her mouth. The flavours were incredible and she quickly ate it, then another, and when he unscrewed the cap on a thermos flask and poured steamy tomato soup into a mug, she took it eagerly.

They ate in silence, the falling snow blanketing any noise from the world outside their little shelter, and Eliza wished that this moment would never end. She wasn't prepared to return to reality. She wasn't prepared to let Jay go.

But let him go she must… and this time tomorrow she would be far away from the farm on Muddypuddle Lane and getting further away with every step of her journey.

♥

Ever since Dulcie had informed him that the ramshackle, abandoned old farmhouse was his if he wanted it, Jay hadn't been able to think about anything else. Sitting in the middle of it with Eliza by his side, he could picture them sitting in the same spot this time next year. The walls surrounding them would be whole once again, and there would be glass in the windows and a roof over their heads. They wouldn't need much, just the basics – as long as they had each other, that would be enough.

Once or twice he almost plucked up the courage to ask her to stay, but when she shivered and brushed a snowflake from her forehead, he realised it was a pipe dream. It would take months, if not years, to make this place habitable again, and that was assuming he would be granted planning permission. Although he had savings, he estimated that the money in his bank account would quickly be eaten up, even if he managed to do some of the renovation himself. Materials were expensive, and there would be some tasks (*many* tasks) that would be beyond his skill set. A bit of whittling didn't a carpenter make. Or a roofer. Or an electrician.

Eliza was snuggling up next to him and staring into the flames, but instead of concentrating on her, Jay's mind was on the issue of access to the property. The overgrown dirt track would quickly become a mud bath as soon as anything heavier than a human came into contact with it, and he had visions of having to tarmac it before work on the building could even start.

No, Dulcie, he thought, thinking fondly of his kind, well-meaning sister, it would take a better man than him to tackle such a daunting project.

But even as he decided that it was a daft idea, he couldn't help toying with it, turning it over and over in his mind, examining it from every angle and wondering whether it could work.

'Eliza, I—'

A shrill jangle made him jump, and for a moment he couldn't work out where the noise was coming from until he saw Eliza slip her glove off and ferret around in her pocket. He had almost forgotten she had a mobile phone, so rarely did she use it.

She examined the screen. 'I've had a couple of missed calls from my mother,' she said worriedly. 'She's left me a voicemail. Oh, god, I hope it's not bad news.' Hurriedly, she stabbed at the phone then held it to her ear.

Jay looked on in concern, seeing her expression change from alarm to bewilderment, then to delighted.

When she let out a squeal, he jumped. 'What is it?'

'I've just had the most brill news!' she cried. 'I can't believe it.' She was beaming, her eyes bright with joy. 'Apparently, a minor celebrity spotted some of my paintings in Arty Smarty, a small out-of-the-way gallery in Aukland, and she bought a couple. She posted about how much she loved them on social media, and the art gallery has had loads of interest. So much interest that they've sold every single one of my paintings and want to know how soon I can supply them with more!' She squealed again. 'Ooh, I can't believe it! Mum said they've been trying to get hold of me and when they couldn't, they contacted her because they knew I was her daughter.' She studied her phone, scrolling rapidly. 'Blimey, I did have a couple of emails last week, but they've gone into my spam folder.' Eliza blew out her cheeks. 'Thank god they contacted my mum… Ooh, I'm so happy!' She hugged herself with excitement, screwing her eyes tightly shut.

He was thrilled for her, and he knew how much it meant to her that her mother approved of her art. But how could he ask Eliza to stay with him in Muddypuddle Lane now?

With the decision taken out of his hands, Jay's heart ached anew as the realisation that they only had a few short hours left stabbed him in the chest.

How was he going to carry on without her?

♥

Eliza thought she must be all sobbed out, but she was wrong. With every hug and every kind word or kiss on the cheek, she burst into tears all over again.

'I'm going to miss you all so much,' she wept, as Beth swept her into an embrace and hugged her fiercely, until Walter wrestled her free for another hug.

'You especially,' she told him.

'Give my regards to your mother and sister,' he said, 'and come back as soon as you can. I mean it – there'll always be a home for you on Muddypuddle Lane.'

'I can't believe I'm leaving,' she wailed. 'I feel like I've known you forever.'

'In a way, you have,' Walter replied, patting her back as he held her. 'Emrys and I weren't all that different.'

Eliza cried even harder, and didn't stop until she had bundled herself into her coat and stumbled outside for her final walk to the little cottage that had been her home for the last couple of weeks.

As she and Jay made their way down the hill, Eliza's tears dried up, replaced by a sadness so deep she feared it might be bottomless.

In six hours she would be gone, and she didn't know if she would ever be back, despite her promise to Walter, because she didn't think she could face Muddypuddle Lane if Jay wasn't there. He was flying to South America on Friday, and she didn't know if she would ever see him again.

They made beautiful bittersweet love for hours that night. He was tender and sad, gazing into her eyes with such intensity she felt as though he was sinking into her very soul. He couldn't get enough of her, nor she him.

Eventually though, he fell asleep, his arms wrapped around her, whilst she lay wide awake, imprinting those final moments on her memory.

When the time came, she eased herself out of his embrace and crept noiselessly from the bedroom, to dress hurriedly in the dark silence.

He hadn't realised that her case and carry-on were in the living room; he hadn't noticed that her travelling clothes had been placed neatly on the sofa. Or if he had, the significance had passed him by. Because if he had guessed that she was planning on slipping away in the middle of the night, Eliza doubted whether he would have let her go without saying goodbye.

He'd wanted to drive her to the airport himself. But Eliza couldn't cope with a tearful farewell at check-in.

This way was better for both of them. He would wake to find her gone, the only physical reminder that she had ever been there would be the self-portrait she left for him and the note.

She hoped he would forgive her.

Quietly, she let herself out of the cottage, her face damp with tears, and made her way to the lane where the taxi she had ordered would be waiting to take her away from Muddypuddle Lane, her new family, and the man who had stolen her heart.

♥

Jay's arms were empty. There was no soft warm body pressed against him, no head on his chest, and he abruptly surfaced from a fitful slumber where he had been dreaming of wandering through the jungle, calling Eliza's name.

It took him a second or two to realise that the cottage was unnaturally silent, and a few seconds longer to scramble out of bed and stumble downstairs.

But there was no sign of the woman he loved.

She was gone. All that was left of her was a painting and a note.

Jay read it in disbelief, the pain of losing her slamming into him. Even though he understood her reason for sneaking away in the night, he berated her for denying him a few more precious hours with her.

If he hurried, he could—

He sighed, his heart a stone of agony in his chest, and slowly returned to the bedroom to dress. It was over.

It had run its course, as it had always been destined to.

He had to let it go.

Jay wondered where she was now and what time she had left. Was she thinking about him at this very moment? Or was her mind focused on her journey and what awaited her at the other end.

He hoped she would be happy. He hoped she would think of him occasionally.

He hoped that given time, he would recover from loving her.

♥

Another departure faced him when he walked into the farmhouse. His mother and Maisie were also leaving today. His mother appeared resigned. His sister, not so much.

'Can't we stay another week?' Maisie was asking as he stumbled into the kitchen.

'Why?' His mother was sitting at the table eating breakfast. Maisie was leaning against the fridge, nursing a mug of coffee.

'Because it's fun here,' his sister said.

'It was fun because it was Christmas. Christmas is over. It's back to normal now,' Beth pointed out.

'I don't like normal,' Maisie pouted. 'Not my version of it.'

'Some days I'm not too keen on my version, either,' Beth retorted tersely. She turned to Jay. 'What time are you leaving to take Eliza to the airport?'

His reply was clipped. 'I'm not. She's already left.'

'*I* could stay here?' Maisie's voice was hopeful.

'And do what?'

Jay made himself a coffee that he didn't want, but thought he had better try to drink. If nothing else, the routine was familiar and it might prevent him from breaking down – for a couple of minutes, at least.

Maisie rolled her eyes. 'I dunno. I'll find something. I always do.'

'And you lose it again, just as fast.' Their mother's reply was sharp.

Maisie glanced at Jay for support.

Jay had none to give. Mum was right. Maisie was good at getting a job. Not so good at keeping it.

In a huff, his sister stalked out of the kitchen, and a second later he heard her heavy tread as she stomped upstairs.

His mum said, 'I despair of that girl ever growing up. She's twenty-five, going on fifteen.' She pushed her plate away, the toast half-eaten, and when she looked up at him, Jay realised she was close to tears.

'She'll find her place in the world,' he said. 'It's taking her a bit longer than the rest of us, that's all.'

'Remind me, where's *your* place this time?' Beth sniffed and withdrew a tissue from her pocket.

'Belize. South America.'

'So far away...' A tear escaped, trickling down her cheek.

His heart broke afresh to see it. 'Don't cry, Mum. I'll try to come home in the summer.'

'I'm not crying about that. I'm upset because you let love slip through your fingers.'

Jay stiffened. 'I don't know what you're talking about.'

'I think you do. I know you too well, Jay Fairfax.'

He conceded defeat. There was little point in trying to pull the wool over his mother's eyes. He'd never been any good at that and she'd always seen straight through him. 'It wouldn't work,' he said.

'Why not?'

'She's got her life in New Zealand, I've got mine in—'

'Belize? Borneo? Sumatra?' she interrupted. 'You can make your life wherever you want.'

'I can't. I go where they send me, where the work is.'

'Work isn't everything, my boy.'

'That's not what you say to Maisie.'

'*She's* not about to make the biggest mistake of her life.' His mother's tears had dried, but her expression remained sad.

'I know what I'm doing,' he replied, his untouched coffee going cold.

'I doubt that.'

Exasperated, he growled, 'What do you suggest, Mum? I can't ask her to go to Belize with me. For one thing, I'll be in the middle of the jungle so it's not the easiest environment to live in, and for another, she's got a home and a family in New Zealand.'

'If she won't – or can't – go with you, it's up to you to go with her.'

Jay barked out a laugh. 'To *New Zealand?* What if she doesn't want me to? She left in the middle of the night – I was supposed to be driving her to the airport, remember?'

Beth tutted. 'Oh, for goodness sake, I expect she did that because she didn't want you to see how upset she was. How long will it take to get to Heathrow?'

Jay replied automatically, 'Three or four hours, depending on the traffic.'

'Then what are you waiting for?'

He blinked. 'You think I should go after her?'

'Don't *you?*'

'Well, yes, but—'

'Stop making excuses. If you want her, go get her. If you can't live without her, you need to tell her so. And if you have to give up your new life in some godforsaken jungle so you can be live hers, then that's what you'll have to do.'

'I can't just—'

'You *can!*' His mother got to her feet, took the mug out of his hand and propelled him towards the door. 'If you don't, you'll always think *what if...* and you don't want to be doing that for the rest of your life. Get a move on,' she urged. 'You've got to get to her before she goes through security, because if she does that she won't be spat back out until she gets to the other end.'

She was right, he realised. He *would* regret it. He had to try.

Impulsively, he swept his mother into a hug.

'Text me,' she ordered when he released her.

'I will,' he promised.

His last sight of her as he raced out of the room was her satisfied face as she called after him, 'You better had,' followed by, 'My bloody kids will be the death of me one of these days.'

Jay was packed and on the road in fifteen minutes.

♥

The world outside the window of the train looked as dreary as Eliza felt. She was exhausted, heartbroken and so utterly sad that she felt like howling. Instead, she settled for a plastic cup of dishwater coffee, and tried not to wonder whether Jay was awake yet.

The thought of him slumbering on in the cottage, oblivious to her having already left, made her tummy turn over. What would he think? Would he hate her for running out on him? Would he be relieved not to have to face such an emotional farewell at the airport?

She would probably never know.

Compulsively, she checked her mobile for the umpteenth time since she'd left Muddypuddle Lane, half-hoping to see a message from him.

Jay hadn't messaged her, but her mother had. **Call me as soon as you get this. Urgent.**

Eliza felt a stab of guilt. She should have replied to her mother yesterday, but she had been a little preoccupied. She had managed to email the gallery though, although she wouldn't get a reply yet because today and tomorrow were national holidays back home.

As soon as her mother answered, Eliza began, 'Hi, Mum, I got your message and I emailed the gallery. Thanks for letting me know the good news. They did try to—'

'That's not why I wanted to speak to you,' her mother broke in. 'I've just had your uncle on the phone.'

It took Eliza a second to realise who she meant. '*Walter?*'

'The very same. Look, I can't pretend to understand what you've been up to, but he's worried about you. He thinks you're making a big mistake. He mentioned a man called Jay? What's going on, Eliza?'

Wait... *Walter* had phoned her *mother?* About her and Jay? *What on earth?!*

'Who is Jay?' her mother demanded. 'And what's this mistake you are supposed to be making?'

'It's a long story. I'm on the train at the moment. I'll tell you about him when I get home.'

'You'll tell me about him *now.*' Her mother's tone brooked no argument.

Eliza bowed to the inevitable and began to explain. 'Walter doesn't own the farm now, a woman called Dulcie does. Jay is her brother.'

'How old is he? What does he do?'

'He's thirty-four and he works in bioacoustics.'

'Do you love him? Walter seems to think you do.'

Eliza sucked in a breath. 'Yes.'

'This is like Barry Skomer all over again.'

'Hardly,' Eliza huffed. 'I'm not about to move to Galway, buy a boat and take up crab fishing for a living.'

There was a pregnant pause, and then her mother spoke. 'The beauty of doing what you do, is that you can do it anywhere.'

'Do you mean paint?'

'You don't need to take up fishing, or find a job in a bar, or pick fruit for a living. You can paint your pictures anywhere. You can sell them anywhere.'

That wasn't strictly true, but Eliza knew what her mother was getting at. A thought suddenly occurred to her. 'Mum, how did the gallery know I'm your daughter?'

'I told them.'

'But… you never visit galleries.' Eliza didn't add, *not even the ones where your daughter's work is displayed.*

'I visited this one.'

'Why?'

'Because they were selling your paintings and I wanted to see them.'

Eliza was flabbergasted. 'You don't *like* my paintings,' she protested.

'I do. It was painting as a career I wasn't keen on. I thought it was too precarious; but I've been proved wrong. You're good. Very good.'

Eliza swallowed the lump that had formed in her throat. 'I thought you hated it because—' she began without thinking, then stopped abruptly, not wanting to have that discussion right now.

Her mother guessed what she had been about to say. 'Because it reminded me of where your father grew up? Of everything that happened before he came to New Zealand?'

'Well, yes,' Eliza admitted, her heart in her mouth.

'I never hated that you painted. I wasn't keen on it purely because it's not a secure career. And I'll also admit to feeling a bit left out. It was something you and your dad had in common.'

'Dad never painted.'

'I know, but your grandmother did. You reminded him of her.' Her mum paused again. 'Did you find what you were looking for in Picklewick?'

Eliza smiled sadly. She had, and a whole lot more besides. 'I feel closer to Dad,' she said. 'Walter reminds me of him so much. Sometimes, when the light is right, or he holds himself in a certain way, it's like Dad is still with me.'

'Your father will always be with you, Eliza. Never forget that.' She sighed deeply. 'I miss him every day.'

'Me too,' Eliza said.

Her mum chuckled softly. 'He was so proud of you. As am I.'

Eliza was welling up. She had waited a very long time to hear her mum tell her that she was proud of her, and she bit her lip to stop herself from bursting into tears. She had already done so much crying over this past day or so.

'Anyway,' her mother said briskly, clearly back to business. 'Tell me more about Jay.'

'There's not much to tell. We met. I fell in love. He's off to Central America on Friday, I'm on my way home. End of story.'

'Do you *want* it to be the end of your story?'

'No, but—'

'Does he know that?'

'No, but–'

'Then you need to tell him,' her mother urged. 'As a general rule, men have to have things spelt out to them. Sometimes daughters do, too. Where is he now?'

'Um, Picklewick?'

'You need to go back.'

'I'll miss my flight.'

'You can get another. What you can't always get is another chance of happiness. Go buy your boat, Eliza…'

Eliza got off the train at the next stop.

♥

'Dulcie, what do you want? I'm driving.' Jay kept his eyes on the road as he spoke.

'I know. You've got to come back to Picklewick.'

'Sorry. Can't. I'm on my way to the airport.'

'Yes, I know, Mum told me. But you have to turn around. Eliza isn't going to Heathrow.'

Jay faltered, his speed dropping. 'Where *is* she going?'

'She's coming back to Picklewick.'

'Excuse me?'

'You heard. She's not catching her plane today. She's on her way back to the farm.'

'You're joking!' His brain had frozen and he was struggling to get to grips with what his sister was telling him.

'I most definitely am not!'

'How do you know?' He was aware he sounded suspicious, but this was so surprising that he suspected something must be up.

'Walter spoke to Eliza's mother and got her to phone Eliza. I don't know what she said, but whatever it was, Eliza decided she had to come back. Isn't that wonderful?'

Jay hoped it might be, but he wasn't entirely convinced. It all depended on *why* Eliza was coming back.

Then he decided he didn't care about the reason. He was going to see her again – that's what mattered.

Dulcie was saying, 'Eliza's mother called Walter back to tell him that Eliza was on her way, and he told me, and now I'm telling you.'

Jay didn't need to hear it again.

With a heart filled with hope, he came off the motorway at the next junction and headed back to the place he was beginning to think of as home.

But he didn't drive straight to Picklewick – there was someplace else he needed to be first.

♥

Eliza dragged her suitcase off the train, hoisted her carry-on onto her shoulder and walked towards the exit. It wasn't a particularly large station and very few people had got off at this stop, so the platform was almost deserted.

Apart from one solitary figure at the far end, near the steps.

A man was standing there, watching her.

She swallowed hard and came to a halt, her heart thumping, her knees suddenly feeling too wobbly to hold her up.

Eliza hadn't expected to see Jay here. She had expected to find him at the farm, where she would try to tell him how much she loved him, and that their love deserved a chance. She didn't care where she went, or what she did, as long as they could be together.

Hesitantly, she began walking towards him.

He took several steps towards her.

As he grew closer, she could see the love and fear in his eyes, and she guessed those emotions were reflected in her own.

'You came back,' he said, stopping a few feet away.

'I did. You came to meet me...'

'I did.' The corners of his mouth lifted in a tiny smile.

'How did you know I'd be here?' she asked, baffled.

'Walter, your mum, Dulcie.'

'Ah. '

'Eliza, I—' he began, just as she said, 'Jay, I—'

They both stopped talking. He pulled a face, and she bit her lip.

'I love you,' he blurted, at the same time she stammered those very words to him.

Then suddenly she was in his arms, his lips had found hers, and they were kissing frantically, furiously, neither of them wanting to let go.

Finally, another train pulled into the opposite platform, and Eliza became aware that they had an audience, and she reluctantly dragged her mouth away from his.

'What happens now?' she asked, uncertainty washing over her. It was all well and good for them to declare their love, but what were they going to *do?*

'No idea,' he replied cheerfully. 'All I know is that I don't want to spend my life without you. We'll work the rest out as we go along.'

Eliza was content with that. After all, if she hadn't returned to Picklewick, she knew she would have regretted it for the rest of her life. And who would want to live a life of regret? Who would want to settle for Paris when she had the whole world in her hands?

This Christmas had truly been a Christmas to remember, and no matter where she and Jay went, or where they lived, the farm on Muddypuddle Lane would always hold a special place in Eliza's heart.

♥

Blimey it's warm, Eliza thought, swiping a strand of hair away from her face with her forearm. April was normally when the temperature started to drop, but the North Island was having an Indian summer. According to Jay's mother when she had spoken to her on the phone yesterday, she said they were having some good weather in the UK, too.

Eliza finished preparing the patties and took the tray out to Jay, who was on the veranda tending to the barbeque. Her mum was sitting in a deck lounger, sipping the cocktail he had made her. She looked very much at home, and it warmed Eliza's heart to see it.

Someone else also warmed her heart, and that was Jay. Actually, he made it sing with joy, and she was astounded to think she could be this happy. It was positively obscene how in love she was. And if he was to be believed (and she had no reason to doubt him), Jay was just as besotted with her.

It had taken much discussion, but eventually they had settled in New Zealand. As much as Eliza had adored her stay in Picklewick, this was her home, and she simply couldn't imagine living in Belize – even if it wouldn't be forever.

Jay hadn't batted an eyelid when she'd said she wanted to return to her little bach near the beach. He had simply bought a plane ticket and packed up his things. Amongst them were his wood carving tools, and the first thing he'd done when he saw her gorgeous little studio was to build a workshop next to it, where she could see him from her easel as she painted, whittling away, his head bowed as he concentrated. She was delighted that there had already been some interest in his work…

Jay beamed at her as he turned the patties on the barbie, and she grinned back. He looked so happy and relaxed, and handsome… *let's not forget handsome,* she thought.

'He's not a bad-looking bloke, your Jay,' her mother said, noticing the direction of Eliza's gaze. 'You've done alright for yourself. I was telling Cathy that very thing the other day, and she agreed. She said he's a keeper, and you don't want to let him go.'

Neither her sister nor her mother needed to worry on that score, because Eliza had no intention of letting him go. It had taken a flight to the other side of the world for her to find her soulmate…

Eliza put a hand on her stomach and smiled secretly to herself. They would definitely return to Picklewick though, because she couldn't wait to introduce the baby to his or her family on Muddypuddle Lane.

About Etti

Etti Summers is the author of wonderfully romantic fiction with happy ever afters guaranteed.
She is also a wife, a mum, a pink gin enthusiast, a veggie grower and a keen reader.

Acknowledgements

My family deserves a great deal of thanks, mainly for putting up with my incessant daydreaming. Love you to the moon and back xxx

Thanks to my lovely editor and friend, Catherine Mills, for her support and advice.

My friends also get a huge hug for all the love and encouragement, even if they don't understand all the wittering on about story arcs!

Finally, I can't go without sharing my heartfelt gratitude to you, my readers.
You make the writing worthwhile xxx

Printed in Great Britain
by Amazon